Blood on the Taiga

The Earthen Calamities: Nizhny
Book 1
E. Anders

E. Anders

Blood on the Taiga / E. Anders — 2nd ed. New Cover

ISBN 979-8-9891807-0-7 (eBook)

ISBN 979-8-9891807-1-4 (Paperback)

The Earthen Calamities

In the spring of **2016**, the **Aperien Event** forever altered Earth.

In an inexplicable moment, everything humanity anywhere in the world had ever imagined became *real*. No one understood why or how, but the who, what, and when were cataclysmic.

Every myth, every monster. Every story and every dream. All the things that went bump in the night and the virtues descended from various heavens. Gods, demons, vampires, dragons. Magic powers, dangerous alchemy, and a dozen recipes for the elixir of life. Wishes, witches and wendigos. Undead, rebirth, immortality. Apocalypses. Lots and lots of apocalypses.

If there'd been a story about it at some point in human history, it suddenly existed. All of it. All in the same instant.

And as one might imagine, it was a mess.

Blood on the Taiga

In **2243**, the world has largely settled after two centuries of apocalyptic events and heroic interventions.

The **Aperiens**—manifested beings from the **Aperien Event**—exist everywhere. **Dusters**, the result of unions between humans and Aperiens, outnumber pureblood human beings ten thousand to one. The **Icelandic Citadel of Knowledge** oversees the **Accorded Territories**, the nations which rose from the ashes of the Aperien Event. The Citadel enforces a set of magically binding laws called **the Accords**. Examples include the **Human Protection Accord**, the **Anti-Apocalypse Accord**, and the **Vilestars Accord**.

Anyone descended from Lamashtu, mother of monsters, and Lucifer Morningstar's Vilestars offspring are considered some of the most dangerous beings in existence. Violent killers prone to blood madness, they can erase humanity with their black blood. Those with vileblood are imprisoned without the chance of parole under the Vilestars Accord.

Content Warning

This novel contains graphic violence, explicit sex scenes, and mentions of attempted rape.

Chapter 1

Even in his near catatonic state, Gunnar recognized this wasn't the normal amount of light sneaking into his solitary hole. His torpor-infused brain took a few beats to shift from bleary instinct to half awake.

Dark hole. Underground walls. The reinforced and enchanted steel door, with a slot for rolling in his weekly sustain potion, was the only light he'd seen in . . . Damn, he really had no idea how long.

Ah. Right.

He was deep in the bowels of the Manhattan Penitentiary, sub-sect of the Eastern Seaboard Conjunct Accorded Territory. Otherwise known as the only magical prison on Earth with a zero escape rate.

Metal squealed, the door hinges rusted from disuse. *Hells.* His hypernatural senses pained at the shrill sound, and Gunnar squeezed his eyes shut tighter at the widening light beam. What might have once been a growl crossed his cracked lips in a pathetic puff.

"Add the second and third restraints once he's detached from the wall and floor anchors."

The voice boomed in the confined space, Gunnar's head throbbing with each syllable. At least the scents didn't overwhelm him as well; he was so ripe with his own sweat and the piss and shit wafting up from the latrine, nothing else made it through.

Rough hands came at him from all sides, and it burned his ass that he flinched at the touch, his skin tingling as his heart barely pumped. His adrenaline wasn't up to the task yet, his blood circulating like molasses. He didn't resist. No point. He was in no state to fight or kill, nowhere near capable of battling his way free. He'd been rotting down here, forgotten, for too damn long.

Half carried, half dragged, he focused on surfacing from his torpor without letting on to the guards. Whoever moved him must have been big, lifting him with no effort. Trolls, ogres, or half-giants maybe? Working the prisons was one way their kind avoided becoming residents. Whoever led his retrieval was a duster like himself or an Aperien. No human in their right mind came anywhere near a place like this.

Every sound grated against his oversensitive ears. They reached an elevator, rode it for a bit while he kept his eyes pinched tight. His eyes still hurt, and the influx of light got worse once they left the elevator. Tile clicked under heels now. They'd come out above the cell blocks and into processing.

The ground floor, which connected to the outside world.

Gunnar itched despite himself. What the hells was going on? There was no reason to drag his ass out. His kind didn't deserve freedom, a message made abundantly clear his entire life.

Doors, buzzers. Muttered complaints and exclamations of surprise from those they passed. Another door open, shut, and his ass was pushed into a metal chair. Wrist restraints shackled to the table in front of him, ankles bound to the floor. Collar clipped in place, anchored at the chest cross guard, the hum of magical reinforcement. Experienced enchanters liked to add sensory charms, calling cards showing just how good they were at their job.

"Wait outside."

He knew the voice, but he couldn't quite place it in his haze.

It wasn't a big room, he could tell by the acoustics, maybe five feet of space around him in all directions and a low ceiling. Gunnar shifted in the chair, testing. Not much give, but nice having a seat for once. Be nicer if they'd turn down the damn lights; his growing migraine made it hard to concentrate.

A sizzle of radio static. "Send them in."

The doors opened and closed again; he counted at least four different locking mechanisms, not accounting for spell or rune work. Two additional sets of footsteps.

"Archivist Avialian, Assistant Doe," his keeper greeted, tone clipped.

"Warden Kushiel," a smooth male voice returned. "And she is Esquire Doe now."

"Warden," followed a firm but quiet voice, feminine.

"Ah, yes. Esquire."

Warden Kushiel sounded as pompous as the first time they'd met, right before he'd thrown Gunnar down a hole. Not that Gunnar expected anything less from the Ridged One. The angel oversaw punishments on Earth now instead of the particular Hell from his origin mythos.

"How remiss of me," the warden went on, "not to assume a promotion was in the cards given your enthusiastic efforts in overhauling the Vilestars Accord."

"She was instrumental," the archivist replied, airy and casual, almost sounding amused.

"She," the woman said, her voice soft despite the steel lacing it, "is standing right here."

Small feet crossed the room toward Warden Kushiel. Gunnar wondered how far she had to crane her neck to look the angel in the face. Unless she was some kind of air element, she must've been tiny given those featherweight footfalls.

Gunnar inhaled, but he still couldn't parse anything beyond his own stench. Just breathing made his face ache, the room arid compared to his dank, solitary cell.

"His condition violates the most basic standards for prisoner care," the woman went on, her voice pitching higher. "How can you condone this?"

"Because I was *there*," the warden all but snarled, the room warming with his temper. "I fought on the front line to end Lamashtu and Lucifer's very effective campaign to exterminate humanity. I bled to bring their Calamity to heel. I watched millions die, friends and kin among them, and I put two of their heinous offspring to the sword myself."

"Your honorable service in a war that happened nearly a century ago doesn't excuse your behavior toward a man who had nothing to do with it," Esquire Doe returned.

"He is a vileblood. I am—I *was* well within my rights under the Accords," Kushiel answered, his tone back to crisp and controlled.

"An Accord that is since altered," the archivist said. "And adjustments must follow. No one is here to downplay the importance of your role in ending the Vilestar War or your service since."

"Having vileblood doesn't give a blank slate for abusing them, not even within the bounds of the previous version of the Accord," Esquire Doe insisted. "When you look at this man, do you truly see justice?"

"I see a man who, blood aside, is an unrepentant, violent murderer," Kushiel replied, papers shuffling. "One John Dust 78102, captured—legally—for his Accord-sanctioned life imprisonment at age five. After being placed in an approved juvenile facility, he killed seventeen of his fellow inmates before escaping at age ten."

Sounded about right. His early years were a bit of a blur.

A page turned. "Recaptured at age fourteen for crimes including theft, illegal solicitation, and multiple murders of licensed retrieval agents."

All true.

Another page. "Two years in the Madagascar Penitentiary, another ten inmate deaths and three guards killed before escaping again. More crimes, more killings."

He grinned, wondering just how thick his file was.

"Captures, escapes, a knack for killing his fellow inmates with alarming efficiency." Pages turned faster now. "Rinse and repeat for another dozen years before he landed on my doorstep ten years ago after raping and nearly killing a child."

He shifted against the restraints, muscles twitching. That last bit was a lie.

"Those last charges are false," Esquire Doe countered. Gunnar wondered how she knew. "And none of that changes the fact that he is a sentient being with basic rights."

"Which shall be properly observed in the future," the archivist said. It wasn't quite an order but carried weight, laden in the way the air shifted.

"None of which explains why you are *here*," the warden said. "Am I to haul all the dangerous beings in this facility up for your evaluation, Archivist Avialian?"

"You mistake the situation, Warden. I am the assistant in this scenario. Esquire, if you would?"

She straightened herself with a rustle of cheap fabric, very unlike the archivist's expensive silk robes or the warden's starch-crisp uniform. "I'm here to secure his release."

Gunnar blinked, wincing at the stab of light.

What the actual fuck?

The room remained deadly silent for a beat.

When the warden spoke again, his tone had shifted. Overly gentle. Curious.

Cautious.

"You have a promising future as an esquire, after helping appeal such significant legislation. The controversy surrounding it aside. Why would you risk your new found status on this . . . *creature*? Even with the adjustments to the Vilestars Accord, John Dust 78102 is a documented killer. That makes him ineligible for the new parole conditions."

"That's true," the woman agreed. "Which is why I'm going to prove he became a killer because of his forced imprisonment under the Accord's original version."

Chapter 2

What followed was a burst of bitching so intense Gunnar's migraine bloomed into a chainsaw. After about five minutes of that shit, Esquire Doe cut the protests about her safety off at the knees. She needed to interview her client—*him*. She pointed out the warden had bigger problems than her wellbeing if his triple-enhanced runic steel didn't hold a duster, vileblood or not.

Quiet fell after the locks reengaged, leaving him alone in the room with his own personal lawyer.

Her heart raced like a rabbit's.

He might have laughed, but he wasn't sure his tongue still worked.

After a delicate throat clearing, she spoke in a hushed voice. "I can't change the lighting in here, but I brought eye coverings that might help." Sounded like she was fishing around in a bag. He heard her swallow a few times from across the room, a little quiver in her voice that hadn't been there when she'd lectured the Rigid One on his prison policy. "I'd have to touch you to put it on, if that's okay?"

Gunnar had little space to work with, chained by the collar and chest harness, but he managed a minuscule nod. He might not know her motivations yet, but he'd be an idiot to turn down relief.

She came to him with a tight stride. Tense all over, he mused, and he wished he wasn't damn near blind so he could see what he was dealing with here. No helping his curiosity. He might as well have been in a coma for all the stimulation he'd had since they tossed him in that solitary hole.

She stopped on his left side. He inhaled to get a read on her scent but still couldn't smell anything but his own filth.

"On your left," Esquire Doe whispered. At first, he'd thought it was just nerves, but he realized she kept her voice low because of his overstimulated senses.

When fingers rested feather light on his shoulder, he jerked in his chains. Warmth through the thin coveralls, then gone as fast. The fabric ghosted along the bridge of his nose before tucking against his eyelids.

Gunnar exhaled at the instant relief the quasi-darkness provided.

"I'm so sorry," she muttered as her fingertips brushed his scalp, catching on his oily, matted hair as she secured the blindfold in place. "The cuts in the fabric are tiny, but you might see shadows in a few minutes. The rest will come back in time."

Gunnar made out a faint rubbing noise besides her hammering pulse. She must have been wringing her hands. After swallowing around his dry tongue a few more times, he managed a grunt.

"Oh, that's right. They keep solitaries on sustains." Esquire Doe bustled away from him, shuffling through her bag again. "It's enough for basic needs, but for so long . . ." She trailed off with an angry huff. "I have water. Just water, they tested it. It was the only thing I could bring this time, but once we have the paperwork settled, I can—"

He managed a sharper grunt at the mention of water instead of that sticky fucking syrup and opened his mouth.

Her throat clicked when she swallowed, three times, before she whispered, "Can you lift your head a little?"

Gunnar did, as much as he was able, fighting back another twitch when her fingertips rested under his chin against his coarse beard. He didn't really have time to process the sensation, because the bottle pressed to his lips and then the water came, cool and crisp, so cold it made his teeth ache. It tasted like she'd frozen it ahead of time, like she wanted to make sure it was cold when he got it.

Tasted like fucking bliss.

He groaned, urging her to pour faster, not giving a shit about dribbling down his chin and beard and filthy clothes, not until he noticed her fingers trembled. He willed himself down, controlled, careful.

Couldn't afford to scare this opportunity away, not if she really meant to get him free.

Esquire, Gunnar reminded himself. She had an endgame, some sort of baby politician, maybe had her eyes on archivist status. No one wasted time with all that fancy training without a goal.

As he drank, savoring the cold spreading through his chest, his stomach, he wondered what her game was because everyone played, so he'd play along too. For now.

When he finished the water, she mumbled another gentle apology as he licked his lips, catching any spare moisture. Esquire Doe retreated, and after a bit more bag fishing and paper movement, she sat.

Gunnar worked his throat, his tongue, salvia slowly coming.

"John Dust 78102, you—"

"Nnn…Gu…" He coughed once, a dry rattle in his chest. Worked his jaw a few times, stiff from disuse, the single word tangled deep down with his past. Took a few more tries, but he got out, "Gunnar."

"Your name is Gunnar?" His little lawyer caught on quick.

He nodded once.

"I'm sorry, I didn't know. That's not anywhere in your file, just your assigned designation." She sounded much more confident chatting about laws and policies. "Of course, Dust is a surname for duster orphans or unidentified corpses, or … well, victims like yourself who were taken as children."

He didn't know what she looked like, but he imagined her stiffening at the injustice of it all. He fought down a chuckle at the idea she viewed *him* as a victim.

"It's awful no one bothers to come up with anything as a first name besides John or Jane and a number. I guess that's because the naming convention comes from the human equivalent used before the Aperien Event." She exhaled, almost scolding herself as she added, "I'm rambling. I'm sure you know all that."

He did, which made him cock his head, desperately wishing he had better use of his senses right now.

Esquire *Doe*.

She was human.

The one thing in the world that had real reason to stay the hells away from a vileblood. Women especially. Two of the most powerful and dangerous Aperiens had designed his kind through a mutual hatred for humanity. Vileblood were a curse, released on the world to wipe out humans through rape and murder.

She interrupted his spiraling thoughts. "I'm sure you have a lot of questions."

He coughed again when he tried to speak, rolling his neck a bit, forced to chew out every word like he was carving a damn monument. She waited in silence as he struggled through the entire sentence. "Fuck . . . do . . . you . . . want."

"To get you paroled and released," she answered primly, but she sounded uneasy now.

"Why." He managed a smirk as he added, "Jane."

"I'm not Jane." That came lightening quick. She must have been used to making that defense. He'd bet his ass on it. "My name is Audrey." When he didn't give her anything, didn't acknowledge her correction, she went on, "I can have your name legally changed as soon as you accept me as your counsel."

"Why?"

He could hear her frown. "I assumed you'd want to change it?"

"Why . . . help . . . me?"

"Because I'm the girl you supposedly raped and almost killed."

Chapter 3

He agreed to let Esquire Audrey Doe pursue his parole.

Not that he believed anything would come of it, but declining the chance would have made him a fool, and Gunnar wasn't that.

Change came as soon as he signed the paperwork.

They took him to shower directly from the visitation room, the first time since his arrival. Cut him out of his coveralls so they didn't have to remove his bindings and let him walk in alone.

It hurt at first, the warm water pelting his bare skin. He'd cowered under the spray in his chains, acclimating for what felt like hours, drinking the water as much as bathing. He'd been tossed a cloth and a thin bar of soap. Then they shut off the lights, and no one rushed him. Gunnar wondered if they'd just leave him here drenched if he refused to move. The sound was too loud at first but then became steady, like breathing and his own heartbeat, and he welcomed it. The patter against his skin ceased stinging. Sedentary years—*hells, ten fucking years?*—falling away from his aching muscles. The sensations and the warmth helped coax his body further from torpor. By then, being wet—which started out novel and shifted to cathartic—lost its appeal. Dry and clean sounded better, so he signaled the guards he'd finished.

They dried him in dim light and clothed him with enchanted fabric. Only thing that made sense, given they never unchained him to put it on.

Afterwards, they ushered him to a prison wing one level down. Another solitary confinement, but geared for sensory deprivation treatment. His new cell was dim, verging on dark instead of bleak, impenetrable blackness. A bed, an actual toilet, a sink with a small mirror above it. A table with one chair.

"You need to stand still as the chains release, then move immediately five steps forward. Do not turn, do not raise your arms. Do you understand?"

When Gunnar nodded, everything but the collar rattled to the floor as the guard whispered a release command. He stepped forward, unwilling to risk this fresh, clean space. The doors slammed as soon as he was five steps in, locks slotting into place, magical wards whirling to life.

He stood in the room's center—larger than his previous cell three times over—and stared at nothing in particular as he rubbed his wrists. Behind him, the door slot opened, closed again. Gunnar turned, canting his head at the tray on the floor. Water, a slice of bread, and a few thin strips of what smelled like cooked chicken.

No sustain potion.

Gunnar ran a hand through his tangled beard, damp from the shower, and took in the room again. He savored the scent of soap on his skin, the starched linens on the bed. Clean toilet water. Circulated air, stale from conditioning but crisp and dry. Yeast in the bread, the faintest whiff of the charcoal they'd grilled the protein over. The almost acidic tang of magically warded steel.

Goosebumps broke out over his arms; he could hear the ceiling lights, the electricity humming, more sounds than his own breathing and heartbeat. Distant movement—other prisoners in this row or guards walking their rounds.

Hesitantly, he removed the mask, squinting in the near dark as he set it on his pillow. Then he sank onto the bed and put his head in his hands, unable to stop trembling.

For the next week, Gunnar's surroundings shifted in measured increments. The light cycle reached a set pattern: twelve hours of light, twelve of dark. A touch panel on the wall let him adjust the brightness during the daylight hours. His food intake increased to portions more fitting for an adult male.

After the first week ended, Gunnar had the energy for light calisthenics. It felt good to move, better to sweat.

Every three days, they granted him shower access. The rotating hallway opened directly into the single shower stall from his cell. When he went back to his room, the doors shut, the wards hummed, and he barely felt the chamber move back to its designated place. He wondered how it worked—magic, technology, or a combination of the two.

This, Gunnar mused, was *humane* solitary confinement. Efficient, with little danger to the guards, and no chance for escape. Isolation with a heart.

He snorted.

As he finished a round of pushups, he thought about his little lawyer again. Gunnar wondered if she'd given up already or if he'd get to see her for real. Get to smell her, so he could know if she was lying, if this was all some sort of bullshit game with rules he didn't understand.

No one cared what happened to vilebloods. Why should she? A

human woman, of all things, even if she really was that girl he'd saved.

The uncertainty of it all made him wander—two steps in each direction, then back again and repeat. Over to the sink in the room's tight corner and the mirror he'd avoided since his arrival. He couldn't put off looking at himself forever.

It wasn't arrogance to consider himself handsome; the Vilestars descended from Lucifer Morning Star. Of all humankind's imaginings spawned during the Aperien Event, few things were more beautiful than angels.

The gaunt face staring back at Gunnar looked like festering shit.

His naturally pale skin carried a sickly undertone, stretched over his bones like yellowed paper. His lips had healed some, but trenches were smeared under his eyes. Like all vileblood, his irises were as black as his pupils and large enough to nearly overcome the whites. What did show was bloodshot with thick, dark lines, as vilebloods had black blood to match their eyes—and their souls, as it went.

Lifting a thin hand, he scratched at his obscene beard. Not a good look.

He spent the next ten minutes scraping and pulling the coarse hair off and tossing it into the toilet. His raw skin would heal fast enough. It wasn't perfect, but at least he looked something like himself now. His cheekbones cast razorblade shadows under the dim overheard lights, his once statuesque marble face a memory.

Gunnar smirked. Truth be told, he was arrogant. He'd look better than this skeleton after a few more weeks of proper food. The torpor effects were largely gone now, but he'd been down so long, everything felt dull.

With nothing better to do, he set to work on his matted hair next. Black as sin, or so he'd been told. He tore at the matts and tangles, ending up with an uneven mop a few inches above his shoulders. After all the work, it was nice to drag his fingers through it without snags. A gift to be *clean*.

The lights cut off.

Gunnar went to bed, waiting for what might come next.

He tried not to hold his breath.

Chapter 4

Two weeks after the unexpected first meeting that vastly improved his situation, Gunnar's counsel returned. When chains slid through the door slot, he found himself a bit excited. If nothing else, he'd get to leave this room. An idea as appealing as it was shocking.

Also dangerous, when all ... *whatever* the hells this was evaporated, and he ended up back to a cursed solitary existence, worse now for having had a bed and proper food. It would be much, much harder to sink down and forget he existed.

Before he put the chains on, he slipped the mask Esquire Doe gave him from under his pillow and tucked in his pocket.

Once secured, the door opened, and he got a proper measure of his guards for the first time. Giant kin, both men ugly and near eight feet tall. The larger, with a mop of gray hair covering his facial features and almost furry skin, might have had minotaur blood, the wet musk about him pervasive. The other smelled like a duster, maybe a giant and human union a generation or so removed, nothing impressive save the height and musculature. Each had a blessed blade on one hip—he smelled the holy water—and an electric baton on the other. Neither spoke.

They guided him up the bright white hall, into the elevator, and to what he guessed was the same room he'd been shuttled to the last time. The light didn't hurt now. He'd mostly acclimated, but the sheer *white* of everything compared to the dark gray paint in his new cell made his corneas ache. His escorts chained him to the table, then left.

The room was what he'd expected, a ten-by-ten square with two-way glass on one wall, a single entrance, and no windows. Gunner's table was bolted to the floor, another desk out of his reach with two seats. He wondered if Warden Kushiel would make an appearance. The angel probably had better things to do than watch a vileblood swing for a parole that would never happen.

Color him surprised when the locks disengaged and the scent of brimstone, feathers, and disgust wafted into the room, the air temperature warming to Eden. The angel didn't waste any time, striding in like he owned the place—he did—and didn't sit. Gunnar craned his neck to look his jailer in the eyes since he hadn't been able to open them last time.

A glance was enough to make him feel inadequate, but that was by design. Kushiel was angelic in every sense of the tales and religions he'd manifested from. Near seven feet tall with ivory feathered wings, his skin polished alabaster and hair curled, spun gold. Most angels, so he'd been told, bore faces reminiscent of the statue of David. Michelangelo's famous art piece was one of many treasures lost when the Storm Belt Calamity ravished central Europe.

Warden Kushiel regarded him down his perfectly shaped nose, clear eyes like piercing glaciers. He folded his hands behind his back, white robes of pre-Aperien legend exchanged for a well-tailored suit.

A decade ago, when he'd been tossed downstairs and forgotten, Gunnar had baited this very Aperien into a raw rage. Gunnar'd been furious at himself for letting a moment of weakness result in an imprisonment he'd never escape. Pissing off the warden had been a thrashing death knell. He'd never expected to see sunlight again, let alone another breathing creature. Kushiel had all but reassured him of that even before Gunnar picked one last fight.

Now, Gunnar had no snide remarks, no prodding or poking. He didn't quite believe he was sitting here at all, with fancy new imprisonment standards and a possible parole.

Looked like the warden couldn't believe it either.

"I will observe every single second of this farce," the angel said, his voice level and soft despite his scowl. "Any misstep, any inevitable opportunity to bury you back where you belong, I will revel in." A scoff and he shook his head, curls shimmering in the caustic overhead lights. "Applying humanity to the spawn of monsters and devils. Where does it end?"

Gunnar didn't speak, savoring the minuscule flinch in Kushiel's jaw muscle when their gazes locked. It was the most he could risk. The warden was furious, the anger in his scent a living, breathing thing to Gunnar's recovered senses.

Maybe this shit about a parole wasn't all smoke and mirrors.

The warden departed, leaving him chained alone, the warmth leeching from the air with his exit.

Gunnar wasn't sure how long he waited, didn't much care, and he dozed a bit. The exhaustion from being active after so long running on torpor and sustain potions clung to him.

When the doors unlocked again, he snapped to attention and inhaled to measure the newcomers.

The archivist's scent was ten times stronger than the woman. Aside from the scent of parchment, ink, and blood, the man carried an air of frustration, unease and smelled a bit like dragon. Wearing authentic silk, he entered Gunnar's field of view tall, lean, and dark-skinned, his head shorn clean. He had kind, neutral features, save where the faint impression of scales swept along his neck and disappeared under the handsewn robes.

Gunnar kept his attention fixed on the archivist, even though he heard Esquire Doe coming up close behind. The lazy, under-used beast in his blood needed to establish what he was dealing with, because this wasn't a duster, no human blood here despite the convincing, humble form in front of him. This man was a hybrid, a union of two Aperiens. Given the crisp undercurrents to his scent and a flavor that smelled inexplicably like clean sand, Gunnar put bets on him being a demigod of sorts.

Which meant Gunnar, a duster of diluted vileblood with at least three generations of human in the mix, was vastly outclassed. His blood might have come from a fallen angel and the mother of monsters—a goddess in her own right—but his great-great-great-whatever grandparents were memories. This archivist weighed heavy in the room, implying whichever parent was pure god blood, they still walked the waking world.

The archivist studied him right back, bold in his assessment of Gunnar's improved condition. That's right, he'd likely need to make some fancy report about the new prison standards following the Accord's revision.

Then another scent hit him, unremarkable by comparison, and shocked him so hard he jerked in his chains.

Esquire Audrey Doe, the human woman, went stock-still at his sudden attention. An overstuffed, frayed satchel hung over her shoulder, a stack of folders and papers hugged to her chest. His nostrils flared as he stared at her, blinking a few times, and then he puffed out a low laugh.

Yeah, it was her.

He'd been running for his life, sneaking through the Eastern Seaboard Conjunct's poverty and rot when Gunnar caught *this* scent.

She'd been stabbed between the ribs, bleeding out, some lowlife thug trying to rape her. He'd acted without thinking. His instincts had overridden his sense of survival for the first time in his life, the idea of leaving her to suffer and die impossible.

And then all she'd asked of him, while looking up at him like her own personal savior, was that he didn't let her die alone.

Gunnar shook his head, snapping back to the present as he inhaled her clean, untainted scent. No magic, no mixed blood, just a human girl—no, a young woman now. She smelled like nothing more complicated than warmth and sunlight that stirred the deepest part of him. None of the pain, blood, or fear from their first meeting. Or the righteous anger when he'd gotten arrested for taking her to the hospital so she wouldn't have to die after all.

For the first time since they'd pulled Gunnar from solitary, he felt the rest of himself wake up. The beast that made his blood black, the source of the sins of his existence.

If he could curl up at her feet in that peaceful quiet she radiated, he might just do that.

Gunnar inhaled deeper, trying to ground himself, his mind spinning a bit. Did she smell this . . . *good* was a poor word to describe her scent, but was it this good just because she was human?

He'd encountered human women now and again over the years, although they'd rightly steered clear of him, and he'd done the same. But Gunnar'd been close enough to scent them, and every time he'd wondered what all the fuss was about. He'd never gone into some frenzied rut, never had the overwhelming urge to fuck and impregnate because of his vileblood.

And he didn't feel that way now, either. This woman's scent calmed him in a way he couldn't explain, the same damn thing that'd happened when he saved her life that night in the slums; he'd been drawn to the scent first, then overcome by the urge to protect, not rape or kill.

The woman in question blinked a few times back at him, her inhale sharp and almost choked. Hazel eyes widened; eyebrows shot up. Her mouth hung open, unabashed, as she stared right back at him, cataloging him from head to toe, then back around again before settling on his face. She couldn't have been an inch over five feet, with freckles in nonsensical patterns all over her visible skin. Her fine hair, a shade between blond and brown, was pulled back in a tight bun, but a few little curls escaped here and there.

No glamours to make her seem like something she wasn't, no attempts to hide herself. She stood there in scuffed flats, her clothes barely suitable for a lawyer representing their own case. Hand-me-downs with worn seams, but clean and pressed, in a taupe pantsuit that didn't do her any favors.

"Oh," she whisper-exhaled, and then a smile burst free. Gunnar's breath caught as her scent washed bright with joy. In a soft voice filled with wonder, she said, "It's you."

He'd cleaned up a bit since she first saw him, hadn't he? Gunnar couldn't help a smirk. A bit of his former self clawed to the surface under such a blatant assessment. "Like what you see then?"

Her smile faltered, and she *bloomed*. She went so flushed, stumbling to form any words, and embarrassment saturated her scent, sweet on his tongue. Been years since he'd seen or smelled a woman, and he couldn't help but appreciate the one in front of him.

The archivist stepped between them, scowling not unlike the warden. "You will be respectful. This may be Esquire Doe's case, but I have kept the right to end her counsel at any point in this process."

"Theodore, stop." Her scent spiked with concern, watery and sour. Gunnar found he didn't like that scent much at all. "I was being rude. It's fine."

He liked her making excuses for him even less.

"No disrespect intended," Gunnar offered, showing his open hands as much as he could given the chains. "Been awhile since I've talked to anyone, out of practice being civilized."

"You should bring yourself up to practice post-haste." To Esquire Doe, he said, "Come."

When he took her elbow, she shrugged him off. "I can walk without help. Thank you."

Esquire Doe blushed as she sat, glancing nervously at Gunnar. He wondered where that steel spine she'd used to put Warden Kushiel in his place had wandered off to. She shuffled through her papers as she composed herself, pushing back her escaped hair a few times after tucking it behind her ear. The apples of her cheeks stayed pink, but when she regarded him again, Esquire Doe seemed back in control. As tempted as he was to ruffle her more, an impulse as strong as the desire to see that smile of hers again, he behaved.

"I'm not sure how much you knew about the previous version of the Vilestars Accord?"

"Besides locked up for life?" Gunnar smirked despite his good intentions toward respect. "Details didn't really seem to matter."

She winced. "Of course not, sorry." She cleared her throat, and it was almost like a blanket settled over her. "The previous version of the Vilestars Accord dictated anyone with vileblood be imprisoned, regardless of any other lineages. Our work overturned this, opening up the revised Accord to allow children to be monitored but not caged. From now on, vilebloods will be cataloged by the Citadel but not punished for existing.

"Any vileblood currently imprisoned are entitled to a review. Those without criminal records will be released and given reparations. Those who have a criminal history will also be reviewed, and if applicable, released on a conditional parole, with reparations controlled by a designated trustee until the parole period is complete. Any parole violations will cause imprisonment under a sentence appropriate to the crime. Those who have committed crimes assigned as irredeemable will remain imprisoned for life, under regulated, humane conditions, verified annually."

Esquire Doe let out a long exhale after she finished her memorized speech, cheeks still a pleasant pink. This woman radiated optimism while the archivist remained politely neutral, although it was pretty damn clear he didn't want to be here.

"You got me a nicer room. Thanks for that," he drawled. "What I don't get is why're you still here, aside from making sure Kushiel didn't toss me back in a hole as soon as you left."

Her brow knit. "To get you paroled."

This time, he chuckled. "Seems you know your shit, which means you already know what I've done. You really think that angel with a hard-on about my ancestors is going to let me walk out of here?"

"Respectful," the archivist chided.

"He won't have a choice if an Archival Tribunal rules in your favor," she said, and for all the tiny thing she was, she spoke with firm confidence. "And yes, I know what you've done and what you haven't." Her chin tipped up. "You were taken as a child, thrown into a prison ill-equipped to separate children from adults, and had to fight for your survival. Killing, like anyone may have in your situation.

"You escaped when you could—still a child—and did your best to stay free and alive, your only kills outside prison walls the mercenaries who tried to capture you." She scoffed. "You stole food. And you were *still* a child when they threw you into Madagascar Penitentiary, also known as the best example of a hell on Earth—which says a lot, given how many iterations of hell spawned during the Aperien Event. The

Madagascar guards died during a riot, which makes it impossible to blame you specifically for their deaths, and yet they did anyway."

Gunnar wondered how she'd picked out those details about the Madagascar guards. He'd never argued when the blame fell his way, hadn't seen the point.

She kept right on going. "Again, you escaped. Again, you stole to live. Again, you killed only to remain free—only in self-defense. And the charges for solicitation are absurd, applied because you . . ." She cleared her throat, red to the ears now. "Because you were underage at the time, making the transaction illegal. But those specific regulations are defunct now anyway because that Independent holding no longer exists.

"Nothing about your actions shows an out-of-control monster bent on exterminating humankind through serial rape and murder, like all vilebloods are 'destined' to be."

Esquire Doe rolled her eyes at the last part. The way she said it made him grin. She made herself sound all stuffy and prim, likely quoting someone she'd argued with before. She talked with her hands now, becoming more and more engrossed as she lectured him about his past.

He would've kicked up his feet and crossed his arms, waved her on if he could've.

"This is a fundamental problem with chasing after people—Aperiens, humans, dusters, anyone—based on their blood. Humanity has a terrible history with this kind of thing before the Aperien Event, and we clearly passed our flaws right on to all the things we imagined. We've debated nature versus nurture for centuries. It littered mythos and folklore even before it all manifested.

"Was Lucifer himself—your great sire—not a perfect example? If there was anything good imagined, was it not angels? And yet we, humanity, already imagined the fall. But if anyone can fall, it stands to argue that anyone can rise."

The archivist's features softened as he watched Esquire Doe, this human woman, debating the fundamentals of good and evil. He seemed amused but also proud.

"Maybe you would've become a killer regardless," she went on. "But instead of having the chance to rise or fall on your own choices, they decided your path for you. And yet you were strong enough to survive." She cleared her throat again, staring down at her hands. "All of which would be challenging to prove."

The archivist chuckled and patted her hand. "Most worthy ambitions are challenging." He arched a brow in Gunnar's direction. "Which is why, if this man were anyone else, I would have pushed you to start with an . . . easier case. Perhaps one who didn't show a certain enthusiasm for his kills."

Gunnar grinned, toothy and wide, then shrugged. "You heard her. I did what I had to do."

"Not always," Esquire Doe said quietly. When she lifted her head, those hazel eyes dug into him, deep down, and he felt like an exposed nerve as she went on. "You didn't have to save me. You could have walked by—dozens of people already had."

Her hands shook now, and the archivist frowned at her. "Audrey, you don't—"

"No, I do." Her focus never left Gunnar, paling as she remembered the moment that brought them together. He shifted in his seat, uncomfortable, the chains clinking. "Stopping my attacker was more than you had to do. But then you carried me to the hospital to save my life. You knew the risks. You knew you'd most likely get caught. And being inside the Eastern Seaboard Conjunct's borders? You knew you'd end up right here, in the only prison on Earth with a zero percent escape rate.

"You saved my life, and now I believe I can save yours. I'm a living witness on your behalf, a human with nothing to gain from your release." She shrugged. "I believe that's enough to prove your blood does not define your nature."

Gunnar inhaled, and sure as shit, she believed every damn word.

The locks buzzed and hissed, four in succession, and Warden Kushiel swept into the room. "Are we concluded, then?"

Esquire Doe snapped to her feet, her delicate hands in tight fists. "Counsel visitation sessions are an hour." She glanced pointedly at her wristwatch—an analog, Gunnar noted.

Gunnar smelled the satisfaction leaking off the warden, smoky and dense. "Ah, a thousand pardons, esquire. The request must have been logged as his monthly personal visitation—an addition, you may recall, added to the revised Accord. We are still acclimating to these new demands. Personal visits are only for thirty minutes. I would accommodate you, but this room is the only approved space for our high-risk prisoners, and it is booked out for the duration of the day."

Gunnar chuckled, the lie ripe on the air, but there was nothing to prove it.

The archivist knew as well, or at least suspected. He started gathering the paperwork. "Esquire Doe, would you be so kind as to sign us out? I'm sure Warden Kushiel can accommodate me a moment to clean up, as he quite understands the importance of proper record keeping."

The woman in question nearly vibrated with frustration, her anger as palpable to Gunnar's nose as the angel's smug satisfaction. Something unspoken passed between the archivist and Esquire Doe. With a curt nod, she left him with the paperwork.

"Three minutes," Warden Kushiel clipped, never stepping into Gunnar's line of view, and the locks sealed on the echo of Esquire

Doe's heels.

Gunnar reclined as much as he could, which was minimal. "Theo, was it?"

"Archivist or Archivist Avialian will do." He organized the paperwork with care, tucking it neatly back into Esquire Doe's satchel one piece at a time, slow about it.

"Alright. Is this where you warn me, maybe put a few threats on the table like our buddy Kushiel?"

"Oh, I think the warden has that well in hand. I may have fought on the same side as him in the Vilestars War, but his losses during the conflict were much more personal. If it wasn't obvious to you already, he will oppose our efforts at every turn."

"Yeah, that's pretty clear. Though I'm not sure those efforts will shake out, not like your girl wants."

The archivist slipped another paper into the bag. "Because you do not believe the claims she makes? Or that she is wrong about her assessment of your past actions? Or perhaps you believe yourself incapable or undeserving of redemption?"

"Doesn't matter what I think if the deck is stacked. Pretty sure they ward this prison against any kind of wishing or luck."

His comment shaved an inch off the archivist's stony demeanor, and the man actually chuckled. "In that, you are correct. As for the rest, all I can offer you is this: I serve the Icelandic Citadel of Knowledge. My father serves on the Citadel Pantheon. If I believed this an endeavor with no merit, I would not subject Audrey to false hope."

Gunnar grunted. "What's she to you then?"

"A rare heart in a battered world. She is good, Mr. Gunnar, not for the sake of it or the rewards, but because that is her true and uncomplicated nature." He arched a brow. "And you—"

"Are the debt she needs to clear, I get it. And it's just Gunnar."

The archivist laughed this time, shaking his head. He slung the satchel over his wide shoulder, stopping when he reached Gunnar's side. He hesitated, then sighed before patting his arm. Gunnar flinched, but it didn't do any good. He couldn't move more than an inch in these damn chains, and the archivist squeezed in response to his attempt to jerk away.

"You are the man who saved a child who'd been thrown away and gave her a second chance at life. One which she has not squandered. Remarkable, don't you think, how a young woman—a human woman no less—with nothing to her name, climbed her way to esquire status by initiating the largest overhaul to a magical Accord in history?"

"I thought that was your show?"

He hummed. "It was, in name. Audrey sought the Citadel's aid by filing an impressive request for reform, thorough enough to draw high-level attention. Of course, such a sweeping measure couldn't be left to a human child—she was only seventeen at the time—and hope to be given any consideration. They assigned me to the task. She was brought on as my assistant and granted esquire status for her exemplary work when the new version of the Accord passed.

"I offered her much more, not the least of which was an archival position at the Citadel, but she has refused every boon save one: That I help her win your freedom."

Chapter 5

His new lifestyle was an adjustment. Not only being awake but eating, moving, talking. Gunnar had gone from a half-life to living again, with hope dangled in front of his nose like a fucking carrot.

Gunnar smirked as he worked through his morning exercise routine, beginning the moment the lights flicked on. He'd never needed more than four hours of sleep a night, so he spent a lot of time in the dark, wondering if nightly torpor was a thing. Since it wasn't, he spent more time than he liked thinking about this damn woman.

Sure, he'd saved her life, but the lengths she'd gone to to repay that debt? It didn't make a lick of sense to Gunnar. He was locked away, nothing she needed to waste her time on. Yet here they were, a human girl fighting with everything she had so he might see the sun again.

The first month was review, questions, answers, separating out the false records from Gunnar's version of his life. On the second week, they were fifteen minutes late to their Tuesday meet. Esquire Doe grinned when she explained they'd been correcting the prison records. She'd gone through whatever record keeping the Citadel required to change a designation to a proper name.

He was Jonathan Gunnar now, which made him smirk given their earliest conversation. When he'd called her on it, she'd shrugged with a knowing smile and explained he had to have a first and last name on the paperwork. That was the first time she brought him food, a cupcake of all fucking things, to celebrate the success.

The archivist—Theo, Gunnar called him just to annoy the stoic bastard—seemed as dedicated to his case as Esquire Doe, though entirely for her benefit, not his. Warden Kushiel stayed close, escorting them in and out. Gunnar guessed he watched their sessions from behind the two-way glass.

Nine weeks in, Esquire Doe was getting antsy. She felt ready to file their motion with the Archival Tribunal. The archivist argued they should take more time. They'd only get one shot; they needed to make it count.

Gunnar wondered about their relationship. Older brother? Father? Mentor with a prodigious student?

. . . lover?

The last one seemed highly unlikely. Gunnar shouldn't have cared. Who Esquire Doe had sex with should've been the furthest thing from his mind. He still felt a strange sort of satisfaction knowing the demigod didn't have that kind of hold over her.

Good old Theo needed to return to the Citadel for a short time to settle a personal matter. "It will only be two weeks, Audrey," he'd chided her.

That had been last Thursday.

Gunnar hopped to his feet, sweating as he shifted from pushups to jumping jacks. He took his shower days on visitation days. Seemed like the *respectful* thing to do. He finished his set, glancing at the mirror with a nod. Days marched on; he'd gained back more and more of his previous strength. He looked less like a warmed-over corpse at least, and the raw skin around his throat had healed clean.

Breakfast, a shower, and he'd timed it with ten minutes to spare before the guards showed up with his chains. As he latched them in place, he wondered what Esquire Doe might be like without her babysitter.

His senses were used to the trek now, and he didn't flinch at the guards' touch or the locks buttoning him down. Being chained to the chair wasn't the best, but the archivist had negotiated down to arm and leg shackles with about six inches of give, citing good behavior. Now Gunnar could sit up straight, even lean back a bit.

Chained and alone, he drummed his fingers on the table. Glanced at the clock; he'd stopped denying after the first few meetings he looked forward to them. He had nothing else but his own mind forced awake for company. The guards never spoke beyond directions, and he saw no one else besides his counsel.

It helped too that whatever it was about Esquire Doe's scent relaxed him. Helped the beast in his blood stay calm. He'd been crawling the walls those first months down in deep solitary before the torpor tripped on, ripped his skin wide open in a dozen places. Maybe it was more the tease of freedom than the woman, but he felt at ease after these sessions, even when the archivist and Esquire Doe argued like cats and dogs over a sticking point and she left furious or frustrated when their time was up.

Didn't matter, she always smelled like sunshine underneath her emotions.

He checked the wall clock again, frowned a bit. The archivist wanted her to skip these two weeks when he was gone, didn't care for her coming to a place like this alone. Gunnar agreed but kept out of the argument, and she'd convinced him she'd be fine. Gunnar had promised to be on his most respectful behavior. As much as the archivist disliked him on principle, he at least believed Gunnar had no intentions of hurting the woman trying to secure his freedom.

Said woman was fifteen minutes late. He didn't like it. If she'd changed her mind about meeting him alone, Kushiel might not have bothered telling him, but they wouldn't have dragged him from his cell. The warden was many things, but he wasn't impractical. Any time Gunnar was outside full lockdown, there was a risk, however miniscule, he might find an out.

He hadn't yet, and not for a lack of looking.

By twenty minutes, his instincts screamed. Gunnar couldn't smell or hear shit beyond the damn room, but every inch of his skin crawled. Something wasn't right. For the first time since he'd been brought here in chains, he gave his restraints serious attention, running through his knowledge of warding flaws and how to exploit them.

The door locks hissed and Gunnar froze. A near silent growl rumbled in his chest as her scent washed over him.

Fear, raw and primal, pouring from her skin in a fucking waterfall.

He jerked once against the chains, wanting to snap them apart, then closed his eyes and made himself settle. Esquire Doe was terrified; Gunnar wouldn't make it worse.

He took the time to pick apart the notes of her scent as she wandered toward the table, her feet dragging, steps timid. Anxiety, sour sweat. Exhaustion. Humiliation. Salt.

When she finally passed into his peripheral vision, he snarled out, "What the fuck happened?"

She flinched, full-body, clutching her bag tight to her chest.

Shit.

Gunnar exhaled hard through his nose. He forced his voice down to a low timbre, the best he could do for gentle. "Go on, sit down, alright?"

She nodded once as she stumbled toward the chair, and he took her in. She only had two dress suits, and she alternated between the taupe one he despised and a powder blue with brown pinstripes that was barely better. They might be used, but she took good care of them, always tidy in her appearance. Professional.

Today the striped fabric was ruffled, like she'd thrown the clothes on instead of putting herself together like she had every other time he'd seen her. He could tell she never wasted hours primping herself, but her normally neat bun sat loose at her nape, strands stuck to her sweaty skin.

She sunk into the chair, knees tight together, satchel clutched in her lap as a shield. Breathing in pained little puffs, bloodshot eyes unfocused on the bare tabletop between them. She might bolt from the room any second, he realized.

Gunnar licked his lips, her distress making his beast just this side of feral, if only because there wasn't a damn thing he could do about it.

"Audrey."

She startled, blinking up at him with wide eyes. He'd never used her first name before. It hadn't felt right, like something he didn't deserve. Hearing him say it seemed to bring her back to the present, and she released her white-knuckle grip on her bag to wipe her face, those delicate fingers trembling.

She swallowed a few times, dry and scraping, before she whispered, "I made a mistake."

Gunnar rolled his neck, wishing for the collar so he could grind his throat against the metal until he bled. His molars ached. "How's that?"

She squeezed her eyes shut, shaking her head as tears spilled down her cheeks.

The salt stung his nose, might as well have been rubbing it into an open wound.

"A new . . . new bakery, on my walk here."

He frowned, annoyed at the idea of her walking into the prison alone from wherever she lived, suddenly aware he had no idea *where* she lived, how long of a walk it was . . . Not that any of it was his business. "Yeah?"

"They opened today. I went . . . I stopped early, so I wouldn't be late. They . . . it was busy. The owner, she's very . . ." Audrey hiccupped. "Nice. She's nice."

She stared at the table until Gunnar hummed.

"Little cakes, but they're tall and skinny, and they look like flowers." She almost smiled. "I didn't know sh-she used silver." Her expression crumbled around a little sob. "A silver t-toothpick to hold the layers so the flower didn't fall down."

Contraband. They'd snagged her for smuggling contraband, even though anyone with two brain cells to rub together could recognize the innocent mistake. Gunnar's heartbeat drummed in his ears, taking in her rumpled appearance again. He knew what went on in those back rooms.

"They hurt you?" He bit out the words, barely keeping the snap out of his voice.

"No," she whispered.

Good. Maybe he'd make it through the day without trying to kill the guards. His knuckles ached from how hard he gripped his chair arms.

"Audrey," he said, using every ounce of willpower to keep his voice low and level. "You need to send a message to Theo and get him back here."

The smallest smile touched her lips. "He hates when you call him that."

"Oh, I am aware." Gunnar offered her a smirk, levity fading fast as it came. "Go home and let him know what happened. Don't come back here without him."

She frowned. "But we . . ."

"It'll keep. Whatever you think you need me for, it can wait until he's back."

He knew she wanted to fight him; some of that fire was back in her eyes, but then she only sagged deeper into the chair. "Okay."

"Good girl." The words jumped from his mouth, and he decided not to dwell on it. "Go get some rest."

"Okay." She stood on coltish legs, her steps unsure, and he fucking hated it.

Audrey hesitated when she passed by him, a hand catching his sleeve and gripping it tight. He inhaled and held his breath, relieved to catch the sunshine under the mess of her emotions. She'd be okay. She was stronger than letting this shit scare her off.

"I'm sorry."

He scoffed, leaning away as she let his sleeve go. "Don't you ever fucking apologize, not to me."

Another nod, and then she walked on, buzzing at the door com to let them know she was done. The locks and door opened, shut, and locked again, and he was left there alone for the next half hour, his nose saturated with her fear.

Then the warden himself came in with the guards. As they unchained Gunnar from the floor and table, he canted his head at the angel, Audrey's words rattling around in his brain, all that shit about rising and falling.

He wondered just how low a beacon of justice could sink.

Warden Kushiel watched him in return, expression impassive. His scent wasn't smug like Gunnar expected. If anything, he smelled . . . inevitable. Unsurprised and unmoved.

"I'll remember this," Gunnar drawled. The guards tensed when he spoke, used to his obedient silence, but neither of the half-giants would overstep while their boss looked on.

Kushiel shrugged, today's suit navy with an ivory tie and shirt. "And what is 'this' precisely? The dangers to a human girl wandering so far out of their depth? I should hope so."

The warden nodded toward the guards, and Gunnar went back to his cell without further resistance. He didn't sleep, couldn't find enough calm.

On Thursday, the guards brought him from his cell again. Audrey's archivist waited for him alone.

Because she was Audrey now, he realized, more than just his little lawyer trying to repay a debt. He wanted to protect her, was wild with the urge, same as when he found her bleeding out in that alleyway.

They didn't speak until he'd been secured and the guards left, locks in place. They were always observed, of course, but the illusion felt like dignity if Gunnar let it.

"She alright?"

"She will be."

"Got word to you Tuesday?"

"Yes, she requested a looking glass summons. For her to bother, I knew it must have been important. I arrived by the evening, and she's been staying in my housing this week." For all his outward calm and neutral expression, the man fumed under his skin, scent raw with a fury he hid very, very well. "She argued, of course, but I insisted. The compromise is that she'll go home tomorrow."

"She tell you anything else?"

The archivist folded his hands neatly in front of him. "Only how fortunate she was that Warden Kushiel arrived in time to stop the cavity search, citing it as excessive for what was clearly a misunderstanding by one not well-versed in prison policy."

Gunnar felt equal parts relived they hadn't fully violated her and furious all over at the idea of those assholes stripping her naked in a windowless, dark room.

"What a fucking savior."

"Indeed." There was a dangerous glint in the archivist's gaze, and it felt strange to find himself so perfectly aligned with one who'd been begrudgingly dragged along for this entire mess. "Things will likely get worse before this is over."

"Then we'll be careful as we need."

"I'm glad we have an understanding."

"That we do, Theo."

"Tread lightly, Mr. Gunnar," he replied, but Gunnar detected the faintest hint of amusement under all that mutual anger painting his scent.

As the archivist moved to stand, Gunnar cleared his throat. There might not be another moment alone, and he'd found he didn't like when Audrey smelled frustrated, disappointed, or even sad regarding his lack of belief that he'd make this parole.

"Answer me something," Gunnar said, unsure exactly where to start. He licked his lips a few times when the archivist motioned for him to go ahead, his scent curious now. "Why now?"

"I assume you're asking why the change in the Vilestars Accord was a success?"

Gunnar shifted in his chains; he didn't much care for hope, fickle bitch it was, but still asked, "They secretly find some cure for vileblood up at your fancy Citadel?"

The man chuckled. Gunnar kind of hated the sympathetic shift in his posture. "Not a cure, no. As I'm sure you're aware, your blood isn't an infection or a disease, but a curse contrived by two powerful, clever, and extremely thorough Aperiens. That said, there seems to be less potency in the effects of vileblood the further removed your kind becomes from their source."

"Diluted now, all these generations, huh?"

He nodded. "While your kind are still overly prone to blood madness, Esquire Doe's research showed a decline in violent acts by vilebloods. In addition, the vileblood population is at an all-time low, continuing to decline."

Gunnar chuckled. "Right, with all of us locked up, can't exactly make more evil babies. And I've killed more than my fair share of my 'brothers' in the pens."

"On necessity, I'm sure."

He answered with a lazy shrug. "Prone to violence ain't a lie."

The archivist gave him a single nod, ceding the point. "Esquire Doe presented a well-founded case, with extensive statistical evidence. She appealed to those on the Citadel who had always opposed a genocidal approach to the Vilestars and their descendants. Right after the war, your kind were a plague, Mr. Gunnar. No offense intended."

"None taken."

"And as I'm sure you can imagine, killing babes in their cradles, even to save innocents down the road, wasn't a good look for those who were supposed to be the heroes. The Vilestars Accord sought an alternative. The Accorded Territories fell in line, and for a century, no one checked to make sure implementation kept up with moral posturing.

"But Esquire Doe is not wrong in the facts. It has been long enough to reconsider. If the cost of saving humanity is losing our humanity, are we truly the victors? And who better than a human to call out the higher beings on their failings?" The archivist chuckled, the sound humorless. "But I don't doubt for a second Lucifer and Lamashtu sought to ensure exactly such a legacy if their primary goal of annihilation failed." He waved a hand. "And the Citadel could use some good PR, anyway. There are many who don't agree with our stance of neutrality and inaction."

"Guess she found the right man for the job then, huh, Theo?"

"I volunteered," the archivist said, his silvery gaze boring down on Gunnar with the weight of his existence, and then he smiled that half-smile. "And if you're freed, prove her right. Reward such unwavering faith. Because for all the gods who walk, few have it their power to offer what you can give Audrey."

Gunnar didn't have shit to say to that, which worked out just fine because Theo saw himself out.

On Tuesday, Audrey came with the archivist, put together as she'd ever been. She sat down across from him, took out a small box from her satchel, colorful cardboard folded like origami. Gunnar canted his head as she reached out and tugged at the right place. The box collapsed outward.

Inside waited a cake shaped like an open cornflower, no bigger around than his fist. Unlike the one she'd described to him the week before, this cake didn't need anything propping it up, its petals flatted against the parchment paper. It smelled like mint, orange, and buttercream.

When he cocked a brow at her, Audrey lifted her chin, her scent bright and sweet and utterly smug.

Chapter 6

The next five months went quick. The twice weekly meetings kept on without a hitch, and Gunnar fluctuated between ease and uncertainty, equally unpredictable. Kushiel loomed, his displeasure flavoring everything. The archivist played by the books, and the angel didn't seem keen on any more aggression directed toward Audrey. He'd been polite since his men strip-searched her. Gunnar wondered if an angel of justice was capable of regret. Then he decided he didn't give a shit because Gunnar wasn't much for forgetting or forgiving.

And what a circus. Paperwork, documents, archival research. Meticulous wording over his accounting of events. Backtracking through time to recall every fight he'd ever been in, every kill, every reason. The more they dug, the less rigid the archivist became, confidence building as the days passed. Audrey sensed it too.

"I think we're ready," she'd insisted a few weeks back.

"Patience is a notoriously difficult concept for humankind," the archivist had replied, turning a page. She'd huffed at him. "We're close, but let's be certain beyond any doubt. There won't be a second opportunity."

Another month crawled by. "Close" changed things.

Gunnar became restless faced with real possibility. Listening to them talk, chattering through all their strategies and reasonings, he found himself flirting dangerously close to belief. He ran himself ragged in his cage, stuck between burying any thought of a future with a sky and coming to terms with a life stuck in this nicer fucking box.

Failure would mean silence and solitude, but with no more torpor to turn years into a vague sense of oblivion. Gunnar wiped the sweat from his eyes and started his routine again, still a few hours left until lights off, pushing himself as far as his body could take. It took a shit-load of work before he collapsed into an exhausted unconsciousness without dreams. It never lasted for more than a few hours, but it was a reprieve.

But the restlessness in his blood, the part of him that was beast no matter how much Audrey and the archivist wanted to believe differently, remained all too aware of the horizon line. It wanted, scented, chance. And there were nights he gave himself over to it, pacing the square block with all the mindfulness of a rabid dog until his joints ached.

Other times, he thought of Audrey.

He tried not to let himself, but it happened on those longer stretches between visitations. At first it annoyed him, because it wasn't only his human blood craving socialization. If that were the case, he'd think of the archivist too, and Gunnar never bothered.

It must have been because she was a woman. She smelled nice, wasn't hard on the eyes at all, and he hadn't fucked in a decade. The first few times he took himself in hand, he came so fast he didn't really have time to imagine much of anything. The pure novelty of getting off after his extended sensory deprivation didn't last.

Then thinking of Audrey with his dick in his hand, really thinking about her, what she might sound like, that blush of hers, her body tight around him in place of his fist . . .

No.

He'd stopped himself from getting off, because that woman wasn't for him. It didn't matter how good she smelled, how pretty she was, how soft that blushing skin looked. It didn't matter that she smiled at him and cared about what happened to him. Hells, it didn't even matter that she was far and away too good for him, too innocent for him, and everything else that made a good woman like her deserve a fuck of a lot better than a duster like him.

He was a vileblood. She was human. Full stop.

If he ended up having sex with her, he'd sign her death warrant. A slow, miserable death culminating a new, miserable child, just like his monstrous ancestors wanted.

Curses were tricky. Magic didn't always listen to science, making human contraceptives of any kind, including condoms, useless. There were magical means for preventing pregnancy, but even those were shotty because it all came down to the strength of the conflicting magics.

Lamashtu and Lucifer were a dangerous, stubborn combination. They'd created what might be the most powerful curse ever known before or since the Aperien Event. Even generations diluted, Gunnar'd be damned if he took that kind of risk for the sake of getting his rocks off.

He'd fuck his hand if he felt inclined to squeeze one out, and faceless fantasies did just fine.

Thinking about Audrey and sex in the same breath was self-flagellation.

He chuckled and locked those wild dreams of a woman he wasn't good enough to touch, even if it wouldn't kill her, deep down in the dark places of his mind. Self-control had always been his strong suit, and he didn't think of her again when he needed to take the edge off.

Otherwise, Gunnar worked out, paced, then showered until they cut off his water. Anything to pass the time until he *knew*.

He waited at the table on a Thursday, nothing unusual about the afternoon, until Audrey and the archivist walked in. Audrey's scent was distinctly different. He tensed, inhaling deep and parting his lips to taste, rolling the change around in his senses.

Excitement. She vibrated with it as she sat down across from him, her smile brilliant. He'd missed the fresh-baked cookies she'd brought, her scent was that overwhelming, and when she plopped the paper plate down on the table and slid it into his reach, he didn't move. Audrey glanced at the archivist as he settled in beside her, and he gave a nod.

Her attention settled back on him like the rising sun, and his chest lurched when Audrey said, "We're ready."

Arranging an Archival Tribunal wasn't exactly easy, even with an esteemed archivist from the Citadel backing the request. There were two more months before the actual hearing started, and for the last week, Audrey and Archivist Theo had made his case to the summoned deities. Apparently, none of the higher-ups gave a shit about his thoughts on this whole thing.

The guards delivered a simple black suit early in the morning, along with a sachet of the best smelling smoking tobacco he'd ever encountered and a note. Gunnar recognized Audrey's handwriting.

It's time. Make sure you bring the offering.

That was all she wrote, as if she knew empty platitudes would annoy him more than encourage. There were no other instructions, so he'd tucked the sachet away, assuming the purpose would become obvious later.

Today, the Archival Tribunal would reach a verdict.

He didn't dare think of an after not including this room; he'd fought hope off for months, and he wouldn't indulge now. Gunnar dressed. The suit wasn't a great fit, but when he looked in the mirror, a man watched back instead of an empty shell.

He wet his dark hair, smoothed it back; impressions mattered, he knew. His dark eyes won him no favors, his black blood a life sentence until the Vilestars Accord revision. He combed his hair with his fingers a few more times while he waited to be chained.

Once he was bound, the cell door slid open, and Warden Kushiel waited in the hall alone. Impeccable as always, the angel's expensive snow-white suit fit him perfectly as if designed to counter Gunnar's. A show for the Tribunal of how below them a vileblood belonged.

He didn't care. It was all a bullshit circus show. They'd make his case or they wouldn't, and a suit wouldn't be what decided the outcome.

He still chaffed against the collar and tie.

Kushiel looked Gunnar over as if they had all the time in the world, like turning up late to a summoning of six gods was nothing for the angel to be bothered about. Gunnar waited, the obedient dog he was right now, for the invitation to step outside his cell. Damned if he'd give the asshole the satisfaction of messing up on something trivial this late in the game.

Kushiel hummed. "I suppose you're presentable, as we work with what we have." His wings shifted, his scent heavy and mixed. Gunnar had trouble parsing all things the angel felt about this moment, they were so tangled and woven in on each other.

He noted the warden seemed to have misplaced his normal arrogant confidence, but Gunnar kept his mouth shut.

"Come. At the very least, we can avoid embarrassing this facility further." He motioned for Gunnar to exit his cell, and Gunnar fell in line. The angel took the lead. Gunnar followed behind his shoulder, the power move clear as it was pointless, but again, Gunnar had never been an out-of-control monster. "I know well your loathing for me, but many others work here to keep the world outside safe from nightmares." The warden cast a pointed glance over his shoulder as they arrived at the elevator, his gaze glacial.

Gunnar stepped inside and gave a lazy shrug. "Never gave a shit about you. You were just doing your job, following the Accords, getting your justice."

Kushiel didn't look at him as the elevator climbed, one wrist gripped firmly in front of the other.

Gunnar tried to keep his mouth shut, but the rest tumbled out. "At least not until you fucked with her for kicks."

Kushiel hummed again. "I can see how you'd interpret events that way, but I didn't break with policy beyond sparing her additional humiliation. If the consequences of her carelessness scared her away from this place, from helping you, well, I'd have considered the world better for it." He tilted his head, the edge of his lips curling up. "Is this where you threaten me, John Dust 78102?"

"Nah," he drawled. "She worked too hard to throw this chance away on someone like you."

"Ah, yes, someone like me." The angel's nostrils flared, his scent flashing hot before he brought himself back under cold control. Without his senses, Gunnar wouldn't have noticed, as Kushiel's tone remained unchanged. "Shame me in this, for bleeding to end *your* Calamity, for suffering under the loss *your* sires parsed out with glee. For wishing only to keep the world safe from *your* kind for eternity."

Gunnar didn't bother replying. Audrey would have answered that already and eloquently to the people in charge of his chance, more so than he'd ever manage. They rode the rest of the way in silence.

When the elevator doors opened, Gunnar hissed and squinted, about blinded by the gleaming sun off thousands of gilded and silvered glass panels.

Then the rest hit him.

The roof.

He was *outside*.

Fresh air. Blue sky sprinkled with fluffy white. Midday sun warm on his skin.

He huffed out a breathless laugh, closing his eyes and filling his lungs to bursting. A breeze tickled his skin, humid and chilly, goosebumps prickling from head to toe. Late fall, he guessed by the smell and temperature. He'd long since lost track of seasons.

He still had to squint as he forced his eyes back open because that was the York Hub during the day—the entire Eastern Seaboard Conjunct, really. The only real holdover from the 21st century in terms of tech, style, and infrastructure, each hub within the ESC was much the same. Towering skyscrapers with metallic, shimmering windows, littered with glowing neon signs and shimmering magical runes from street level to the clouds.

A complicated lattice of stonework made up the rooftop under his heels, magic so intense the air crackled. There were wards, runes, probably some black and blood magic in the mix too. Twenty stories high, more levels burrowed into the bedrock under the bay and rivers that kept Manhattan Penitentiary isolated from the mainland.

The angel watched him take everything in, but for the moment, Gunnar tuned him out. Over his shoulder, a gathering waited a good hundred meters in the distance, near the center of the oblong building's roof. He tuned that out too.

Gunnar allowed himself to be distracted by the glitz instead, despite the shock of free air against his senses. He'd never seen much of the ESC hubs aside from crawling in the slum alleyways and industrial lanes, the utopia glimmering above his head, far, far out of reach.

Being here, on top of one of the tallest structures in York, well, it was one fuck of a view.

Only the colossal bone obelisks stood taller than the skyscraper city surrounding the Manhattan Penitentiary, the closest anchored in the river to the south. Eerily smooth and featureless, it reminded Gunnar of a giant talon. A massive golden chain attached at the tapered end, which floated upwards against the laws of physics, yet well within the realm of magic. That chain, along with a dozen others like it from each city hub, stretched up to a enormous floating island. And that elevated paradise was reserved for the ESC's ruthless and efficient dictator: Archlich Lawrence Davids, the only head of an Accorded Territory who'd started his life as a human.

Gunnar chuckled, wondering idly if the monster on high had any idea what the girl who shared his humble origins was up to right underneath his nose.

Kushiel gestured for Gunnar to precede him, the angel a picture of patience and calm now that others watched on. Others, Gunnar thought with a smirk, bigger than Kushiel. Gunnar schooled his expression; ego had no place where he was about to stride.

He doubted anything he'd offer would sway the gods awaiting him, if he could speak at all. Audrey and the archivist had made his case, or they hadn't. Until now, a creature like him had no rights at all; there was no sense in pretending things had changed in less than a year.

So he hobbled along the roof in his chains, giving the air of a man properly cowed and respectful of his betters, none of which was exactly difficult to put on. All of it was true, anyway.

The air grew charged the farther he walked, making his skin itch and his nose burn. The fine hairs on the back of his neck stood at attention, sweat tickling his temple. Kushiel at his back wasn't helping, and Gunnar had the absurd desire to know if the gathered gods affected the angel. The angel had fought in a war that killed off a lot of deities, which meant he'd been in the presence of beings greater than himself before.

Gunnar had never had the displeasure before today, certainly never sought their attention, let alone seeking help. This wasn't praying. That required, as far as he understood, the right context and the right god to accomplish shit, but it felt adjacent enough to make him uncomfortable.

Then again, it wasn't really him doing the asking. He tried to catch sight of Audrey or the archivist and frowned. He could make out bodies in the distance, this rooftop center piece they moved toward, but everything was fuzzy. Strange that, given his keen eyesight.

One figure was in focus ahead of the blur, and he stood with the help of a cane in his right hand as they approached, a mutt of indeterminate breed rising with him. He was tall, lean, and night-skinned, making both Gunnar and Kushiel look like snow by comparison. His wide-brimmed straw was an odd sight, but looks tended to be unreliable when it came to Aperiens. He pulled long on his pipe, the exhaled smoke warming the air, and gave a nod in greeting.

"*<<Hello there>>*," the man said, accent thick as he grinned wide, speaking Haitian.

He couldn't be bothered to speak the designated regional tongue? English in this case, Lawrence Davids's roots. But more likely, he knew both Gunnar and Kushiel would understand. Anyone with angel blood was a polyglot.

If his situation wasn't so precarious at the moment, Gunnar might have reminded Kushiel of their commonality.

Instead, he inclined his head respectfully, hoped he didn't butcher the accent too much when he replied, "<<*Afternoon, sir.*>>"

"<<*Good manners, good start, but no need for us to dance around why you've come. I'm Papa Legba.*>>" Another flash of white teeth as he leaned on his cane, taking Gunnar in from head to toes, not showing the least interest in Kushiel's presence. "<<*You'd be Jonathan Gunnar.*>>"

"<<*Yeah.*>>" Gunnar inhaled, not bothering to hide it, finding it strange how unremarkable Papa Legba's scent was. Straw from his hat, damp fur from the dog sitting obediently at his knee. The tobacco was strongest, along with easy sweat and a tinge of dark rum. Spices he didn't recognize, which felt like a tease or memories. Gunnar had never been to Haiti.

The underlying scent of power had a flavor he couldn't name, a warning seated deep in his hindbrain. Papa Legba's dark eyes twinkled under the quiet assessment.

Then Gunnar remembered the sachet. Fumbling awkwardly in his chains, he retrieved the tobacco pouch and held it out. "<<*Pretty sure this is for you.*>>"

Papa Legba nodded, taking it in a weathered, wrinkled hand, the skin around his knuckles dry and cracked. He lifted it to his nose, inhaled deep, then sighed with pleasure. "<<*You've got good ones looking out for you, boy. Go on, then.*>>"

There was a pop in Gunnar's ears, and whatever magical veil or spell or force of will that had been keeping the gathering hidden dissipated. Papa Legba hobbled out of the way; Gunnar realized then he'd been blocking the path forward.

Gunnar said, "<<*Thanks,*>>" and moved on, pretty sure one shouldn't dawdle when a powerful Aperien dismissed them.

Kushiel and Papa Legba didn't speak at all; they must have settled up long before Kushiel came to fetch him from his cell. The angel had likely spent every hour possible up on this roof, arguing for Gunnar to stay under his lock and key forever.

He pushed down the thought of what a victory for Kushiel would mean for him, instead seeking those he called allies. Good ones, that was certain, just like Papa Legba said.

A ritual circle weaved across the roof, because he recognized it now, a summoning circle to get all the deities assembled and channel whatever magic they'd pour into the weight of their decision.

Audrey and Archivist Theodore sat near the circle's outer edge in plain wooden chairs. A few more archivists stood around the border, witnesses or facilitators maybe. He really wasn't sure how all this worked.

Audrey wore her taupe suit. She looked exhausted but smiled when she saw him and gave a little wave. Archivist Theodore nodded, his expression shuttered. Gunnar's feet moved on their own toward the gathering's center, his senses inundated with exuded energy.

Six powers from the Icelandic Citadel of Knowledge's vast pantheon awaited him, their visages blurred.

Chapter 7

G unnar stared at the elevator numbers as they counted down.

Despite the verdict in his favor—*conditional parole granted, his freedom beginning now*—he tensed as the floors counted down deeper. But then they hit L for lobby with an unceremonious ping and sure as shit, the doors opened.

Gunnar stared down a plain hall he'd never seen before. He tested the air, staggered by the overwhelming glut of sensory information.

He smelled dozens of people of all stripes, their scents circulated through cool, conditioned air. Kushiel frequented this hall, so did his guards. There were smells of detergent, paper, electricity, and protective wards. A cleaning solution used on the floors, wax to keep it polished. Ink, enchanted and not. Dirt tracked in from the outdoors on leather shoes, the metal tang of runed prison bars. The sharp bite of holy water-soaked weaponry. He heard the hum of voices down different hallways. Bright, buzzing lights, and there, far down the seemingly never-ending corridor, daylight for the second time in a decade.

Gunnar huffed, shifting his ankles before he stepped, not used to his own weight without irons. He still wore the ill-fitting suit, a dark shadow against his pale skin, the fabric suddenly itchy.

"I reserved a room for us down the first hall to the left," Audrey said, holding the elevator doors open while he stared and listened and smelled.

He blinked down at her. He'd almost forgotten he wasn't alone. "What for?"

"Oh, um." She gave him a half-smile. "To talk about what comes next for us."

Apprehension licked up his spine. He'd thought this was a done deal. Gods said so, hadn't they? He couldn't quite help his sneer.

"Your reparations, for one," the archivist said, voice smooth. "Esquire Doe has done research into options you may find appealing once you're ready to travel."

Gunnar exited the elevator, Audrey following. The doors swished shut behind them.

"Not sure what the hells that has to do with either of you."

He didn't miss the bloom of concern in Audrey's scent.

Good old Theo, though, he only smelled annoyed as the conversation continued. "One might find themselves more grateful, given all that has been done on their behalf."

"Far as I understood it, this was a debt being cleared." He jerked his chin in Audrey's direction. "I saved her life, she saved mine."

"Ah, of course," the archivist said. "Why would you see this as anything beyond a transaction?"

"Theodore, don't."

"Maybe you should've been clear you had expectations from the get, not act like I owe you when you fought for me to be fucking free."

"The time and effort we both put in on your behalf is astounding. Audrey . . . Esquire Doe in particular. You do not know what awaits outside these doors."

"Same shit as before. Fucked up world, big ass mess," Gunnar drawled.

"All of this, leading to your release? The Eastern Seaboard Conjunct is the last holdover of 21st century ways before the Aperien

Event," the archivist went on, ignoring Audrey's hand on his forearm. "Media is controlled, used as both entertainment and weaponry. The change in the Vilestars Accord, along with your review, has been the height of fearmongering for well more than a year, culminating in today.

"Walking out the front door? You'll be assaulted by the ESC press, which hardly holds a favorable view of your kind. Walking a block outward? You'll have thrill seekers looking for a fight, vigilantes aiming for your throat, all brainwashed into believing your release is the first step toward a fresh Calamity."

"I've faced worse," Gunnar drawled.

"Enough." Audrey's cheeks flushed red, her scent brimming with frustration.

The archivist took her hand in both of his. "Perhaps this isn't the wisest course."

She jerked away. "You don't get to make that choice."

"Your safety is my concern, Audrey."

Gunnar scoffed. "What, you think I'm gonna hurt her now? With this parole hanging over my head?"

"Perhaps I'd be more convinced if the parole wasn't the only thing holding you back."

The archivist swelled a bit as he spoke, as if losing hold on whatever mantle he kept in place around lesser beings. The scales on his dark skin became more pronounced, the cloying scent of dragon heavy in the narrow hall.

It made Gunnar's skin itch, but he didn't dare flinch. It pissed him right off, this asshole thinking he'd hurt her. And he was *done* being muscled around by anyone—angel, god, demigod, or otherwise.

"He won't hurt me. You know that, so stop. Just stop, Theodore." Audrey sighed, turning to Gunnar. "I'm sorry. I should have asked, but I figured you'd need at least a day to settle. I . . . I didn't want either of us to have to deal with the mob outside." She smelled nervous now, despite her frustration, and embarrassed. Hopeful too, which he didn't understand.

"The press has not been kind to Esquire Doe," the archivist said. "Most times, she is more the enemy than you."

"I have a single-use gate," she said. "Directly to my apartment. From there . . . well, you can do whatever you want, but at least you'll be away from the crowds out front." Audrey's fists tightened around her satchel strap.

But she clearly wasn't scared of him, and he doubted Theo really thought he'd do anything to Audrey or he'd never let them leave together. But bringing him into her home? Excessive. Way more than she needed to do for him after getting him out of this shithole. As far as he was concerned, they were clear—not that he'd viewed her in his debt before—and the last thing he wanted was to start out his new freedom owing someone.

Single-use gates were expensive magic. Only extremely talented mages could handle that type of craftsmanship; hells, it was easier most times to make foundations for permanent travel portals. How the shit did this girl, who could only afford two suits, secure one? And why the hells would she bother?

It must be more for her than him, Gunnar decided, the only thing that made sense. She didn't want to deal with the press. Maybe the two of them worried if the press got ahold of him, he'd make Audrey look worse.

Not for the first time, Gunnar wondered if Audrey was in some kind of debt to this demigod. Magical bindings didn't have to be infernal; lots of benevolent creatures bound lesser beings for a whole host of reasons, protection not least on the list.

Gunnar distinctly disliked the idea that Audrey had sold herself on his behalf. Had she bartered part of her soul for this fucking gate?

Gunnar inhaled again, but she didn't smell like magic. Only human, through and through, same as the day he found her dying in that alley.

"I have some supplies," Audrey offered, taking his silence as hesitance. "Statistics show convicts released on parole with no kind of support are far more likely to be incarcerated again. It doesn't matter if they were innocent or guilty the first time." She sounded stiff again, reciting memorized facts at him. Her voice went hushed as she added, "Having nothing is almost impossible to build from for anyone."

Right. She'd been a homeless runaway when he'd saved her. They'd never talked about her past despite all the deep dives into his. He realized with striking clarity he knew almost nothing about this woman, aside from her outsized devotion to helping him.

"Fine. Wouldn't do for me to kill a reporter five minutes after being freed."

Chapter 8

Gunnar'd taken a few gates in his time, but never a single-use. It was a ring of blue metal about the diameter of his fist. Audrey recited the correct incantation, and they left the prison behind.

Unlike a fixed travel gate, which felt kind of like wading into an ocean, then getting rolled carefully back onto shore, this shit was like being tossed into a whirlpool and pissed out at full force into a brick wall.

They both stumbled when they arrived, and he caught her arm before she fell face first onto the linoleum flooring of her kitchen unit.

Gunnar's ears hummed, his sinuses aching. Audrey ripped away from him and puked in the sink. He leaned against the counter and closed his eyes for a few seconds, his equilibrium returning. The vomit gave him something concrete to center on. He wasn't much better off than her, he wagered, just better at containing it.

"Sorry," she gasped. He cracked an eye, found her bent over the sink as she flipped on the water.

The white noise grounded him further. He pushed away from the countertop, mumbled, "Don't worry about it."

She apologized too damn much. Audrey grunted, and he chuckled at her embarrassment as he took in their surroundings. His first impression? Being an esquire must pay fuck all. The place had two small bedrooms down a narrow hall, a bathroom about as big as a cupboard, and a sitting area barely large enough for two folding plastic chairs and a matching table.

It was clean, meticulously so, which only helped so much with the peeling paint and cracked flooring. The carpet was threadbare and stained, and she'd tried to hide it beneath her meager furniture. Mismatched bookshelves were lined up next to the front door, stuffed to overflowing, papers sticking out every which way with more piled on the floor. The place smelled like her, bright and warm, the sensation aided by the canary yellow of her handmade curtains.

Blue sky and cityscape taunted him through the window, but Gunnar controlled the twitch in his hindbrain because he wasn't being hunted. He didn't need to escape this place.

He didn't believe it yet, not entirely, his instincts ratcheted high. It wasn't every day one got judged by a pantheon of gods, he thought with a smirk, less so that it turned out well.

"Sorry," Audrey murmured again, shutting the water off. She set a full glass next to his elbow at the counter. She drained a glass that didn't match his. When she was done, she wiped her mouth with the back of her hand.

Then she grinned at him. A big, goofy grin. When he cocked a brow at her, the expression thinned. "Sorry, I just . . . I believed we'd get you out. I always did. But you're here, and . . ." Audrey blew out of breath and gestured at him. "You're *here*."

She seemed far too comfortable about that fact.

"Sooner we get this shit sorted, sooner I can be gone."

Her disappointment soured her scent. "I . . . well, I made up the second room for you. I put some things in there for you too. Clothes and stuff. I figured . . ." Audrey gave him a smile that was more of a grimace. "You might want to change, or whatever. Then I can show you the options Theodore mentioned."

She wrung her fingers as she watched him, like a fucking puppy waiting for any scrap he might toss her. Gunnar grunted, left the glass untouched, and strode away from her down the hall.

"I can make food, if you're—"

"Don't bother, won't take me that long."

He tucked into the room before she answered, scanning for escape routes in long habit. The door to her room across the hall was open. Both rooms had simple cots, but they were clean, and so were the linens. She had a few plastic storage tubs and an electric lamp in hers, nothing else he could see from this vantage. His cot was the same—hardly the worst place he'd found himself.

But he couldn't shake his sudden, violent dislike at how she lived.

Likely not the worst she'd had either, and he liked that less.

Gunnar shook his head. He didn't need an opinion on the matter at all. Grabbing the heavy canvas backpack from the floor, the nicest thing in the entire apartment, he tugged the largest compartment open and overturned it.

A canteen tumbled out, along with waterproof matches, flint and steel, a substantial first aid kit, and sunglasses. A hunting knife—damn good quality too, with an eversharp rune etched on the blade. A plastic rain poncho, a tarp, and enough rope to rig up a small tent or hammock. Field rations, enough for around two weeks in a stretch, a packet of jerky, and a chocolate bar. Two pairs of shoelaces, a bottle of multivitamins, a travel sewing kit, and a plastic bag with all the basic toiletries. A paper map of the ESC York hub, published seven months ago, along with a compass. An analog wristwatch, brass with a fabric band.

Beside the bag sat neatly folded clothing. Shorts, two pairs of pants. A sweatshirt, two T-shirts, and a thin long-sleeved shirt. Six pairs of boxer briefs, six pairs of socks, and a black wool hoodie. Leather gloves.

A pair of steel-toed boots waited on the floor near the cot's edge.

It all smelled new.

Gunnar repacked the bag, then stripped off the suit and prison-issue skivvies, tossing them to the room's far corner. The underwear, jeans, and T-shirt worked well, all dark colored. The socks were soft, and the boots fit like a dream.

He sat on the cot as he laced them up, trying to figure out what this girl was about.

Why did she live like a damn roach, even though she had a good job and a title to match? It was like she'd skimped to make sure *he* had everything he needed. She wouldn't have known until today if he'd be out, yet it was clear she'd worked on this gear for weeks, if not months. Maybe longer.

Gunnar stuffed the other clothing into the backpack and hauled it over his shoulder. Best to get on, not waste time thinking about it. He'd be gone, and she could do whatever she wanted.

When he emerged, she waited in the kitchen unit, which had a two-burner gas stove, the sink, and a half-fridge. She'd covered the counter in more papers, and he recognized her tight, looping handwriting. Audrey smiled up at him, though it didn't light up her entire face this time.

"The clothes fit? Shoes too?"

He cleared his throat. "Yeah."

"Good." Her gaze fell to the backpack, but she kept her expression cool. She smelled unsure. Not afraid or anything, just unhappy. "I . . . They didn't give you a full explanation on the reparations?"

He shook his head, annoyed by the slight shake in her hands. He didn't like her nervous, not when related to him. Gunnar wanted to throttle the archivist then, wondering what the fucker had said to her when he'd taken her aside before they used the gate to her place. When he didn't reply, too busy grinding in his own head, she gestured to the paperwork.

"It was part of why I had your name changed so early. They created your reparations account when the revised Accord passed, same as for any imprisoned vileblood. Yours, however, remained empty until they granted your parole. Since you didn't have any next of kin, they allowed me to take on the role of trustee, since I was your representative for your parole case."

Gunnar didn't know how much money was in that account, only that they'd calculated it based on years imprisoned. Being that they'd caught him the first time when he was five years old . . .

Pieces shuffled into place, uncomfortable in his mind, and while Audrey didn't smell like deceit . . . "So what? You decided since you helped me get out, you get my money?" She blinked up at him, confusion on her scent, but this was the only fucking thing that made sense to him. He took a few steps forward, leaning on the counter across from her. She didn't retreat, only watched him with her brows furrowed. "I ever say I wanted you as my trustee? I don't remember that fucking conversation."

She flinched at his harsh tone. "No, but . . . You didn't have anyone else who would qualify. Not even Theodore, since he was acting as my advisor, not your counsel. It's stupid," she said, her frown deepening. "If I didn't step in on your behalf, you would have lost your reparations."

"And you just forgot to mention this until now." He waved a hand around the room. "Once we're here, on your turf, so you can what? Tell me your terms where no one can hear you?"

"My terms?"

"Oh, you're just going to give me my money, huh?" Gunnar chuckled. "Nothing in it for you? Like getting out of this shit stain of an apartment? Get yourself some clothes that actually fit you right?"

Her arms hugged around her middle; she glanced down at her worn taupe suit. "No."

"No?"

"I don't want your money. I just didn't want you to lose it. There are limits to what you can take since you're on parole. It's spaced out over three-month intervals until you finish your parole, and then whatever's left defaults to your name. When that happens, I'll no longer have access." She didn't look at him. "There's an ESC branch a few blocks from here. We can go tomorrow morning. I'll take out as much as possible and give it to you."

"Do it now."

"They're only open for a few hours in the morning for this type of thing. They need an overseer present who has the proper magical access to alter the accounts."

He inhaled, deep, and her face jerked up, the flush crawling across her cheeks hardly pretty. A bit of anger peppered her scent now.

"I'm not lying. I didn't gain access as trustee until after they ruled in your favor. The account didn't exist until then."

She wasn't lying. She smelled hurt and angry, but she was telling the truth.

"What do you want?"

"To help you."

"In exchange for what?"

She swallowed a few times, then gestured at the paperwork. "I did some research on places that might be good for you. You can't stay in this hub of the ESC. Anywhere in the Eastern Seaboard Conjunct would be bad. You're famous and not in a good way." She gave him a helpless shrug. "We did what we could, but Warden Kushiel made sure the media got involved as soon as we challenged the Vilestars Accord.

"Anyway, the Collation of Creatures is always an option, but I didn't think you'd like the idea of being confined behind the labyrinth walls, so I didn't place an appeal for sanctuary. I can, if you want."

When he just stared at her, because she'd ignored his question, she barreled ahead as she unrolled a world map, pointing as she talked. "There are a few places in Western Europe that aren't very populated. The Portugal coast has several small Independents who hire outsiders without background checks, magic or otherwise.

"The Sahara is desolate territory, but there's a propagation project underway. They're taking anyone willing to work and giving them a stipend and housing. And then out here, in northeast Siberia, I thought this looked the most promising. There's a second generation Aperien who founded a town of self-proclaimed outcasts, but the territory is rough. She needs hunters to kill off dangerous wild creatures, but she also needs workers in town. Bookkeeping, cooks, stuff like that, so we'd both be able to work. Well, at least I'd be able to do more work than I could digging ditches in the desert."

There it was.

She'd finally given him the answer, but it wasn't what Gunnar had expected.

She thought she was going with him.

He laughed, a sharp bark that stopped her rambling. Audrey's lips pressed in a thin line, and he couldn't miss the thread of determination in her scent, right beside a ribbon of fear, sticky and acrid.

"We?"

The air went out of her sails, a sunset with none of the lingering warmth. She dropped her gaze, picking at the map's edge.

"There's . . . You heard Theodore. I'm all over the ESC media as much as you are." She waved a hand, her smile mirthless. "'Enthralled human campaigns for vileblood; is she possessed? Enslaved? Pregnant with his spawn? Brewing with blood madness? What protections for the public will she undo next?'"

"Theo said you got an offer from the Citadel."

Audrey stiffened. "He had no right to tell you that. And it doesn't matter, anyway. Theodore helped me instead."

"That's what you're fishing for? You control my money, so I have to haul you around if I want what I'm owed?"

"No, why would you think . . ." Audrey rubbed her face. "No, of course not. You can tell me where you go and I can—"

"Still a leash, knowing where I am so you can tug my chain when you need something, huh?"

She surprised him then, surging around the counter, all five foot nothing, and poking him hard in the chest.

"No!" She poked him again, and he let her, staring down at her as she fumed up at him. "I would empty the account for you tomorrow if I could, and you'd never have to hear from me again if that's what you wanted." Her scent lanced again with unhappiness, and she backed away from him as if suddenly realizing how forward she'd been. "You don't owe me anything. I just thought . . . I wanted . . ."

Audrey laughed then, a humorless exhale.

"You can't get anywhere tonight. Look at my research, sleep here, and in the morning, we'll go to the branch. Theodore can help you if you don't trust me. We can have him write up a magical contract sealing my word that I'll never ask you for anything if that's what it takes for you to believe me."

Audrey, the human who'd stood against Kushiel unflinching, offered him another flat smile before waving a hand at her pathetic kitchen. "Help yourself if you're hungry. I'm tired. It's been . . . it's been a long day."

She left him there in the kitchen, the linoleum creaking as he shifted his heels.

Nothing from her had been a lie, not since the moment he'd met her for the second time. Her desire to help him was as genuine as anything he'd ever tasted, along with her desire, for whatever fucking reason, to stay with him while she did.

Could her life be so bad she'd take her chances digging in the Sahara or facing down the Siberian wilds? It didn't make a lick of sense, but the money didn't matter to her.

Gunnar snatched the backpack, gathered up all the papers she'd worked so hard on, and retreated to the second room. Her door was shut. No sense letting her hard work go to waste. He knew it'd be thorough. Audrey didn't do anything by halves, he'd learned.

They'd get him some funds in the morning and he'd be on his way. Alone, just like he always had been.

Best for everyone.

Chapter 9

Sleep never came easily for Gunnar. It was worse in unknown places. That said, it wasn't every day he faced down the judgement of six gods and came out on top. He'd dozed as he read over Audrey's notes and eventually gave in, tossing the papers beside his packed bag. The cot was more comfortable than anywhere he'd slept in as long as he could remember.

But it wasn't really the cot or the clean sheets. It was her, which he disliked as much as it lulled him into a quiet, dreamless slumber. That scent of hers, light in the darkness, lingering on everything she'd touched. Sunshine. He'd never thought of sunshine having a smell before he met her.

Gunnar bolted upright, no idea how long he'd been out, but his blood roiled. Wrong, his instincts screamed. He shoved his feet into the new boots, grabbing the hunting knife he'd stuffed under the thin pillow and the bag.

He needed to get what mattered and get the fuck out.

He bullied his door open, didn't hesitate across the narrow hall, and kicked down Audrey's door next.

She jolted up with a shriek, and he grabbed her by the upper arm when he caught the scent.

Hellfire.

"What are you doing!" Audrey yelled but didn't fight him as he jerked her out of the bed and shoved her behind his body, then picked up the cot and threw it at the doorway.

Crimson flames exploded from ventilation system as the ductwork melted. Gunnar barely had time to turn, growling as heat washed over the room. Audrey screamed, her pain lancing through his senses and drowning out his own, and that dark part inside Gunnar snapped the leash.

He punched out the window, clutched Audrey against his chest, and swung them outside.

Third floor.

Fire escape.

He made the jump easy, the rusted metal protesting. Smoke billowed after them, filled with hellborn magic, burning flesh and fabric. The brick face melted, screams in the near distance cutting off short. Hellfire burned fast, hot, and out of control if it didn't have an anchor. Flaming tongues rolled up and down the building, weaving in and out of windows, glass evaporating and the air red and black.

Audrey buried her face in his chest. He kept her tight to him as he vaulted to the next fire escape. The entire building whined, molten metal and sparks flashing, then an explosion shook the foundation.

Gas pipes.

Less time now.

With a hard kick, the fire escape ladder dropped with a squeal. Sirens echoed through the night. Burned flesh. Death. He climbed fast, but not fast enough, those hungry flames biting, chewing, burning.

They were still five feet off the ground when the fire escape lit up and melted, and they plummeted.

Gunnar turned midair, landing hard on his back. The air was forced out of his lungs, the backpack crushed against his spine, but Audrey was cradled safe against his chest. He coughed, sucking in smoky air as he hauled them to their feet. The nearby asphalt bubbled. A few patches of grass and shrubs blackened and disintegrated.

"Jonathan," she gasped. He caught her face in both hands. He smelled her pain over the hellfire and ash and snarled. She blinked a few times as he stared at her, into her, words out of reach. She seemed to understand, shuddering as she whispered, "I'm okay."

Enough for now.

They ran. He didn't stop with crossing the street. Away was the goal, and not just from the immediate threat of the liquifying building, falling debris, and fire. Away from the hellfire's source.

About three blocks over, he stopped, tucking them behind a dumpster. The sirens grew louder now, the air thick with smoke. The ground shook, a violent, rolling rumble he felt in his bones. Her apartment building had fallen, thankfully not in their direction.

He closed his eyes for a few seconds, focused on his breathing. Letting his instincts rise and overpower him was easy in times of overt danger. Calling it down, that took more work. He buried his face in Audrey's hair, searching for that sunshine, seeking a tie back to his humanity before he completely lost his shit.

Gunnar exhaled, shaking his head as intellect overrode instinct, and he pushed her back to arm's length. Audrey let out a hiss of pain, and he let go, but she didn't, her fists clenched on his shirt, knuckle-white. That sound. Her pain? It snapped him into focus right quick.

He cupped her cheek, making her look at him. "We're clear."

When she gave him a shaky nod, he turned his attention to the rest of her. They were both singed, barely caught by the fringes. Hellfire burned through flesh like a knife through hot butter. They got lucky. Real fucking lucky.

She'd gone to sleep in an oversized T-shirt, and the left sleeve had burned off. That side of her body was bright red, a seam running from her shoulder to her elbow of more severe damage. When he reached out, she flinched but didn't let go of his shirt. He pulled the backpack off, tossing it between them. Part of the bag had burned away. Thankfully, the medkit was still there.

"Anything for burns in this bag?" Gunnar asked. When she just stared at him, he tried again. "Audrey, you're burned. Need to treat it if we can. The kit you made for me, anything for burns?"

She blinked, owlish. "Um . . . yes. For burns." She closed her eyes and shivered. "And pain ease."

Good. Last thing he needed was her going into shock. It took a few seconds to wrangle the items out, the burn cream non-magical, but the pain ease was in potion form. He peeled one of her fists from his shirt, shoved the vial against her palm. "Drink it."

"It's for you."

"I'm fine. Drink it."

"But I got it for you." Audrey's chin jutted out.

"It's mine. I get to do what the fuck I want with it. Drink. It," he growled. "This cream is gonna fucking hurt."

She drank, then buried her face in his shoulder and whimpered as he rubbed the cream on the worst of her burns, his teeth grinding at those pained sounds. He bandaged her up, as quick and gentle as he could.

"What about you?" she asked, clinging close to him as he tucked the supplies into the battered pack.

"I'm not human enough to be at risk for infections like you are. Come on, we need to keep moving." Gunnar was used to pain. It was easy to channel it into adrenaline until he knew they were really safe.

Audrey wiped tears from her face, wincing when she touched her burned cheek. Hopefully, it wouldn't blister too bad, and the hair that had singed away would grow back. It wouldn't make her any less beautiful.

He stared at her for a second, registering just how close she'd come to dying.

There'd have been nothing left of her, not even ash. Hellfire didn't just burn. It devoured.

And hellfire didn't just show up.

"What happened?" She kept his shirt in her right hand, fingers pinching his skin, but he didn't mind because she was alive.

Gunnar shook his head; he needed to focus, and he didn't want to pull the darkness forward again. He didn't want to scare her more than she already was.

"Hellfire."

Audrey drew a shuddering breath, peering out from the alley at the pillar of inky smoke and sunset fumes filling the sky.

"My apartment . . ."

"The entire building is down. Come on." He pulled the knife out, stuffed the sheath in his pocket for now, and tested the weight again. She'd picked a good piece for him, heavy enough to do some damage in a fight, although she'd likely picked it for survival. Then he smirked to himself; she'd probably picked it for both. Thorough.

He took a step, but she didn't move, her gaze fixed on the hellish sky.

"The entire building? But . . . hundreds of people live there . . . that was everything. Everything I had. All my work," she whispered.

"Come on," he repeated, tugging her along. "Worry later. Now we move."

She leaned into him, swaying as they walked, and he kept her going, foot over foot.

The slums weren't far. She'd lived on the edge, the border barely visible from her third-floor window. A few more blocks and they could disappear until they figured out what to do. It wasn't hard to chase the scent. The wind moved in their favor, desolation and smoke billowing over the glistening cityscape, neon and gold and magic shimmering uninterrupted against the night.

"Someone did this," she whispered.

"Yeah."

She shivered again, but he couldn't let her rest, not yet.

The line between slum and gilded city came up stark. The block was double wide, and that was it. No fencing, no other border. Gunnar wondered what kept people out or in, or if it didn't matter.

He'd always known which side of the line he belonged on. He stepped forward.

Audrey didn't move.

When he tugged at her, she let go and cowered away from him. No, not him. She didn't look at him. Her attention was over his shoulder, her face bloodless. And she shook now, her entire body. The air was cool, not cold, but she only wore a T-shirt and underwear. He cursed when he saw her dirty, cut up feet. He should've noticed sooner.

"I'll carry you," he offered, gesturing to her feet, but she shook her head.

"I can't."

Gunnar inhaled, taking in her scent. She was more terrified now than she'd been when they'd hung off the fire escape as the building melted around them. "Audrey?"

She stared toward the slums. "I can't go back there."

The place where she'd been starving on the streets, almost raped and killed, would have died if he hadn't happened along and intervened.

"You can," he said, stepping closer, keeping his snarl down when she retreated from him. "I got you," he added. "Kept you safe before. I'll keep you safe now. We need to hide, then get to Theo." He hesitated, but he'd decided the second he'd smelled the hellfire in her apartment, so there was no point fighting it now. "Then we figure out where to go next." Gunnar held out his hand. "Me and you."

Audrey drew a shaking breath and took his hand.

Chapter 10

Six Months Later

Gunnar could damn well handle tracking down and killing this dragon on his own.

No, not dragon, he reminded himself; they were called zmei around here. It was a small one anyway, only three heads, but the Longest Night was tomorrow, making the Siberian taiga around Nizhny more dangerous than usual.

More relevant, Audrey had insisted a joint venture with their new neighbor was the right move. He'd been skeptical, but Audrey was as stubborn as him when she thought she was in the right.

Gunnar smirked behind his wool scarf; the woman was right more than he liked. And pretty much always when it came to social maneuvering.

He dropped to his knees in the snow, the tracks here fresh, each print as long as his forearm and twice as wide. Small, he thought again with a chuckle, but still not the kind of creature to be left wandering the settlement fringes.

"<<*What funny?*>>" A rough voice carried easily on the sharp wind, speaking broken Russian.

Gunnar motioned to the obvious trail. "<<*All this fuss over a baby lizard.*>>"

His fellow hunter Zhadan laughed—as much as a chuchuna *could* laugh. It came out more like gurgling snorts, but Gunnar had spent enough time around the yeti-like creature that he recognized the sound. More than seven feet tall, he wasn't the hairy beast of other yeti mythos. The chuchuna was more Neanderthal, with a full coat of dark, thick body hair. He still needed heavy furs to stay warm in the Siberian winter.

"<<*Mate wants, mate gets. Zmei smells makes scared for coming cubs.*>>" Zhadan lifted a meaty hand to scratch frost from his hairy face. "<<*Meat, bones, skin, more. All good for using.*>>"

Gunnar grunted. No argument there. Of course, all the zmei parts could've been his and Audrey's, traded toward a better place for her than the small cabin they shared on Nizhny's northern edge.

He could almost hear Audrey's voice, going on about him being part of a community now and needing to think about this town as a long-term investment instead of a stopover. How he wasn't on the run, not anymore . . .

"<<*Problem?*>>"

"<<*No.*>>" Gunnar dusted his hands and rose. "<<*Another hour or less, given our current pace. You still good with the plan?*>>"

The chuchuna gave him a toothy grin. "<<*Yes, yes. Me big bait, wash out zmei.*>>" He let loose a few growls, waved his arms. "<<*You quiet, pull the tail. Then . . .*>>" He smacked a fist on his open palm. "<<*Dinner.*>>"

"<<*It's flush out, not wash out,*>>" Gunnar corrected. Hells, Zhadan's Russian was almost as bad as Audrey's. "<<*But that's the gist of it.*>>"

"<<*Good, good. Hungry.*>>" Zhadan patted his thick middle.

They spoke little after that. About another thirty minutes north, they split off, the chuchuna making enough noise to wake the damn dead. Gunnar kept his mind clear, dropping deeper into his instincts as he prowled through the thickening trees.

They were well outside Nizhny's claim now, the zmei's range to the northeast, but near enough for its scent to drift in when it wandered this way. Deep in the dragon's territory now, notable in how little else in the way of magical beasts or even the mundane held a presence. Just frozen peat, fresh and old snow, and the sharp scent of broken pine. Gunnar settled himself between a few fallen trees ripe with the zmei musk. They didn't nest without a mate as far as he understood it, but they marked like bears or rutting deer.

About fifteen minutes later, things got loud again, and Gunnar couldn't help a grin. This was going to be fun. He pulled the eversharp blade from its place on his thigh. Fresh zmei musk hit his nose at the same time as Zhadan's damp fur and the sound of boot falls on snow and needles, crunching over fallen branches. The zmei's three heads hissed through shared lungs, its tail thrashing the forest as Zhadan lured it right into the thick.

The chuchuna darted by his hiding place in a dark blur. The fucker was laughing his ass off between whooping hoots. Gunnar shook his head; damn good thing this hunt didn't call for finesse.

The zmei plowed through the bowers, melting snow dripping wildly from the thing's hot breathing and sheer body mass. Long and lanky, and thin for a dragon of any kind, it snapped at Zhadan's heels three times in succession, then reared up on its hind legs when the chuchuna suddenly stopped running.

Gunnar didn't hesitate, the placement perfect. Two steps from the brush, he cut across the beast's hind leg, hamstringing it. A quick roll put Gunnar back on his feet, cutting through scale and muscle on its good leg just as it compensated. The zmei toppled sideways with a furious roar.

Zhadan was on it as soon as it fell, claws and teeth on the closest neck. Gunnar cursed as he scaled up the dragon's spine, throwing all his weight forward at the middle head as the jaws snapped shut just shy of taking off Zhadan's scalp.

Gunnar's momentum crashed the center head into the third and then he collided hard into the packed, frozen dirt. He grunted with the impact, a growl bubbling up. He took his frustration out on the yellow eyes, eight of them in a mess of blood, gore, snapping teeth, and lolling tongues. A few tears in his sleeves, a scratch on his forearm, and it was over. He dropped back on his ass, sitting on the zmei's shoulder as it drew a final, shuddering breath and went still.

Zhadan was covered in ichor and bright green blood up to his elbows. Gunnar pointed his bloody knife at him.

"*<<You're a fucking idiot.>>*"

That just got the bastard laughing again, all hoots and snorts as he cleaned himself with snow. "*<<Is good. Is dead.>>*" Zhadan made a mouth with his hand and flapped it opened and closed a few times. "*<<Why goose?>>*"

"*<<What?>>*"

"*<<Goose.>>*" Zhadan sucked his teeth, thinking for a second. "*<<Whining, you. Why?>>*" He patted the dead zmei. "*<<Is dead, not us.>>*"

Gunnar snorted. Fucking hells, was he really splitting hairs over vocabulary—again—with this tall bastard in the middle of the damn taiga? Being a polyglot had become a massive pain in the ass since arriving in Nizhny six months earlier. Gunnar tried to imagine explaining this moment to a previous version of himself and came up empty.

"*<<You're as bad as Audrey with your fucking Russian,>>*" Gunnar grumbled as he stood. "*<<Grouse. You mean grouse.>>*"

"*<<What said. Goose.>>*"

"<<*Whatever. Grab the tail, we got a long walk home.*>>"

It took them a few minutes to get situated, Gunnar trying to balance two dragon heads, one on each shoulder, the third dragging along in the snow while the chuchuna gathered up the zmei by its haunches about ten feet back. They headed out from the trees on to the open hard pack. It was late morning now. They'd gotten lucky finding the zmei this far south in its range. If they pushed, they'd get back before nightfall. Zhadan would approve.

He'd been restless since his mate became pregnant, part of the reason they were out on what should've been a rest day. But Gunnar never backed down from a challenge. This zmei was outside their weekly hunt quotas required by the settlement, meaning the massive corpse was profit heads to tail. Skin, bones, meat, and alchemical and magical ingredients galore.

Rina, the Aperien Independent who controlled Nizhny and the surrounding area, would be pleased, especially since less than twenty-four hours from now, they'd be up to their ears in mythos climbing out of the forest, marshlands, and lakes during the Longest Night's hallowed darkness.

They needed to get home. Gunnar and Zhadan's homesteads backed into each other, a new development as of two months back. Rina wanted to expand north and had selected the pair of them to tackle the new expansion. They got on well enough, him and the chuchuna, and it added some extra security for both Audrey and Zhadan's mate, since they trusted each other well enough. Audrey being soft for Lyubava and her impending cubs only helped matters. They'd settled on the midway, Gunnar and Audrey's log cabin about half a mile from the chuchuna's cave mounds.

And now they'd all sleep better without a feral dragon near the borders.

Zhadan hummed loudly. "*<<Is good for soup.>>*"

"*<<What?>>*"

"*<<Yes, yes. Soup.>>*"

"*<<That's it? With all this?>>*" He gestured up and down the length of the corpse, which they'd divide evenly back at the homestead. "*<<Soup from boiling the bones and nothing else?>>*"

"*<<No bones. Meat and insides parts. Juicy. Thick. Scoop.>>*" Zhadan gestured with one of his massive hands, shoveling at his mouth, struggling with the zmei's ass end as he did.

Again with this shit. Gunnar turned so the bastard wouldn't catch him fighting back a grin. "*<<Stew, Zhadan, for fuck's sake. You mean stew, like Aster makes at the tavern. The chunky stuff most of us use spoons for, not our damn hands.>>*"

"*<<Stew, yes.>>*" Zhadan grunted as they resumed walking, and after a few paces he asked, "*<<Audrey cook?>>*"

"*<<Not sure she's worked with dragon meat before, but you can ask. Lyubava not good for it, huh?>>*"

Zhadan snorted out another chuffing laugh. "*<<No.>>*" He got the emphasis right this time, the *hell no* kind of no, and Gunnar chuckled despite himself. "*<<Mate no know how cook. But likes.>>*"

"*<<Yeah, we're all turning so bloody civilized, aren't we? I'm sure Aster will trade you lots of stew for a share of this meat. We'll toss some of ours in too. Audrey'll want to make sure Lyubava is eating well.>>*"

"*<<Good. Good.>>*" Zhadan smelled satisfied. Gunnar caught it easily with the wind blowing at their backs. He found he couldn't disagree.

They passed the trek home in companionable silence, Gunnar surprised the chuchuna knew how, but he didn't miss the steady uptick in Zhadan's anxiousness. He was just as eager as Gunnar to get back. Finally, they crested the last meager, snow-covered hill. Gunnar's cabin came into view, smoke winding from the chimney.

"<<*In the back,*>>" Gunnar said, motioning toward the stone patio and wooden decking he was still building up in his off hours. It was large enough now for the butchering block and the drying racks rowed up beside the humble smoke shed. No way the whole corpse would fit, but not like they'd be wrestling the damn thing indoors, regardless.

As they trudged down, the cabin door swung up and there was Audrey, stuffed into so many furs he couldn't make out her face. She waved, and the zmei body jerked around as Zhadan waved back and shouted, "<<*Little!*>>"

She met them halfway, panting and pulling down her mask to grin up at Gunnar, hazel eyes twinkling. "You found it." She leaned to the side and waved again at Zhadan.

Gunnar smirked down at her. "Didn't think we would?"

She laughed. "Never had a doubt." Then she frowned a bit as she took in the zmei. "I'm not sure we'll get the whole thing processed by train day."

He shrugged. "Whatever we don't will keep for next time." Over his shoulder, he called, "<<*Move it, this fucker's heavy.*>>"

A grunt. "<<*Wait for you, much talking.*>>"

"<<*Play nicely,*>>" Audrey said.

Zhadan chortled and snorted as they hauled the body. Once they set it down on the snow, Audrey asked after Lyubava. He bared his teeth and growled while he stuck out his belly and rubbed. Audrey laughed, the sound airy, one of Gunnar's favorites he'd discovered over the last six months.

"<<*Same trade?*>>" Gunnar offered. They often helped with processing the chuchuna's kills for a share of the materials, meat or otherwise. Zhadan was a sloppy butcher, and Gunnar and Audrey had invested in far better gear at this point.

Zhadan glanced the direction of his den and mate, then back to the zmei. This wasn't some bauk or vodyanoy. Even the chuchuna, uneducated as he was, understood dragons carried inherent value. Gunnar could smell his uncertainty, but he obviously didn't want to mess with the working relationship they'd developed.

Audrey stepped forward and patted Zhadan's massive arm. "<<*Check Lyubava. Later, we . . .*>>" She glanced at Gunnar for translation help. "See to the details?"

"<<*Ain't gonna short you, Zhadan. Go see your woman, come back after. Bring her round, if she's up for it.*>>"

Zhadan relaxed and offered a toothy grin that might have been terrifying if they didn't know him. Then he gave a mock salute—Gunnar had no idea where the hells he'd picked that up—but then stalled, his scent hopeful when he asked Audrey, in English, "Cookies?"

She giggled. "Yes, cookies. <<*In the oven.*>>"

"Good, good." He nodded a few times, calling over his shoulder as he lumbered off, "Lyubava much happy for cookies."

Damn liar. He ate way more than his mate whenever Audrey baked.

"I better make more, so she actually gets some," Audrey said with a hum, echoing his thoughts.

"They really still in the oven?"

"Theirs are still baking. *Ours* came out a few minutes ago. Still warm too."

Gunnar grunted.

She made damn good cookies.

Chapter 11

I t turned out plain old, human-made chocolate chip cookies were the key to greasing just about any wheels out in the Siberian wildlands.

After the attack on Audrey's apartment building, she and Gunnar spent two days hiding out in the ESC slums before reconnecting with Theo. The archivist proved worth his salt again. Once they'd decided as a group Nizhny was their best option, he got them out of the Eastern Seaboard Conjunct himself—on dragon back. His back, as it turned out.

Theo didn't want to make a show when they arrived, so they'd landed a few stops earlier on the Trans-Siberian railway and then rode it to the ass-end. Once in Nizhny, Theo made the introductions to Rina. He left on the train out the next morning.

Rina put Gunnar to work immediately, setting him and Audrey up with temporary lodging at the town center, an impressive train station that had survived well over two hundred years of calamities and hard winters. While Gunnar hunted, Audrey rooted out ways to be useful to the community, starting with cookies.

After getting permission to use the tavern kitchen from Aster, the cornflower wraith who ran the place, she baked for days, insisting that first impressions mattered. Gunnar knew she didn't want to be a burden. Audrey had learned everyone's name by day two, and by the end of the first week, Gunnar was escorting her around the settlement to hand out baked goods.

They were met with amusement or confusion, bewilderment, and in one case, hostility. An Aperien harpy named Celaeno acted as Rina's scoutmaster, and had set herself up in a rundown electrical pump house on Nizhny's west side. Reputation preceded Celaeno; she hated everyone and wanted to be left in isolation, enjoyed throwing out hexes at those who bothered her. Audrey insisted on paying her a visit, unwilling to treat anyone unfairly.

Rina joined them, shouted out a greeting and warning, and then she and Gunnar hung back while Audrey trotted up to deliver the baked goods. Everyone walked away with their skin intact. Audrey's only comment as they walked back to the town center had been that Celaeno "seemed nice, but maybe a little bit lonely."

Gunnar watched her now as she carefully removed the eyes from the third dragon head, gloved hands steady despite being covered in viscera.

She hadn't stopped with the cookies, dedicating all her free time to studying local mythos and struggling to learn Russian. She handled their trade, keeping their books beyond Gunnar's quotas, and had helped others in town maximize their profits after learning how to best preserve the various bits and pieces used for profitable alchemical ingredients. Rina said her efforts helped get the train coming four times a month instead of three. Exports were up that much since their arrival.

All of which was fantastic. Everything was, really. Gunnar had never found himself more at ease. The beast in his blood was content; he hunted most days, brought in kills that kept his territory clear and he and Audrey beyond well-fed. There was a brothel at the station for when his baser urges clawed up, and he'd garnered the respect of his fellow hunters.

He'd never had an obvious purpose before, always on the run, just trying to make it through the day. Gunnar found he enjoyed the simplicity of sleeping in the same place each night and not worrying where his next meal would come from.

There was really only one problem, and he was staring at her right now.

Gunnar, now he belonged in a town filled with dangerous creatures, way out on the fringes of civilization. Deserved it really, given who and what he was. Hells, he was thankful. He wasn't buried in some cell, rotting underground and barely alive. He was free, more than.

But it shouldn't have cost Audrey everything.

He frowned a bit. Her nose was pink from the cold where it poked out of her scarf, her brows knit in concentration as she put the eye into a vial filled with a preserving agent. When she finished, she hummed and nodded to herself, then screwed the lid on before she caught him watching her. She blinked at him, hazel eyes bright in the fading sunlight.

"Do you need help?"

Gunnar chuckled; he was elbows deep in the chest cavity, fishing after the zmei's second heart. "Nah," he drawled, catching the concern in her scent. They'd learned each other in the last few months, living and working together in such proximity. She'd worry too quick, so he shrugged and offered, "Just realized you never told me where you learned to make those cookies."

He could tell she grinned under the scarf, with the way the skin crinkled a little around her eyes. "Oh, from Whistelae, the healer who took on my fosterage after they released me from the hospital. Her mother was human."

Gunnar extracted a few more ribs and tossed them in the growing pile for smoking. "Druid, right? Odd place for them to turn up."

Audrey nodded, back to eyeball grabbing, and he relaxed with her attention off him. "She came from the Coalition for a teaching exchange, which was how I met Theodore, actually. He acts as a liaison sometimes."

"Heard from him at all?"

"No. He told me not to expect anything, but I'd hoped . . ." Audrey sighed. "It's safer this way."

Meaning how Audrey was assumed dead.

The ESC had blared the headlines about her death. The terrorism of it, media speculating if Gunnar himself had opened a hells gate with his demonic blood to pay her back for her good deeds. Seemed like fearmongering didn't require even basic knowledge about vilebloods, just whatever made the best story bait.

Gunnar'd expected some pushback from Theo when he'd told the archivist he planned on taking her with him, maybe more lectures about gratitude or his manners, but he'd agreed it was the right call. It was strange to lockstep with the good guys, but whatever bastard he was, Gunnar knew the math.

Audrey lost everything for him this time around, and fuck if he'd leave her hanging, not after she'd dedicated her life to his freedom.

He wasn't sure how he'd clear the debt, and it bothered him, day after day.

He figured the best start was saving up enough trade to get Audrey her own place, remove that forced sort of dependence she had on him. She'd been doing just fine for herself outside the hunting quota he took care of in exchange for both their Nizhny residences.

Maybe there was some secret magic in those cookies, he thought with a chuckle but dismissed the thought as quick as it crept up.

It was really just her.

Just Audrey, this human girl who deserved far, far better than being tied to a monster like him for the rest of her life.

"This might be enough to push us over," Gunnar said, cutting the heart loose and setting it on the table. He let her handle the more delicate work; she had steady hands and smaller fingers. "Could get you set up in your own place in the station instead of all the way out here."

Audrey's movements stalled. She tried to cover it by setting aside the knife and cleaning her hands. "Oh?"

"Said yourself, dragon bits are a big deal."

"Zmei," she corrected, grabbing some cured leather to wrap the hearts. "I guess we'll see after the next two train days? No rush really," she added, avoiding eye contact now.

Gunnar leaned against the table while she tied off the bundles. "Thought you were excited about getting a new place?"

"Sure, but I figured . . ." Audrey fiddled with the string. "I enjoy being close to Lyubava. I could babysit the babies. No, the cubs, I mean." She laughed, waved a hand. "And we share the trade and work, so it seems silly to drag corpses all the way into town, right?"

"Not that far of a walk. We could do the grunt work up here." Gunnar rubbed his chin, skin cold. They'd need to take a break inside soon; she shouldn't be out so long in the cold, even with the open fire furnace running on the deck and the smoker chugging away. "Figured you'd be happier with your own space."

"Oh, I'm not bothered by sharing space." She waved a hand again, wandering around their work area like she suddenly couldn't figure out what to do with herself.

"Inside," he ordered, snatching up the gear too valuable to leave outside.

She nodded and followed suit. Gunnar sighed when they stepped into the cabin's warmth, pulling down his scarf, and kicked the packed snow off his boots before he shut the door behind them. He inhaled, long and deep, her soft scent all over everything.

The cabin wasn't much, built in a rush before winter set the ground hard. Rina wanted Gunnar helping with Nizhny's next expansion over the dark months. The foot print wasn't bigger than that apartment Audrey had back in the ESC, but it was nicer by a thousand miles.

Stone pine had a mild scent Gunnar appreciated, the log cabin walls rustic and easy on the eyes. They'd imported the windows, the soft tint warming the lighting in the large sitting room that doubled as her little library. They each had their own bedroom, along with a rather modern shared bathroom, complete with a copper tub and shower, and kitchen.

A drop door led into the basement, a stone-sealed cellar that doubled as a workshop and storage facility for their trade between train days. It also housed the boiler, which connected to enchanted piping that ran all the way back to Nizhny's town center.

Another wheel greased by cookies. The town smith, a dvergar—not to be ever called a dwarf, not if you valued your balls—who only went by E, was a notorious grump despite his skills, and apparently with a previously undiscovered obsession with human baked goods.

According to Rina, they should have been chopping wood for heat and boiling their own water through the winter, but E had been unexpectedly cooperative about running and enchanting the pipes before the hard freeze. And a week after they'd moved into the new place, Audrey had a passing conversation with Aster one night in the tavern. She was all apologies for the latest batch of cookies being overdone, muttering about wooden stoves baking unevenly.

Not even two days later, an enchanted Dutch oven, the perfect size for a dozen cookies and magically primed maintain the perfect baking temperature indefinitely, appeared on their doorstep with a hastily scrawled, unsigned note about the importance of settlement morale during the long winter season.

Gunnar was certain if Audrey wanted, she'd be welcome at the train station proper. Hells, E would probably make some excuse about connecting her kitchen directly to his forge if it got him more of her cookies.

Now Gunnar wouldn't enjoy being further away from her, unable to check in on her whenever he felt the itch, but the train station was one hells of a step up from a cabin on the fringes. She'd never whispered a single complaint, though, not in all the time they'd been here. Far as he could tell, she was fine with their situation, happy even, and he really couldn't understand *why*.

She should want more. She deserved it. If anyone fucking did, it was her.

Instead, she was here with him, shaking snow off her furs and hanging them near the furnace to dry, washing her hands and setting up tea for herself, coffee for him, and lunch for them both.

He'd push more later. Talk her into what she deserved, Gunnar decided, inhaling again as her content scent of sunshine permeated the room.

Audrey went about her day, humming a song they'd heard last train day from a traveling music troupe. He basked in the moment and pretended he deserved it, maybe even earned it by keeping her safe.

At the very least, he'd take it. He'd always been a greedy bastard; it was in his blood.

Chapter 12

"**G**o yell at Rina, not me."

Audrey crossed her arms. "I'm hardly yelling, Jonathan."

Gunnar cocked a brow at her. She always said his first name like that—the one she'd given him when she changed his records—when she was serious. Or annoyed at him. "Then give her the dirty looks."

She pursed her lips, amusement and frustration painting her scent.

"You know all the things crawling out of the swamps and lakes tonight eat little girls like you."

"I'm not a child," she snapped as she packed her bag on their kitchen counter with more force than necessary. She smelled pissed now.

"No, but you are human. The only one in town. And you're not a fighter, Audrey."

"I'm not asking to fight. I'm just saying I could help with any injured. Bandages can save lives." She wrinkled her nose. "That sounds stupid. They can buy time, I mean." She sighed, picking at the stitching on her satchel. "I hate feeling useless."

Yeah, that's what he'd thought this was about. "You're not, and you know it. Only combatants outside on the Longest Night, you heard it from Rina. Everyone else is in the station, no exceptions, until dawn. Any injured will get tossed inside the barriers, then you can help them." He grinned at her back. "Besides, you packed stuff to make cookies for everyone?"

When Audrey glared at him, there was no heat in it. She barely held back her smile. "I have more to offer than baked goods, you know."

He laughed. "Believe me, I am aware."

Gunnar checked his weapons over one more time, including the eversharp hunting knife. He favored close combat, which let him make use of his speed and sharp reflexes, but he'd become a clean shot with the crossbow because silver-tipped bolts were never a poor bet. He used the single-handed battle axe he'd gotten from the Úlfheðnar clan less than the crossbow, but weapons were weapons, and tonight would be a battlefield, not a hunt in the woods.

Despite her complaints, they left the cabin a few minutes later, bundled in furs against the deep winter bite. Sunset was a still a few hours off; Rina wanted everyone gathered with time to spare, a non-negotiable request from the settlement leader to give everyone time to bunker down and for the fighters to divide up coverage for the town's defense.

Audrey locked the door behind them, and although theft was low on the list of concerns this evening, they had a goldmine in dragon parts stashed in the basement until train day. She pulled her scarf up over the bottom half of her face and gave him a thumbs up as she stepped down onto the snow.

The train tracks were only a few feet out from their front door, the terminus about a mile north from their location. Everyone worked together to keep the tracks clear of winter snow and debris. They hadn't had a fresh snow in a few weeks now, making the mile and half walk to the station easy.

A clear, cloudless sky welcomed them, blue stretching endlessly to the horizon. The land out here was remarkably flat, with marshes and tree lines in all directions. Gunnar still felt exposed when they walked the train tracks, but most of the local wildlife and mythos knew better than to approach Nizhny's territory in broad daylight.

That didn't stop Gunnar from watching all directions, tasting the crisp, frostbit air for anything out of the normal.

"Are you worried?" Audrey asked, her breath coming through her scarf in little puffs.

He gave her a lazy shrug. "Nah. They've all done this before, know what to expect. This is what, seventh year?"

"Yes, but you haven't been here."

"Same shit I hunt day to day, just a bunch at one time." He inhaled. Her scent was muffled by the furs, but he tasted her worry. "What's really bothering you?"

"Hmm?" She blinked up at him, then wrinkled her nose. "Nothing, I just . . . I don't want you to get hurt, that's all."

He gave a little snort, not sure why that mattered. "I'm used to it. I heal fast anyway, you know that."

She huffed. "It *is* a big deal. You still feel pain, Jonathan."

Gunnar canted his head at her, not sure what she wanted from him. It had been nearly a year and a half, having her in his life. First as his counsel while he was in prison, then here in Nizhny after. He still wasn't used to anyone giving a shit what happened to him, let alone worrying about his well-being.

"I'll be careful," he offered, the words almost coming out in a question. Was that what she was digging for? He wouldn't make a promise he couldn't keep, but he'd never been the type to be reckless in a fight, anyway. Cold control was more his style. "Besides," he drawled, "I'll be keeping Zhadan's ass out of trouble. Last thing I need is you moving us in with a widowed Lyubava and her cubs."

She laughed. "Only if she didn't come after you for letting him get himself killed. I doubt cookies would help against an enraged, pregnant chuchuna."

"I'll keep that in mind."

The station proper came into a view, the building an impressive holdover from the pre-Aperien era. What was once a plain building of beige and white concrete now acted as the town hub, decorated with colorful prayer flags along with etched and painted wards. Empty all around aside from the tracks, it painted a stark picture of their lives here: isolated and removed, with only the weekly train as any form of contact with the rest of the world. The most expensive part of Rina's initial investment into the settlement had been the snowplow engine to clear the railway to Nizhny station.

Gunnar found he liked that aspect of Nizhny just fine.

The town's patroness—mayor, boss, dictator, all the above—leaned against the main doorframe, talking with Zhadan and Lyubava.

Katerina "Rina" Yaga cut an intimidating figure, as one would expect from a hybrid Aperien of her heritage, the daughter of a folk hero warrior and a witch goddess. The woman stood toe to toe with Zhadan, only an inch or two shorter, her muscular frame clear under the folded arms and well-kept leather armor. She wore a fur cloak, bearskin, her right shoulder bare. An ancient great sword that looked too big even for her meaty and capable hands leaned against her thigh.

Rina tipped her chin up at Gunnar and Audrey's approach, her pale blue-gray eyes focused on the chuchunas' needs.

"<<*Yes,*>>" Rina said in Russian, gesturing to the station behind her. "<<*E is warding, as promised. It's a contracted agreement between the town and Clan Bödvar already, if we want the Úlfheðnar tranced and fighting tonight.*>>" She gave Zhadan a rough pat on the shoulder, then a nod to Lyubava, who didn't seem impressed by them discussing her safety. *"<<Have I given any reason for doubt since you two arrived, Zhadan?>>"*

The chuchuna shook his head, grumbling and growling a bit, before he said, *"<<No, except treeman.>>"*

"<<And I told you, we'll figure that out after the Longest Night.>>" Zhadan snuffed, but took the dismissal for what it was, and he and his mate ventured into the station. Rina rubbed her chin, turning her attention to Gunnar and Audrey in full.

"Good, you're a bit early." Rina gave Audrey a warm smile, speaking English for Audrey's benefit. Her accent was thick, her voice a deep baritone for a woman. "We're just waiting for the rest of the Clan then we'll begin."

"Anything I can do?" Audrey asked before Gunnar replied. He grinned over her head, catching Rina's amusement despite her stoic exterior.

He was pretty sure she only tolerated his presence because of Audrey.

"We feast with the dawn," Rina said. "Aster could use the help in the kitchen, but she's also set space aside for your baking."

Gunnar chuckled, and Audrey shot him a glare. He held up his hands in surrender. "Told you, dirty looks for the boss lady, not me."

"She's not laughing at me at least," Audrey said, chin up, but then she sighed and adjusted her bag. "I'll help with whatever we need."

"Thank you," Rina said, genuine, and Audrey gave a half smile before she ducked into the station. As soon as she did, Rina arched a brow at Gunnar. *"<<Little wanted to fight, is it?>>"*

"<<Nah. More like she hates feeling like a burden. That and she gets restless when she worries, especially when she can't do anything about it.>>"

"<<Fair,>>" Rina said, then grinned a little, conspiratorial when

she added, *"<<She believes so little of our abilities? I think my feelings are hurt.>>"*

"<<You have those, huh?>>"

Rina threw back her head and laughed, a heavy braid tossed over her shoulder. Then she sobered, made a thoughtful hum. *"<<Audrey will stay inside?>>"*

Gunnar inhaled. Rina's scent wasn't concerned, not exactly. Audrey, for all her endearment to Nizhny's people, had no qualms about letting everyone know when she disagreed with something. After a few uncomfortable conversations, Audrey agreed to bring up any grievances in private from now on, but she'd never disobeyed a directive.

Rina smelled protective. Possessive, almost. This town was her livelihood, her everything really. A home, the backbone that made Rina a true Independent power. She regarded those under her umbrella as family, at least those who'd proven themselves worthy.

Audrey had certainly done that. For any mild headaches she caused, she solved a dozen more. She made a settlement filled with grumpy dusters and meaner Aperiens *smile*. She just had a way about her.

"<<Yeah, she will,>>" Gunnar said, and he didn't doubt it. She wouldn't cause trouble without good reason, and she knew she had no place in a fight. She hated the violence of his quotas, even if she understood the reason and helped process the dead.

That was enough to satisfy Rina.

They headed inside when Clan Bödvar came into view down the railway, the berserkers already chanting battle hymns as the sun sunk low behind them. The dire wolf pack, twenty plus strong and counting, Rina's own personal hunting beasts, answered with echoing howls at the promise of bloodshed.

Chapter 13

Dawn

The tavern smelled completely different as early morning light drifted in through the wall-sized windows on the eastern side. Most notably the blood of all varieties, some long dried and some fresh, most belonging to the dead piled around the settlement. They'd deal with clean-up over the coming days, because now was a time to celebrate before everyone fell over and slept.

Nizhny had survived the Longest Night without a single causality.

Gunnar grinned, couldn't help himself, three pints deep into Clan Bödvar's homebrewed honey mead. He sprawled on a chair near the front doors, elbows on the table behind him, watching the people he'd fought to the teeth with all night make asses out of themselves.

The only serious injury of the night fell on one of the younger Úlfheðnar, a boy named Uffe who had a reputation for being reckless even among his berserker kin. He'd chased down a wounded bukavac to its lake, got gored when the six-legged beast fought back at the last second.

An odd thing to witness, since the Úlfheðnar fought with their spirits. The boy's wolf had battled to the end, then collapsed and vanished like smoke. There was lots of noise from his fellows—wolves and boars and bears—but they'd kept on fighting, trusting those back at the station to take care of Uffe when he woke. The boy fell pretty early, maybe one in the morning. When they'd all trudged back here at first light, Uffe'd been waiting, bandaged and bitter over missing the bulk of the battle.

Gunnar snorted as a verse got bawdy. Afi Frode, the enormous man as furry as his bear spirit and Clan Bödvar's head, stood on the table swaying with his two sons, his daughter, and Rina all linked arm to arm. Unlike the berserkers, Rina was absolutely filthy and didn't seem to give a shit about the mess she was making of her tavern.

Old Norse wasn't a tongue Gunnar had needed before coming to Nizhny, and they were so fucking drunk a lot of it slurred into nonsense. He'd caught something about fucking and fighting and mayhem and not getting enough of the former after the latter? Everyone cheered. Gunnar took another drink, grinning into his mug.

He'd never been part of anything like this before. All the rough shoulder pats, the howls and cheers every time he killed, or nods of thanks when he helped drag someone's ass out of the fire. No one flinched at his black eyes here; he was a brother-in-arms in a war, a monster they were all happy to have on their side. They stayed comfortable with him even now; the mood was relaxed and fevered and exhausted, unwilling to let the moment of victory go just yet.

Gunnar still kept himself back. Anyone who walked by greeted him, toasted him, but it was a lot of noise and bodies. The smells merged into sweat, blood, and dirt, all that stony soil and loamy moss heavy on the air. He'd met everyone at least once, not enough for him to really know people, not yet. All he smelled right now was the unified ease that everyone had survived the Longest Night this year.

He'd gathered that hadn't always been the case.

Gunnar glanced up as E wandered over and sat with a seat between them, mead horn in one hand and a plate of cookies in the other. The smith set the plate between them, motioned with a rough palm for

Gunnar to help himself.

"Didn't know you shared these," Gunnar drawled. It didn't go with the mead, but he'd already gorged on Aster's bounty, his gut heavy with rich meat and vegetables too damn good to be called healthy.

E smoothed his thick beard, shrugged as he took a deep drink. The man rarely talked to anyone, including Rina and Audrey. Right now, he smelled well and truly drunk off his ass. "Your girl made them for everyone. She's been running the ovens with Aster since sundown."

"She didn't sleep?"

E snorted, leaning back in his chair; his feet didn't quite reach the floor. Gunnar's skin prickled under the focused attention. The dvergar was obviously an Aperien, likely one of the original manifestations given the power underscoring his scent. E was otherwise unpresuming. Without his senses, Gunnar would have dismissed him, which only made the man that much more dangerous.

Despite being in a village of outcasts, Gunnar couldn't help wonder who E was or what he'd done, in mythos or reality, but it was none of his business.

Gunnar scanned the room for Audrey, who was most decidedly his business, starting with the fact she hadn't slept. She'd greeted him when he'd come back, of course, saturated in worry, then relief, before ushering him to a seat and bringing him an overflowing plate. Once she'd settled him, she gave him a tired smile and then raced back to help Aster get food and drinks for everyone else.

Before he found her again, Gullin lumbered over, blocking his view and reminding Gunnar about the pitfalls of staying in one place too long.

The Aperien towered near eight feet tall, ducking around the antlered tavern lights, his honey-colored beard swaying to his knees. He was as a filthy as Gunnar, coated head to toe in dried blood and muck. Twigs and leaves matted his hair, more shoved between the creases in his leather armor. He thumped his oversized wood axe on the empty table.

"Da," he greeted E with a nod, reeking of honey mead. When his icy gaze shifted to Gunnar, Gullin smirked. "Vileblood."

Gunnar took another drink from his mead horn. Ignoring the asshole was worth the flared nostrils and the sharp sting of annoyance flavoring his otherwise strange scent. The Aperien always smelled like metal and magic that reminded Gunnar more of a powerful weapon than a living being. He really couldn't parse Gullin beyond that by scent, not on any meaningful level.

That didn't make Gullin less of a prick, at least toward Gunnar, but fortunately, he didn't spend more than a few days at a time in Nizhny. Audrey had gathered bits and pieces of his story over the last six months. Gullin and E both searched for something, but Gunnar didn't give two shits what it was as long as he didn't have to deal with Gullin.

"Go on," E said, breaking the tension with that gravely grumble of his. "This night is for honoring the living and old sacrifices, not pissing."

"Not worth my spit or piss," Gullin said.

Gunnar didn't look at him. "Plenty of other places for both."

"Came to talk to my da, not you."

"Yeah, well." Gunnar shrugged. "I was here first."

"We were here when Rina set roots. Seven years we've held this ground."

Oh, he was getting mad now. Anything Aperien just *loved* when their lowers didn't bend and lick their boots. Gunnar cocked a brow up at him. "I heard all about it while I was out there slaughtering with the rest of you."

Gullin grimaced, all blustering, loud, and irritating when he started in with, "Rina should have never—"

Only to have E cut him off at the knees. "Rina decides for Nizhny."

The smith's steel gaze settled on his . . . whatever they were to each other, because Gullin clearly wasn't a dvergar. Gullin defused, not bothering to address Gunnar again before he gathered his axe and left for the tavern's far side. E's scent remained as calm as a frozen pond.

Gullin would be gone before train day; with any luck, it would be months before their paths crossed again.

Gunnar drank more.

He'd always be vileblood. Nothing would change people hating him for it, despite being exonerated for existing. Gunnar caught sight of Audrey then, who watched the singing and table dancing from the bar as Aster tapped another cask.

Aster was another Aperien in town who was unassuming, the cornflower wraith tended both the tavern and the summer fields here. Everyone knew to follow her rules and not piss her off. Odd, because at first glance she looked no more threatening than Audrey, a slim woman with long golden hair who always wore deep blues. Her eyes though, they gave it away, a piercing azure that took in more than any human ever could. She'd taken to Audrey the same as everyone else, appreciating her help in the kitchen. It helped Audrey's interest in learning about everything never came off in the prying kind of way that drove a lot of Aperiens and dusters to suspicion.

Everyone laughed then, the group stumbling, tipping the table. Gunnar picked out Audrey's laugh over the din, watched her instead of the show, his frown lessening.

Missing a night of sleep hurt no one, but he was protective of her, had been since that moment in the alley, her safety one of the few things that kept his nature subdued. That part of him wanted her to take a damn nap as soon as he convinced her to go home for the day.

She looked tired but happy. Her nose wrinkled as she watched the chaos, hands covering her mouth as Rina and Frode's stumbling devolved into a wrestling match that sent food flying and chairs crashing. Aster yelled about brawls and breaking things before throwing entire loaves of bread into the fray. Frode's wife Hertha, ever the voice of reason, shouted at them both.

"Idiots," E grunted.

"Cheers to that," Gunnar drawled.

The wrestling settled down, songs dwindling maybe an hour later as fatigue set in. A few of the Clan left first, younger children who'd fallen asleep in the corners carried home. The harpy flew out on silent wings. The only one she'd interacted with the entire morning was Audrey when she offered her food. A broken table got Aster throwing hexes until Rina intervened, their fearless leader drunk as shit. Rina took over the bar so Aster could retire, slurring promises about "clean-up day before train day after rest day."

Gunnar chuckled. E yawned, gave Gunnar a nod. He hesitated, then grabbed up the rest of the cookies and wandered off to his rooms. He hadn't fought with them, instead fortifying the station to keep those inside safe during the long dark, a task just as vital. Gullin followed him, saying his farewells to everyone save Gunnar, which suited him just damn fine.

Across the tavern, Audrey yawned as Rina talked louder than she needed in Russian, so fast and slurred he knew Audrey only caught every other word of it. The general idea became clear when Rina lifted Audrey off her feet in a bear hug and she returned it with a giggle. Back on her feet, she searched the room, and he waited until she found him in the darkened corner and lifted his mead horn in her direction.

She rolled her eyes, made her goodbyes to Rina and the rest, then joined his quiet corner.

"Well, all that was exciting," Audrey said, sitting in the chair beside him with a huff and slumping toward him.

He leaned toward her when she did, inhaling her particular, sweet scent with a hidden smile. It'd been hard to pick her out in the crowd, and he was pleased to find she smelled content, happy, and tired but not entirely exhausted. She also smelled like sugar and spices from all the cooking.

She smelled good. Really good.

He slung an arm behind her, ran a hand over where her braid was coming apart. She let out a little sigh and rested her head on his shoulder. He gazed down at her, feeling lazy and content with her back where she belonged.

Gunnar frowned.

He'd learned a long time ago being a vileblood granted a resistance to most venoms, toxins, and poisons, thanks to the Mother of Monsters' contribution to his heritage. This included alcohol, killing almost any chance for him to get drunk, or even a good buzz going.

Whatever those damn berserkers brewed, whatever magic they wove into the drink? He wasn't burning it off like he normally did.

Between the mead and the hours of fighting and the adrenaline dying back, his entire being purred at Audrey's proximity.

Not good.

He cleared his throat and shoved his drink away, rising on slightly unsteady feet. "Should get you home."

She blinked up at him with a yawn, then nodded.

They made it about halfway up the rails before Gunnar slung her over his shoulder like a sack despite her protests and laughter; the girl was falling asleep on her feet.

As he shut the cabin door behind them, Gunnar let out a long breath, realized how spooled him up he'd been at the tavern. He couldn't relax, not entirely, not with so many other people around him. He was used to never relaxing if anyone was nearby, but now "anyone" excluded one person. He chuckled as Audrey told him to put her down, grumbling about him being a big oaf, but he didn't argue since she was right. Gunnar stumbled as they reached the bathroom, wincing as he set her down.

He thought he'd hid it, but she was on him in a second, a frown turning down her pretty mouth.

He shouldn't be thinking about her mouth.

Fucking honey mead.

"Are you hurt?" Audrey put her hands on her hips.

Gunnar leaned on the doorframe. "Not really."

"Not really," she deadpanned back at him, then sighed. "Why didn't you let me patch you up when I was helping everyone else?"

"Don't like being exposed around so many people, you know that. And they don't need reminders of what I am."

Seeing his black blood, he meant. She didn't like that thinking, he knew, but she didn't argue with him this time. He wondered if she'd overheard Gullin, but probably not. She'd been too far away.

"Go sit down and let me see it."

"You need to sleep."

"And I won't if you're bleeding."

He let her move him toward their sitting area. With a growl, he slumped down on their couch, a hand-me-down from Rina. It had taken weeks for it to stop smelling like anything but him and Audrey. He closed his eyes for a few seconds while she gathered her homemade healing kit. This wasn't nearly the first time she'd patched him up.

He liked it, he'd realized early on, and it gave her the sense of purpose she always chased, being useful as she called it. Gunnar rubbed his face as he waited, wondering when she'd realize her just being, just existing? Having her around was more than enough. He'd never had anyone around. Never kept anyone around.

Never *wanted* to keep anyone around.

He frowned again.

He shouldn't be thinking about keeping her. She wasn't his. Couldn't be.

Fucking hells, this damn mead.

And all the more reason to get her a place of her own. He didn't need to get dependent on anything. Sure, this was working out, but shit went tits up at any time. Being prepared was the best call, another reason he was glad everyone in town saw her value.

Audrey set her bag on the table, poked him in the shoulder. "How bad?"

He shrugged. Their definition of bad rarely aligned. "A scratch."

He pulled his shirt off, the dark fabric damp from blood, but there was a reason he wore dark colors. The slices came from a strzyga; one snuck its claws under his guard while he dealt with a flight of them. Zhadan fared worse, but together they'd brought them all down. His undershirt showed four claw marks through the thin fabric, along his side and lower ribs. Gunnar tossed the shirt to the floor, knowing Audrey would insist on stitching it up for him.

She was on him in seconds, kneeling beside his chair as she examined his wound. He breathed through his nose, not liking the bitter tang of unhappiness coming off her skin.

"Jonathan." There went that name again. "This would have only taken a few minutes, but you sat there and bled for hours instead? And you were drinking. It thins your blood."

Gunnar shrugged again, and she glared up at him. There was flour on her cheek. He brushed it off, showed her his fingertip.

Audrey blushed. "I made a lot of cookies last night." Her cheeks stayed pink as she washed away the blood with a warm cloth. It stung, but he didn't flinch.

"E took a whole plate back to his rooms."

"I wondered where the rest went. You know, he still won't admit he made that oven for me."

He watched her work, frowning at the way the inky black of his blood stained her fingertips, deciding to stare at the ceiling instead. "Man doesn't talk much."

"He really doesn't, but you two sat together for a while today. What did you talk about?"

"Nothing."

She laughed, grinning up at him when he smirked down at her. "Why am I not surprised?" She washed her hands, and Gunnar relaxed more once she poured the bowl in the sink and brought back clean water.

He'd never mentioned how he felt about his blood touching her, but she seemed to know. She never washed up when she treated someone as much as she did for him.

"Gullin as friendly as always?"

"Mhm."

Audrey rolled her eyes. "At least he's always traveling," she muttered. "I'd offer something for the pain, but then we'll have a whole debate about how you don't need it, and I'll say how it will make it easier, and you'll go on about how pain is no big deal and I should save it for someone else."

"You're sassy when you're tired."

"You try waiting tables for eighteen berserkers. See how you feel."

He chuckled, watching as she stitched. The way her brows pinched in concentration, the way she chewed her lower lip as she worked.

He hunted overnight most times to hit his quotas. A lot of the more dangerous mythos around here were tied to the dark. He'd come in quiet, but she'd always be on his ass in the morning if she'd slept through his return, demanding to treat each minor cut or bruise.

The light came in the windows differently now. Warmer. Made her hair lighter in the mid-morning sun. It was a clear day, the entire room brighter than he normally cared for, but he found he didn't much mind, not like this.

He canted his head, his body a bit heavy, lazy as he studied the curve of her cheek. The slender column of her neck. If he closed his eyes, he could hear her heartbeat. Gunnar let out a long sigh, which made Audrey giggle.

"You're tired too, you know."

"Mhmm."

"Almost done."

"Mmm."

He found himself transfixed by her soft fingers taking care of him. Another person, a good person, willing to touch him at all. Always there, waiting for him, looking forward to him. Smiling. Beautiful.

He inhaled on impulse, leaning forward as she pressed the bandages to his bare skin, his body dwarfing hers. He was watching the fine bones in her wrist move as she worked, her scent blooming, pleased, when she said, "There, finished."

And she smiled up at him, expression warm and open, cheeks flushed with pride and fatigue. Her fingertips lingered against his skin, lips parting to ask him a question.

Hmm, what would the sound coming out of those lips taste like, he wondered, the darker part of him rolling over in delight at the idea of finding out.

He jerked back.

The fuck.

This was Audrey.

Audrey, not some woman to slake his lust. His beast.

Fuck. *Shit.* These were not thoughts he allowed. Ever. He needed to get away from her while he was out of control like this.

He pushed to his feet, grabbing his dirty shirt. "Thanks. Get some sleep."

Audrey rocked back on her heels, confusion saturating her scent. "What about you?"

"I'll be back," Gunnar said, throwing on his jacket. "Just need to take care of something."

He stepped out into the cold without looking back, the iced air helping beat down that heat inside him. Gunnar jogged toward the station, needing to get this mead the fuck out of his system.

Chapter 14

Gunnar made it back to the Nizhny station in half the time. Nearing midday now, he kicked snow off his boots as he stepped inside. The mood was drastically different now, the tavern area that connected to the main doors empty. It was a mess, reeking of spilled mead and broken wood, blood and leftover food. Rina hadn't been kidding; clean-up day was going to be its own marathon.

He moved through the station with purpose, past the kitchen entrance and the general trade area. Past the stairs to Rina's offices and the long hallway toward private quarters in one direction and guest rooms in the other. He reached the familiar ornate double doors framed with red silk curtains and neon signs shaped like angel wings, and let himself in.

Gunnar winced. He always did when he entered the brothel. Spicy incense wafted, but it only did so much to cover the stale and fresh scents of sex and sweat. The greeting room was clean, but the private rooms were only a few feet away, separated by brocade curtains enchanted to cover sounds, not smells.

"And here Virtue didn't think you'd show today," a male voice crooned from the room's far corner, its owner sprawled across a maroon velvet chaise.

Innocence wore a pink kimono that reached mid-thigh, ankles crossed and drink swirling in his free hand. The duster's features became more feminine as he gestured to the open chaise beside him, the end table set with clean glasses and an open bottle of absinthe. He appraised Gunnar without a hint of shame, his scent ripe with interest, sexual and general, licking his lips before smiling with perfect white teeth.

"She busy?" Gunnar asked.

"She is," Innocence said, emptying his drink and setting the glass down. "But I'm clearly unoccupied."

"Told you before, I don't fuck men."

He shrugged a lithe shoulder; it was funny how subtly Innocence could shift his appearance, by inches at a time. Few had that kind of finesse, a stark reminder he was dangerous. "And I've told you, I suck cock far better than my sister."

Gunnar smirked. "I'll wait."

"She has all the fun." Innocence pouted, slumping in the chaise, pretense dropping as his features shifted back to his natural appearance. Still handsome, or beautiful, whatever, with lavish blond curls and sea-green eyes. He smelled hungry despite dropping the seduction attempt. Gunnar leaned against the wall, wondering if anything could fully sate him or his sister. Memories from their first encounter flitted to the surface.

Virtue and Innocence were half-siblings who shared the same incubus father; Gunnar'd picked that up over a few beers earlier that day. Innocence, however, was a duster. The man lingered back a bit, all pretty as he watched Gunnar with a hungry expression, but it was Virtue who stepped forward to greet him, her head tilted.

The difference wasn't a matter of beauty or sexual preference. Gunnar wasn't appraising for an evening partner yet. Aperien power steamed off the woman approaching him.

As the hybrid daughter of an incubus and succubus, no one needed to explain why she'd found herself out here in Siberia. Gunnar had a hard time imagining any Accorded Territories welcoming a being with her kind of appetite.

"I was wondering when you'd make an appearance, Jonathan," she said, her voice low and sultry. Easy on the ears, but it grated real hard against the name that didn't belong in her mouth.

"Gunnar," he corrected, crossing his arms. Only one person got to call him by his new first name, and he wasn't letting Audrey anywhere near this place.

Virtue nodded, the heavy braids draped over her well-muscled shoulder laced with gold thread. He'd never seen skin so dark, save maybe Papa Legba on the top of the Manhattan Pen. Somehow, it didn't clash with her sea-green eyes. Everything about the Aperien was smooth and natural, down to the thin shift hugging her ample curves, teasing at darker nipples. A tall woman too, only an inch or so shorter than him.

While plain wasn't a word he'd throw anywhere near the woman, she didn't wear makeup or jewels, and her feet were bare. No paint on her finger or toe nails, no perfumes either. She moved like water down steam, not a care for anything, all grace and liquid sexuality.

Then he frowned, because she was shrinking right in front of him, those curves slimming down and her skin lightening. Eye color shifting to an all too familiar hazel.

Gunnar knew exactly where this shit was going.

"Don't," he growled. "You're fine."

Innocence, who'd been a silent observer—almost forgotten given the air of sex and promise rolling off Virtue to lure Gunnar in—hooted like a fucking monkey. The spell, illusion, magic, whatever Virtue radiated snapped off, leaving the room chilled.

"Did you hear that, sister dear? Former Mistress of the Velvet Empo-

rium, Aperien whore of legend. You're 'fine?'" The duster doubled over, slapping his knees.

Virtue watched Gunnar with the kind of look that killed.

Shit, not the impression he'd intended.

"You can see yourself out, yes?" Virtue asked.

Right. Gunnar gave her a curt nod. Not ideal, but . . .

"Not you."

Innocence righted himself, still cackling as he waved a hand and sauntered down the back hall. "Yes, yes, off I go. Though I expect a report later, dearest."

They waited until he'd excused himself entirely, likely behind silencing charms. Gunnar kept his arms crossed, pretty sure the next thirty seconds decided if he'd be stuck jerking off for the foreseeable future.

"Not trying to offend," he drawled, doing his best to sound stupid. He doubted she'd buy it, but it might help soothe those ruffled metaphorical feathers. "Just figured we could cut all the bullshit."

Virtue raised both brows, her huffed laugh incredulous. "Bullshit, is it?"

"Your kind needs to eat. My kind needs to fuck." He shrugged. "Rina said we pay for the sex here by letting you feed. Me? I just need to scratch that itch before it becomes an issue. You can just take what you need, no song and dance. And I'm damn sure you can feed deeper on me than the other dusters around here."

Her expression relaxed slightly, her scent shifting from annoyed to curious. "Vilebloods do have more sexual stamina than most." Virtue ran her thumb over her bottom lip, her gaze a living thing as it wandered over his body. "You surprise me. Most leap at the chance to indulge in what they consider forbidden."

"Sounds like a good way to frustrate yourself into doing something stupid."

"Or experience that which one must deny oneself. For whatever the reason."

He bared his teeth. "Not interested." Then he gestured between them. "And if what I'm offering don't work for you, fine. I've gone years without fucking. A few more won't kill me."

Virtue only smiled, as if the game suddenly closed. The score, he didn't entirely know yet, but she said, "No, it sounds . . . pleasant, to be honest." She gestured down the hall. "Last room to the left. Would you like me to bathe first? I know your senses are more heightened than most."

He leaned in, sniffed. She didn't take offense. Sure enough, he smelled someone on her skin, but he didn't know the Clan well enough to tell who she'd fucked last.

"If you don't mind."

"Not at all. I won't be long."

"Alright." Gunnar scratched the back of his head. All this was too easy? Simple? "That's it then?"

Virtue laughed as she headed toward the stairs. "Did you plan to leave without partaking?"

No. A hard, uncomplicated fuck was exactly what he needed. "Nope."

"Then make yourself comfortable." Virtue canted her head at him, flashing another serene smile as she ascended toward what he guessed was her personal quarters. "You're not what I was expecting when Rina said a vileblood had come to town. With a human girl, no less."

"Yeah, she won't be stopping by."

"Of course not."

"Now look what you've gone and done, Gunnar," Virtue called as she stepped into the sitting room's warm light and leaned against the doorframe. "I owe my brother a drink."

"Like taking candy from a baby," Innocence mused from the chaise, tossing his curls. "But that can wait, of course. Business first."

Gunnar ignored him as he crossed the room to Virtue, who watched him with a curious expression and the same electric gaze as her sibling.

Neither had fought during the Longest Night. They instead waited to soothe their clientele after, lovers not fighters and all that, and they'd both used their magic to help E fortify the station. He smelled the lingering effects.

Virtue stepped aside when he reached her, motioned down the hall; he knew the way. "I'll bathe. Make yourself comfortable."

Gunnar nodded, familiar with Virtue's chambers now, and ducked through another set of enchanted curtains. He inhaled deeply, wondering why the enchantments that kept her room scentless couldn't work on her skin. Same with the bed, though she'd mentioned simple cleansing magic worked fine between patrons.

He stripped down, tossing his clothes on the chair in the room's corner, grinning as he recalled fucking her bent over it a few times. He stroked his hardening cock as he sat on the bed's edge, making sure his thoughts stayed exactly where they belonged: on Virtue.

The Aperien made it easy. Over the years, he'd always needed to be careful with working women. He'd always been dominant in every aspect of his life, and fucking was no different. He liked things rough; he required control. His stamina tended to cause issues for dusters if nothing else did first, which left him unsatisfied after most sexual encounters.

Even if fucking Audrey wouldn't risk killing her because she was human and he was vileblood, this part of himself—well, all parts really, but his sexual urges especially—didn't belong anywhere near someone like her.

Someone good, everything he could never be. Someone he'd never deserve, even if by some miracle he *could* have her.

"Deep thoughts?" Virtue asked as she stepped into the room. Her natural scent—an unmoored mix of inviting and danger—appealed to him, the beast in his blood humming under his skin.

Virtue could handle him. Those darker parts of him wouldn't hurt her.

That said, she'd never truly satisfied that deeper itch in him. Virtue might submit to him, but it was a service, not a fundamental truth.

"Nothing new," Gunnar drawled, leaning back on one elbow as he watched her.

Virtue didn't put on a show, but her entire existence was seduction. She didn't need to try. It helped her attraction to him was genuine.

He'd been right, what he told her that first night they met. The drain she took from him, the sexual feeding, she could take more from him than most others because he wanted it gone. He wanted her to root out his lust, let him pretend he was a civilized man, even if it only worked for a few days at a time. And he never pleaded for her to leave off.

Virtue always quit first, fears of her own nature keeping her from crossing whatever invisible line she'd drawn.

She didn't waste any time now, dropping the gossamer robe, miles of perfect legs, full curves, and night skin on display. Virtue smacked his hand from his cock, and a heartbeat later, he was buried to the hilt in her wet, welcoming cunt. They both let out satisfied moans.

"You're injured," Virtue noted, fingernails digging into his shoulder blades.

He fisted her braids, jerking back her head, his teeth on her jaw. Guiding those thick hips with a heavy hand on her thigh, squeezing hard, enjoying the way she filled his palms as he fucked up into her. "And?"

"An observation, nothing more."

Virtue already fed; she never waited with him, didn't hold off for the burst of sexual energy during an orgasm. It felt like fingertips inside his spine, his lower back, his groin. Cool and hot at the same time. An electric, unnatural jolt as she clenched her inner muscles around each thrust.

"Did Audrey patch you up?"

Gunnar flipped them with a snarl, driving her into the mattress. She arched up to meet him, heels digging into his ass, the sharp spike in her feeding making him lightheaded. He shook his head once, trying to hold off against the sensation.

"Didn't come here to talk."

He closed a hand around her throat. She leaned into the pressure; her eyes glowed as she licked her lips. Her pulse didn't so much as stutter, a steady drum for all her panting.

"Here I thought . . . we'd become . . . friends, *ah!*" Her voice caught on a particularly violent thrust, their hips smacking together, louder now. She pressed a palm against his bare chest, reacting more than goading him.

He didn't relent until the Aperien tumbled into an orgasm, because he had to *concentrate* to keep himself from following her right over the fucking edge when she practically sucked his soul out of his dick. And her feeding spiked harder when she came, his skin tingling all over, his heartbeat stuttering violently.

His instincts flared at the inherent danger.

Being vulnerable, even as the woman under him shattered and screamed.

Gunnar snarled.

It wasn't enough. He was still too restless, too aware. He wanted to give over and let her drain him dry, even as the beast that made up his vileblood bucked in protest.

Like always, the man won, and Gunnar bit his cheek until he bled, ignored his blackening vision, and pinned one thigh to her chest as he growled and grunted with each relentless snap of his hips.

Virtue stopped feeding, gasping, moaning under him. She licked at his skin, nibbled, purring.

Relaxing.

"We're not done," he gritted out.

"Of course not."

"Then keep fucking feeding."

They didn't talk much after that, the only sounds heavy breathing and flesh on flesh, moans from her. The drain on his senses, his life force, continued as he railed against Virtue's body and wrestled down the instinct to break her neck before she killed him. It was dangerous, telling her to feed this long, but her eyes were glazed now, her entire body singing with magic and power as she pulled more and more. Devoured.

The beast inside him thrashed, but the man always won. He used his vileblood, not the other way around. His muscles burned, thighs cramping from the effort; all the while, Virtue's pulse remained a steady drum under his palm.

Her brow furrowed. He shook his head. "More."

"Gunnar."

"What, suddenly too much for you?" He bared his teeth inches from her mouth. Hooked an elbow under her other knee.

Virtue's magic spiked as she grabbed his wrist, her pointed nails breaking skin this time, black blood and sweat mingling before dripping down on her chest.

His hips stuttered. "Fuck, *fuck*." The sensation was lightning through his veins, making his cock twitch and pulse, and he had to stop so he didn't spill. His head swam, his lungs lurched, his heart leaping against his ribs.

But then there was a surge of pheromones from Virtue, followed by a very deliberate, slick flutter around his cock, and Gunnar came with a hoarse shout.

He rolled off her as exhaustion chased him from all sides. The fucking mental hurdles, the night-long battle, the Aperien's feeding. "Hells."

Virtue stood, putting on her robe and moving his clothing so she could settle on the seat across from him, her posture lazy. "I thought the Longest Night would be enough for you," she mused.

Gunnar shrugged, much as he could lying flat on his back, still catching his breath. The room was cool, sweat already drying on his skin. He pushed himself to sitting. "You know what I am."

"Doesn't it ever get tired? Tossing around your nature so casually?"

"Must not." Gunnar yawned, rubbed his face. His body felt heavy—exhausted and almost empty. The booze had burned off, and his mind felt quiet. Perfect. He'd be able to sleep a few hours now. He fumbled into his clothes, his fingers numb. "You?"

Virtue's legs crossed as she settled deeper into her chair. "I have to feed or I'll die, Gunnar. We aren't comparable."

He tugged on his shirt. "We are what we are, nothing to change it. Sounds the same to me." Gunnar laced his boots, giving her a nod as he saw himself out. "Thanks. See you around."

Chapter 15

Train day was always a shitshow as far as Gunnar understood it. When Rina struck out to claim Nizhny seven years ago, she'd paid heavy tolls to get trains coming in from Moscow down the line to the ass end of Siberia. At first, they limited it to imports at ridiculous markups. Once the exports started and news of Nizhny spread, people started coming down the rails as well.

Rina didn't allow for tourists, but with the increase in the town's exports warranting a train every week, more and more unfamiliar faces came to sniff out Nizhny. Anything from investors to alchemists, and poachers to the occasional desperate soul seeking sanctuary.

Rina allowed for an open market of sorts for whatever wasn't assigned for exports. Aster ran the tavern for meals and drinks, E kept a stall for anything from weapons to jewelry, and the Clan usually sold treated furs and leather armor. Innocence and Virtue entertained, of course, while others made themselves scarce, like the harpy and the chuchunas. Gunnar would have liked to do the same, but Audrey loved having a stall on train day.

He needed to make extra trips today for the zmei parts, a gods' damned fortune coming their way. This was his second sled load, but he needed to make a stop before the market. The north end of the station proper housed the local pack, a mix of Aperien dire wolves, normal wolves, dogs, and various half-breeds.

He'd promised Audrey he'd drop off the frozen broth cubes she'd made for the puppies. The larger beasts, including the alpha pair, made themselves scarce with strangers in town at Rina's request. She liked to keep some of her cards close, he'd learned.

Gunnar whistled when he reached the pack encampment. A series of shelters, lean-tos, and dens dug into the hard pack. A muddy mess, and it reeked of dog piss, but even he couldn't help a chuckle with the dozen puppy faces poked out of the closest den. One howled, and that set the entire group off, and then they charged him, barking and yipping. This group was mostly wolf, barely a trace of magic in their blood, which made them little more than sled dogs, although smarter than average.

"Alright, alright," he grumbled, unpacking the ice chucks and sliding them away, the pups tripping all over themselves to chase the blood and broth pucks. A larger wolf, one of the older females in the pack, watched from the den entrance, eyes gleaming yellow from the shadows.

"Audrey says hi," he called, and the wolf chuffed at him, then disappeared back underground.

That done, Gunnar picked up the pace. Audrey was already at the market, and he didn't much like her there without him. They'd never know what—or who—the train might drag in.

Audrey was supposed to be dead. He wasn't sure anyone on this continent would recognize her face. The Eastern Seaboard Conjunct was one of the few places that kept on with twentieth century technology, but the Moscow Dominion made up another pocket. Would anyone all the way the fuck out here recognize the human who helped change the Vilestars Accord? Unlikely, but the idea put his teeth on edge every time the train rolled in.

She'd lost so much on his behalf. Gunnar tugged a little harder than necessary on the sled straps, picking up his pace. He'd keep her from losing anything else.

A few minutes later, a hundred unfamiliar scents mingled together, along with the cacophony of train day. Yeah, train days couldn't go by fast enough for him. He headed directly to the loading area first, to make sure the materials from his kills made it out on this train and to give his senses time to adjust.

Gunnar rubbed his chin as he walked, recalling the brief conversation about their savings and Audrey moving to the station. Maybe she was just trying to be polite, but she hadn't smelled like deception. She never did. They'd need to talk more about it, because this load from the zmei was a shitload of trade, and it wasn't even half their share of the creature.

He greeted Frode and Hertha, the eldest pair of the Clan overseeing loading as usual. Kept the Clan kids out of trouble on train days, which everyone needed. Uffe stepped over as Gunnar settled his pallet near the open freight car.

"*<<How's the wounds?>>*"Gunnar asked. Uffe startled at his use of Old Norse. Before the Longest Night three days back, he'd never really spoken to the kid aside from their initial introductions.

Uffe shrugged at him, chest puffed out as any fifteen-year-old might. "*<<What wounds?>>*"And to prove himself, he slung a burlap bag of dragon bones over his shoulder. Gunnar held up his hands, overlooking the way the boy stumbled.

Once Uffe was out of earshot, Frode grunted. "*<<Stubborn boy, that one. And we never thanked you properly.>>*"When Gunnar raised a brow, Frode waved a hand. "*<<Too drunk that morning.>>*"

That was the fucking truth. Gunnar grinned, wondering how much Aster had taken out of his hide—and Rina's—for all that broken furniture in the tavern. "*<<It's nothing.>>*"

Hertha stepped down from the train car, dusting off her callused palms. She looked at him like she wanted to hit him, but her scent was calm and clear. Still, short as she was for a Viking berserker, Gunnar was pretty sure Hertha's word was final for Clan matters.

"<<*It's far from nothing. That boy was a fool, and without you and the chuchuna, we might have lost him. The Clan is the last of our kind, and family. We've lost enough over the years, many on the Longest Nights.*>>" The woman gave him another once over, then a sharp nod. "<<*I wouldn't have let you near this place, but you've more than proven yourself.*>>"

Gunnar inclined his head. Wasn't this just cozy? He excused himself and left the sled; he'd get it later this afternoon or tomorrow.

It was amazing the difference having a few dozen outsiders in town for the day made. The train always rolled in near first light and left by dawn the next day. Occasionally, Rina would arrange stay-overs for the week, but she kept a tight lid on her business and a polite sort of iron fist over her guests. Living on the fringes of town, Gunnar made a point of going the whole week without the pleasure of socializing with someone new on those rare occasions. The static population of Nizhny was far and away enough people in his life. Too many, honestly.

He brushed by strangers, all of them carrying scents he associated with the Moscow Dominion. Old industrial and regimented magic, lingering touches of wards used to keep the winters out and population within the laws and bindings. As far as Gunnar understood it, and he never cared much for politics aside from what Audrey shared over dinners, a large majority of the Dominion's magic came from its queen of sorts: Jaga Baba, the eldest of the Baba Yaga sisters, who was Rina's aunt. The Aperien witch had married Koschei the Deathless, both known for leading a productive but strict regime.

He smelled a strange witch's dark magic now, thicker than normal for proprietors passing through. Gunnar homed in on the scent but doubted the woman herself had made time to visit. Rina didn't speak with much fondness for her aunt. If Jaga Baba had come calling, they'd all know about it by now.

Gunnar frowned when he found the source waiting in line at Audrey's stall. She thanked another visitor before the man Gunnar scented stepped forward. He was unremarkable aside from the magic in his scent and wealthy clothing. It reeked of witch and power, more power than any duster, despite appearing remarkably human. Two bodyguards flanked the man, both duster trolls. He'd bet his nose on it.

The stranger removed his gloves as he stepped up to Audrey, who greeted him in careful Russian.

Hells, her accent was still atrocious. Gunnar couldn't help smirking; they really needed to work on it.

The man answered her in a clipped tone, asking Audrey where her keeper was.

"<<*Keeper?*>> I'm sorry, I'm . . ." Audrey cleared her throat, beginning again. "<<*I am sorry, my Russian is poor.*>>"

"<<*You are human, yes?*>>" the man asked, pointing at her for emphasis.

Audrey patted over her heart. "<<*Human, yes.*>>" Her smile didn't waver, though it didn't reach her eyes now. She gestured toward her table. "<<*Buy?*>>"

When the man smiled, Gunnar's skin prickled, but he held back from interrupting just yet.

"<<*Yes, I'm interested. If you have no owner, you can return with me to the Dominion in the morning.*>>" The stranger didn't wait for a reply, instead doling out instructions for one of his guards to head to the station now to book an extra seat.

Gunnar cut through the crowd, a growl building in his chest.

Audrey struggled to translate. "<<*Owner?*>>" She pointed to the stall, to their goods. "<<*This is me and my partner's. We own.*>>" She shook her head, frowning. "I'm sorry, I really don't understand what you're asking. Do you speak English by any chance?"

The stranger caught Audrey's chin. When she tried to move back, protesting, he held tight. "<<*Another human? I suppose I could purchase them as well to secure owning a human as sweet as you, dear.*>>"

Gunnar snatched the man by the wrist, ripping his fingers from Audrey's skin and muscling him back a few paces. He swore and struggled, unable to break from Gunnar's grip.

"<<*Don't fucking touch her.*>>"

"<<*Unhand me, now. Do you have any idea who you're talking to?*>>"

The trolls had their axes out, snarling as they circled in tighter, Audrey yelling from behind him to stop. Gunnar let go, but not before shoving the man so he stumbled over his fancy shoes.

He straightened himself, smoothing his pompous jacket front and waving down his guard. The man had icy blue eyes and a flop of dark blond hair tucked under his wool hat. He gave Gunnar another once over, then motioned to Audrey, who held Gunnar's forearm in both hands.

"<<*You know this human, then?*>>" When Gunnar only stared at him, the man huffed and rolled his eyes. "<<*Well, does she belong to anyone? I'm not here to stand out in the cold all damn afternoon. If she's not claimed, I'll arrange her purchase and take her off your hands.*>>"

The answer left his mouth before Gunnar gave it a single thought. "<<*She's mine.*>>"

The man blinked a few times, his witch scent bursting with annoyance. "<<*I see no markings of ownership. I'm to believe a vileblood has gone through the proper, legal channels to secure possession of this girl?>>"*

"<<*She's mine,*>>" Gunnar repeated. "<<*Touch her again and I'll kill you.*>>"

That got the trolls up in arms again, all snarls and broken, yellowed teeth under beady black eyes, but the witch-man didn't seem bothered. He seemed determined now, entitled in a way that made Gunnar's muscles twitch.

"<<*I'll speak to my cousin then and get this sorted out properly. Honestly, Rina must be more desperate than I imagined, allowing something like you inside her borders.*">> A tsk, and the man turned his back on Gunnar, a clear dismissal. His trolls were smart enough to guard his back until they all moved out of reach.

Gunnar watched them go, his hands in bloodless fists.

"What was that about?" Audrey asked, her scent laced with concern. "I couldn't follow everything. Does he think we stole something?"

"No," Gunnar said, a snarl low in his throat. "Do me a favor and go help E with his stall until I get back."

"What's wrong? Jonathan? Hey, don't just boss me around and walk off!"

"Misunderstanding," he muttered through gritted teeth. "Need to fix it before it gets more complicated."

"I'll go with you then," Audrey said, shuttering their shop and making a hasty apology to those waiting, but Gunnar shook his head when she was done. She planted her hands on her hips. "Why not?"

"I'm not sure what he'll do." Gunnar watched the stranger and his bodyguards disappear into the station proper, no doubt headed right to Rina. His cousin. "Don't want you around him until we know." When he inhaled to test her scent, she watched him with her brows furrowed. Worried, but as always, for him and not for herself. He rolled his eyes. "I won't pick a fight, not unless they make me."

She rolled her eyes back, but she wasn't amused. "Be careful. He reminds me of some of the wealthy Aperiens in the ESC. Like he thinks since he has money, he can do whatever he wants." She folded her arms, her scent unhappy now, so he nudged her with his shoulder.

"Go piss off E, it'll make you feel better."

She pushed him away. He let her move him and grinned, but she headed E's direction without further protest. Gunnar's amusement dropped cold as soon as she turned.

Chapter 16

Gunnar didn't knock when he reached Rina's office, just shoved open the door and stepped inside, acting like he belonged, and he did. Audrey was his business, full stop.

Rina was behind her desk with her elbows on the surface, woven fingers cradling her chin. She smirked at his entrance, then sighed as the rich man shielded himself between the troll dusters, who advanced on Gunner with weapons out.

"<<*Enough,*>>" Rina said, rising to her impressive height. The trolls balked, looking to their master for guidance, who offered none in the moment. To her cousin, she ordered, "<<*Send them out. This isn't a conversation you need your little pets for.*>>"

The man scoffed but didn't fight the demand, and the trolls shoved by Gunnar on their way out. Rina sunk back into her seat, annoyance clear.

"<<*You two've met then?*>>"

"<<*Not formally,*>>" the man said with a sniff, crossing his arms with what Gunnar could only describe as a flourish.

Gunnar snorted. "<<*Don't need to get acquainted. I need it made perfectly clear Audrey isn't for sale.*>>"

Rina held up a hand before her cousin could protest. "<<*Gunnar is one of my best hunters. Gunnar, this is Dimitri syn Koschei, the Deathless's oldest son, and . . . what is it now? A duke in the Moscow*

Dominion?>>"

"<<*Your cheek has never been the endearment you think it is, cousin,>>*" Dimitri said, then gestured at Gunnar. "<<*He claims the human girl in the market is his. Is this true?>>*"

Rina hesitated; it was brief, barely noticeable, but Gunnar caught the spike of frustration in her scent. "<<*I know you think the Dominion's authority extends to wherever your boots fall, but this is my territory. An independent settlement outside your father's jurisdiction.>>*"

"<<*A settlement which would never have gotten off the ground without his generous support,>>*" Dimitri returned.

"<<*I cleared my debts the first year, in case you're not included in territory affairs.>>*" Rina clunked a dirty boot down on her desktop, crossed her other ankle on top, ignoring how her cousin bristled. "<<*And the rail line is more than paying for itself, profitable to all involved.>>*"

"<<*And this has what to do with our current conversation?>>*" Dimitri asked.

"<<*Not much, beyond the part about humans requiring a patron. I don't peddle that here.>>*" Rina said. Dimitri's scent spike with triumph, but Rina continued before he could respond. "<<*Which just means I don't enforce it. Gunnar and Audrey came here as a pair.>>*"

He wondered what she was playing at exactly, so he just shrugged and repeated himself. "<<*She's mine, told you that outside.>>*"

"<<*You expect me to believe this farce? Dominion rights aside, there's nothing that prevents me from claiming a human who is without a proper keeper.>>*"

"<<*Nothing except me,>>*" Gunnar said.

Rina sighed rather dramatically. "<<*Look, cousin, you want to fight a vileblood for the human girl he considers his? I can't stop you, but I'd really rather not have to explain to my aunt and uncle why I had to ship you home in a box. Let it go, Dimitri. The girl is spoken for, and it's not just him. She's part of Nizhny.>>"*

Dimitri shook his head, nose turned up as he tsked again. "<<*This is what you stake your reputation on? A human girl and a vileblood. You're lucky that your economic value has increased, or you might find my father losing patience with your little endeavor.>>*"

"<<*If he does, he'll let me know through official channels.>>*" She leaned forward and shuffled her papers a bit. "<<*Nothing here about this visit being more than a holiday for a bored politician. Speaking of, you'll need to head home in the morning. I don't have an open room at the station this week.>>*"

A blatant lie, but in the end, Dimitri didn't question it, striding stiff-backed from the room with that stick still six feet up his ass.

Rina shot Gunnar a wry smile once he'd left. "Family is such a joy, no?"

"Wouldn't know. Is he going to be a problem?"

"He's had eyes for Nizhny from the gate, but that's another matter entirely. As for Audrey? Likely not, because despite his lineage, his father is the Undying. He doesn't value heirs." Rina chuckled but then sobered, giving Gunnar a thoughtful look. "You could save yourself future hassle and just make it official. Others might come from the Dominion and make asks after her, long as she stands unclaimed."

Gunnar drew a deep inhale to make sure Rina wasn't fucking with him. "You're serious."

"Before you get up in arms about it, it's common practice under the Dominion's umbrella. It's their way of fulfilling their obligation to the Human Protection Accord, like ESC uses welfare and fosterage. Most of the wealthy Aperiens own humans in name but let them live their lives. Having a benefactor keeps them safe from unsavory circles. Those happen, of course, but . . ." Rina trailed off in a shrug, as if to say "what do you do."

"You're telling me what exactly? Brand her ass or something, make her my slave to protect her?"

Rina expression was bored now. "You really do like being difficult when it suits you. Most ownerships Dominion side are paperwork based on magical seals. The humans wear identifying jewelry for their house benefactor." She put up her hands. "And I'm not telling you to do anything. I was simply making a suggestion. You're the one barking 'she's mine' like some sort of barbarian."

"She is," Gunnar snapped, then sighed. "She's mine to protect, Rina. You know how we ended up here."

"All the more reason it wouldn't hurt for her to have an official benefactor," Rina replied with a shrug, then a smirk. "Even if we are at the ass end of nowhere."

"No, I . . ." He rubbed his face. "I can't do that to her. Bad enough she's stuck depending on me, stuck with me around at all. I'm not going to take away her having a choice in the matter." Logical or not, another level of protection or not, he wouldn't force her to be *his*.

Rina watched him, almost like she had something more to say on the matter, but then shrugged again. "You know her better than any of us."

"Maybe," Gunnar offered, then grunted. "Thanks for . . ."

"Not letting him take Audrey? Please, I should thank you. I haven't had a good fight with that asshole in almost a year. He swings by every few months, always with a new way Nizhny would be better off if he was involved." She stood, stretching until her back cracked in a few places. "I've had enough of this office for today."

Gunnar nodded, wanting to follow and make sure Dimitri didn't get any ideas, and to let E know what was going on. And to get Audrey the hells out of the market until the train left tomorrow morning.

When he opened the door, unfamiliar scents smacked him hard in the face.

Two men waited outside, talking in low tones, but Gunnar already knew they were vilebloods, both of them, black eyes watching him as the beast in his blood snarled.

"It's true then," one said. "This is a haven for vilebloods?"

Chapter 17

While Rina didn't directly invite Gunnar into the conversation, she gave him a nod of approval when he stepped inside and shut the door behind the four of them.

"I don't run a charity," Rina said once she'd settled back behind her desk. The two newcomers—vilebloods—sat in the chairs across from the ancient piece of furniture.

"'Course not," the shorter vileblood said, licking his lips, nervous. "Sorry, that's not what I meant. Just seeing another one of our kind here, walking around, figured it at least meant we won't get stoned or some shit."

Rina explained a bit about Nizhny, since it was clear these boys weren't from this continent. Suited Gunnar just fine, because it gave him a few minutes to breathe, which kept him from cutting throats.

Nothing like a damn mirror to remind Gunnar about the dangers of his kind.

He exhaled. He wasn't killing anyone, not right now at least. If that was what Rina wanted behind closed doors, she'd have reached for her sword, not her chair. And she knew about his ability to scent emotions and intentions. She wanted his insight as much as they both wanted information from what would hopefully be a first and last meeting with these two.

It's true then, the one had said. They'd somehow gotten word that a vileblood lived in Nizhny, which wasn't exactly something they went around advertising. He needed to know if they knew who he was, if they knew Audrey was alive.

They both smelled filthy and tired, like old, adrenaline-tinged sweat and the thick dirt that came with being on the run. Their fatigue was genuine, the same as their uncertainty, and they were half-starved. Optimistic but tempered. The shorter of the pair, he didn't really seem to believe anything would come of this, yet they'd spent days on a train to the middle of nowhere. He introduced himself as Mateo, the other Tomas, his younger brother.

So far, the brother thing was the only lie. They weren't related; they both smelled like distinctly different Vilestar lineages.

While black blood carried a flavor none of his kind could escape, there'd been twelve Vilestars born before the war. The six males spawned six vileblood lines. Each carried an animal aspect, though it wasn't overt. Gunnar didn't look like a canine from having the Wolf-star as his great-great-great-whatever-grandsire. Beyond that, there wasn't much information on the subject—the goal had been to kill and imprison.

The younger man, Tomas, smelled . . . well, familiar was the only way to really explain it. He had more human in him than Gunnar did, more generations removed from the Vilestar source, but there wasn't a doubt in Gunnar's mind they came from the same Aperien. It was the oddest damn thing, feeling comradery on the first whiff. Made him realize he'd never encountered one of his kin before today.

Mateo's scent was entirely different. Gunnar didn't have context beyond knowing his own origin, but this vileblood wasn't carrying the same magic. Similar, without of a doubt, but not the same. And like Tomas, his blood wasn't nearly as concentrated as Gunnar's.

If Gunnar bled midnight ink on white parchment, they'd pen a sloppy, watered-down gray.

That didn't mean they weren't dangerous. Didn't mean two on one wouldn't present a challenge.

Physically, they were unremarkable aside from their black eyes. Both spoke like they came from the ESC territory. Haggard, too thin, and wearing clothes that didn't fit right. Tomas was pale under his tanned skin from malnourishment and exhaustion, black curls matted against his forehead. Mateo kept a shorn scalp, shorter and stockier than his supposed brother.

They both kept glancing at Gunnar, meaning they had enough instinct to be uncomfortable with another predator at their backs. Gunnar wondered if their senses were as a good as his. He did his best to keep his emotions clear, away from killing and territorial urges.

Rina went on now about how the quotas worked. How she wasn't sure if now was the best time to bring on new mouths to feed, being they were deep in winter now. Both claimed they'd have no trouble hunting for their keep; they'd dealt with worse.

"How so," Rina asked.

"You learn to fight or you die when you're in a prison for dangerous creatures." Mateo shrugged as if he talked about the weather. "We did what we had to inside, then about four months back, we got pulled out of the general pen—something about laws changing—and they let us out since we'd done nothing to anyone outside the prison."

"We did what we had to, you know?" Tomas added, and that skirted the very edge of a lie, but Gunnar couldn't fault him. He'd done more than he'd needed to down in the dark, fighting for his life, and he never felt ashamed of it either.

"Anyway," Mateo said, shooting Tomas a look; he was the smarter of the pair, didn't want to risk messing this whole thing up now that Rina hadn't immediately sent them packing. "They gave us some money for our troubles, but nothing's changed how people feel about our kind. We've been trying to avoid trouble, but trouble keeps finding us. It's been made real clear we'll be right back in a cage if we fuck up."

"People don't want us around. Think we should all be dead or worse," Tomas mumbled. He stole a glance at Gunnar, seeking his agreement, but Gunnar gave him nothing. He rubbed his nose. "We get chased out from everywhere. All we've done is run since we got out."

"And then you hear some golden story about Nizhny?" Gunnar growled out. Rina arched a brow.

Mateo turned on him fully for the first time, dark trenches under his gaze, but the man didn't flinch. "A letter one day at the homeless camp, talking about how if we could get here, we'd have a place to work and could avoid going back to prison. Said killing needs to be done, but it's sanctioned by the local Independent." He gave Rina a respectful nod. "Like I said, we're no strangers to violence, and we're happy to work to earn a place to sleep and eat. We blew everything we had to get out here, so . . ." He ended with an unremarkable shrug, already resigned to rejection.

Rina did a good job radiating neutrality. "I don't make calls about my town lightly, and you weren't on my inventory." She held up a hand to stall the excuses about how they'd gotten on the train illegally. "I need time to consider before I decide." Directness worked for Rina. Her no bullshit methods were how she kept a town of monsters in the outer limits of civilization in check. "Go on down to the tavern, have yourself a meal on the house. I can tell you need it, and while I can't guarantee you'll be staying any longer than the train out in the morning, I also don't let visitors starve. Aster can get you settled."

They knew the dismissal, and Gunnar moved from the door as the pair got to their feet, all thank you ma'ams and head bobs, keeping their posture non-threatening. It wasn't a hard sell given the shit shape they were in, but Mateo cast Gunnar one last look on his way out the door, appraisal in his dark eyes but no challenge. The fellow animal knew his place, at least for the time being.

Once they were gone, Rina let out a long exhale. "This day just keeps getting better." By better, she clearly meant fuck all. "What's your take on them?"

"They're vilebloods." When Rina gave him a tired look, he shrugged. "No lies about what got them here, but they weren't offering details either. Who knows what they consider keeping their noses clean? And they're not brothers, at least not by blood."

"We're expanding ahead of my goals," Rina said, crossing her arms as she paced over to the map on her wall. The landscape extended miles beyond what they'd already claimed in her name. "We've got excess stored up, enough for two years if we face unexpected bumps. Four trains a month are making us a killing."

Rina rubbed her chin, tapped a finger toward the eastern side of the map, all untamed territory besides the tight acreage the harpy kept clear around her perch at the pump station. Celaeno's primary contribution was scouting in all directions, not clearing out beasts for Nizhny's expansion.

"No one comes looking for work in the winter," Rina went on, her expression all cool business. "Two more hands could go a long way before spring."

Gunnar didn't want the fuckers here, but that wasn't what Rina was asking him. She didn't give a shit about posturing—aside from herself coming out on top—and she'd put Nizhny first every time. "Not sure what you want from me."

"I want an honest assessment."

"What, vileblood to vileblood? They're dangerous. You know that already because you know me. Yet you let me in."

"They don't come with a future favor from a Citadel Archivist."

Gunnar huffed out a sour chuckle. "Theo, huh?"

"I thought you knew," Rina said, then shrugged. "I wouldn't have let you within a hundred miles of my home, given what you are. The archivist got here first, told you and Audrey's story. It's a good one, don't get me wrong, and I'm glad as hells I took you both in. But I didn't know either of you, and I don't give a shit about Accords that don't affect me."

Another shrug. She watched him closely now, and he scented a bit of regret on her, but Rina was a sledgehammer and she'd already swung.

All of it just reinforced what he'd always known. Even with the Vilestars Accord changing, his kind were still shit. Gunnar smirked, this time with more mirth. None of that changed the fact he wanted to throw Mateo and Tomas out on their asses, no hesitation.

But he'd fooled himself into thinking he'd somehow made a place for himself on his own merit. Now he knew; he was still running on the good graces of good people when they should have left him to rot in the dark. None of it was a surprise, but it was real fucking annoying. It *bothered* him that Theo had bribed his way into this place he'd started to call home.

What a fucking joke.

"I want you to have some drinks with them, see if their story holds up."

Gunnar jerked; he'd been staring at the floor like an idiot. "What now?"

"Use your senses, get a read. Tell me if it's worth the risk of taking them on."

"Why the fuck are you asking me?" He half-laughed out the question. "You sure you can trust my judgement?"

Rina's jaw ticked, annoyance threading through her scent. "No promise would have kept you here if you didn't prove worth your salt, Gunnar. Don't go soft on me because the truth is a bitch." She gestured at the window, the midday sun painting shadows across the taiga. "Time is business, and that keeps us all alive. And in case it wasn't clear? This isn't a request."

Gunnar exhaled hard.

"Take it seriously, because you'll have the last word. I wouldn't have homesteaded you near Lyubava if I didn't trust you. We good?"

Aside from the fact that he had no interest in what she was ordering, he nodded. The rest, well, Rina smelled like she always did, which was crisp honesty, and it eased the sting a bit. Then he wanted to shake himself for feeling anything about it at all.

"Yeah, we're good. I want to get Audrey home first. I don't trust Dimitri not to harass her, if nothing else. Same with those vileblood, not until I know more."

"The train leaves early, with or without them, and if you fuck this up, you'll be babysitting until the next train day."

Gunnar let out a low growl as he strode out of the room.

"I would have kept Audrey, no questions," Rina called after him.

"You'd have tried," he called back.

Chapter 18

Audrey was, to Gunnar's relief, right where he asked her to be, regaling E with a story that required waving arms. A quick check as he strolled through the stalls around the station didn't turn up Dimitri and his guards or the vilebloods. He wanted to get her back to their cabin without encountering either group again.

E saw him first, the old Aperien fixing Gunnar with a glare. Audrey's scent washed with relief as he strode up.

"You've been gone a long time," she greeted. Her cheeks were pink from the cold, eyelashes rimmed in frost.

"Yeah, took a bit to get that shit sorted." He nodded over her shoulder at E. "Thanks."

E spoke in old Norse. *"<<And what's all this about?>>"*

"That's rude," Audrey said, but it didn't phase E in the least.

"<<You familiar with how the Moscow Dominion views humans?>>" Gunnar asked.

An affirmative grunt from the smith. *"<<There going to be a problem?>>"*

"<<Not sure.>>"

Audrey huffed. Gunnar held up a hand to soothe, asking for her to wait. Pissed her off, and he didn't blame her.

"<<The Deathless's son saw her in the market, asked to buy.>>"

E's furry eyebrows lifted. He jumped down from his stool and started packing things away. "<<*And then?*>>"

"<<*Told him she was mine, but he pushed and went to Rina. She backed me up, but there's no paperwork if he digs.*>>"

"<<*He leaves with the morning train?*>>"

"<<*Far as I understood it. Rina certainly didn't welcome him.*>>"

Another grunt from E. Audrey shuffled between her feet, her annoyance fading into concern. "What's going on?"

E motioned for them both to help shutter his goods. They joined—it did no one any good to fight E if he wanted something done. To Audrey, E said, "If you need to be alone this afternoon, stay with the chuchunas until the train leaves."

"Alright?"

"Good." To Gunnar, he added. "<<*I'll spend the afternoon at the station, watching Dimitri. He's a greedy boy with none of the patience of his father. He comes, he complains, he tries to find a reason this place should be his. I assume you'd be watching him already if there wasn't something else.*>>"

"<<*Two vileblood came in on today's train. Rina wants me babysitting to decide if keeping them to hunt is worth the risk.*>>"

"<<*Trouble comes in threes.*>>" With the tarp pulled and tied over the last of his goods, E gave a satisfied nod. He stepped to Audrey and gave her upper arm a squeeze—a reach for him, as he barely came up to her shoulder. Gunnar wasn't sure he'd ever seen the smith so gentle around anyone, not even when she brought him cookies. "Thanks for helping me with the stall."

With that, the dvergar smoothed down his gray beard and strolled off toward the station

Before Audrey could ask, Gunnar jerked his head toward their homestead. "Let's walk while I fill you in."

"You're scaring me."

"Yeah, well, it ain't great," he grumbled as he took her elbow and led her away from the pop-up market, north toward the unused portion of the railway's dead end. A few minutes of walking and Audrey was about vibrating out of her skin with nervous energy. "You heard about how the Dominion deals with its human population?"

"Yes, though benefactors and contracts sounds like a fancy way of saying slavery," she said with a grimace.

"Yeah."

"The man at the market wanted to buy me?"

"Pretty much. I went to Rina, got it all sorted, but he'll be around until the train leaves tomorrow."

"Who is he?"

He didn't want to worry her more, but he'd never lied to her and didn't intend to start over this asshole. "Dimitri syn Koschei."

Audrey stopped walking, fear saturating her scent through the thick furs. "Koschei? As in Koschei the Deathless?"

"His son, yeah."

"Rina's cousin then, but he . . . Why . . . What would someone like him even want with me?"

Gunnar set his hands on both her shoulders. "Who gives a shit? He's not taking you. Got it sorted with Rina already. That's where I went."

"But you're worried," she accused. "You sent me to E."

"Because I didn't know what was going on."

"E has never had a conversation that long with anyone since we've been here." Audrey poked him in the chest. "And E never worries about anything."

Gunnar shrugged. "Dimitri would be a fucking idiot to pick a fight over this, especially when he has no proof you're not contracted already."

"But I'm not." She swallowed a few times, her voice pitching higher. "You're both worried he's going to take me. Why are you lying about it?"

"Hey, I'm not lying about anything. This is Rina's turf as an Independent. Dominion doesn't mean shit here, and he knows it. I don't think he's going to grab you, Audrey."

"Then what *are* you worried about?"

He was more worried about the vilebloods, but they hadn't even gotten to that part yet. "He might harass you, try to bully you into going with him." Or nobility like him might give her the offer of a lifetime, not that he believed Audrey would ever sell herself like that. His frown deepened at the thought. "Dimitri's not the only shit going on today. Come on, you're gonna freeze."

She rolled her eyes but followed him as he started walking again, agitation in his stride. She jogged up to his side, and he forced himself to slow down for her shorter legs.

After a few minutes, she mumbled, "Train days used to be just fun."

He snorted. "For you maybe. I've always hated them."

"What else happened?"

Gunner exhaled with a growl. "Two vileblood came in. They got word about me being here, came looking for a place to live."

"Oh." Audrey hesitated, then said, "And that's bad?"

"Of course it's bad. Why the hell wouldn't it be?"

"Are they criminals?"

Oh, how he hated that prim and proper tone of hers, convinced she was in the right before they'd even started talking. It might have helped him get out of prison, but right now . . .

When he didn't answer, she prodded. "Well, are they?"

"They claim they aren't."

"Did they smell like lies?"

Gunnar sneered at the horizon line instead of her, fists clenching and unclenching at his side because he knew exactly where this was going. "No," he ground out, his jaw aching from the effort.

"Then how is this a bad thing? Rina wanted more hands for this winter season, but nothing turned up before the freeze. The newcomers could help."

"They're vilebloods, Audrey. You really need a reminder of what that means, you of all people? They'd spent their whole lives in prison. They're killers."

"Because of their imprisonment?"

Their cabin appeared on the horizon, Gunnar desperate to get her shoved safely inside and get away from this fucking conversation. "According to them."

"And when they told you this, they were telling the truth, as far as you can tell. With your incredibly accurate senses."

"Audrey, you—"

"Worked very hard to change the Vilestars Accord." She talked over him when he tried to interject. "And changing the Accord changed it for everyone with vileblood. This shouldn't come as a shock."

"And they just happened to hear about me living here?" He kicked their door open, not bothering to take off his boots or furs. "Get whatever shit you want for Lyubava's. You're heading over."

She paused in the middle of taking off her jacket. "Why? Where are you going?"

"Rina wants me to vet the vilebloods."

"Jonathan . . ."

"What?"

"They deserve a chance, especially if they've been incarcerated since they were children, like you were."

"That chance doesn't have to be here."

"And why not?"

"Because we don't know fuck all about them, that's fucking why. They're dangerous." He held up a hand when she protested. "I'm dangerous. We all are. You know that, whatever else you think is right and fair aside."

"Rina gave you a chance," Audrey protested. "How should it be any different for them?"

Gunnar laughed, the bitter sound barking out of him. "She didn't give me shit. Theo bought our way in, promising Rina a future favor for letting us stay."

"That . . . he wouldn't . . ." Audrey's cheeks flushed; he normally liked when she blushed—something sweet about it—but this was blotchy and red with anger.

"He sure did," Gunnar drawled. "Rina told me today, wouldn't have let me stay otherwise, would have told us to fuck right off. Because she knows the risks."

Audrey lifted her chin. "What changed then? Theo isn't granting favors for them, so what's different?"

He scowled at her. "I'm stuck fucking babysitting, that's what. She seems to think since I've played nice, it's worth rolling the dice."

"Played nice?" Audrey laughed. "Jonathan, you're one of the best hunters in Nizhny. You've made yourself indispensable to this community."

"Bullshit," he shot back. "You did that, not me. They tolerate me because all the monsters like having someone around who's not treating them like garbage for two seconds of their lives."

"That's not true."

"You act like you don't do shit, but you do. Everything you do adds value to this place." He smirked. "And to me. They'd have gotten sick of me a long ass time ago."

"Don't do that," Audrey said, pointing a finger in his face, trying to intimidate him. It would have been funny if he wasn't so pissed about the entire conversation. "Stop talking about yourself like you're nothing. You know I hate it when you do that."

"Sure, I'm good at killing. And having a brothel down the street keeps the beast in my blood from getting out, for scratching that itch. That doesn't mean something inside me couldn't break or snap."

She rolled her eyes. "You're not a werewolf."

"What the hells does that mean?"

"You talk about your vileblood like it's some separate part of you. It's not, Jonathan. You have powerful urges." She blushed, hurrying on as she waved her arms. "So what? There's no rule book for anything that's happened since the Aperien event. Every duster is a new person with new powers and needs and struggles, with no preexisting mythos to define or guide them. That doesn't mean you're a monster just because of your blood. You've proven that repeatedly in your life, yet you still see yourself as nothing but your blood."

"There any other dusters they made a fucking international magically binding Accord over?

"The Accord was wrong."

"Yeah? If everything is perfect now, why are these two vileblood starving and running?"

She threw her hands up. "All the more reason they deserve a chance! To prove they're more than their blood, just like you have!"

"There isn't good in everyone, Audrey. Not everyone can or deserves to be redeemed."

"Are you talking about yourself now?" she snapped, hands on her hips. "Are you not redeemed? Was I wrong to see good in you? In the man who saved me from being raped and killed in that dirty alley?" Her eyes shone. He could smell her tears; he hated when she cried, especially for him, or worse, because of him. "Why is it so hard for you to see yourself the way I see you?"

He tapped his temple, bared his teeth at her. "Because you're not in here. You don't know all of me."

"That's your choice, not mine," she bit back.

He laughed at that; yeah, not gonna happen. She wasn't getting anywhere near the dark corners of his mind. The darker corners of him. How he got off on killing, how much he liked it, how much he needed it. How much he needed to fuck too, and how sometimes, when he looked at her . . .

He shook the thoughts away. "I've got to get back, and I'm not leaving you here alone with a human slaver and two vilebloods loose in town. You're not safe."

Audrey crossed her arms, more to hug herself than posture. "I will because you're worried, not because you think you can order me around." She stalked into the kitchen, packing her bag louder than necessary.

Gunnar leaned against the doorframe, trying to maintain a calm exterior. Inside, he roiled, annoyed as hells at her continued insistence at helping when it put her in danger. Two more vilebloods living in Nizhny was a risk. And what made him more furious was the guilt she'd carry, as if it was her fucking fault if they didn't get to stay here. As if the entire world's problems belonged on her tiny shoulders.

Audrey walked back over after a few minutes, not looking at him. "I'm ready."

He sighed, motioned for her to lead the way. They strode back into the cold, the path to the chuchuna cave well marked. The icy snow crunched under their feet, the silence otherwise heavy between them. Didn't take long for Audrey to crack, and he grinned when she spoke first; she hated silence, especially when she had something to say.

"All I ask is you give them a fair assessment," she said. "I trust you, and I trust your judgement. If you think they're a poor fit for the town, then of course they should leave." She glanced at him, then away. "But don't send them away just because you're worried about me."

He snorted. "And why not?"

"Because you thought everyone was dangerous when we first came here. You didn't want me talking to the harpy, you didn't think I should go near the wolf pack, and you warned me off the Clan too. And E. And Virtue. And Innocence."

"I'll warn you away from Innocence every day of the fucking week," he growled. He'd made it clear to both Virtue and Innocence they weren't to touch Audrey, let alone feed off her. The thought of them . . . with her . . . "I stand by that."

"He's been nothing but extremely polite to me, Jonathan."

"That's because he'd probably die if I cut his nuts off."

Audrey let out a choked laugh, trying to glare at him, but she was blushing too much. She cleared her throat. "My point is, while I appreciate your concern, and I understand you worry about me because I'm just human, that doesn't mean you need to cast these two vilebloods away for my sake."

"You're not just anything," he muttered. Realizing she'd never let this drop, he added, "I'll give them a fair shake. But if they start any shit, believe me when I say I will finish it."

This time, her expression was amused. "You should put that on a shirt." She held her mitten-covered hands out wide, punctuating the air. "'He who finishes all shit that starts.'"

"On a shirt?" He quirked a brow at her, and she laughed. He liked the sound, liked how she relaxed now under the trust she had in him. Much better than her being pissed at him, that was for sure.

"Yes, it's a thing. Or it was, with human clothing. All sorts of stuff printed on cloth. Pictures and words and sayings. I bet you could buy shirts in this station, like souvenirs, when people came to visit."

"Who the fuck would come visit here?"

She laughed again and shrugged, and they settled into a comfortable silence as they approached the chuchuna cave. Zhadan poked his head out, sniffed the air a few times, then waved when he saw it was them before ducking back inside.

"Jonathan?"

"Hmm?"

She'd stopped walking, so he did too and turned, surprised to find her twisting her fingers and not looking in his direction. "What did you mean when you told Dimitri I was yours?"

You are mine nearly left his mouth, and he swallowed a few times to contain the words.

She wasn't his. He didn't have any claim on her. He owed her, not the other way around. And he sure as shit didn't have any rights to own her, contract her, any of the shit they did in the Dominion, and he wouldn't want that anyway.

It didn't change the fact that saying she was *his* in front of that bastard had been natural as breathing. Even now, his blood rolled at the thought, the single word: *Mine.* He shivered, trying to shrug away the feeling, how it coiled tightly in his chest and made his lungs ache. Didn't matter, none of it. He didn't deserve to breathe the same air, let alone pretend she could ever belong to him. Lucky she considered him a friend, which still baffled him.

And here she stood, hazel eyes looking into him, her scent nervous.

Right, him saying that made her nervous. Fuck.

Gunnar ran a hand through his hair. "He can't prove there's no paperwork behind it. Figured it was the fastest way to get him to leave you alone. Rina backed me up, so it should be enough."

"Right, of course." The words rushed out of her with a held breath, her shoulders slumping. Her scent became a wild mix of embarrassment, frustration, and fatigue. She gave him a half smile, then averted her gaze. "I'll see you later."

"Yeah," he said, for lack of anything better, not sure why she seemed almost sad. She shouldn't worry over these strangers. Gunnar grumbled as he headed back to the station, hoping the two vilebloods would make things easy for him.

Chapter 19

Gunnar joined the vilebloods without a greeting. He threw himself heavily in the chair across from them and slapped three mugs of Clan honey mead on the table. They huddled close, talking low as they ate their free meal, tucked in the tavern's far corner. Black eyes watched as he made himself comfortable, slinging his fur coat over the chair back and claiming a mug for himself.

He knew his limits, knew the mead and how it might affect him. Maybe these two men were belligerent drunks, then he'd have a solid reason for Rina to pack them. Gunnar took a deep drink.

Neither man rose to the bait. The younger, Tomas, carried apprehension and fear thick on his sweat-drenched scent. Mateo kept himself better controlled, but he was nervous too.

"You need something from us?" Mateo asked, tapping his fork on his empty plate. They both still smelled ravenous.

Gunnar wiped his mouth, shrugged. Lies didn't really suit his kind. They all knew it, and he wasn't in the mood for anymore bullshit today. "I'm here to decide if you're trouble." He nodded to their empty plates. "If you're still hungry, eat. Rina's good on her hospitality."

Tomas was on his feet, plate in hand. Mateo jerked him back down by his sleeve. "Relax."

"What?" Tomas protested. "We don't hurry, there might not be any more."

Gunnar recognized that deep prison mentality from places like the Madagascar pen. They let the inmates run in packs and let those packs sort out their own issues. Meant starving. Often.

He waved at Aster, who'd been watching their table since he'd sat down. She headed over, smoothing her cream-colored apron over her deep blue smock. Gunnar wanted to see how they acted toward a woman.

"What will you have, Gunnar?" Aster glanced at his company, nodding. "Gentlemen." Her ethereal gaze washed over them, polite, but quick.

"Nothing for me, but Rina's guests are still hungry. They didn't know they could ask for more," Gunnar said.

Tomas hunched now, embarrassment wafting off the boy. Gunnar wondered if he wasn't much past sixteen or eighteen. He didn't look at Aster at all, looked anywhere else he could find.

"This is true?" Aster asked, brows raised. She did her job well, made it easy to forget she was an Aperien and not some low-level duster. Radiated human in her mannerisms, but both these vileblood should be able to tell she was more from her scent.

"Yeah," Mateo muttered. "Free meal, she said, so didn't want to assume."

"It is no worry," Aster said, waving off his concerns. Gunnar knew she didn't give a shit about anyone who wasn't part of Nizhny, but she took her duties to the settlement seriously. "What Rina says goes around here, so if you are hungry, eat. More of the same for you both?"

"Please," Mateo said, Tomas nodding along.

Silence stretched after Aster left. Gunnar took another sip of mead, spread in his seat like he wasn't there for any reason.

Mateo cleared his throat after a few minutes. "Is this an interview or something then?"

Gunnar smirked. "Not really."

Frustration and desperation pressed Mateo's scent now, reminding Gunnar of a nervous animal backed into a corner. Good. He needed to know if they were the kind to bite at hands or piss themselves, or whatever might go in between.

"That's it then? Just going to sit there glaring at us until we fuck up enough you can ship us out?"

A lazy shrug. "Sounds fine to me." He glanced up at the antique clock face near the rafters. "Only so many hours until dawn. I've dealt with worse."

"I'm sure you have," Mateo bit out.

"I don't get it. What's the problem?" Tomas all but whined the question, and he seemed genuinely confused. "You know what it's like, but you fit in here. What's wrong with us trying the same thing?"

"I don't give a shit what you try, just don't want you doing it anywhere near me."

"Okay? We can leave you alone. We're used to lying low," Tomas went on, then kind of trailed off as Mateo scowled.

"You're a selfish fucker."

Gunnar chuckled. "Are what we are. Selfish for one, dangerous for another." He quirked a brow. "Or you boys going to deny that?"

"We haven't denied shit," Mateo snapped, his nostrils flaring. "Yeah, I'm fucking selfish. I don't want us to starve to death out on these damn icefields. Yeah, I'd like a bed under our backs for a change, a roof over our heads." He scrubbed his face a few times, a snarl thickening his voice as he went on. "And yeah, we're dangerous. And hells if it doesn't sound nice to get to make a living off it. Is that so hard for you to get? Or maybe you'd like to ask us actual questions instead of pissing all over the place."

Mateo threw up both hands. "We get it. You're stronger than we are. I could smell it as soon as we stepped off the damn train. You were here first, yada-yada, so you tell me what the hells you want from us."

Gunnar took another drink, knowing his scent must be ripe with annoyance, because Mateo was asking for exactly what Audrey had asked from him. To give them a fair shake. To hear them out before he made the judgement based on his own desires.

"When'd they get you?"

Mateo leaned back in his seat, his scent and expression cautious. "I was around seven. Shoved me in the youth section in Manhattan. Moved into the open population when I was twelve. There were a few more vileblood, and they let me run with him." He lifted his chin at Tomas. "He was born inside."

Tomas shifted in his chair, and when Mateo glanced at him, he nodded.

"They threw a woman in about four months pregnant. The guys I was with got her right when they dumped her, smelled her from miles off. A whore from some dark rites brothel in York, and when they found out the father was a vileblood," Mateo shrugged, "she traded sex for protection and made us promise we'd take care of her kid if it was a boy, kill it if it was a girl, and put her down if she didn't die during the birth."

"Fuck of a thing, watching her get all twisted up as the days went by." He shook his head, then went on. "After Tomas was born, she went batshit, and they killed her. Two days later, the guards came and wanted to take him away. They caught me with him, offered me a room back in the youth prison if I'd take care of the baby." Mateo grinned over at Tomas. "Was better being a big brother than the low man of the pack." His expression sobered. "They were all gone once Tomas hit twelve and they shipped us back out into general. Dead most likely.

"Then what, six years later? They come down, tell us shit changed, and let us out the front door."

Tomas stared at the wall now, his expression vacant, no hiding the bitter guilt from his scent.

Gunnar sighed before he said, "Human women never make it out if they get pregnant from our kind. It's the curse, the whole point."

Tomas winced, but his scent was curious now. They really didn't know shit about themselves, did they? Most days, Gunnar wished he knew less.

He added, "Maybe the kid lives, maybe it doesn't, but it's not like we can do shit about being born."

"How do you know all that?" Tomas asked, brow furrowed.

Gunnar chose his next words carefully. "I met the archivist who changed the Vilestars Accord. Got to learn a whole lot about our history, more than I really gave a shit about, to be honest. And like you said, the Accord changing didn't do much aside from us being thrown out on this side of the bars."

"Do you know what we are?" Tomas pushed. Gunnar got the impression Mateo didn't much give a shit about heritage, but Tomas's interest was genuine.

Aster came back with the food, they thanked her, and she was off again. The men both dug in, unashamed, and Gunnar figured it didn't hurt to share the knowledge Theo and Audrey had imparted upon him.

"You know anything?"

Mateo snorted. "Devil spawn. Demon blood. Monsters." He waved his fork. "Not much else for conversation when everything is trying to knife us for our food in the pen."

"Lucifer Morningstar and Lamashtu, goddess of monsters and beasts, got together and made a go at snuffing out humanity. Twelve

Vilestars, six men and six women, each infused with a different animal nature. The women were all twisted on the outside, ran around eating babies and shit. Real nightmare stuff.

"The men, they were beautiful like their father but hungry for violence like their mother. While their sisters hunted down pregnant human women and newborns, the men seduced or raped human women to start new bloodlines." Gunnar spread his arms, indicating the three of them. "Backup plan. If eradication failed, they'd corrupt the rest of humanity and bolster their numbers.

"The war to end them was one of the biggest calamities after the Aperien event. Good won in the end, but it took years. Lucifer, Lamashtu, and the twelve Vilestars all fell, but they'd done a lot of damage first. Crippled the human population for one, nearly made them extinct. And they made us."

"So we're part animal and angel and . . ." Tomas grinned a bit. "And god?"

Mateo snorted into his roasted potatoes.

"Don't get too excited," Gunnar drawled. "Pretty sure we didn't get much of that last part, but you can understand almost any language you hear, speak it with a little work?"

They both stilled, Tomas with a mouth full of food and glancing at Mateo for direction. The other licked his lips. "Yeah, that's a thing."

"Polyglot," Gunnar offered, "from angel blood, no matter how thin."

Mateo made a thoughtful noise as he kept eating. "You said the men were rapists."

"That part of what you had to do to get by?" Gunnar asked, flat out.

"No," the reply came fast from both of them, not a lie, but Mateo elaborated, "Strong drives, though. For sex and fighting."

Tomas cleared his throat. "I heard someone talking about there being a brothel here, but you don't pay, you just let them feed on you." The kid's cheeks flushed now—because he was, Gunnar realized, not much more than a damn kid. "Feedings like take energy out of you, so maybe it would be really good for the itching Mateo is talking about?"

Gunnar was not about to share anything personal with these two. "Already said we're different, you'd have to figure that out yourself if you end up staying."

"You're considering it, then? Us staying on?" Mateo sat up, his plate forgotten. His black eyes held Gunnar's, that desperation in his scent dusted in hope now.

Fuck.

All I ask is you give them a fair assessment.

Yeah, he'd done just that, hadn't he?

Gunnar sighed and took a deep, deep drink of his mead.

Chapter 20

When Gunnar headed up to Rina's office at about three in the afternoon, he'd surprised her. He'd been gruff, saying to give the boys a week, see what happened. He had no idea if they'd settle in or be shit at hunting, but Rina would sort that out.

He'd thought so, at least.

But apparently, him babysitting extended for their first trial week. She ordered Gunnar to show them the ropes, like Zhadan had for him.

Fuckers.

Audrey wasn't exactly smug when he told her as much, but it was a near thing. She'd smiled and patted his arm, told him he'd done the right thing.

Gunnar wasn't supposed to meet up with the other vilebloods until after lunchtime today. Doing the right thing sure felt like a fucking punishment.

He was enjoying a quiet cup of coffee, Audrey with her tea, when a meaty paw beat at their front door before it swung open.

Gunnar set down his cup and crossed his arms. The chuchuna smelled absolutely furious.

"Is Lyubava alright?" Audrey was already up, rushing over to the snarling monster.

"Treeman!" Zhadan roared. "Treeman still there!"

"A leshy has territory overlapping with the expansion plans," he said to Audrey when she looked confused. "Rina said we'd figure that out after train day, Zhadan."

"After train day now," he snorted.

Gunnar shrugged. "Why you yelling at me about it?"

"Come with." Another snarl. "Danger tree. Cubs come soon." Zhadan gave a few more snarling huffs, the chuchuna radiating a posturing musk. Smelled worse than a wet dog, more like wet skunk. "Come, tell Rina. Now. Not later. No more waiting."

And then he stormed out the door, leaving it wide open.

Gunnar sighed, not sure when he'd become the go to for everyone's fucking problems around this damn place.

"I'll get my coat," Audrey said.

Rina weathered Zhadan's loud entrance and louder bitching with no expression beyond wincing at a high-pitch roar. Gunnar leaned at the door frame with his travel mug, drinking as he listened, Audrey covering her mouth to hide her grin. The rant went on a good ten minutes, Zhadan switching between broken English and broken Russian and what sounded like Tibetan at one point.

When the chuchuna finally paused, his chest heaving, Rina set down her mug.

"I'm not sure how anyone can be this angry this early in the gods damn morning about anything, but yes, it's after train day, so." Rina stood and motioned to the map on her wall. "Show me."

Gunnar joined the pair, sharing what he'd picked up about the area. The leshy territory was likely huge, but he'd only detected signs of its presence in the last few miles on the northern projected border.

Close enough that they were encroaching at this point. Both Gunnar and Zhadan had steered clear as much as they could, but pretty soon they'd need to push out deeper to keep clearing for Rina's plans. If they hunted in the leshy's territory, it'd likely turn hostile for spilling blood on its claimed soil.

"Simple, really," Rina said when they finished. "Leshys aren't pushovers, but we have more than enough muscle to take it out. You two rally the Clan and whoever else isn't out hunting yet. Gunnar, grab the vilebloods too. This will be an excellent test run. See how well they can follow orders. We should have this settled by lunchtime."

"You're just going to kill it?"

Gunnar, Rina, and Zhadan all turned on Audrey. The other two seemed to have forgotten she was there. She smelled alarmed now. And pissed.

"Yes," Rina answered as she moved around her desk.

"But they're not just beasts. They're intelligent. We can reason with it."

"Reason for what, Little? They don't leave their land, ever." Rina cocked a brow.

"And you have more claim to this land than the leshy does?"

Gunnar rubbed his jaw to hide his smirk.

Rina appeared genuinely flat-footed, like she couldn't believe what had just come out of this human's mouth. "Excuse me?"

"What claim do you have to its forest? Aren't leshys small Independents in their own right, given they're sentient?"

"Did you miss the part where we've been killing all sorts of sentient things since you came here? And for years before you arrived?" Rina's voice was steady, but her posture tensed now, her scent ripening with anger. She wasn't used to being questioned. The woman led a tight, efficient ship, and most of the time, there wasn't a reason to argue.

"A leshy is not malevolent," Audrey countered. "Sharing a border with one could be a boon for Nizhny."

"If I want council on running this settlement, I'll ask for it," Rina said, her tone brokering finality, but that kind of shit was wasted on Audrey when her little righteous fire got going.

"Killing this leshy just because it's in your way is wrong."

Rina took her great sword from its place against the wall, slinging it over her shoulder. "Did you two miss my orders?"

Zhadan left without another word. Gunnar shrugged at her; Rina knew he wouldn't leave without Audrey.

"You should try to talk with it first," Audrey insisted, following Rina as she moved toward the doorway. "Please."

"Maybe I don't want to talk with it," Rina said. "Maybe I want to take care of this problem instead of wasting time on shit that won't work. This isn't the first time we've dealt with shit like this, and there's always a cost."

"But you don't know that until you try."

"It won't leave, Audrey. And I'm about to walk out this door." Rina stared down at Audrey, who'd grabbed her sleeve. "You've said your peace. I've made my call."

"I haven't said enough. You didn't even consider an alternative!"

"I've made my call."

"Your call is wrong," Audrey shot back.

When Rina scowled at her, Gunnar lazily crossed into her vision. The Aperien glanced at him, then back to his fiery human. "You don't like it? You know when the next train leaves."

Rina left, calling over her shoulder, "Gunnar, get to work," as her heavy boot steps echoed down the stairwell. Audrey's fists clenched at her sides.

"This isn't right." She turned on Gunnar, cheeks flushed and her frown severe.

Gunnar didn't care much either way, aside from not wanting to get kicked out of Nizhny. "She's the boss here. And you can't save everyone."

"Don't patronize me. All I'm asking is for her to have a conversation before she kills a being who has probably called that stretch of forest home since the Aperien Event!"

Gunnar gave her braid a tug. She slapped his hand away. He shrugged again. "Things worked this way long before the Aperiens came. Bigger stick wins, so I'm just glad we're swinging instead of dying."

Audrey stormed from the office with Gunnar on her heels. "There is also a long history, before *and* since the Aperien event, of successful diplomacy and unifications. Everything doesn't have to end in bloodshed for people to get what they want."

It impressed Gunnar how loudly she stomped down the station stairs, but he kept his grin to himself. When they reached the doors, he grabbed her elbow. She stalled, her shoulders hunching.

"I hate this."

"Yeah, I know you do. But Rina's no hero and she's never pretended to be one."

"I was just asking for her to take a chance."

"Say she did," Gunnar offered. "And say the leshy killed her."

Audrey's eyes shot up to his, wide. "That . . ."

"Could happen. Maybe not the most likely outcome, but not the least likely either. She goes down, Nizhny goes with her. And all these people who depend on this settlement are out on their asses."

"But she—"

"Has to weigh the risks. All of them. She's not just being cruel or cold."

"This is about expanding, not protecting what she already has. She didn't even think about it, Jonathan. Not even for a second."

"That's her choice. She's the one taking the risk either way, not you."

Audrey's lips formed a thin line. She was still furious, but she sighed. "You're right, I know that, but I still don't like it." Another bigger sigh as she chewed her bottom lip. "I hate feeling so damn useless. So . . . *human*." Then she glared up at him. "She might have listened if it wasn't coming from me."

Gunnar chuckled. "She's listened to you more than half the people in this damn town, woman. Come on, why don't you head home? Rina'll prep for this in the tavern. No reason for you to be part of it."

"I know about it, Jonathan. That makes me part of it."

"You did what you could, no need suffering for it. Staying with Lyubava might help Zhadan relax, though." He took her by the shoulders and turned her toward the exit. "I got to go find the other trouble, the ones you roped me into. You did that, so quit feeling useless, alright?"

She wrinkled her nose at him, trying not to smile. "I made a suggestion. You followed through. You can't blame me every time you do something good, you know."

He shooed her away as he said, "Can too."

Chapter 21

By the time Gunnar brought E up to speed at his forge and roused the vileblood brothers from their temporary housing at the station, Zhadan had returned with the available Clan members. Rina had spread a map over one of the long tables and stood at the bar talking in hushed tones with Aster, who looked unhappy. E joined them, the smith's expression by contrast unconcerned.

"What now?" Mateo asked as they entered the tavern proper, and Gunnar waved him and his brother toward the Clan, where Frode discussed terrain with Zhadan. The chuchuna was all flailing arms and grunts, impatient now that things moved forward.

"That big man is Afi Frode, leader of the local berserker clan. He lays the groundwork for shit like this. Rina deals in the overhead. Introduce yourselves," Gunnar said. When neither of them moved, he chuckled. "Everyone already knows about you."

"This a test?" Mateo asked as Tomas trotted over to join the others without hesitation.

"Everything is for the next week," Gunnar said with a shrug. "And the weeks after too. I won't complain if you go ahead fuck things up before the next train."

Mateo gave him a sideways look, his scent laced with apprehension as he inhaled Gunnar's. He left the vileblood standing there. They tripped up and were gone in a week? It'd be no skin off his nose.

He picked up bits of conversations as he stepped over to Rina to check in, but her chat with Aster and E captured his attention. The cornflower wraith smelled absolutely furious, and while E smelled as he always did—like ash and molten steel and powerful magic, with no more tells than a brick wall—his posture read uncomfortable.

Rina scoffed. Aster held out an open palm, almost a peace offering, but Rina shook her head, her tone low. "No, we're taking care of this now. My way. This is no different from what we've been doing since we broke ground here."

Gunnar sidled up next to E, who ignored him. He'd sat in on conversations like this for months now, his insight as valued as any of Rina's hunters.

Unless she disagreed, apparently.

"There are others," Aster said. "Word will spread. You have the benefit of surprise this time."

"And we'll cross that bridge when we come to it," Rina insisted. "For all we know, the others are miles beyond concern."

"You push when you should bend, Rina," Aster hissed out, her gaze piercing. Made sense, being she was a steward of the land, not so unlike the leshy. Gunnar never got the full story about how Rina worked things out with Aster when they first came to Nizhny. He knew that if Aster didn't want it happening, not a damn thing would grow on the fields they depended on come spring.

Rina stood up tall. "Noted." And left them at the bar.

Aster tsked, then asked Gunnar, "Anything for the road?"

"Nah, I'm good," he drawled, rubbing his chin. "Funny, Audrey said about the same thing to her earlier today."

E snorted into his mug but added nothing else. Aster only sighed, wiping up the bar with her towel even though it was spotless, her frustration palpable.

Things moved along about how he expected. With everyone present, Rina gave a rundown of the leshy and its capabilities and what Gunnar already knew about the terrain they'd be hunting on.

The main doors swung open, Uffe running in breathless, the Clan boy stalling as he neared the main table.

Gunnar caught the scent of panic.

Rina straightened, Frode and Hertha both picking up on the boy's hesitance as well. Gunnar leaned forward, but Frode was faster, calling out in Old Norse. "<<*What, boy? Speak, before the flies take to roost in your mouth.>>*"

Uffe swallowed a few times. "<<*The wolf pack is gone.>>*"

"<<*What the hells are you on about?>>*" Frode said, scoffing at the same time Gunnar's stomach churned.

Rina glanced impatiently between them; she wasn't fluent.

"<<*They're not at their den out back. I triple checked and ran around the station twice. Yuri and the pack are gone.>>*"

"Fuck," Gunnar muttered, heading for the doors as Frode translated and Rina about exploded. He knew she'd be hot on his heels. It was a short walk from the station's main entrance to the pack's dens. Gunnar moved quick, ignoring Rina calling after him because he needed answers before she drew her own conclusions.

The scent of wolf, heavy wet fur and musk, saturated the entire area, as well as blood, meat and marrow, fresh and old. The pups he'd fed a few days ago were barely old enough to hunt with the pack, but Uffe was right. Every one of them was gone, leaving a very obvious trail northward. No effort to sneak, they'd just all up and left.

Gunnar paused near the main den, inhaling deeper. Audrey had been here. Recently.

Recent as in as soon as she'd left the station for home.

"Fuck," he snarled, running a hand through his hair. "Shit."

"Gunnar! What the fuck is going on!" Rina was on him, heavy footfalls on the ice and snow, her voice damn near a roar over the cold air. She'd come alone, and Gunnar didn't know if that was a good or bad thing.

He grunted out a strained laugh. "You can't guess?"

Rina surveyed the empty dens, brow furrowed. She studied the snow, but it was so iced and packed down from the wolves. There wasn't much to track, and she didn't have his nose, but he saw the moment it clicked in place, the muscles in her jaw jumping.

"Did you know about this?"

"No," Gunnar said. "Far as I knew, she headed home to wait this out with Lyubava."

"She took my wolves."

"They followed her, not sure she . . ." Gunnar cleared his throat under the death stare, Rina's heaving chest and the white clouds puffing from between her grinding teeth. "Smells like it, yeah."

Rina saddled right up on his ass, and she had him by half a foot flatfooted, a little more with her shit kicker boots. "Take care of this. Now. Or I swear on my mother's name, I will see you both out of my town on the next train."

Following a wolf pack as large as Yuri's, with multiple dire wolves and hybrids in the mix, was easy as tracking a blazing forest fire. Besides that, Audrey's scent was so ingrained in his nose, she may as well have been screaming at the top of her lungs for as hard as it was for Gunnar to follow. That was good, he supposed. She clearly had no qualms about getting caught.

He jogged up the rails, pausing between the homesteads to make sure Audrey hadn't somehow made a sensible choice and gone to Lyubava, but no, her scent kept right on with the wolf pack's. Past the staked borders of Nizhny and into the wilds he patrolled for dangerous creatures.

The taiga closed in around him, blotting out the early sunlight, the needles thick and the ground uneven, but he knew this landscape like the back of his hand. A few weeks into settling on their homestead, he'd mapped it all, including Zhadan's neighboring patrol zone and the unmarked area toward the east. He liked knowing what he was dealing with, and it helped him root out monster dens and burrows. Gunnar knew exactly where the leshy's borders started, and he'd avoided them with purpose.

Now he didn't have a choice, because the wolves and Audrey were pacing a direct line to the leshy's home.

"Fuck," Gunnar grumbled. Not much longer now. He'd be on the pack soon, their scent heavy and scat fresh, paw marks clean in the otherwise undisturbed snow and needle fall. Fifteen minutes later, he saw the first wolf.

A dire hybrid, patrolling south of where the pack must have settled. She perked her ears at him, sniffed the air. The hybrids were smarter than a normal wolf by a mile, but nothing like a purebred dire wolf's human—and sometimes greater—intelligence. The pack's scout recognized him, raised her head to give a short yipping howl.

"Easy girl," Gunnar mumbled as she brushed by him. She sniffed his hand, licked his fingers, and let him scratch behind her ears. A cursory tail wag, and the wolf settled in to shadow him.

She seemed relaxed, too much so for them easing up on a bigger predator's territory, though a leshy coexisted peacefully with the animals in its habitat. The near forty strong wolf pack lead by an Aperien beast didn't exactly scream hospitality, though.

His skin prickled. Not too far now. It was a feeling more than a smell, though the scent was there too. Old magic, an original Aperien they'd be dealing with, settled in like the roots of this forest. Very dangerous potential hidden somewhere between all the peaceful sounds of nature. Even the air felt still, like the snow only fell or the wind only blew here if the power at be decided it was alright. He crested a stout ridge, found the pack waiting about twenty to twenty-five feet back from the leshy's line, utterly content.

The pups chased each other and wrestled while others napped about. The adults all lounged, as if this didn't differ from being at their den in Nizhny. He didn't count heads, but a quick scan showed Yuri missing and Audrey was nowhere in sight.

A demanding woof drew his attention, and Liral, Yuri's mate and another full-blooded dire wolf, stretched and lumbered to her feet. A gorgeous beast, she had silver-white fur, unusual compared to the typical black of her kind, and a dark muzzle and paws. She shook out her fur and padded over to him, knocked at his hip.

"You guys are in deep shit with Rina," Gunnar said. Liral gave him a yawn that ended in a whine, then turned toward the leshy's border with a huff. He didn't speak wolf, but he was fairly certain that was the sound of a disapproving mate. "Did Yuri go in there with Audrey?"

Another single woof, then a low growl.

"Don't look at me, she thought this up all on her own."

Liral sneezed a few times, then trotted off.

Gunnar drew himself up and headed toward the invisible border, noting how the scent changed as he stepped past the leshy's threshold. Everything smelled richer and more alive than a deep winter forest, rich and heady. The greens were brighter, and despite the crisp snow and dangling icicles, the air felt warmer. A snowshoe hare darted through the underbrush, birds chattering, the wind more a caress than a bite.

Audrey's scent was easy to follow, the dire wolf with her. Nothing else off, aside from the general oddness of a magically inhabited stretch of woodland. Gunnar's skin still itched, that sensation of a big predator nearby under his skin, but nothing felt overtly threatening. He kept moving, not attempting to mask his approach, pretty sure the leshy knew as soon as he stepped a foot on its land.

It didn't take long to find what he came for. Sooner than he expected, only two hundred yards in before the trees thinned, and Gunnar hit the clearing.

Audrey sat on a stump, talking with her hands in painfully slow Russian. The dire wolf lay beside her on a pine needle bed. The huge black wolf blinked lazily, thumped his tail once, and went right back to napping.

And there was the leshy, within arm's reach of Audrey, attentive to her chatter. A tall, lean man in shape, he had a green beard of moss and pine reaching down to his spindly legs, which were crossed at the knee. Leaned forward on an elbow, fist propped under his chin, nodding casually as she spoke. No clothing, his skin ashen brown like the surrounding trees, so much so he almost blended in to the old growth he sat upon, which bent around him in a high-backed seat. His arms dangled like branches, his hair mottled lichen. In his lap, a plate of half-eaten cookies.

The Aperien could've been someone's grandfather, the kind expression at odds with the danger radiating in the air now that Gunnar was closer. And damn, did that change when he looked toward Gunnar, the gaze so vast his hindbrain twitched. Everything about the leshy's appearance was a carefully crafted lie.

Audrey followed the leshy's gaze and leaped to her feet when she saw him. "Oh! Jonathan! Um . . . *<<This Jonathan Gunnar. Very good friend. He worries.>>*" She smiled, bright and wide, a damn ray of sunlight in the dark forest. "It's alright. I think we have things worked out."

"Worked out?" Gunnar didn't dare move closer.

"Yes," she insisted. The leshy hadn't moved, stone still as the tree beside it now, eerie and ancient, almost as if all the time it had existed in mythos before it manifested into reality was accounted for in its presence. "His name is Aspen, after the tree that grows here."

Gunnar inclined his head at the leshy, offered in Russian, "*<<Good to meet you, Aspen.>>*"

The leshy's voice came from all around at once, the lips not moving. "*<<That name is a blessing for the girl, not you.>>*"

"*<<Okay.>>*"

"*<<You seek what belongs to me.>>*"

Gunnar crossed his arms. "*<<That'd be Katerina Yaga, not me.>>*"

Audrey shifted toward Gunnar, her hands placating. "I've negotiated terms with Aspen on behalf of Nizhny."

Gunnar rubbed his forehead, then his mouth, fighting the urge to laugh. Given that Audrey was fine, the whole thing was a bit funny. The risk she'd taken still pissed him off, but Rina was going to shit herself—and maybe in a few weeks, come around and thank Audrey.

If it all worked out.

He side-eyed the leshy. "*<<You're willing to talk?>>*"

"*<<Not all savor violence.>>*"

Gunnar inclined his head at that. Him and Zhadan had been slaughtering things at the leshy's borders for months now. Rina was rallying the whole damn settlement to axes.

Audrey rested a palm on his forearm, her hand warm through her mittens. "This is going to work out, I promise. Aspen won't attack

Rina unprovoked, and there's really nothing to argue over regarding what he wants in return."

"You sure about that? Your Russian is shit."

She pursed her lips. "I'm not that bad."

"How bad is good enough for high-level negotiations?"

"Don't be a jerk," she hissed at him, fighting against a smile.

"<<*What she lacks in words, she makes up for in intention.*>>"

Ah, so the fucker spoke English. Gunnar cocked a brow at the half-tree, half-man, and motioned at the plate in the thing's lap. "<<*And cookies.*>>"

The leshy didn't reply, his attention back to Audrey as she bowed deeply. "<<*Thank you greatly. I am appreciating your time. I return soon.*>>"

Gunnar winced at her grammar, but the leshy only bowed his head in return as Audrey beamed at him and gathered papers into her over-stuffed satchel. She patted Yuri, who got lazily to his feet, apparently unmoved by this entire outing. The dire wolf trotted by them both without so much as a backwards glance. Audrey took Gunnar's arm and tugged him after her. He didn't look at the leshy again, trusting Audrey to have done her research about proper behavior.

She didn't say a thing as they fast walked to the leshy's borders, Yuri already there with his mate. The rest of the pack watched on, at attention with their alpha back with them. Audrey didn't hesitate, racing over to the dire wolf and throwing her hands around his thick neck.

"Thank you," she mumbled into his fur. Yuri licked her face a few times, woofing softly as he looked south. Audrey let him go and nodded. "Jonathan will see me home." She waved at the wolves they could see. "Thank you, everyone!"

Liral hip-checked her, almost knocking her over, and Audrey

laughed. Then Yuri lifted his head in a long howl, answers sounding from all directions, and the wolf pack departed.

Audrey damn near glowed, cheeks flushed and grinning from ear to ear. She swung her arms a few times, breathless when she said, "We should get back, right? And tell Rina." Audrey's expression fell slightly. "How mad is she?"

Gunnar just stared at her.

She blew out a breath, hard enough to ruffle the hair poking out of her fur cap. "Right, really mad then." She winced. "And how mad are you?"

He considered, then said, "Half."

"I knew what I was doing," Audrey said, glancing at him sideways as she adjusted her satchel and started walking. He caught her elbow and steered her in the correct direction. They walked for a few minutes before she spoke again. "I've studied the local mythos in depth. A leshy isn't hostile, not if you have good intentions and harm nothing in their forests."

"Mhm." He wasn't going to make this easy on her.

He didn't miss her little huff. "And I took Yuri and the pack. I didn't go alone. I'm not stupid."

Gunnar chuckled. "How'd you manage that little trick, anyway?"

"Oh." She grimaced. "I promised the pack zmei bones and meat." A swallow. "Everything that's left."

"That including Zhadan's half?"

Audrey lifted her chin. "He wanted the treeman taken care of, didn't he?"

Gunnar laughed. "You're telling him, not me."

"I'm not afraid of Zhadan," she said, but her scent reeked of nerves now that they headed back to Nizhny. Hells, she hadn't smelled nervous at all sitting next to that Leshy, but now that she'd have to face the music, she was sweating.

He grinned at her back. Yeah, he was fucking pissed she'd run off on her own. If she'd talked to him first, which hadn't been an option given Rina breathing down his neck, he'd have tried to talk her out of it. But she was better at talking him *into* things than he'd ever been at trying to change her mind once she'd set it on something she felt was important. Dog with a bone, his little human.

Not his, he reminded himself.

"Jonathan?"

"Yeah?"

"Are you really half as mad at me as Rina is?"

He sighed, knowing he'd probably regret admitting it. "No, not even close."

Chapter 22

They didn't even get a foot in the station doors, and Aster was on them like a shot. Gunnar'd expected it to be Rina, but a glance showed her tucked in at the bar, deep in a drink and talking quietly with E. She scowled at them both as she rose. Behind her, E shrugged. The rest of Nizhny's hunters waited around the tavern, no doubt on Rina's orders. The room silently screamed with the marinating tension.

"Audrey, you went to the leshy, yes?" Aster spoke in English, which showed just how anxious she was, given how she harassed Audrey about her garbage Russian on a regular basis. Aster glanced back at Rina, who was closing in fast, then back to Audrey with an expectant expression. "Yes?"

"I did," Audrey said as she took off her hat and scarf, setting them on the nearest table.

"And?" Aster prodded.

"He's willing to work with Rina to find an agreeable arrangement with Nizhny." Audrey smiled. "And he told me his name."

Relief flooded Aster's scent, her smile brilliant. Then she spun on a heel, marching right into Rina's path as she stormed toward them. It surprised Gunnar when Rina didn't shove right by her, instead coming up short, her expression severe. Aster had to reach high to rest her hands on Rina's board shoulders.

"Listen first. Please," Aster asked more than stated in a voice that didn't carry, then released her.

Rina closed her eyes for a second, exhaling harshly through her nose, before she pointed at Gunnar and Audrey, then jerked her thumb at the stairs. "My office, now."

"Yes, of course," Audrey said, stumbling over herself to go, now, her gaze skirting away from Rina's as she all but ran by her. Gunnar took a more casual approach, hands in his pockets.

Gunnar took his post beside the door, wincing when Rina slammed it behind her. Audrey sat, satchel in her lap, her leg jumping with a mix of nervous energy and excitement. He crossed his arms, inhaling deep; Rina was outwardly calm, but her scent reeked of frustration. Not the best state of mind for a powerful Aperien who was furious at them.

Rina still didn't look at them, the cold shoulder childish on the surface, but Gunnar sensed she was doing her best to control her temper. She wasn't a volatile woman. In the time they'd been here, he'd never seen her this angry. He wondered what exactly had her temper up so high. The defiance from someone she'd trusted? The embarrassment of the disobedience being so public?

That she'd been wrong?

Rina stood in front of her map, back to them. "My wolves?"

"At their dens, all accounted for. No injuries or anything like that," Audrey said.

"And how did you manage to take my entire pack?"

"I promised Yuri all the zmei meat and bones we have left for the pack." Audrey blushed now, speaking faster. "All I asked was for an escort through the woods. I thought maybe Yuri would come alone, but he brought all of them and then Yuri insisted on accompanying me into the leshy's forest . . ."

Rina rubbed her forehead.

"I wanted to help," Audrey added quietly.

Rina spun, snarling as she flattened both palms on the desk, leaning in close to Audrey. "You want to help by ignoring my direct orders?"

Audrey's spine stiffened.

Ah shit, here we go. Gunnar knew what came next.

"You didn't give me direct orders beyond ending our conversation. *You* didn't want to try." She lifted her chin. "You never said I couldn't try."

Gunnar had never seen Rina so utterly baffled, and Audrey took her stunned silence as permission.

"The leshy doesn't want conflict. He understands you're building a home here. If you're willing to guarantee the continued respect of his territory, he'll create a road through his forest." Audrey used her esquire tone now, and she spoke with confidence despite her scent radiating nerves as much as stubbornness. "He will allow residents of Nizhny passage unbothered, provided they remain on the path. If any threats to Nizhny enter his forest, he'll prevent them from reaching the settlement proper.

"While the leshy does not need to leave his forest, he agrees to abide by your laws as the greater Independent territory he resides within, provided you agree to his terms. He would retain the right to punish those who break this agreement himself."

Rina scoffed as she pushed away from the desk. Audrey swallowed a few times, and Gunnar did his best to be a statue. The Aperien was coming around; he didn't dare disrupt this delicate transition.

"Aster is crawling up my ass, as if this place wasn't a dream that could be ripped out from under us at any time." Rina laughed, shook her head again as if chasing away thoughts she didn't dare give voice. "And then you, a human girl, wander off into the damn woods and treat with leshy in my name."

"Not in your name. I told him this all depended on what you decide. I would never speak for you. I know that's not my place."

Rina waved a hand as she spoke. "You did everything else in my place."

"I know you're mad I went against your wishes—"

"Wishes, but not orders, is it?"

"Please don't throw away this chance at a peaceful solution because you're angry with me." Audrey glanced back at Gunnar. The look she shot him was apologetic, and then her attention was back toward Rina. "I'll go, if that's what you want. For . . . I don't know, an example? If you don't . . . if you don't want me here anymore."

Gunnar snorted. So that's what that look was about. "She goes, I go."

"He had nothing to do with this," Audrey said, grabbing at his sleeve. "Gunnar is the best hunter you have. He's good for Nizhny."

"You're fucking nuts if you think I'd let her throw you out on your ass alone," Gunnar growled down at her.

Audrey shook her head, giving him that jutted chin, that fierce, righteous streak of hers. "You don't have to—"

"Fucking hells, enough. Both of you." Rina leaned her head back to stare at the ceiling, fists on her hips. She rattled off a string of curses in Russian that really didn't amount to much more than *fuck*. When she gestured at Audrey, she spoke to Gunnar, incredulous. "She can barely speak Russian."

"Yeah, I know. She's shit."

Audrey punched him hard on the shoulder, hard for her at least, and he gave her a grunt in response.

"Get your jackets. We're settling this today." Rina headed toward the door, muttering and cursing, half at the ether, half at them, before she added, "And if anyone breaks our agreement with the leshy, *I'm* dealing with them, because that would break *my* fucking rules." And then she vented more of her frustration by hammering down the old wooden stairs.

Audrey let out a shuddering breath, gripping Gunnar's forearm. Her cheeks were flushed, and now that Rina was out of the room, she trembled, but the fear in her scent slowly evaporated.

He nudged her shoulder. "Nice job, Esquire."

She giggled, giving him a brief grin, and he inhaled the burst of happiness coming off her skin. It pleased him, almost obscenely, to bolster her with a few words.

"We're not done just yet."

Gunnar nodded toward the door. "After you."

Chapter 23

The meeting between Rina and the leshy went smooth. Aster and Yuri accompanied them, everyone else sent off to mind their own business for the afternoon. Midway through talks with the leshy, Rina's scent shifted from general frustration to relief, then pleased. Gunnar didn't mention it when they walked home. Rina remained stiff toward both of them but agreed when Audrey offered to draft up a document so E could magically seal the agreement.

After dragging all the zmei meat and bones—a damn fortune—to Yuri and the pack and dealing with Zhadan's bitching about it, everything more or less went back to normal.

Almost.

Gunnar spent his evenings with Mateo and Tomas, as per Rina's demands, meeting them at the tavern after sundown. The third day, he arrived a bit early.

Rina remained standoffish, while Audrey busted her ass over drafting the agreement. Until that was done, they only had words, nothing binding with the leshy. He supposed that kind of thing might make him twitchy too.

Virtue might have had some insight into Rina's mood, though. It was common knowledge they were lovers beyond Virtue's services.

When Gunnar stopped at the bar, Aster greeted him with a wide smile. She set a mug of Clan mead down like she'd pulled it out of her sleeve.

"Evening, Gunnar," she said, her voice singsongy.

"Evening." He took a sip, wary about the warm welcome. Sure, Audrey deserved that kind of affection. He'd done nothing but escort her home from meeting the leshy, yet Aster hadn't stopped grinning at them both since.

Gunnar cleared his throat. "Audrey loves those flowers," he offered, trying for casual conversation even though it made his teeth hurt. "She keeps them on the kitchen table and waters them every day."

Aster wrinkled her pert nose. "Humans are so strange. I told her they will not die unless I do."

He and Aster kept a companionable silence until he finished his drink. "You seen the new guys?"

"Virtue's."

Another reason to stop by. "Thanks."

When he stepped into the brothel, the greeting room was empty, but he didn't have to wait long. Innocence and Tomas wandered out of his room a few minutes later, reeking of sex and absinthe. The incubus had his head ducked against Tomas's ear, whispering, the young vileblood flushed to his ears.

"Ah, Gunnar! My favorite visitor who never visits me!" Innocence winked, his kimono barely tied at his narrow hips. He let go of Tomas with a pat on the man's ass, sauntering over to pour himself a glass of absinthe from the corner bar, faerie lights twinkling in gold and pink. "Virtue is still busy, but my offer stands as usual. You can ask Tomas here if you need a referral into my mouth."

Tomas made a choking noise, his scent near panicked before he muttered a goodbye and bolted from the room.

"Tactful," Gunnar drawled.

Innocence shrugged. "He wasn't complaining a few minutes ago."

Gunnar couldn't help a smirk but sobered quickly. "She with Mateo now?"

"Mmhmm." Innocence drew out the sound as he flopped on the couch. He swirled his drink, gaze dragging lazily over Gunnar's body.

"First time they came?"

Innocence snickered into his drink. "First, second, third. At least for young Tomas."

Gunnar walked right into that one. "I mean the vilebloods coming to the brothel. Need to know they're not causing trouble."

Innocence rolled his eyes. "All business, no fun. But yes, today was the first time they visited."

"They behave?"

"Why, Mr. Gunnar, do you truly want me to answer that question?"

He threw up his hands. "Never mind. I'll just ask Virtue, since you're such a pain in the fucking ass."

"Oh, darling, you have no idea." Innocence tipped back his drink, then set the empty glass aside, waving a hand at Gunnar when he snarled. "Sorry, sorry, here I am playing while you're being so very serious about my well-being. Tomas was fine, polite even. Quite naïve, actually, but very, very excited to learn." Innocence studied him for a moment, the endless sexual bravado peeling back. "Do we have reason to be concerned?"

"Dunno," Gunnar said honestly and gave Innocence a brief rundown of what he knew about the men so far and his role as babysitter. "They're young, not much exposure beyond being locked up."

"And we're worried what freedom might inspire?"

"Can argue all you want the Accord was wrong, but it happened for good reason."

Innocence hummed again, crossing his legs and leaning forward on his elbows. "Imagine talking about one's nature in such a removed way. How the Accord that buried you in prison for your entire life only for the crime of being born was there 'for good reason.'" He bared his teeth, perfect white, pointed tips flashing. His scent spiked with power and a raw, wounded rage. "Let them all burn, on high, assigning fates as if they don't have the capacity for far, far worse in their oh-so-righteous hearts."

"Doesn't change what we are," Gunnar said, unphased by the bristling incubus. He'd just fed, and while he was powerful, Innocence wasn't a fighter.

A huff, and he returned to his bar. "As if control can't be learned. Or better yet, taught." He poured a second glass, sauntering over to Gunnar and offering it between two finely manicured nails. When Gunnar accepted, Innocence clinked their glasses. "Cheers then, to the monsters at the cold-ass end of the Earth, apparently where we belong."

He could drink to that, but winced at the burn.

And at the intruding thought of Audrey being stuck here with the monsters.

Innocence said nothing else, wandering down the hall and disappearing into his room, his scent a kind of melancholy Gunnar had never caught on the man before.

Virtue emerged with Mateo then, who was clearly more comfortable in this setting than Tomas. He smiled at Virtue, hooked elbow to elbow with her, and she seemed pleased as punch.

When Mateo saw Gunnar, he stiffened.

"It's still early, just came to talk to Virtue," Gunnar said, setting his empty glass down with the others.

"Alright." Mateo glanced between him and Virtue, then shrugged. He kissed Virtue on the cheek, mumbled, "See you soon?" She nodded, and he saw himself out.

"You can settle in the room," Virtue offered, adjusting her robe. "I'll shower."

"Not today," Gunnar said, gaze jumping to her face. "Just checking in."

Virtue perked an elegant brow as she leaned against the brocade wall. "About?"

"The vilebloods, for one. Innocence said this is their first time around."

"Worried about their control?"

"Yeah."

"They're fine." She canted her head slightly, studying him. "If that changes, we'll tell you."

"Good."

"And?"

Gunnar couldn't help but chuckle. Virtue didn't mince words if fucking wasn't involved. "I wanted to ask you about Rina."

"Tread carefully, Gunnar. We might be friends, but we're not that close."

She didn't smell like lies when she said it, but he still had trouble believing she considered him an actual friend. Didn't really matter though. "Just wondering how long she's liable to be bent out of shape about the leshy. Audrey's worried."

"Hmm, can't have that. You're so restless if your human is unhappy."

"She's not—"

"Hush, Gunnar. We all got the memo the day Rina's cousin came through." She folded her arms, her scent smug, her expression worse, and he hated the damn twinkle in her glowing eyes. "Rina will come around when she's ready and not before. Give her space. And try to avoid directly defying her again if you can help it?" A small pause, and Virtue sighed. "Audrey was right, and Rina knows it. Getting the magical anchors in place around the agreement with the leshy will help ease the sting."

"Figured as much. Thanks." Gunnar turned to go, then hesitated. "You might want to check on Innocence."

A pause. "I will." When he reached the doorway, Virtue added, "Thank you for looking out for us both."

"Yeah, sure. Just doing what I'm told." He ducked out before she could respond.

The vilebloods were clean trackers and efficient hunters. On the fourth night, Gunnar shadowed, watching them work their assigned area. Their quota for the first week was lean, being they were two hunters sharing a single land parcel. Gunnar didn't doubt they'd meet it. He left them around midnight, after they brought down a pair of roving bauks with minimal struggle.

Three more days until the next train. No trouble so far from any quarter, but Gunnar still didn't like it.

He hated the way they smelled. Mateo came from a different vilestar than him, and the knowledge just sat right under his skin and itched like mad, keeping his instincts on high alert. Tomas was worse, because his scent made Gunnar feel . . . he didn't fucking know what, but he found it hard to hate the kid.

Maybe it was just a space thing; he'd been in forced proximity with them for four days. If they ended up part of the settlement, he'd do his best to avoid them altogether.

Gunnar slowed as he approached the cabin, keeping his steps light. Audrey slept by now, no sense waking her up with his stomping around about irritating dusters. He sighed as he opened the door, tension leaking out of him as he inhaled, drinking in sunshine at midnight.

He didn't expect to find the source of that sunshine passed out at the kitchen table, papers spread everywhere, books stacked around her head. A cup of cold tea too, he noted as he stripped his outerwear and kicked off his boots. He crossed the room on cat feet, grinning at the ink smudged across her nose and cheek. Audrey's chest rose and fell in a deep sleep, the papers near her face rustling. Aster's gift, a beautiful bouquet of blue cornflowers, sat in the middle of the chaos.

Of course, she used an ink pot and quills even though modern pens would do the job. Until E magically bound the agreement, it was just words on paper. Gunnar shifted the inkpot to the other side of the crowded table so it wouldn't spill on all her hard work.

Her Russian dictionary was one of the open books. He chuckled, tucking her hair behind her ear. Audrey leaned into the gentle touch with a soft murmur.

Gunnar drew back his hand, swallowing. He considering waking her; she was drooling on her papers, couldn't have that, but she looked so damn tired. Mind made up, he plucked the quill from her half open hand, then scooped her up in his arms. She grumbled, then she blinked up at him, half-asleep.

"You fell asleep working, putting you in bed."

"Oh." She yawned, then nuzzled into his chest as those delicate fingers, spotted with ink, curled around his shirt. "Okay."

Gunnar chuckled; he was pretty sure she was already asleep again. He toed her bedroom door open, kneeling as he set her gently on her bed. She grunted again—almost sounded like a snort, and he bit his cheek to keep from laughing. Her forehead scrunched up, but she didn't open her eyes again, her hands chasing after him as he rocked back on his heels. He wasn't sure why, but he brushed his thumb over that unhappy crease between her brows. She sighed in her sleep, the tension abating and her little frown fading into an almost smile.

Gunnar lingered, watching her sleep, watching her breathe, snippets from his conversations between Virtue and Innocence wading through his mind.

He'd call her his to keep her safe from the likes of Dimitri, sure, but she wasn't his. No, a man like him didn't get to have someone so pure and good, just wasn't in the cards. But he let himself steal a moment, as she smiled in her sleep, reminding himself all that didn't matter, so long as she was safe.

He could give her safety, so he would as long as she let him.

Chapter 24

Two days later, Audrey finished the paperwork. They'd accompanied E and Rina to seal the deal between Nizhny and the leshy, literally, that morning. As far as Gunnar could tell, everything went off without a hitch. Rina called an all hands for the same evening. Her mood seemed improved, less stiff toward him and Audrey.

Such meetings were a normal thing, once a month, to update everyone on news outside Nizhny, hear any grievances, and a share a meal as a community. Attendance wasn't optional, much to Gunnar's chagrin. He saw Audrey off to help Aster prep, then spent the afternoon hunting to put himself into a mood better equipped to handle the looming social demands.

It sleeted all morning, sky dark and dismal. Fitting, he decided with a growl.

As he dumped a dead vodyanoy on their deck, Gunnar wondered why he was more bothered than usual about the upcoming meeting. Not like he couldn't hide in the back; that's what E always did.

Been a long week and still not train day, he reminded himself as he went inside to clean up. He threw on some fresh clothes and dry furs and headed down to the station.

Maybe it was the vilebloods. They'd be here for another two days at least, and he hadn't found a reason to kick them out. Today they'd meet everyone, including all the Clan kids. Gunnar didn't see either of them out to hurt children. Really, they'd only shown interest in surviving so far, painful as it was to relate.

He shoved his hands deep in his coat pockets.

Maybe he'd just had enough of Audrey being in danger to last himself a fucking lifetime. Tonight, she'd meet the vilebloods.

It wasn't for lack of trying on her part, but Rina'd kept them busy with Gunnar, running them through the ropes. They spent a good deal of their off time at the brothel, but no signs of abusing their welcome. According to Aster, they remained polite over meals and drank little, maybe a beer, but never the Clan mead. They met their trial quota a few days in, seemed to lie low while they waited for Rina's verdict, which they knew hinged on Gunnar's approval.

Truth was, Mateo and Tomas were outmatched by just about everything in the settlement, and they had the good sense to recognize it. Aster was arguably a weak link considering her limited and specific capabilities as a cornflower wraith, but she was still a full-bloodied Aperien.

But Audrey was just a human girl, exactly the thing most at risk from vilebloods.

They'd be idiots to try anything with Audrey in front of anyone. They'd be stupid to try anything period if they valued their chances in Nizhny. And they really, really seemed motivated to stay.

Gunnar sighed.

Once Audrey met them, they'd become another cause for her to champion. Hells, they already were. She'd make them cookies. Smile at them, welcome them, and encourage him and Rina to let them stay because she believed they deserved the opportunity.

Then he let out a low chuckle at his churning annoyance, because it wasn't at Audrey, aside from the fact she'd walk into danger head held high if she thought she could do some damn good.

He was annoyed at himself because he was *jealous*.

Jealous these two men might take part of her attention. Jealous at the prospect that she'd want to take care of them like she had him. She'd dedicated her entire damn life to changing the fucking Vilestars Accord; that kind of devotion didn't just go away. Gunnar scratched at his chest, scowling as he approached the station.

Unless something drastic happened tonight, the little fuckers would stay, because lying to get them kicked out, well. Audrey would be furious with him. And having her upset at him, truly upset . . . He didn't much care for it.

He cracked his neck, exhaled, because what mattered most was Audrey being safe, secondary only to her being happy.

The vileblood weren't a direct threat to her as far as he could tell, and after meeting them tonight, she'd know it.

"Fuck," he grumbled. There really wasn't shit to do about it except kill them both if anything changed.

Silver-lining then, he thought with an attempt to grin, but it was more a grimace.

Probably too late to gut them and dump the bodies in the swamp.

He fucking hated train days.

When Gunnar reached the station, the wolves were out of sight, all tucked away in their dens to escape the weather, the sleet coming down harder now. Only Yuri and his mate came inside for the all hands, or else the entire tavern would smell like wet dog for weeks. He was almost late, always avoiding the crowded confines as long as possible. He scanned for Audrey as soon as he stepped inside, found her milling around with Aster behind the bar.

The Clan, as per normal, occupied the back half of the room, the younger ones running in circles around their elders. He forgot sometimes how damn many berserkers made up Nizhny's population.

He had little reason to interact with the Clan beyond gatherings like this one.

The harpy lingered in the rafters; he smelled her but didn't see her. E sat alone at the bar's furthest end, Innocence and Virtue talking quietly at a nearby table with Zhadan and Lyubava, the latter looking extremely round. Gunnar wondered just how many baby chuchunas they'd be dealing with in a few weeks. He had to step over Yuri and Liral to get inside, damn furry, giant doormats who didn't bother looking up from their naps. Rina wasn't there yet.

The vileblood were though, crowded up to the bar as far away from E as possible. Gunnar grimaced again; them being here for the all hands about settled shit, because Rina'd been prodding him for updates and he'd had nothing to offer but "fine."

Then Audrey caught his eye and waved, urging him to come sit with them.

"Fuck," he muttered again but made his way over.

Audrey was all glowing smiles, pride in her sunny scent. "I finally met Mateo and Tomas. They're very grateful for all your help, you know."

Yeah, this shit was a done deal. "Just work," Gunnar grunted, nodding to the pair.

Audrey rolled her eyes at him but kept right on smiling. "Drinks?"

They all three said yes, and she scooted off, calling back, "On the house," as she went, in case Tomas and Mateo didn't know.

They both watched her leave, Gunnar's back to her now, and he stared right at them until they realized he was watching. Tomas looked away, but Mateo just grinned at Gunnar.

"Never thought I'd find a human woman all the way out here." Mateo rubbed his chin, all scruff like he was working up to a beard. They'd both cleaned up, making it easier to read their emotional scents without all the caked-on dirt.

Mateo's interest in Audrey? Way too much for his liking. Gunnar didn't hide his displeasure, frowning as his gaze bounced back over Gunnar's shoulder, undoubtably in Audrey's direction.

"She's a pretty thing."

"She's not for either of you, that's for fucking sure," Gunnar bit out.

Tomas glanced up with wide eyes, then to his brother, and Mateo finally gave Gunnar his full attention as he leaned his elbows on the bar. "That so?"

"Yeah," Gunnar said. In for a penny, in for a pound. "It is."

"I heard something about that this afternoon when we were getting the rundown on train day tomorrow. That if anyone came asking about buying her, she's spoken for. That's you then?"

Gunnar wondered if murder was a scent he could radiate.

"Makes sense, protecting her and all." Mateo leaned in and inhaled, then shook his head. "But you're not fucking her." At Gunnar's snarl, Mateo held up his hands. "Hey, I'm just trying to get the lay of the land. Not looking to step on anybody's toes, but there are protections against knocking up humans, you know."

Gunnar leaned in. "The lay of the damn land is you keep the hells away from her, because I can tell you right now, she won't be fucking either one of you."

Mateo and Tomas's gazes both flicked behind him. Gunnar smelled Audrey's anger and embarrassment the second before she slapped three mugs on the bar top between them.

Shit. He canted his head at her, her cheeks blotched red and her hazel eyes daggers. She crossed her arms, looking at each of them before she bit out, "Who I sleep with is no one's business but my own."

Tomas wouldn't even make eye contact with her. Mateo played it humble even though Gunnar caught whiffs of satisfaction and arrogance on his scent. Whether he'd baited Gunnar into Audrey hearing or not, the asshole clearly didn't mind the results.

"Sorry, no offense intended," Mateo offered, clearing his throat. "Thanks for the drink."

Audrey's gaze bored into the back of Gunnar's head, but hells if he'd show any belly around these two. She huffed and left.

Gunnar took his mead and went to find an empty table as far away from everyone as possible. Maybe there was time to tell Rina he'd changed his mind, and this shit wasn't fucking fine at all, but Nizhny's fearless leader called the meeting to order as soon as she entered the tavern.

He nursed his drink while Rina filled everyone in on the accord between Nizhny and the leshy. She gave Audrey credit without cutting herself down or belittling Audrey's efforts, and the entire gathering lauded the decision. He caught Audrey blushing at the praise, along with a meaningful look from Rina reminding him to keep towing the line

She officially welcomed Mateo and Tomas to the settlement, the next half hour spent on introductions and welcomes from the community. Gunnar sensed hesitance from most quarters, the same as he'd received upon his arrival. They wouldn't have Audrey to buffer their presence like he did.

Good.

After Rina finished, everyone settled in to eat. Gunnar grinned behind his mug when Mateo tried to talk to Audrey again and she gave him the cold shoulder. He'd enjoy it for now, even though his reckoning was no doubt coming.

With the meal done, the tavern emptied. Gunnar worked his way over to the bar again, giving E a nod and leaving three stools between them. When Audrey came close enough to hear him, he said, "Hey, you ready?"

She walked right by, not even looking at him when she said, "No."

E chuckled from downwind, and when Gunnar glared at him, he held up his hands, then headed off down the halls to his smithy and private rooms.

And that was how Gunnar closed out the tavern with an empty mug while Audrey helped Aster do every little thing she didn't need help with until the cornflower wraith shooed her off.

"Ready now?" he asked as she took off her apron and stepped from behind the bar.

"I don't need a babysitter," Audrey snipped as she walked by. He followed, because he'd walk home with her if she liked it or not. Night had already settled, the days short this time of year.

She ignored him while she put on her coat, hat, and gloves and didn't hold the door for him as she slipped out into the cold, her cheeks red before she hit the chilled air. She walked fast, much faster than normal, so Gunnar threw on his coat and followed just far enough so she could pretend he wasn't with her.

He gave her about half the walk home before he called out, "You half as mad as Rina was?"

Her shoulders tensed, and she stopped walking. He could tell she had her hands in tight little fists inside her mittens.

"All things considered, probably only a quarter as mad," she mumbled through her scarf. When he chuckled, she started off again, but at a slightly less aggressive pace. "That doesn't mean I'm not mad."

"Alright."

Audrey huffed. "Do you even care?"

Gunnar considered how to answer for a few seconds, then offered, "That you're mad at me, yeah, but I'm not sorry for putting them in their place."

"Which is not your place."

"How you figure that one?"

She stopped walking again, hands on her hips as she glared at him—ridiculous with how short she was compared to him. All he could see were her angry eyes between the scarf and the hat.

"Shotgun and shovel talk, really? What gives you the right?"

"I'm not sure what shotguns or shovels have to do with this, but my job is to protect you." He folded his arms, glaring right back. "I don't trust them, less with you than anyone."

"Why? Because I'm human?"

"For starters."

"Jonathan."

"They want to get you on your back."

What he could see of her cheeks went bright red again. "That's . . . No, they were just talking to me before you started threatening them."

She was beautiful, perfect. Innocent. Of course a vileblood would want to claim her. There was a part of him, deep down, that he kept caged, which wanted the same—exactly why he never let that want surface. And he damn well knew better. Even if he wasn't a risk to her—any magical protections from vileblood? They'd need to be damn fucking powerful to be one hundred percent safe—she wasn't for a man like any of them.

But all he said was, "I smelled the want coming from Mateo."

"What's next then? Barking out that I'm yours again just because they look at me or talk to me?"

"If that's what it takes, sure."

"That's not fair," she snapped. "You're . . . you can't act like that."

"Why the fuck not?" Now he was getting pissed. "You almost died because you got me out of that cell. The fuck if I'm letting anything happen to you. I don't trust them. Yeah, they're not lying, but a week isn't enough time to know shit about anyone. If I need to scare them off to keep you safe, I'll do it every fucking time."

She threw up her arms. "And I'm just supposed to what? Hide in your house until you give me permission to speak to anyone?"

He frowned down at her; why was she twisting this into something else entirely? Last time they talked, she didn't want to move.

"It's our house, but I told you, we'll get you settled somewhere else soon." Then he sneered when he added, "If you hadn't given away all that zmei meat and bones to help someone else, you could've already been in your own place."

And just like that, all the anger washed out of her.

"No, I don't . . ." She sighed. "Just . . . Never mind." Another deep breath and a shaky exhale, then she motioned north toward their homestead. "It's been a weird week. I don't want to fight with you. Let's just go home."

"Didn't mean to start a fight," he offered into the quiet night around them, between them. He hated her upset. "You always think of the good first. Doesn't always work out like that way."

"I'm not naïve."

"No, you're not that." He rubbed his forehead. "Promise me you'll be careful around them, that's all, and I'll drop it."

"Are you really worried, or is this about something else?" She sounded tired when she asked, almost defeated.

He thought about the sting of jealously he'd felt earlier, seeing her talking to them, smiling at them, but that wasn't her problem. "Only been a week. Better to be cautious until we really know them."

Another long pause. He almost asked if she heard him before she quietly said, "Okay, Jonathan. Whatever you say."

"You'll be careful then?" He needed to hear her say it.

"Yes, if that's what you want."

For some reason, it didn't feel like a win.

Chapter 25

Time had a way a flowing when things were unremarkable.

For all the fuss of that one week—Dimitri, the vilebloods, and then the leshy—everything went back to quiet winter days and long silent nights. Trains came and went, nothing interesting in or out. Rina warmed back to her typical chilly exterior toward both him and Audrey. Audrey made extra cookies and introduced the settlement to hot chocolate with tiny marshmallows. Lyubava grew so round, she didn't leave the den at all anymore.

Gunnar kept to his parcel in the north. Mateo and Tomas expanded their patrol areas to the eastern side. They'd cross paths for the all hands and on train days, little in between, which was just fine by him.

Audrey came around, things between them back to the comfortable Gunnar enjoyed—no, depended on. His interactions with her were the best part of his days. He didn't burn the apology note Mateo left the morning after he'd pissed her off; that probably helped.

He kept on quota, his newer, extended parcel shouldered up to the leshy's area. Went through it once to examine the promised road, which was easy to follow and hazard free. He'd yet to see the leshy again but always felt those eyes whenever he skirted the line or needed to pass through.

Zhadan made Rina redraw his quota lines so he'd never have to be anywhere near the leshy.

The chuchuna was half losing his mind at this point, his mate set to burst any day now. Gunnar ran him ragged as much as he could, hoping he'd sleep during the days instead of getting thrown out of his den for pacing like a madman. Gunnar was getting sick of the wet fur smell in his cabin every other day, but Audrey always invited him in and soothed him with cookies.

Audrey's library had expanded since the incident with the leshy. She wrote up more than a few dossiers for Rina on other creatures they might encounter as they continued expanding. Rina took the information without discussion, but it seemed to work for them. Might avoid Audrey getting in the shits with Rina again anytime soon.

The only new information of note came at the last all hands two days ago.

Celaeno ran scouting sweeps during the days, and she'd been turning up mutilated beast corpses at the settlement's far edges. Nothing stood out in terms of a pattern, so they'd all agreed to keep an eye out while the harpy kept tracking the oddities.

As Gunnar poured his coffee, Audrey closed her book.

She'd woken up a few hours earlier than him this morning. It was a long night running the entire perimeter of both his and Zhadan's parcels, an extra check for anything strange. He'd come up dry, again. No mutilated bodies, no odd smells or traces, nothing out of the ordinary. Normally, he woke sooner than her regardless, only needing about four hours of sleep to her eight on any given night.

"Almost everything from local mythos really enjoys drowning things," Audrey said with a grimace.

"Probably from all the flooding in spring," Gunnar said. "The temperature swings between seasons are pretty intense."

"Hmmm." She rested a chin on her hand, lips pursed. "Nothing fits with what Celaeno is seeing. I've been over all my books twice now."

"Rina'll appreciate that."

Audrey smiled, shrugged a bit. "I'm glad to stay busy. But it really could be anything. Aperiens travel everywhere. And when you consider hybrids and dusters? It's been more than 200 years since the Aperien Event. There's really no end to what might have wandered into this region."

"She hasn't seen anything in the north. That seems to be the only consistency."

"Zhadan is still worried?"

Gunnar finished his cup, headed to the stove to refill his mug. "He's on edge, but that's more to do with Lyubava." He poured his coffee and grabbed more hot water for Audrey's tea.

"She thinks it could be as soon as next week."

"You plan on helping her out?" He sat down, the chair creaking as he leaned back and canted his head toward her bookshelves. "Saw your new ones. Anatomy and midwifery?"

"I think she'll let me?" Audrey worried her bottom lip. "Amma Hertha offered her services since she's delivered all the grandchildren in the Clan, but the berserkers and the chuchunas don't seem to get on very well."

"Hm."

"You may need to help too."

Gunnar sputtered into his hot coffee, then cursed and rubbed his mouth on his sleeve. "What now?"

Audrey laughed. "You might need to distract Zhadan so Lyubava doesn't murder him."

"Hm."

Audrey refilled her tea, adding too much honey in his opinion, her chin still resting on her hand. Content, he recognized. None of them were too worried about whatever might be creeping on their borders, despite Audrey's preemptive research.

He tapped his foot a few times. "Quota is already done for the week."

"That's early, even for you." She flashed him another bright smile.

"Means the rest is profit. Maybe Zhadan and I can scare up another dragon."

"Zmei," she corrected him, exactly why he'd said it wrong, but her smile dropped as she started clearing the table.

"Even if we don't, we'll have plenty of excess trade built up in another month or two." Then they could deal with their housing situation, see about getting her a nice set up in the station.

"Hm," was all she offered, drying her hands on the towel Aster had helped her embroider a few weeks back. "How are Tomas and Mateo settling in?"

Well, if she wanted to change the subject, that would do it. "Why, they bothering you?"

Audrey smirked at him, a real smirk. He narrowed his eyes, which made her roll hers. "I almost never see them. I was more curious if you're still spying on them."

"I observe, from time to time," Gunnar said. "Like Rina told me to."

"And in the last six weeks?"

Gunnar took a drink of his bitter black coffee. "They've kept their noses clean. Making their quotas, but nothing else. Lazy ain't a crime, though."

"Or maybe they deserve a little rest?" Audrey asked, closing up her books and shelving them in the proper order. "They were so worn down when they first got here." She frowned, her busy work stalling. "Not as bad as you when Warden Kushiel brought you up that first day."

Gunnar stood then, draining his mug. "No need to dive down those memories."

She shivered despite the cabin being plenty warm, rubbing her arms. "I know."

He hated her getting all sad remembering how shit off he'd been. Hated the way her scent dimmed, clouded by memories of him, by memories of the ESC. Memories of her apartment burned to ashes for helping him. Memories of her starving on the streets, almost dying before he'd found her.

He dumped his mug off in the sink, then went over so he could pinch her chin in his fingers, make her look at him. "That shit's done and over with."

"I try not to think about it, you know? It just happens sometimes." She squeezed his forearm, her fingers warm. "I don't know why it happens when it does. Quiet times like this? Everything is great. I don't know . . . Why I would think about that when we're happy?"

Gunnar caught her tears with his thumbs, then pulled her into his chest with one arm. She hugged him tight. He tried not to be casual in touching her, but sometimes she really needed it.

Sometimes . . . sometimes he needed it.

He indulged himself a bit, resting his chin on the top of her head, letting her warm, bright scent wash over him, still the best thing in his life even when she felt a little sad.

A little sniffle. "Thanks."

He didn't really have anything that needing doing just then, so they stood in the kitchen like that for a few minutes, the outside world snowy, brisk, and silent.

Audrey spent the rest of the morning baking. When she wasn't feeling her best, she always tried to brighten others' days. Gunnar settled on their worn-out couch and thumbed through a few books while she worked, knowing she needed the company although she'd never ask. By midafternoon, she'd exhausted her baking supplies, wrapped about six dozen cookies—snickerdoodle, a new recipe—and asked him to join her for a walk to the station.

Audrey disappeared into the station kitchen with Aster shortly after they arrived, because the cornflower wraith insisted on learning the new recipe after one bite. Turned out she really liked cinnamon.

Idle hands left Gunnar restless, and he realized he hadn't been to see Virtue in a while. He didn't have any urges at the moment, no more than normal, but he hadn't checked in with them either.

Might as well make sure the vilebloods were still being polite, he decided as he headed down the hall to the brothel. Might be worth asking Virtue about Innocence as well, since the incubus was unusually bleak during their last encounter.

Gunnar ducked through the angel wings, finding both Virtue and Innocence seated in the lounge area. Innocence rested his head on his sister's lap, her lithe fingers playing with his golden curls as she hummed what sounded like a lullaby. Eerie eyes cracked open at the swishing curtains, and Innocence blinked lazily up at him.

"Oh, look who deigns to grant us his presence," the incubus slurred, waving a finger around in a circle.

"Still in a shit mood?" Gunnar asked.

Virtue laughed, patting Innocence on the forehead. He swatted her away, pouting. "Maybe." Then he pointed at Gunnar. "You were supposed to be watching."

Gunnar cocked a brow at Virtue, whose mirth faded, her expression a bit of a grimace. He sat down across from them, leaning back on the velvet couch. "More of a doer than a watcher."

Innocence gave an inelegant snort.

Virtue went back to soothing him with a sigh. "He means Mateo and Tomas. We've been meaning to catch you. You," she said as she gestured dismissively at him, "haven't had need of me lately it seems."

"Oh, ho, ho, has he finally slaked his thirst at the most elusive of wells?" Innocence grinned, his teeth tapered to points as he licked his lips.

Gunnar ignored him, the fucking idiot. "Been busy is all," he said, which wasn't really true. Things had been quiet, calm, and he hadn't felt an urge strong enough to require attention. Apparently, quiet was good for him. Go figure.

But he wasn't babysitting anymore, not like Rina wanted that first week, and he'd done his best to avoid the pair. They'd left Audrey alone, which had been good enough for him, but not if they started other trouble.

"What's going on?" Gunnar swallowed a few times. He'd expected if a problem showed, it'd come from Mateo, not Tomas. "Are they, uh, acting like me?"

The stark shock that hit his nose, the blatant disbelief in both their scents, Gunnar didn't understand. Innocence sat up, blinking at him with bleary eyes, and even Virtue seemed at a loss for words.

Then Innocence laughed, a single bark. "He's bloody fucking serious, isn't he?"

Teach him to show a bit of concern.

Virtue laid a hand on Innocence's arm, but he slapped her away and stood. Virtue followed, and Gunnar did too.

"No," Innocence said, shaking that pointy finger in Virtue's face. "No, this pandering is relentlessly exhausting." He wheeled on Gunnar. "You want to know if they're like you, hmm? How so? If they can walk into the brothel and have a conversation? Hm? If they can leave without fucking?"

"Innocence." Virtue's tone carried warning.

"No. He's a fucking idiot, and it's tired, Virtue. I'm tired." He waved a hand, flippant, and Gunnar snarled at him. Innocence clutched his chest, gasping. "Oh, so scary, because he's a vileblood. You're boring, Gunnar, that's what you are. A drole, pathetic duster, using your blood as a crutch."

"You want to say that again?" Gunnar growled, grabbing him by his silken robe.

"Yes. Again and again and again." Innocence twisted free easily, his eyes gleaming, and not just from the alcohol. "What I wouldn't fucking give to have the control *you* have. What I wouldn't give to be able to turn down a fuck, to have a choice in my feeding. To have a life beyond my nature.

"You ask if they're like you? Gunnar, they're here every night, sometimes two or three times a day if their quotas are done. They can't even walk in here without climbing one or both of us."

Gunnar glanced at Virtue, who nodded. "They hurt either of you? We need to take care of this?"

"Still ignoring the actual conversation, how charming. I'll be in my room." Innocence sauntered down the hall, vanishing behind his curtains.

"The fuck is his problem?"

Virtue didn't smile. "You've added to it, but you're not the source by a mile. And their appetites aren't a worry. I can handle a hungry vileblood." She tsked. "But I became concerned a few days ago when Innocence questioned my time with you and Mateo. He wanted to know what was normal for vilebloods, because Tomas is becoming hungrier. Needier." Virtue slumped down on the couch. "My brother cares for that boy, you know."

Gunnar didn't say a thing, tasting the worry in Virtue's scent, briny and thick.

"Tomas has never come to me, only Innocence. I didn't expect them to become so close, so quickly, if at all. Innocence has always been keen on keeping his feelings closed." She sighed. "I joined them last night. Tomas tastes like the beginnings of madness."

Shit. "Blood madness, yeah?" He rubbed his face, and grumbled, "Only a matter of time, huh."

Virtue studied him for a moment, the succubus he'd learned a long time ago, clever as a whip. Observant, much more so than her brother. "Blood madness can happen in any duster. You know that. Any mixed blood has the chance to break away from humanity and lose the mind. I've seen angels weep for their children gone mad from beauty. Dragon whelps eat their own bodies. Siren spawn drown themselves to stop their own voices.

"Feeding on Tomas is stalling the problem, but I'm not sure how much longer. I planned to tell Rina tonight."

Gunnar crossed his arms. "Why not kill him? I can take care of it in five minutes."

Virtue turned from him but not fast enough to cover her frown. "Blood madness can be cured." She drummed her nails on the side table, her gaze straying down the corridor, her scent laced with a sudden sorrow, bone and ages deep.

Shit. "It happened to your brother."

"He doesn't want to abandon them to the fate that almost took him. He wants to help Tomas until we can arrange for a blood mage, but he can't. I won't risk him going mad again for anything."

"And you?"

"I have no human blood," Virtue said, giving him a smirk, but her expression was dark. "But truly holding madness at bay for an extended time, that would require me to feed from him in ways I've abandoned. Ways we both did, to keep ourselves . . ." She stalled, considering Gunnar in a way he wasn't entirely comfortable with. A small nod, as if deciding something. "Like you."

He narrowed his eyes. "He bitches at me and now you're circling back around."

"Yes, because apparently you truly are willfully obtuse when it suits you."

"Oh, you gonna enlighten me then, huh?"

"Do you want to be the monster, Gunnar? The rapist and murderer, hunting and bloody, tossing your seed far and wide as you end the human race?"

He rolled his eyes.

"Same as neither my brother nor I wish to be nothing but sex demons who feed so deeply we steal the souls from those we fuck. We are monsters by definition, designation, fate predetermined, yes? And yet we choose who we are. We choose to keep the dark where it needs to stay, the monster right at the edge, to protect that which we wish to see preserved. Things—people—better than we ourselves could ever dream to be."

Gunnar swallowed; he really hated thinking of Audrey in any context when he was in this damn brothel.

"But we're in control. Of our monsters, our demons, our blood, because we *choose* to be in control. I've never met a vileblood more balanced with their humanity than you, Gunnar. And these two men? They are nothing like you. Tomas will lose the fight for his humanity if he doesn't receive proper care. Mateo, well, he might not be mad, but he has no aims to live a better life than required of him."

"You want to help them? When it's fucking up your brother like this?"

"Don't use my brother to shield your desire to kill them for the smallest infraction because you worry about Audrey. I might not have your sense of smell, but I'm not a fool."

Gunnar ground his molars.

"And what would Audrey desire, anyway? If I'm to guess, she'd want to help. Isn't that the only reason they're still here in the first place?"

"Rina's in charge," he deflected, but it was weak and he knew it.

"That she is." Virtue stood. "And I'm requesting she help secure a blood mage and whatever else we need to see Tomas well."

"And Mateo?"

"For now, he doesn't matter, but if he started going blood mad? I'd help him too."

"Be careful, Virtue," Gunnar drawled as she headed down toward her brother's room. "Mad or not, in control or not, vilebloods are always a risk."

"We all are, Gunnar."

Chapter 26

Audrey wasn't happy with the news. At first, Gunnar considered not telling her, but that felt too risky. Who knew what the fuck would happen in the next few weeks? He'd told her over dinner at their cabin. Now they'd finished eating, and she pulled books from her shelves one after another.

"And she's sure it's blood madness?"

"Got the impression they've both fed on it before."

"I know little about it," Audrey said, stacking another tome on the table before retaking her seat. When she shoved one toward him—*Duster Studies Portfolio 2143*—he quirked a brow at her. She mirrored his expression. "We both know you're too worried about me to go hunting tonight. Instead of sitting here brooding about it, why don't you help me try to find a solution?"

He opted to clean the dishes instead, which he never did, if only because Audrey always beat him to it. Not brooding while he did it, though. He didn't . . . *brood.*

He frowned.

Did he?

"Maybe the solution is sending them somewhere else."

She'd already opened another book, *Human/Aperien Medical Condition Crossovers*, and didn't look up as she ran a finger along the index. "Maybe it will be, if that's what Rina decides. Or maybe she can arrange help to come here on the next train day." She turned the page. "It's still two days off."

After a few minutes of scraping paper and clanging flatware, she muttered, "I wish we could contact Theodore."

"He's not where all these new books are coming from?"

"Maybe some of them?" She said, granting him a wrinkled nose with a snarky little grin. "I regularly get books with no sender marked, but I've also ordered several of them from traders in the Dominion." She pointed to a thick volume on the shelf with gold leaf on leather; *History and Policy of the Moscow Dominion, Ver. VII.* "That one was a gift from the head bookkeeper in Moscow proper. I export ink to him every week now for new reading material."

Gunnar grunted and went back to the dishes, later plopping down across from her again when he finished.

"This entry says blood madness can be treated if caught early, but also that the treatment varies drastically depending on blood composition. You might get your wish after all, at least temporarily. The Dominion has some talented healers, both science based and magic users."

"Read that in the fancy book?"

Audrey laughed and flattened her hand on the spine. "However did you guess?"

Gunnar tapped a finger on the book she'd pushed at him. He had an idea, but he didn't much like it. He tapped again, considering the book in front of him, Audrey's furrowed brow as she studied. Innocence's melancholy and Virtue's concern for her brother.

He cleared his throat, grumbled out, "Might be worth talking to Virtue and . . ." He grimaced. "Innocence about all this. Maybe they know some shit that won't be in these books or can tell you what to look for."

Audrey paused, and when she looked up from her reading and propped her chin on both hands, he knew he couldn't walk it back. Her grin was entirely shit-eating. "Did you just tell me to visit the brothel?"

"No."

She squinted at him. "Are you sure?"

"Pretty fucking sure." Gunnar's lip twitched, but otherwise he stayed stoic as her scent threaded with more mischief.

After a pause, she asked, "Do you really hate reading that much?"

"You want help carrying your books or not?"

Gunnar tried not to be a complete asshole, but watching Audrey at a tavern table between Virtue and Innocence gave him trouble. To his credit, Innocence hadn't made a single innuendo, subdued as he drank tea and listened, offering an occasional tidbit. He'd even left a seat between himself and Audrey without Gunnar insisting. Virtue sat close, her focus entirely on the research at hand, but she was still an Aperien apex predator.

And while Audrey did her best to stay attentive, she blushed the entire time she chatted with the pair, and every time Virtue gave her any praise or encouragement, she got flustered.

Natural response, he reminded himself. Any duster would have trouble around these two; a human didn't stand a chance no matter how hard Virtue and Innocence suppressed their natures.

"Gonna go hunt," he grumbled after about twenty minutes of pacing around the tavern, and he pointedly ignored Virtue's smirk, Innocence's eye roll, and Audrey's confused expression. "If I'm not back when you're done, walk her home."

"Jonathan, I can walk home by myself," Audrey groused. "They need to w-work when we're done, anyway." She cleared her throat but kept her little chin up high.

Virtue canted her head at him, her smirk devilish from behind Audrey's shoulder. "Audrey is very capable, Gunnar. I'm sure she'll be just fine."

That Innocence didn't join in for an easy barb spoke volumes. And he needed to get out of here before he started being irrational. Audrey wasn't in any danger; she was well protected between two powerful creatures, both of which were grateful for her help.

His hackles were up anyway, hindbrain overruling logic, which made him growl. "Don't wait up."

Gunnar shoved out the doors, thankful for the winter bite, sunset inches away. He cracked his neck, rolled his shoulders, irritated at his frayed control. The fresh air helped; his nose cleared out long enough for his instincts to fucking relax.

This wasn't a normal response.

They lived in a town full of dangerous beings. Rina was Baba Yaga's daughter, for fuck's sake. He didn't know who the hells E really was, but the man reeked of old, deep power. Gullin was a raging dickhead on a good day. The harpy wasn't overtly threatening to him, but she could easily rip a human to pieces. Same was true for Aster, Zhadan, and Lyubava. Same was true for the entire Clan, not to mention a thirty-strong pack of dire wolves. A leshy lived a few miles beyond their cabin.

And then whatever the train brought through every week—like that fucker Dimitri. A roulette every time, and while he kept himself on guard during those days at the market, he'd never let his instincts rankle like they did right now.

And as dangerous as Innocence and Virtue were by nature, Gunnar knew they'd never hurt Audrey. Hells, Gunnar was pretty sure Virtue was a friend to them both at this point, and as much as Innocence was a pain in his ass, the man was alright. They'd protect her same as they'd protect anyone who called Nizhny home.

He stepped down the station stairs, still growling and grumbling, because he knew exactly what was going on and admitting it wouldn't do shit about him getting territorial around a girl who didn't belong to him.

Gunnar scoffed, but he couldn't help a smirk. As Audrey said the bar that night, who she fucked or didn't was none of anyone's business. Yeah, well, she could think that all she liked, be right about it, and he'd keep his mouth shut. But none of that changed the truth.

If anyone touched her? He'd kill them.

Gunnar'd never felt so certain about anything in his life and never so out of control at the same fucking time.

"Shit," he muttered, rubbing his face.

The fresh scent hit him before he heard the footsteps, a shadowed figure stumbling from the western tree line and collapsing after only a few paces.

Mateo. And by the smell, he was bleeding out.

Gunnar inhaled deeper as he stalked toward the vileblood, picking apart the nuances as he crossed the rails, boots crunching against the icy snow.

A gut wound, the rich, heady stain of organ blood. Adrenaline, sour and wild, tangled with frustration, anger and fear. Regret? Exhaustion, right on the edge of passing out. Gunnar realized he wasn't just scenting Mateo.

Tomas's blood too, and a lot of it. And fuck if he didn't taste madness in the dark scent of that spilled black blood.

Blood madness didn't have a flavor he could readily associate it with. Anger tended to read hot, spicy. Sadness, by contrast, might come across cool on his senses, often reminding him of rain—or a rainstorm if tangled up with other emotions. Happiness felt warm, could carry sweetness for some reason, rich and almost fruity other times. Arousal, depending on the person, could be decadent or sour—but always invasive.

Madness wasn't bitter—like lies tended to be, probably because madness couldn't really hide once it really gained ground. Acidic, antiseptic? Not really rotten, not overripe, either. But like many things, Gunnar knew it when he smelled it, and Tomas's blood carried the taint. Whatever happened since yesterday? Not fucking good.

"The fuck's going on?" Gunnar yelled, keeping a good ten feet between him and the downed vileblood. Mateo's blood smelled clear of madness, but he was a wounded, vulnerable predator.

Mateo rolled his head, groaning as he shifted his weight. Blood drenched his furs in wet black, a smear spreading on the surrounding snow. Blood, blood, and more blood, everything reeked of it. "Gunnar?"

Frost and frozen blood peppered his hairline, bruising forming around both eyes and his left cheek. His bottom lip was split wide open, his teeth black when he winced.

"The fuck happened?" Gunnar repeated, dropping to a squat with his palm resting at the knife on his thigh.

Mateo wheezed out, "Tomas."

"Yeah, I can smell him. He dead?"

Mateo's eyes flashed, all pitch and pain. "No. He's mad, though. He . . ." He licked his lips a few times. "I thought we . . ."

"You fucking knew?" Gunnar snarled, wanted to grab the fucker and shake him. "For how fucking long?"

"Few weeks." He coughed, holding his stomach as he bent in on himself. "Tried . . . tried to help him."

Gunnar blinked. "Those corpses, all fucked up on the borders. That was him?"

"Tried to . . . work it out."

"You fucking idiot. You should have told someone."

He shook his head. A brittle laugh bubbled out. "What, so you'd kill him?"

"If only I fucking could," Gunnar growled. "No, once you're here, you're part of it. Innocence and Virtue picked up on his madness. They're already going through Audrey's books, trying to figure out the best way to help him. Rina'll get a blood mage out soon as she can."

"They . . . really?" Mateo's scent washed with disbelief.

Gunnar rolled his eyes, checking over his wounds. Yeah, the worst was his stomach, wide open, guts tangled in his fists. "You gonna shake this off?"

Mateo grunted. "You need to find Tomas . . . He was worse off." His head lolled a bit, and Gunnar smack his cheek a few times. "I had to hurt him," Mateo mumbled. "You're going to have to put him down . . ."

He regretted that part, Gunnar could tell from his scent, even if he didn't regret hiding that Tomas was slipping.

This shit was not how Gunnar had expected the night to go. When he pulled at Mateo's arm, set to drag him to the station, the vileblood shook his head.

"I can manage."

Gunnar inhaled, because the blood was all tangled between the two vilebloods, but he hadn't picked up a lie anywhere in Mateo's scent, so he left him in the snow.

The trail cut a stark, dark line in the otherwise pristine landscape.

Gunnar hit a fast jog he could maintain for a few miles. If Mateo was this worried, Tomas might die before he reached him. Or he fully expected Gunnar to finish what he'd started and put the kid out of his misery.

He veered off the main railway area, following the bloody footprints toward the taiga proper. He let his beast rise, easy with so much blood on the wind, saturating his senses with heady violence. Idle days were fine, Gunnar'd gotten used to them, but he hunted harder and fought messier after a few days off. That conversation with Virtue and Innocence simmered in the back of his mind; he might as well make use of his blood, what made him a monster. What made him good at being a monster.

He was the best tracker in the settlement, hands down. His senses, his endurance, and the way he could drop into a mode not so unlike torpor, everything else falling away besides what he needed to do: find Tomas before he died, because if he could be saved, it would make Audrey happy.

The terrain was easy, and he ate up the distance. He swung wide around the expansive swamp Mateo came in from, as nasty things came out to play there at night. Mateo and Tomas hadn't cleared this parcel yet. He'd find Tomas there, he wagered, out on the far, frozen edge.

Breathing heavily now, Gunnar slowed. Tomas's scent thickened, along with the scent of him and Mateo's blood. Viscera mixed in. He inhaled deeper, other scents sparse as he veered further away from the nearest swampland. Audrey'd been right about most nasties around Nizhny favoring wetter terrain. Good for Tomas, though. Maybe nothing had come upon him yet.

Gunnar squatted at the edge of a clearing. Broken branches, smears on the snow, what looked like a body dragged over the next mounding snowbank. He drew the eversharp blade, flexed his knuckles. Maybe all the vileblood chased everything else off.

He crept forward, crouched low, the cocktail of Tomas just up-wind, over that next bank. He crested, finding an unmoving lump at the bottom of the dip, half covered by a cluster of fallen trees. Damn, they'd torn this place apart, but there was no movement, no heat.

"Shit," Gunnar muttered.

He heard a snap.

A body collided with him full force, a blade digging through his coat and deep into the meat of his shoulder, before they rolled wildly through the snow.

Chapter 27

Muffled curses, fresh blood, and Gunnar shook loose, his attacker sliding across the pine needles. He stumbled away, putting space between them as fast as possible, because the wound fucking *burned*. Having resistance to poisons didn't mean he'd instantly shake the effects, so he needed to get *away*, defense more important than offense.

Especially if he wanted to avoid killing this kid.

Gunnar stayed crouched as Tomas picked himself up from the snow, dusting off his coat. The moon hung bright; the sky was cloudless. He flipped the odd-looking blade a few times, Gunnar's blood flicking to the snow between them.

"Manticore," Tomas said, a quake in his voice and hand. "They kept them in the Manhattan Pen's general population, you know? They were prisoners too, but didn't stop them from eating us. Every once in a while, we'd bring one down, eat it back, and keep the quills for shivs."

Gunnar's fingertips tingled.

Manticore venom was nasty shit. It wouldn't kill him, but it would slow him way down. He didn't rise, staring at the man in front of him, teeth bared. If he stood now, he'd get even more lightheaded. Also explained why he was bleeding like a motherfucker, his coat already soaked.

He needed to keep his shit together.

Because despite the amount of blood littering the snow, covering Tomas's clothes, blowing out his senses, the kid didn't seem injured at all.

"I didn't want to do this, you know? But Mateo." Tomas swallowed a few times, swaying. "Mateo said you'd kill me if you found out."

Gunnar blinked a few times; charge and overpower? Another prick of that knife might leave him too dizzy to fight. He swallowed around the cotton taste and texture of his tongue.

Tomas seemed skittish. It was hard to grab scent details; so much blood, that tang of madness. Maybe he was too far gone? Odd, because he seemed pretty damn lucid despite being twitchy.

Buy some time, let his body burn off the venom.

"Do what?" Gunnar slurred.

"Kill you. Make it look like an accident." Tomas licked his lips, then again. "He says you're out to get us. Keep us from what you found here." The boy nodded a few times, as if convincing himself. Or reminding himself.

"Don't like you," Gunnar admitted. "Wanted you gone, but Rina's the boss." He wheezed as he spoke. Fuck, the quill must have come off an adult manticore.

"But you would. Kill us and leave us for dead. You'd do it."

Gunnar shook his head, his ears ringing, pain stabbing behind his eyes as the venom circulated. It'd get worse before it got better. If Tomas was smart, he'd make his move quick. The kid had to know he'd never take Gunnar out in a fair fight.

Then he remembered their talk the first night the pair arrived. How they'd known next to nothing about vilebloods. If they'd never dealt with being poisoned, bitten, anything like that, they probably didn't know about their innate resistance to things like manticore venom.

No idea that given another ten minutes, Gunnar wouldn't be at his best, but the symptoms that really fucked up his abilities in a fight would be long gone.

Stall then.

"No. Just send you back on out on the train. Gone, not my business."

"We have nowhere else!" Tomas lunged as he spoke, shaking the quill, his other hand tight in his messy black hair. "I have to do this. He told me! He said I had to get under control by more killing and sex, more and more of it, but it's not working! He said you'd figure it out because you'd smell me. He told me this is the only way we can stay."

His vision swam as the pieces came together. "He gut you himself?" Gunnar nodded toward the stained and torn tunic under his open coat.

Tomas jutted out his chin, his face pale. "You wouldn't have believed it without enough blood. And he cut himself up good too, not just me."

He must have used healing potions, the only thing that made sense for Tomas to be this lucid after a wound like that. His brother hadn't taken it easy, did everything to make this gambit convincing, otherwise Gunnar would have smelled the lies, scented a light wound instead of organ blood.

"Mateo told me you've been killing the stuff at the borders. Can't help yourself from making it messy."

"He wants to protect me. No. Stop, stop," he muttered to himself, pacing back and forth while Gunnar remained utterly still, unthreatening. Docile. "Stop stalling, stop talking. Just do what he said." Tomas grimaced, mumbling more under his breath, not even watching Gunnar now. "Mateo wants to protect me."

"So does Innocence," Gunnar said.

The boy stopped, eyes wide. "W-what?"

"He knows that you're going blood mad. He figured it out from feeding on you."

"He . . . he knows?" Panic laced his scent, so strong it overpowered the blood in the air, and his expression crumbled. Looked like the kid had it as bad as Innocence did.

"He wants to help you, him and his sister both. And Audrey," Gunnar added with a wheezing chuckle, "because the girl can't let anyone suffer if she can help."

"No." Tomas shook his head, pulling at his hair, biting his lip so hard a black drop trailed down his chin. "No, no, there is no help. Once you're sick like me, that's it. Mateo said so."

"Ever think maybe Mateo doesn't fucking know everything?" Gunnar drawled. "Or doesn't tell you everything?"

"He's my brother. I . . . I wasn't big like others in the pen. He looks after me. He's always looked after me."

"He sent me out here to kill you, kid."

"You're a fucking liar!"

"Yeah? Is that what you smell on me? Lies?" He bared his teeth, Tomas backing up half a step before he rallied and lifted the quill between them. "You smelled a single fucking lie on me the entire time you've been here?" Tomas's nostrils flared. The spots in Gunnar's vison had faded, but his muscles still twitched, his body sluggish. Getting easier to breathe, though, slowly but surely. "What's next? Innocence knows about this shit, you gonna kill him too?

"What? No, why—"

"Think you or your brother have a shot at taking out Virtue?"

Tomas laughed at that. "No." Another laugh. Another headshake. He squeezed his eyes shut, held them shut, while Gunnar kneeled a foot away from him, weapon in hand.

He really was just a damn kid.

Gunnar managed a smirk; Audrey really was going to love being right, because yeah, Tomas deserved a chance. He wasn't a threat. Gunnar wasn't sure if he knew *how* to be one.

"Blood madness can be cured, even for vilebloods," Gunnar said, shifting his weight a bit as the feeling slowly came back to his feet.

He worked to remain as non-threatening as possible, but the more he talked to Tomas, the less mad the kid seemed. And if Innocence had only just picked up on it from feeding, even if the incubus denied it for a few days, it appeared less and less likely Tomas had snapped enough to warrant Mateo deciding trying to kill Gunnar was the only way to keep living in Nizhny.

Mateo and Gunnar needed to have a little chat. On the end of Gunnar's blade.

"Why today?" Gunnar pressed as Tomas continued pacing and pulling at his hair. "You've been mutilating shit for weeks."

"I don't know," Tomas muttered. "I don't know. He said I was going to get worse. That we need this now, not later. That he's sick of waiting for someone to find out. Sick of waiting for you to be out of the way."

Gunnar lurched to his feet, the burst of raw rage driving him. He swayed, a snarl rumbling deep in his chest, and Tomas almost fell on his ass.

"This ends one of two ways, kid." He opened his arms wide, pushing through the venom's lingering effects for show. "You need me to put you down? You that fucked up? Because it don't look or smell that way to me."

"How . . ." He shrank back a bit more, eyes darting between the amount of blood Gunnar'd left behind on the snow and dirt, his weapon, and the dwindling space between them. "The venom . . ."

"Another thing your brother don't know," Gunnar drawled, letting a growl bleed into his voice, crowding up on the kid while he fumbled around. "Venom doesn't really work on vilebloods."

"Shit," Tomas whispered. He held up his hands, too spooled up to realize what Gunnar meant was the venom wouldn't kill him—not that he was currently operating on about seventy-five percent bravado and sheer fucking willpower.

The entire back of Gunnar's jacket had soaked through, the wound still leaking, and despite shaking down the venom, if he didn't get patched up soon, blood loss was going to become a real fucking problem.

If Tomas went all out? Right now, he might win.

An actual threat, a real predator, would have figured that out.

"You want to live? See if we can get you fixed up? Give me that quill and sit the fuck down," Gunnar bit out.

Tomas handed it over and sat.

Gunnar tucked the quill in his back pocket.

"You patch up with healing potions?" When Tomas nodded, staring up at him like a fucking lost puppy, Gunnar sighed. "Stay here. I know you won't freeze to death. You wait until someone comes for you, prove to me you're not completely fucking lost, you got me?"

"Mateo—"

"Mateo, I'll deal with." Gunnar turned his back on Tomas, the utter defeat in the kid's scent over taking everything else.

"Are you going to kill him?"

"I ain't promising shit, aside from the only way he's staying in this town is if he's in the dirt. And you need to think real hard if the man willing to gut you and leave you out to face me alone is really who you want watching out for you."

He considered Tomas for a few seconds, considered what he might find once he got back to town if Mateo was really gunning this hard for him. He wrestled his coat off, tossed it at the kid's feet. No way Mateo didn't have his own healing measures on hand if this was his plan.

What was the game, though? Lie in wait in case Gunnar limped back into town instead of Tomas? Fucked up as he was, if Mateo was at full steam? Gunnar needed an edge to counter the venom still pumping through his veins.

To Tomas, he said, "I'm gonna need your jacket."

Chapter 28

It took way too fucking long, but Gunnar finally hit the Nizhny's edge. His teeth chattered, but Tomas's coat, soaked and frozen, insulated him from the worst of it. He limped, his muscles tight from head to toe. Kept the hood drawn tight, scarf wrapped around his entire face, and his posture hunched to make himself seem small. He had to expect Mateo at his best, while Gunnar was stumbling along at barely half of his capabilities.

He paused when he reached where he'd encountered Mateo. A lot of blood and mussed snow, but the man was gone. Gunnar kneeled at the spot, grunting at his body's protests.

If Mateo meant to play this up, make some claim that Tomas was mad, that Gunnar died trying to fight him down, he'd have dragged himself bleeding to the tavern. If he'd been waiting to ambush Gunnar if he came back alive, injured and crippled by manticore venom, Gunnar would have smelled him by now, or they'd already be rolling in the snow.

No, he smelled healing potion, sticky-sweet. A few red drops spilled among the mess. And Mateo had made no effort to hide his tracks, which headed directly north up the rails.

This fucker . . .

Tomas had said he wanted Gunnar out of the way. He'd assumed it was the same shit they'd been whining about from the start, how

Gunnar was being selfish and not wanting any other vileblood in his territory. No.

Mateo was after Audrey.

Gunnar lurched to his feet but only got a few steps before he caught Audrey's scent on the wind. She'd left the station while he'd been after Tomas. He followed her footprints a few steps, saw the convergence. Mateo followed her, no signs of any kind of struggle, the tracks continuing toward their cabin.

With the rails under his boot, Gunnar moved fast, his head less foggy now. Pure, violent rage had that kind of effect on him. He kept the hunting knife Audrey gave him tight in his fist, tucked under the heavy, bloody fur coat.

Mateo needed to think he was Tomas for maybe five seconds. That might buy him enough time to get Audrey out of this fucking mess unscathed.

He coughed, cursed, but he could breathe deeper now, fuller. The wound on his back still burned like hells but was superficial compared to the venom and blood loss. His head pounded with each step, but each step put him closer, so each step fed the hatred threatening to consume any part of himself he ever considered human.

The cabin came into view, lights on. Nothing outside. Door shut. He hugged to the darker shadows, thanking whatever gods might be listening—which was none—for the cloud cover that had rolled in. Mateo's fresh tracks ended on the front porch. A tangible silence hung over their house, as if the entire taiga held its breath.

Fuck, how long had she been in there with him?

His skin felt tight, hot. His joints ached, his jaw grinding.

If Mateo touched her . . . If he hurt her . . .

He smothered the growl before it erupted from his chest, struggling against the bloodlust threatening to unmoor him completely. He was a vileblood, a fucking monster like the one in his house right now, but *he* was in control of the beast that made up his darkness.

And he was going to use that control to make Mateo wish he'd never existed.

Gunnar stopped short, a quick glance in the window showing the medkit abandoned on the table. A chair overturned. A few of the books she'd had on the table carelessly tossed around to the floor. Aster's vase of flowers, broken, the unnecessary water Audrey gave them puddled on the wooden floorboards.

Mateo came to her asking for help, pretending to be injured, and she'd let him in, because why wouldn't she? Gunnar gave Rina the all clear. They'd lived in Nizhny for weeks, keeping their heads down, not causing any trouble.

Gunnar opened the door, didn't stop. Not when he smelled human blood, her blood, not when he heard Mateo's voice floating from down the hall.

"Tomas! Ha! I knew you'd do it! I can smell him, pet. He did it, killed that selfish fucker you holed up with."

Gunnar's eye twitched; focus. Smooth movements, no delay. He knew this house, knew exactly how many steps from the front door to her room, and crossed them in full strides, reaching her door as Mateo leaned out to greet Tomas, and he swore he heard Audrey's voice, a low, desperate whine, and that was it.

Gunnar about climbed the walls as he charged, Mateo's expression flickering from triumph to confusion to panic in a heartbeat, and Gunnar was on him, full body, slamming him back into Audrey's bedroom.

She screamed, screamed like she was fucking alive, and Gunnar didn't even look to confirm, instead eviscerating the threat. Head-butted Mateo in the face. Slammed him against the wall, lifted him bodily, hunting knife sliding like butter into his groin, savoring the guttural howl of pain and shock, and then threw all his muscle upwards, up, up, breaking through the sternum, gutting the fucker nuts to neck, viscera and organs slopping at his feet. Black blood sprayed as he reclaimed the knife and brought it down again, at the heart, then deep into the neck, then Gunnar let out a howl of his own as he severed Mateo's spine, bending his neck back at the gaping hole, and sawing until he could drop the head, Gunnar's chest heaving, the body falling limp to the floor.

Gunnar swayed, shoulder colliding with the wall, rolling so he rested his back against the doorframe for support, sucking in heaving, gulping drags of air, trying to taste his sunshine.

He wiped his face, smearing the mess around, but there she was.

Audrey stood on the far side of her bed. There were scratches on her delicate forearms, bruising already staining her soft skin around her wrists. Her beautiful eyes were wide, red and puffy from crying, her hands clutched over her heart.

Black blood had sprayed everywhere. On her bedsheets, the wall, the ceiling. Spreading over the floorboards toward her bare feet. Dotting her clothes. Staining her.

She swallowed a few times, her voice hoarse. "Jonathan?"

Gunnar cursed under his breath, yanking off the scarf, throwing the hat across the room. "Yeah, it's me, Audrey. It's me."

She blinked, shuddering violently. She clutched her shirt tighter. "He said you were dead. He said he smelled his brother and your blood, that you . . ." A sob, her entire body spasming with it.

"Audrey, sweetheart, I'm here." He didn't move though, didn't go to her. Fucking hells, blood and viscera covered him from head to toe.

Shit, she'd just watched . . . that.

But before he could gather his painfully scattering thoughts, Audrey crossed the room, burying her face in his chest. He almost pulled back. He didn't want her covered in this fucking mess, but she held tighter. "He said you were dead."

Gunnar pulled her closer. He couldn't stop himself, arms tight around her, pressing his face into her hair. "You're safe, sweetheart. I'm here. I've got you."

He tried to peel back; he wanted to make sure she was alright, but she just buried herself tighter against him every time he shifted.

"Audrey, did he hurt you? Baby, are you okay?" He gathered her face in his bloody hands, but her eyes stayed scrunched closed as she shook her head. He couldn't tell if that was an answer or not. She trembled against him.

"There was so much blood. I thought he was hurt. I let him in and got the healing kit and then he . . ." She shook her head again. "He told me you'd be out of the way, then he smelled Tomas, and you . . ."

"I'm not dead," Gunnar growled, and her eyes blinked open. He tried to smooth away the tears, but they kept coming, and his gloves left an inky mess on her cheeks. He grimaced; fuck, she was covered in vileblood. The room was drenched.

Gunnar scooped her up and stepped into the hallway, shutting the door behind him. Mateo could wait; he needed to make sure Audrey was okay, and right now all the pain and fear and panic in her scent damn near overwhelmed him.

He put her at arm's length, and she sagged against the wall, grabbing at his arm as he struggled out of his coat and dropped it on the floor in a filthy heap. As soon as he did, she was back against his chest, her little hands clinging to his shirt.

"Audrey, we're a mess. Come on, let me get you in the shower."

He tried to move her into the bathroom, and her scent spiked so hard with raw fear, Gunnar's heart stuttered.

"Don't leave," she whispered as she grabbed at him with shaking hands. Shit, he'd never seen her like this, not even when her apartment burned to the ground by hellfire. She babbled on, her voice hoarse. "I don't want to live anywhere else. I want to be with you. Don't leave me. Don't—"

A knock thundered on their front door like a battering ram, and Gunnar put his body between her and the sound.

"Little! Gunnar!"

Zhadan. Hells, he'd never been so glad for that damn oaf, and a second later the chuchuna kicked in the door, his wide nostrils flaring. When he saw Gunnar, he bared his teeth and took in the mess in their front room.

"Smelled blood. Little?"

"She's here, she's okay." Gunnar took a steadying breath; Zhadan understood Russian better than English. "<<*Fucking Mateo tried to take me out, used Tomas going blood mad as, I don't fucking know, some kind of opening.*>>" He tilted his head down the hall toward the closed bedroom door, black leaking from underneath. "<<*He's dead. Tomas is alive. He's waiting for someone to come bring him in.*>>"

Zhadan snarled, loud enough to rattle the window glass. Gunnar blinked a few times, gritting his teeth as Zhadan took a few steps closer—but not close enough to be a threat.

Because he wasn't, he was an ally. A . . . friend. Audrey mattered to Zhadan too, and he . . . Gunnar was still fucked up. And she needed him, and hells if she hadn't told him repeatedly they weren't alone here in Nizhny.

Gunnar swallowed, gritting his teeth as he managed, "<<*I need help.*>>"

"<<*Anything*>>," Zhadan snorted out, not a lick of hesitation, the chuchuna's scent washed in worry and conviction. "<<*How help?*>>"

"<<*Get to Rina while I make sure Audrey's okay. Tell her about Tomas. Innocence will want to know about the kid too. I'll deal with the rest.*>>"

The chuchuna chuffed out an affirmative, a deep frown creasing his enormous mouth as his gaze drifted to Audrey, and then he stomped out of the house, slamming the door behind him.

"Just us now," Gunnar said gently, keeping his voice a low rumble deep in his chest.

"Don't leave me," she whispered, her voice broken.

"I'm not going anywhere, sweetheart. I promise."

Chapter 29

They were both covered in blood, but Audrey wouldn't let Gunnar go for anything. He couldn't stand it much longer, her skin tainted by his kind, so he coaxed her into their tiny bathroom.

"Need to get you cleaned up, sweetheart," Gunnar said, gentle as his voice allowed, her nails digging into his forearm as he turned on the shower. The copper piping groaned against the cold, steam filling the air in seconds. He owed E a mead next time he saw him. "Get in."

Audrey shook her head.

"Audrey, I'll be right outside."

She shook her head again. "Don't leave me."

"I'm not going to leave you, sweetheart. Hey, look at me." Gunnar cupped her face in both hands. Her chin trembled against his palms, and he tried to ignore the black smears all over her skin. "Just a shower, just for a minute."

Another head shake, Audrey muscling her way against his body again.

Gunnar held her; he didn't know what else to do. The water drummed against the copper tub. He blew out a breath. "Okay, okay, whatever you need."

He got her to sit on the toilet and let go long enough for him to peel off his gloves and toe out of his boots and socks, kicking them out of the way.

Audrey remained seated, palms open in her lap, staring vaguely at the floor. Gunnar kneeled down, hands on hers, gave a squeeze. She shivered. She was so damn pale. Modesty would have to take a backseat.

"Arms up," he said, and she obliged him while he tugged the shirt over her head, adding it to the pile of things they'd need to fucking burn. Gunnar spared a glance at the simple white cotton bra, stained with black, and swallowed dryly as he helped her stand. Turned her so her back was to him, that'd be better, because he didn't need to be looking at all her skin like this.

Audrey didn't seem to care, standing limp in front of him as he helped her out of her jeans, steadying her with a hand on her hip as he gritted his teeth. He hadn't seen this much of her since the night they fled her apartment, barefoot and in a T-shirt and underwear. He wanted to ignore it, he really did, but she was all soft skin and delicate curves, tiny under his huge hands, stirring that hungry, dark part of himself he kept buried any time he looked her direction.

She was beautiful, always had been, much as he tried to ignore it, and now was the worst time to be reminded. The scars on her arm and shoulder from the hellfire attack had faded, a reminder of how close he'd come to losing her, long before he'd really come to understand just how important she was to him.

He cleared his throat and stood, gaze falling between her shoulder blades when he noticed a faint shimmer.

Every thought vacated when he saw the delicate spell work. Runes colored nearly the same as her skin. He growled, couldn't help himself, grabbed her by one shoulder as he ran his fingers over the marks.

"What the fuck is this?"

Audrey didn't tense at his tone, didn't really react at all beyond turning slightly in his direction. Her eyes were glassy, and she made a small questioning sound.

"Who fucking marked you?" Gunnar snarled, everything forgotten beyond the runes, what they could mean.

Was she bound? Had someone enchanted her? Possessed her? How and who and when? The questions hammered into his skull. She reached over her shoulder, touching the runes; at least she knew they were there, that was something . . .

"Oh . . . Theodore," she answered, dropping her hand. "Before we left the ESC."

He'd kill him. It'd be work, but he'd find a way.

"Just protection spells," she added, her tone emotionless.

Gunnar ran his fingers over the marks, pressing with his thumb. One-way spell work? The kind of shit E did with the copper pipes to keep water warm, or the oven he'd made Audrey for the cookies.

But these were on her *skin*. That archivist fucker had branded her.

"What did you pay?" he asked, because he needed to know if he was swimming to Iceland.

"Nothing. He was worried, and he said it was the easiest way for him to help me since he couldn't come to Nizhny." Her fingers came back up, brushing Gunnar's near the almost invisible runes. "Four protection runes. From hellfire, persuasion, possession, and undesired pregnancy."

Made sense, what Theo'd picked, and he could confirm later that Theo hadn't done more than he'd told Audrey. They'd been attacked by hellfire; it could be used against them again. Both persuasion and possession were common and effective tactics against humans and had plenty of sources.

As for the last one . . .

Undesired pregnancy. It shouldn't have made his blood race, his mind stutter. His body shouldn't have been reacting to the idea she was protected, as protected as possible by a demigod's magic, against his vileblood.

The first thing in his head should absolutely not have been the ringing, deafening realization that he could have her, touch her, be with her, and she'd be safe from his blood's curse.

Gunnar scoffed, the sound loud and ugly in the tiny bathroom.

Yeah, there was a reason he was a fucking monster. Here Audrey was, vulnerable and in shock, and he was thinking with his dick. And a protection rune didn't change the fact he didn't deserve to touch, nor the undeniable truth that she'd never want someone like him, safe or not.

He needed to get his head out of his ass and take care of her.

"Sorry," he grumbled, guiding her into the tub, but she grabbed his arm again when he reached to close the curtain.

"Don't leave."

"I'm right here."

"Please," she whispered. "Please, just stay with me right now."

Gunnar closed his eyes and cursed. He could do this. He could be what she needed, not some fucking lecher. With a jerky nod, he tugged his shirt over his head, hissing as it reopened the wound on his shoulder.

Audrey frowned up at him. "You're hurt?"

"Not serious." Not anymore at least, though he'd take a few days to bounce back from the blood loss. He kicked out of his pants, keeping on the shorts underneath. Blood soaked them, but he did not need to be naked in front of her. Gunnar adjusted himself as he turned.

Her palms pressed on his chest, trying to look at the wound, and he planted his hands firmly on her shoulders and kept her facing away from him, into the hot water, then closed the curtain behind them. "Worry about you first, then you can patch me up."

"I'm . . . I think . . ."

"You're not fucking fine," he growled at her, running his hands over her arms, trying to scrub the black from her skin. "I stayed like you asked, now let me get this blood off you before I lose my fucking mind." He closed his eyes, exhaled through his nose, and added, "Please."

A pause, and then she gave a small nod, still shivering despite the hot water. Gunnar focused on cleaning her, and when she stripped out of her bra and underwear, he refused to acknowledge how his pulse jumped, how his cock twitched. Eyes on the top of her head, he turned her and tilted her head back, washing the blood from her hair, smoothing it away from her puffy eyes.

"He said you were dead." She shuddered, and before he could argue, she flattened a palm over his heart. "I didn't believe him." Her brow furrowed, clearly important to her he understood. "I didn't."

"I know, Audrey."

He didn't think this time, holding her tight as she quietly cried, a hand cradling her nape. He soothed her. He didn't really know what he said, half of it wasn't even words. It was killing him, the pain in her scent.

Gunnar would do anything, he realized then, anything to bring the sunshine back into her scent, anything for the precious woman in his arms.

Once they were both clean, he shut the water off. Wrapping her in a towel was a challenge, but after she let him sit her down long enough to strip off his wet shorts and get a towel tied around his waist, he scooped her up bridal carry. Her arms went around his neck, and her face nuzzled at his throat. Gunnar paused at the sight of her in his arms reflected in the polished steel mirror above the basin.

Perfect came to mind.

The front door opening snapped his attention. He pressed his lips against the top of Audrey's wet hair, nudging the bathroom door open just enough to poke his head through.

Rina strode through the living area, her face twisted in a scowl, blond hair messy and loose around her shoulders. Aster and Virtue came in close behind her. When she saw Gunnar, she showed her open, empty hands. Kept her distance, not stepping into the narrow hall.

His lip curled back. If any of them tried to touch Audrey . . .

No.

An impossible task, but he needed to fucking relax. These people were on Audrey's side. Part of him expected Rina to bust in the door and demand answers, demand he step the fuck back, let her handle things. Take Audrey away from him, because that was probably for the best, wasn't it?

But they weren't doing that. This was fine. They were here to help, because he'd asked for help. He'd asked Zhadan to get help. He realized then Rina had only brought women to help. Good call, given he was acting like a territorial beast in a damn rut. Gunnar licked his lips, gave Rina a hesitant nod.

"Audrey?" Rina asked.

"She's not hurt," Gunnar replied, relaxing a fraction when Virtue closed the front door, a brow arched, but she stayed silent. Aster had already moved into the kitchen, cleaning up without a word.

"What do you need?"

Gunnar jerked his head toward Audrey's room. "Clean up Mateo. Tomas is alive, out on their parcel. He's waiting, told him not to move until someone gets him."

Rina nodded. "I've got things covered for tonight. Get some rest, both of you."

"Yeah," Gunnar drawled, glancing down at Audrey nuzzled against his chest, both of them still wet and in towels, wondering what they all must think. If they were smart, they'd step in. All three of them should have had opinions about a vileblood damn near naked with a human woman in his arms, but nothing came.

They trusted him. By the expressions, they were just as worried about him as Audrey. He didn't know what the fuck to do with that knowledge.

"Thanks," he mumbled, nodding to Rina once as he ducked into his bedroom with Audrey still in his arms, closing the door and locking it behind them.

The room was dark, as he never bothered lighting his space, the bed crisply made, nothing else in the utilitarian space besides a trunk for his clothing, an end table with his under-used oil lamp, and a single wooden chair tucked in the far corner.

Audrey wasn't crying anymore, her expression vacant, her scent pained and exhausted and driving him nuts. He considered getting her some of her own clothes, but that would mean wading through what was left of Mateo, and the smell was bad enough with two doors between them and the body. Instead, he helped her into a plain black T-shirt of his, big enough to be a nightgown of sorts on her. He dressed himself, then pulled down the covers and helped her underneath. When he moved to tuck her in, she grabbed his wrist.

"Don't leave."

"Audrey . . ."

Her grip tightened, and he stopped fighting himself, forcing his way through the borders he'd built up between them. Because she needed him.

Gunnar barely got into the bed before she curled up against him, her head tucked under his chin, holding her against him the most natural thing he'd ever done. She sighed, the sound bone deep. Gunnar only let himself close his eyes when he scented sunshine in the darkest part of the night.

Chapter 30

Wakefulness clawed its way to the surface, leisurely and slow, probably the most relaxed Gunnar had ever woken up in his entire life. He blinked a few times, eyes crusted with sleep, bright light creeping in through the half-drawn curtains. Fuck, he was exhausted, despite knowing in his bones he'd passed out last night and slept hard and long.

Felt warm too, and when he shifted, he frowned, because the warm had a shape: Audrey curled tight against his side, her cheek on his bare chest.

Right, the night before.

But before the memories crashed over him in force—Mateo, Tomas, the horrible things Audrey had watched him do in her own fucking bedroom—she let out a little snuffling snore, and he couldn't help a stupid grin.

All he wanted to do was watch her for a minute, fuck the rest.

She hadn't moved much in the night far as Gunnar could tell, but then again, neither had he. The last thing he remembered was crawling in bed with her to soothe her, and then she curled up just like she was now, trusting and soft and gods damned beautiful. He must have passed out seconds after.

Her full weight rested on him, like she'd pressed as close as she could get without climbing on top of him. She was drowning his shirt, an arm across his chest, loose fist resting by her chin. Paler than normal, dark circles smudged under her close eyes, delicate eyes lashes fanned across her cheeks. Mouth hanging open a pinch, another soft snore.

Gunnar brushed the hair back from her forehead, grazing her skin, which felt normal. A soft noise and Audrey nuzzled closer.

He should get up, he thought, let her sleep. Last thing she needed was him creeping on her after what she went through last night.

Gunnar didn't move aside from idle fingers playing with her hair, dozing in the warmth and light. Moving might shake her awake, couldn't have that. She seemed comfortable, smelled content. His eyes drifted shut; he wasn't sure he'd ever napped in his life, was that what this was?

Audrey twitched; Gunnar had no idea who long it'd been when she jolted upright in the bed, fear lancing her scent.

"Hey, you're alright," he said, rubbing her arm. She shivered once, letting out a shuddering breath before rubbing her eyes. Then she flopped right back down on him.

"You're alive," she mumbled against his skin.

Gunnar nuzzled against the crown of her head, inhaled as the fear faded from her scent. "Yeah."

They said nothing else for a few minutes, the only sound their breathing, her eyelashes brushing his skin every time she blinked. He'd never just . . . laid or slept with a woman without sex. He always left after, no reason to linger with the exchange completed. Sure, he'd chatted with Virtue a few times after they'd fucked, but only while they got dressed.

This, though, he had no idea what to do with it, except that he didn't find himself in any hurry to move, but as much as he didn't want to break this peace, he needed to know she was alright.

"He didn't hurt you?"

"No, just . . ." When she moved, he almost growled at the loss of her warmth, and then she showed him her right arm. "He grabbed me pretty hard, then scratched me when I pulled away, but that's all."

They weren't deep at all, barely broken skin, but he still hated the red lines against her fair skin. "I'll bandage them for you."

"What about you? He hurt you, I remember from . . ." She blinked a few times, avoiding his gaze. "From the shower."

"We can take turns patching each other up, how about that?" he offered with a chuckle. She gifted him a shy smile in return, which made his chest ache for some reason. "I'll get the healing kit."

"I'll go with you." She slipped off the bed before he could protest. Last night she'd been terrified for him to be out of her sight, so he didn't argue.

"Alright, just let me . . ." He remembered how they'd left the place and grimaced. "Let me check things first."

"Okay." Audrey shifted between her feet, clutching at her borrowed shirt.

As soon as he opened the door, relief flooded through him. Smelled crisp and clean, so much so the place didn't smell like him or Audrey anymore. Aster and Virtue must've used magic to clean when they came with Rina the night before. Gunnar cracked Audrey's door, found the room as pristine as the hall. Same with the main living space, their clothing from the night before folded on the couch, no trace of Mateo or blood anywhere.

He nearly bumped into Audrey when he came back to his room. "We're good, come on." He didn't even think about it, just held out his hand, and she took it.

"Your shoulder looks terrible," she mumbled.

He didn't doubt it. He found the healing kit on the kitchen table, fully restocked next to Aster's fixed-up cornflowers, and brought it over to the couch as Audrey sat down.

"What happened?" she asked, like she wasn't sure she wanted the answer.

"We're going to have to go through all the shit from last night with Rina, top to bottom. We could wait, do it once." When her brow furrowed, he added, "Doesn't bother me either way, just want this easy for you." Gunnar hesitated, then reach out to cup her cheek; he didn't know why, but felt like the right thing.

Audrey leaned into his touch. "Okay," she agreed, "but I'm patching you up first."

External wounds treated, all dressed, coffee and tea finished, Gunnar and Audrey headed to the station under the late afternoon sky. The only hiccup came when Audrey asked him to get clothing from her room, but he didn't hesitate. As soon as they left the cabin, she'd linked her elbow through his and refused to let go, even when they stepped inside the station proper.

Aster was the only one in the tavern, a quiet time between lunch and dinner, and raced over as soon as she saw them, all gentle words and hugs for Audrey followed by concerned glances at Gunnar when Audrey claimed she was fine. Rina's greeting was much the same.

Gunnar ran through everything, doing his best to keep things brief and the more brutal details for another time. Audrey sat with her hands fisted in her lap, so damn pale, but she put on a brave face. She confirmed when Rina needed it and did her best not to cry when Gunnar explained the manticore quill. He passed it over; Rina would give it to E for safekeeping.

Everyone else was fine. Mateo's body—what was left of it—was being buried about two days' trek to the south. Frode was happy to send a few of the Clan boys out on the excursion. Good exercise, he'd said. Tomas was with Virtue for now, kept in one of her rooms under constant supervision. She'd confirmed what Gunnar suspected; Tomas would recover with proper treatment.

The whole damn thing would have made more sense if Mateo was the mad one, but no, turned out he was just an overreaching asshole.

Good fucking riddance.

Rina ordered Gunnar to take a week off from his quotas and rest, which also applied to Audrey. If they needed anything, ask. When they came downstairs, Aster gave them enough food for a damn feast, insisting they take it. The basket included a new cast-iron pan from E.

From there, they had nothing to do but go back home. Zhadan stopped by with Lyubava about an hour after they returned to the cabin. The chuchunas shared a meal and then headed back to their den.

After they left, Gunnar cleaned up while Audrey sat on the couch, knees to her chest as she quietly watched out of the window. He let her be for a few minutes, taking his time despite feeling restless. Her scent wasn't right, too much clouding up her normal disposition. Combined with whatever magical cleansing Rina, Aster, and Virtue had whipped up, their home didn't smell like it should and it aggravated the hells out of him.

When Gunnar settled on the couch next to her, Audrey leaned into him. He slung an arm around her shoulder and pulled her close, resting his chin on the top of her head as she sighed, and he waited.

It didn't take long.

"I'm sorry," came her quiet whisper.

He figured it might go something like this, so he just said, "Bullshit."

Audrey pushed away from him, wiped her face, all puffy again. "You were right. They were dangerous, and I made them stay."

He rolled his eyes at that. "In case you haven't noticed, no one makes Rina do shit—except talk to a leshy, apparently." When he smirked, she shook her head.

"Don't joke around. I'm serious."

"So am I."

"You wouldn't have let them stay here if I hadn't talked you into it. You would have told Rina to send them off, and she would have listened to you." Her voice hitched as she stood, arms tight across her chest as she paced the room, her scent absolutely miserable. "You could have died."

"You know vilebloods are resistant to poisons. I'm fine. Another day, it'll be like it never happened." Audrey winced at that, and he shook his head. "I'm not talking about you."

"You're the one who got hurt because of me. Because I'm always trying to see good where it isn't, being such a naïve, stupid—"

He surged to his feet so he could snarl right in her face. "Knock that shit off. You're not naïve or stupid. You're good, sweetheart. I don't know how you're so good in this fucked up world, or why I get to be a part of that. I sure as shit don't deserve it, but you're exactly what this world needs, you hear me?"

She blinked up at him, tears flowing freely now. He wiped them away, frowning at her. He hated seeing her like this, so he smirked down at her then, trying a different tactic.

"You didn't let fucking Kushiel get you down, don't let that dead asshole do it either. Besides," he added, giving her a lazy shrug. "You're never getting rid of me. Fucker didn't even get close." Gunnar tugged her in for a hug, and she clung to him, sniffling still, but her scent had warmed a fraction, a bit of light peeking through her uncertainty and fear.

She'd need more time, he knew, but it was a start.

She sighed against him, then patted over his heart. "You saved me first, you know. The only reason I get to be around is because of you."

"Hmm."

Chapter 31

Having a week off—a vacation, Audrey called it—was strange. It was one thing to be ahead on his quotas and take it a little easy but another thing entirely to check out. A good thing though, because Gunnar was weaker than he wanted to admit after the manticore venom and so much blood loss, and Audrey still wasn't entirely herself.

The night after he'd killed Mateo, he'd walked down the hall to find Audrey staring at her closed door, shaking so hard he could hear her teeth rattling. He didn't say a word, just steered her into his room, then got her some sleeping clothes from her closet. He'd planned to tough it out on the couch for a few days, but when she whispered don't leave, sounding almost as broken as when she'd thought he died, Gunnar found he couldn't refuse her, and didn't want to, anyway.

After that, they crawled into bed each night with her curled up against him, and Gunnar slept better than in his entire life. Waking up to her sleepy smiles was its own kind of treat.

They fell into other unspoken patterns. He watched her cook, which turned into helping when she offered to teach him. She wouldn't let him help with the cookies, couldn't have him stealing her only magic, she'd said with a silly grin. He taught her how to sharpen their various tools and treat skins to leather, one of the few skills she hadn't learned yet for processing his kills. On the third day of their week, they reorganized the basement storage.

Audrey took a bath every day, because it was vacation, but she left the door open, and Gunnar settled on the couch with a book, so when she came out looking for him, he'd be right where she left him.

The few times he'd left her sleeping alone, even just to take a piss or if he got up early, she woke up screaming, her dreams tricking her into thinking he was dead. She'd cry, he'd hold her, then when she calmed, she'd tell him about the nightmares. Ask him not to leave her; he'd promise he wasn't going anywhere.

They had one serious conversation about her living at the station; Gunnar needed to confirm living with him was really what she wanted going forward, needed her to tell him when she wasn't hysterical, and she calmly informed him she had no intentions of living anywhere he didn't, ever. After, they'd spent a few hours sketching out an expansion for the cabin, speculating how many cookies they'd need to throw at E to get what they wanted.

On the fourth day, they talked about Tomas.

"You're sure you're good with this?"

"Yes," Audrey said, that Esquire tone of hers surfacing. "He's not to blame. Mateo . . ." She clutched her tea cup tighter. "He manipulated him, used his madness as a distraction. Tomas deserves a chance to get well, and Rina has the resources to get a blood mage out here to help." Then she cleared her throat, blushing a bit when she added, "And doesn't Innocence like him? Maybe he won't flirt with you so much now."

Gunnar growled at her, but she only laughed—and it felt damn good to hear the sound.

They cooked, ate, read from her books. She taught him Blackjack and Poker, even though she was terrible at bluffing, and he showed her Nine Hands. She accused him of cheating; he told her it wasn't his fault she was terrible at card games.

On the fifth day, Audrey's sunshine scent became stronger, and she stared out the window less. She laughed more, and he laughed with her. That night, he watched her sleep and wondered if he'd ever enjoyed living without her around.

It snowed heavily, covering the settlement in fluffy white and a peaceful blanket, almost like the entire town had taken the time to just be for a few days, appreciating all they'd built.

Neither of them felt the urge to leave the little bubble their unique situation presented. They could have gone to the tavern, handed off the insane number of cookies she kept baking, maybe gone for a walk. He figured maybe they were both avoiding stepping back into normal.

One thing gnawed at him though, every time Audrey walked by and he caught himself staring at that space on her spine, right between her shoulder blades. Those marks Theo put on her.

The beast in him, well, Gunnar wagered all that was just pissing. His instincts acting like a bit of a possessive, raging, territorial asshole about the idea of anyone else having any claim on Audrey. He knew he was all of those things, so he kept pushing it away, brushing it off like it wasn't a big thing. Control. He had control, so the rest of the shit could take a seat and shut the fuck up.

But the itch about it wouldn't leave his brain or his blood. There was more to it, as much as Gunnar wanted to deny it. First, that shit with Rina—a smack in the face, that Theo'd bribed his way into Nizhny. Sure, she'd said pretty words about how he'd proven himself, but without the archivist's reassurance, he wouldn't be here.

Now, knowing about those marks on Audrey's back, he'd started wondering if she'd needed the same reassurance. Conditions to make Gunnar worth the risk of being around.

In the apartment, before it'd burned, she'd seemed disappointed in his desire to go at it alone. At the edge of the slums, she'd seemed reassured when he'd promised it would be the two of them going forward. Then they'd hid out for two days in the alleys, and then more time at Theo's condominium in the Eastern Seaboard Conjunct before they'd finally gotten out of the ESC's borders.

Lots of hours to reconsider or get scared. After all, she'd lost everything. And then Audrey had time alone with good old Theo, which was apparently enough time to talk her into four ritual runes permanently etched on her body. From a demigod. That kind of spell work? Theo had given up part of his magic, his raw power, *himself*, to put that on her skin. And as far as Gunnar understood, unless Theo died, there was no undoing it. Only an Aperien more powerful than the archivist might unweave the work, and it'd be hard to find one willing to make that sort of sacrifice for a human.

So why?

He understood the hellfire, persuasion, and possession. It made sense, still did. And Gunnar believed Theo did it to look out for her.

That last one, though. Undesired pregnancy.

Did Theo insist? Or did Audrey ask?

Was it the only reason he had her in his life, another bribe to make the risk worth taking a chance on a man like him?

"What is it?"

He blinked up from his coffee mug at Audrey's voice, no idea how long he'd been staring at the black liquid. It was cold.

This was what? Day six of them alone in the cabin? Gunnar frowned, pushing the cup away, set to brush the thoughts aside—again—but the tremble in her voice, the shadow crossing her scent . . .

No, he needed to clear his head.

"Those runes." Gunnar lifted his chin in her direction. She went utterly still, caught between refilling her mug and returning to sit with him. Fitting, somehow. "I got questions."

Audrey swallowed, giving him a shallow nod as she set her steaming mug on the table. She offered him a refill, but he knew the delay for what it was and shook his head. "Alright. What did you want to know?"

"You pay anything?"

"You already asked, I think? That night . . ." She shook her head. "No, Theodore didn't ask for anything. No binding, no geas. He doesn't have any influence over me." Audrey rubbed her nose. "I told him it was too generous with his magic when I had nothing to give him in return, but he insisted."

"Why?" Gunnar leaned on his elbows, licked his lips a few times as he watched her. Her scent floundered between embarrassment and worry—did she think he was angry? He tried to keep his expression calm, but it was a challenge.

"He worried if anyone found out I was alive, they'd come after me again. It made sense to make me immune to hellfire." A half-shrug. "I told him that was more than enough, but he said possession and persuasion were . . . well, you know why." She waved a hand, her tone self-deprecating. "I'm human. I have no innate resistance to any of those things."

"Sure. What about the last one?"

Her cheeks pinked, averting her eyes and fiddling with her mug. "Just more protection."

"From me?"

Audrey's gaze shot up, brow furrowed.

"He figured you'd better be protected in case I ever went feral on you? Theo always thought I should be more grateful for everything you did for me. Always thought I was an uncivilized animal, didn't he?"

"That's not true." She paled, her scent souring. He wasn't sure with what, her emotions were so tangled up.

Well, that was certainly an answer. He stood. "I get it. Better safe than sorry."

Audrey jerked to her feet so fast she knocked her tea over. "No, none of that is true, Jonathan." She struggled for more words, her jaw working, before she gave up and snatched a towel.

She didn't smell like lies, for all that her scent rolled. Gunnar crossed his arms, leaning against the counter as she cleaned, refusing to look at him at all now.

Ah, so it was her then. She'd asked for the rune, for the protection against him. He scoffed, half a laugh, rubbing his chest. This pretty little bubble of the last few days? Yeah, what a load of shit. All this time, he'd thought she trusted him, but if it was only because of that magic on her skin . . .

The words snarled out of him, low and acidic. "Needed a bribe just like Rina to keep me around, huh?"

Audrey stiffened, anger flooding her scent along with . . . pain? Then she tossed the towel on the table, rubbing her temples with her back facing him. "Is that really what you think of me?"

When she turned, her hazel eyes, those gorgeous eyes, blazed with indignation. Gunnar went perfectly still, instinct warring with logic, because he felt like something critical hung on this next moment of his life, and he didn't know what to make of the feeling.

But he didn't like—hated, in fact—the grief peppering her expression, her scent. The way she deflated in front of him.

"After all we've been through, you don't think any better of me than when you first got out of prison and thought I wanted to steal your money?"

When he said nothing, Audrey gave a snarl of her own as she stormed around the table, and he yielded a step. And then he snarled back, realizing he was being pushed into a corner. And fuck that.

Fuck that, because he wasn't the one not making sense.

He caught her wrists, no pressure on them, careful of her bruises, but he would not let her fucking push him, not without an answer. Not without her giving him a *reason*.

"Why would you think that!" she all but screamed at him.

"You tell me then, huh? What the fuck am I supposed to think?"

Audrey let out a little shriek of frustration, and he let go as soon as she struggled against him. Her chest heaved like she'd run miles, staring at him like he was stupid. When he sneered down at her, she laughed at him.

"You—"

"You want me to tell you?" she shouted over him, and Gunnar didn't know what he'd meant to say, only she kept right on talking, her voice shrill. "Yes! I asked him!"

Fucking hells, the wind left his lungs like she'd kicked him in the chest. He blinked a few times, not sure why hearing her admit it was a shock.

"Are you going to ask why? Or do you want to make up another story that paints you as a horrible monster instead of thinking, maybe, just maybe, there might be a good reason?"

Audrey moved closer, suddenly all fury, so angry he felt like he'd lost the thread of the damn conversation somewhere, because *he* should be the furious one, not her, but he'd never seen her this angry before.

"No?" She tilted her head at him, as if daring him, and when he only sneered again, she scoffed at him. "Fine, I'll tell you. I asked him because I thought," she started, then stopped, swallowed a few times. Audrey closed her eyes, taking a deep breath, then said, "I asked him because I hoped that maybe someday, if you . . . That you might . . ."

Her expression crumbled slightly, the fire fading from those bright eyes.

"That you might see me," she trailed off in a whisper and made a frustrated little noise he couldn't make sense of, and he smelled salt and she was wiping tears, of all fucking things, gaze fixed on the floorboards now. "You might see me as more than an obligation."

Gunnar stared down at her. They stood so close; he felt her heat, felt her trembling even though they weren't touching.

It had started that way. He wouldn't lie, but since coming to Nizhny, protecting her had gone from a debt to a pleasure. A fucking gift.

He hesitated—he shouldn't, he knew, but he still reached out, catching her chin.

"I don't," he mumbled, but he still didn't see how the lines connected, because she was safe with him if she was an obligation or the best thing in his life. She didn't have runes on her skin for any of that. "Not anymore."

Her breathing hitched, her expression softening as she looked up at him. She reached out, flattening and flexing her palm over his heart. Then Audrey ran her fingertips over his neck, then they rested on his cheek and she was up on her tiptoes, pressing her lips against his.

There was a split second where he was so fucking shocked, he didn't move, couldn't. The world narrowed down to her, her soft lips pillowed against his, sunshine and warmth filling his nose.

That you might see me as more than an obligation.

The lines connected, neon, the word *more, more, more* making Gunnar's fucking brain stutter.

But just like that, it was over, Audrey pulling back, covering her mouth with a shaking hand as she flattened her feet. Her cheeks flamed, bright red all the way to the tips of her ears, down her throat, her scent flashing cold with embarrassment, because Gunnar hadn't reacted at all.

"I'm sorry," she gasped out.

That wouldn't fucking do. Like hell he'd let her be sorry for that? For the best thing he'd felt in his entire damn life?

Because she was safe from him, from his blood. She'd *wanted* to be safe from him, sought the protection that meant he could touch her. That he could . . .

"No," he bit out, the word loud, and a growl, so much so that she startled, but by then he had his hands on her cheeks, and this time his mouth found hers. She let out a surprised sound against his lips, but then she melted into him and whimpered.

Gods, fucking hells, she tasted better than she smelled. Sweet, perfect. Everything about her made the world a brighter place, drowning his senses. Gunnar nibbled at her bottom lip, sucked on it softly when she gasped, pulling her closer, closer. He needed more, more of her. Just . . . more.

So soft, so delicate and tiny, this human woman. He wove his fingers through her hair, angled her head, pulling back to kiss the side of her mouth, her cheeks, her nose, living for the tiny giggle that slipped out of her, right before he found her mouth again, this time their kiss far less chaste.

It only took the tiniest coaxing, and she opened her mouth for him, and Gunnar was *lost*. Lost on her little kitten whimpers, the way she tentatively slid her tongue along his in reply, the way her fingers pinched his skin as she clutched at his shirt.

The way she utterly, entirely submitted to him at the barest touch.

He groaned into her mouth when her arousal touched his senses, her desire, desire for him. *Him.*

How long had she wanted him?

Long enough to ask a demigod to make it possible.

"Fuck," he whispered against her mouth as he relented, blinking down at her face cupped in his huge hands, her eyes closed, her lips already swollen from his kisses. The pretty blush painting her pretty skin. He wasn't sure what possessed him, but he nuzzled his nose against hers, then dipped forward, kissing along her jaw, bumping his nose under her ear as he whispered, "You want me?"

Her only response was another of those whimpers, followed by a spike in her pheromones that went straight to his cock. He nipped at her throat, gentle, be *gentle*, then soothed with his tongue before scooping her up by her thighs. Another gasp, her arms flying around his neck, and Gunnar growled, after her mouth again as he walked until her back pressed against the cabin wall.

It was doing something wild to his hindbrain, his instincts, the always restless beast in his blood. How small she was compared to him, how he surrounded her. How she'd never be any safer than she was right here, right now, with his body between her and the entire fucking world.

She panted now, and he smiled against her lips, licking into her mouth, groaning when she slid both hands into his hair, her fingernails scraping at his scalp.

She had no idea.

No idea what she was doing to him, no idea how he'd craved this and denied himself even the thought, how much he wanted to bury himself into her tight little body and make her scream for him, make her feel better than she made him simply by letting him exist in her orbit.

He pressed his hips forward, rubbing against the apex of her thighs, warm and wanting, and they both moaned together. His hands gripped tighter, his fingers wrapping around her waist, touching. This delicate, beautiful girl.

Maybe she could be his. More importantly, maybe she *wanted* to be his.

"Jonathan," she gasped. He let out a low growl, chasing her jaw, her neck, peppering any skin he could reach with kisses.

She deserved a million. She deserved everything.

But then she said, "Don't," before cutting off in a whimper.

Gunnar pressed his nose to her throat, her racing pulse, inhaling against her skin. Checking himself, because nothing about her scent said "don't."

"What, sweetheart?" Another kiss, gentle, there at that spot behind her ear that made her entire body shiver again, those sweet, sweet pheromones about to smother him.

Her scent shifted, not with fear, but with something close. Uncertainty? Fretting, suddenly, when she'd been falling into him seconds before. He pulled back, finding her eyes pinched shut, her forehead furrowed.

"If this is just an urge for you. . . Please don't do this if it doesn't mean anything to you."

He stared down at her pained expression, trying to figure out what the fuck she was asking him. His mind was blurry, fuzzy, all the blood drained south. Sure, sex was an urge, but it damn well felt like she was having the exact same urge right now.

But asking, "What do you want it to mean?" clearly wasn't the response she was looking for.

Audrey shook her head, leaning away, and he set her down, gripping his cock, trying to calm himself the fuck down.

"I'm sorry, I can't. I shouldn't have kissed you. I'm sorry," she stammered as she stumbled away from him.

"Why the fuck not?" Gunnar screamed inside at the distress flooding her scent, overtaking everything else, blotting out the sunlight.

Did he scare her, was that it? Too rough? Too forward?

She stood with her head bowed, clutching the sink edge, whispered, "Because I'm in love with you."

Gunnar retreated this time, his thoughts stuttering. "You don't mean that."

Damn, did her scent shift. She spun on him, her eyes glassy with threatening tears, but she was back to all fiery anger now. "Excuse me?"

She was giving him fucking whiplash. Scowling, he waved a hand. "You heard me."

"I tell you I love you, and *that's* your response."

"No one wou—"

"Don't you dare finish that sentence!" Audrey crossed the gap, her finger in his face. "Don't you dare tell me no one would ever love someone like you. I refuse to listen to you go on about being a vileblood and monster. Not right now, after you stopped touching me the second I asked you to stop." When he tried to speak again, she lifted her hand higher, speaking over his attempt. "Not when a week ago you saved me from an actual monster. *Again.*"

Gunnar caught her hand, lowering it down out of his face. "That doesn't mean you owe me shit."

Her brows knit. "You think I love you because I owe you?"

"Only thing that makes sense to me."

"Jonathan," Audrey said on a hard exhale, almost a whine, then rubbed her face with both hands. "Loving you is my choice."

She searched his face, seeking something from him. If she was smart, which she was, she'd make a better choice, and he couldn't understand why she didn't. The bloated silence stretched until she turned away with an exhausted sigh.

"I can't have sex with you if it doesn't mean anything to you,

Jonathan." She hugged herself now, closed off. "It would break my heart. I shouldn't have kissed you, not before I told you."

The way the ground was shifting beneath him. First, the frustration at thinking those runes were from a lack of trust, but no, they were her hope. A minute ago, he'd felt maybe the best he'd felt in his damn life. Sure, he'd kissed women before, but it felt nothing like that, like her.

And now she was saying she shouldn't have done it. The regret in her fucking scent, he wished he didn't have a damn sense of smell.

"It's fine," she whispered.

It wasn't fine, but he still didn't understand how she went from kissing him to telling him he loved her—she really shouldn't, it was idiotic, absurd; she was probably just confused—to telling him things were *fine*. He didn't know what she wanted from him, aside from the desperation in her scent begging for things to be *fine* or she might not survive it.

His hands fucking itched to touch her again. His lips were burning, his blood on fire. He'd never wanted anything more in his entire life, but the words that left his mouth were:

"If that's what you need."

"Yes," she said, but it was a question, another one he didn't know how the fuck to answer, aside from the fact that if having sex with her was going to break her heart, he wouldn't.

Obviously.

What the fuck had he been doing touching her in the first place, a monster like him? He should have pushed her away, so she'd figure out her mistake sooner. Sure, thanks to some magic, he wouldn't kill her if he fucked her, a bar so low he almost tripped over it.

"It's getting late," she offered, not looking at him.

It wasn't. It was barely after sunset.

"Yeah."

"I'm going to take a bath, then get some sleep."

"Sure."

Gunnar didn't know what to do with himself after she walked away from him and shut the bathroom door behind her. He got some water, stepped outside for a few minutes, trying to clear his senses, but when he walked back inside, she was everywhere.

Whatever she needed, he reminded himself as he wandered into his room, flopped down on his bed and stared at the ceiling, gave up trying to understand, because he was chasing after an ending that didn't belong to him. She didn't belong to him, with him, any of that.

She was in love with him.

He closed his eyes. He didn't know what the fuck love was. How the hells was he supposed to deal with this?

Why'd she'd reach for the one thing he wasn't capable of?

Gunnar must have dozed off, steps on the floorboard snapping him awake. Night in force now, even though it wasn't that late, just the way the dark crawled in this time of year.

Audrey stood in his doorway.

They watched each other, neither sure of what came next until she whispered, "Can I still sleep in here with you?"

"Yeah," he answered without hesitation. She crawled into the bed, this time her back toward him, and the inches between them could have been miles.

Anything she needed, he reminded himself, and nothing more.

Chapter 32

Lyubava went into labor early the next morning, the last day of their assigned break, on train day. They woke to Zhadan banging on their front door, and they didn't have time for anything awkward as they packed up medical supplies and food and headed out to the chuchuna's den.

Audrey barely looked at him.

By noon, everyone was ready to strangle Zhadan, and when Gunnar tried to coax him outside, all hells broke loose.

And that was how they ended up outside, Gunnar panting and holding the sweaty chuchuna face first in a snowdrift about a hundred yards from the den. He twisted the oaf's arm harder, which got him a muffled, frustrated roar.

"<<You fucking done yet?>>"

Wet snarling, something in broken Russian about feeding Gunnar's entrails to his cubs.

"Not yet then," Gunnar grunted and settled in to wait, grinding the chuchuna into the fresh snow.

About an hour and a few dozen creative threats later, Zhadan went completely slack, the chuchuna's scent washing with defeat, exhaustion, and a burst of fresh worry for his mate. Gunnar let his arm go and rolled off the bastard, lying next to him and trying to catch his breath.

"<<You're a pain in the ass.>>" Gunnar grumbled, closing his eyes

as the falling snow cooled his skin.

Zhadan didn't argue. A few minutes later, he asked, "<<*Little okay?*>>"

"<<*Doing better. Still has nightmares.*>>"

Zhadan sat up, brushing snow from his fur. "<<*Take care good care of mate.*>>"

"<<*She's not my mate.*>>"

Zhadan snorted.

Audrey emerged from the den, waving her hands and yelling, her smile miles wide. "Zhadan, you're a dad! <<*Father, father!*>>"

The chuchuna sprang up, snow flying every direction as he half crawled before making it to his feet and rushing to the den. When he got to Audrey, he scooped her up in his arms, spinning her in a few circles while she laughed. He deposited her on wobbly legs, then ducked inside. Gunnar dusted himself off with a chuckle, figuring they were done here, but Audrey waved him over. Together, they peered inside.

It was a sight, Lyubava nursing two wrinkly, hairy newborns, the third cradled in Zhadan's enormous hands as he snorted and cooed and chirped at his cub.

"Two girls and a boy," Audrey whispered. "Everyone is healthy."

Zhadan crawled up onto the furs with Lyubava, nuzzling her, praising her, the mother of his new cubs snuggling back. Felt like intruding, watching such a tender, private moment, so Gunnar nudged Audrey with his elbow, and she smiled up at him—warm and bright. She didn't bother to gather her things for now. They snuck out, leaving the new family to bond.

Audrey walked with her hands tucked in her pockets, humming softly as she smiled at the brief break in the falling snow, dark clouds already blowing back in on the horizon. Her cheeks were bright pink, her eyes shining in that way she got when she was truly happy, a little wrinkle in her nose.

She smelled like sunshine, but she was sad underneath.

He nudged her shoulder. "Nice work."

"Thanks," she said, tucking her hair behind her ear, shy almost. "I told Lyubava we'd let Rina know about the cubs so no one comes near the den for a few days."

"It's train day, so better get on that. We rarely get wanderers, but she should make it clear. It's early yet," Gunnar said, nodding south. "Still got time to set up a stall."

Audrey kicked at the snow as she walked, shrugged. "No, not today. I think . . ." She worried her bottom lip, shrugged again. "I'm just not feeling up for it. Do you mind running down to tell Rina about the cubs?"

"Yeah, I can do that." Gunnar reminded himself it had only been a week since someone had kidnapped her in her own home. She'd been doing better, but new people might put her off for a bit still. Probably had nothing to do with how she shouldn't have kissed him. "I'll head down now."

"Okay."

"You good walking back?"

She smirked, half-hearted. "I can literally see our house."

"Yeah, so?"

Audrey's smirk faded into a soft smile. "Yes, I'm good."

"Alright. You . . ." He hesitated, not liking the idea of her alone in the cabin, but she might want time away from him after yesterday. Gunnar frowned, not wanting to be away from her, not when he was supposed to protect her.

She closed the gap between them, squeezed his forearm. "I'll meet you at the tavern for a late lunch?" She sounded hopeful.

"Whatever you want."

She nodded, hesitating, but then she gave him another half-smile, the kind that didn't reach those beautiful eyes, and walked away from him.

It was early still, the train just in, stalls up and the pop-up market crowded with unfamiliar scents. Gunnar ignored it, pushing his way into the station proper with his hood up, then climbing the stairs to Rina's office. All she had time for was a quick update on the chuchuna cubs, ass deep in imports and exports paperwork.

He found himself idle, time to kill before a late lunch, as Audrey said, not sure exactly when to expect her. Gunnar ended up at the bar, talking with Aster for a few minutes before travelers came in for a meal.

Innocence plopped down beside him, drink in hand, and the duster smelled tired. "Gunnar."

"Innocence."

Silence for a few minutes, and Innocence leaned into his field of view, lips pouted. "I'm not very good at," he waved a hand around, "gratitude." Then the incubus chuckled. "Well, at least ways that don't involve my kind of favors."

"Still a no."

"I know, I'm not . . ." Innocence trialed off, his scent frustrated. Annoyed. "I wanted to thank you. For sparing Tomas." He tapped a nail on the bar top, restless in his seat. "I'm sure it would have been easier to kill him."

Gunnar grunted. "Not a big deal."

Innocence turned on him fully, and Gunnar faced him, because the full attention of a predator wasn't something good instincts could ignore. His sea-green eyes gleamed, but not from hunger. "But it is. I find myself . . . charmed by the boy, inconveniently so." Another, very put-upon sigh. "He's a good man, but young and hopeful." He swirled his glass, then frowned, setting it unfinished on the bar. "Certainly, too good for the likes of me, yet I find my affections returned. Not being able to help him through this . . ."

An odd thing, sitting at the bar sharing feelings with the one person in this town he was certain he'd never find commonality with, yet here Gunnar was, relating. Maybe even feeling bad for the asshole, at least enough to continue the conversation.

"Been out of the loop for a few days. The blood mage come in this morning?"

"Yes, a highly regarded talent from the Dominion's fancy clinic. They're reading his lineage now, then it will just be a matter of finding the right formula." Innocence rested his elbow on the bar, chin on his hand. "Until then, Virtue's feedings can hold him at bay. Worst case, the mage can put him in stasis."

"Tomas'll be fine," Gunnar offered. "Mateo was full of shit, using him, convincing him he was worse off."

Even thinking of the dead man made Gunnar's blood churn, wishing he could kill the fucker all over again. He didn't realize how long he'd been glowering at his empty glass until Innocence cleared his throat.

"Is Audrey well?"

"She's doing okay, I think."

"And you? Manticore venom is nasty business."

"Fine." Gunnar sighed when Innocence just stared at him. "You want something else?"

"Besides world peace and the hope diamond all for myself? If it still exists, of course. No, nothing really. Just feeling a disquieting urge to forward some of the well-being passed unexpectedly in my direction as of late."

Gunnar chuckled. "I'm that obvious?"

"Only to those with eyes." Innocence smiled, the expression remarkably free of his normal sass. "No secrets between my sister and I, you know. Your girl will come around, be back to her chipper self soon enough. Humans are more resistant than monsters, I've found, at least with mental health matters." When Gunnar didn't respond, Innocence frowned. "Virtue might help. She's worked with victims before. Feeding can sometimes ease the memories."

"No, it didn't get that far." Gunnar cleared his throat, worked his jaw. Not sure why he felt the urge to talk about it, to Innocence of all people. "Mateo had her in our house. Her bedroom. He convinced her I was dead, and it didn't help the way I came in on him." Gunnar tapped the empty mug, spun it, then pushed it away. "I butchered him right in front of her."

"Hmm."

"She went into shock over the whole thing, crying about me leaving her. Worried about me after all that, I just . . ." Gunnar swallowed. "She can't go in her room, even though it's clean. Can't sleep alone. Nightmares about it."

"Time helps with trauma. It's only been a week," Innocence murmured, gentle. Sad, but firm. "The girl's too bright not to shine, Gunnar. She'll heal."

"She said she's in love with me."

Just like that, it left his mouth, out in the air. Gunnar winced.

"Oh, so this is the true worry then, hmm?" Innocence chuckled. "And now you're here at the bar, with an empty drink, struggling to understand this most unexpected of revelations?" Gunnar scowled at him, but Innocence didn't flinch back. "Genuine love is a gift, my friend, and we don't get to decide if we deserve it or not, because we already have it. Believe me, I've been struggling to accept it myself."

"She shouldn't," was all he managed.

"And yet she does."

Innocence stiffened beside him, sudden absolute fury roiling off his scent, entirely at odds with his demeanor a second before, just as a new scent rolled over him, carried on the breeze of the opened station door.

Brimstone and feathers, expensive fabric. Heavy, powerful Aperien magic.

Gunnar turned on the stool, Innocence scoffing beside him. "And here I believed myself free from such beautiful righteousness."

Warden Kushiel stood in the doorway, filling it with his folded wings, his perfectly tailored suit, the air warming as he brushed fresh snowfall off his shoulder.

"You know him?" Gunnar asked.

"Oh, yes. We are very familiar."

"Yeah, same."

"How interesting."

The angel's stark blue eyes scanned the room, but any attempt to hide was pointless; the bar was directly across from the doorway, and when Kushiel's gaze found Gunnar's, a perfect brow lifted, followed closely by a dangerous smile.

"Virtue and I had the pleasure of that one's company in the Velvet Emporium, oh, a century or so ago, and not in a fun way." Innocence tsked. "Imagine coming there of all places, hellsbent on starting a new war over demons and their feeding habits, just a few years after such triumph in the Vilestars War."

"Real funny," Gunnar drawled, "considering how he likes to go on and on about the Vilestars War and how bad it was for everyone. Bad enough he fought changing the Vilestars Accord a few years back. It really pissed him off when I got let out on parole."

Innocence hoisted himself up on the bar, crossing his legs. "You or me then, do you think?"

The angel wove his way through the tables, more than a few gaping at his passage, likely wondering what the hells an Aperien like him was doing in the ass end of nowhere. The Clan in the tavern watched him with open suspicion, the rest a mix of merchants and other guests in town until tomorrow's morning train.

No one knew the full story behind why he and Audrey showed up here six months ago besides Rina, unless she'd had reasons to share he didn't know about. Right now, Gunnar didn't see a reason not to quietly say, "Or Audrey, if he has some reason to stop believing she's dead."

Innocence's scent spiked with alarm and surprise, but he remained calm and collected on the exterior. "Sounds like you and I have some stories to swap over tea sometime, then. I promise not to proposition you."

"You're a shit liar."

Innocence laughed, really laughed, and by then Kushiel had almost reached them, adjusting the buttons on the front of his three-piece suit, gold pinstripes against ivory cloth

"Get to Rina before this gets messy, yes?" Innocence said as he hopped off the bar, stretching like a cat as a pair of leathered bat wings uncurled from his shoulders and his silk kimono braided away into black leather pants and a half-open poet's blouse. A devil tail, exactly out of all the pictures in Audrey's books, swayed lazily. Loudly, he called, "Well, well, if it isn't my holy lord and savior, come from across the sea, to deliver sinners into the immaculate, effervescent grace of the saints."

Kushiel sneered, otherwise composed, his scent laced with hatred and calculated control. Innocence was all flourish, the attention of the entire tavern on the pair, including Aster, her expression alarmed. Gunnar strode toward the stairs, his skin prickling at the idea of running from a fight.

If Audrey was at stake, Gunnar could shelve his pride, and he took the stairs two at a time, feeling eyes boring into his spine as he went.

Chapter 33

Gunnar shoved the door to Rina's office open, not bothering to close it behind him. She didn't look up right away, forehead resting on her fist as she read over shipment manifests.

No sense bullshitting around. "Kushiel is here."

"The Rigid One?" Rina snapped to her feet. "Where's Virtue?"

"Dunno, but Innocence is in the bar with him right now."

"Why?"

"Buying me a minute to get up here."

"Fuck," she hissed out, set to push by him when footsteps echoed up the stairwell, a voice following.

"So charming, this place at the ends of the Earth," Kushiel said, heavy boots creaking the old wooden stairwell. The angel paused at the top platform, glancing down at his fancy shoes and the bits of mud and snow he'd trailed in after him. "Katerina Yaga, I assume?"

He canted at the waist, the barest echo of a bow.

Rina at her full, impressive height was still about six inches shy of Kushiel's golden, well-kept curls. She walked right up to him, all cool business outward despite that spike of fear over Virtue. Gunnar leaned back against the wall.

"Rina is fine," she said, extending her hand in greeting. They shook, both pointedly ignoring Gunnar's presence for the moment. "I have to admit, I'm getting a little tired of important guests showing up unannounced." She folded her arms and leaned on her desk, a brow cocked. "There's a passenger manifest for a reason."

"Ah, forgive me." Kushiel bowed, deeper this time, hands tucked behind his wings. "I didn't wish to draw unneeded attention before my arrival." He turned then, hooded gaze in Gunnar's direction, a smile turning his lips up. "Imagine my surprise to find John Dust 78102 here in Nizhny."

Fucking liar, he reeked of it, and by his expression, he didn't give a single shit.

"Go by Gunnar now," Gunnar said, shooting back a lazy shrug, calm until he needed to be something else entirely. "Should have been in my release paperwork."

To Rina, he said, "I assume as you're acquainted with Mr. Gunnar here, you're aware of the changes in the Vilestars Accord?"

"Old news, sure." Rina said.

"Because of course you would have handed him over to the proper authorities in the Dominion, had you not been aware?"

"Neither here nor there, really, unless the current Accord shifted again?"

"It has not, but words on paper and magical bindings do not change the nature of a thing simply because of wants and wishes." Kushiel smiled, thin-lipped. "I am doing my due diligence, being that two vilebloods, both released from the Manhattan Penitentiary of which I oversee, have taken up residence here in Nizhny. I've come to ensure they are treated fairly under the new Accord regulations."

More lies, and the angel let them fly without a care, knowing damn well Gunnar smelled each and every one.

"That number, however, did not include Mr. Gunnar who, unlike the other two men, was a documented criminal before his release. And it seems my reasons for coming all this way have increased."

Rina smiled too, her grin toothy, her scent dangerous. "I'm not some wilting flower. I'm an Independent, and this is my territory, proven again and again over the years. If any vileblood had given me trouble, I'd have taken care of it."

"Yes, daughter of the missing Baba Yaga and a dead human legend, your efforts are becoming known. The monsters at the edge of civilization, carving their place in the dark and cold. No shock then, to find this criminal," Kushiel gestured at Gunnar, "among others you keep comfortable at your table."

"Do you have a point?" Rina asked, gesturing at her desk as an answer. "Because I've got shit to do, which includes making sure you have a ride home in the morning."

The angel chuckled, shaking his head. "I'd heard you favor directness. How very human of you."

"Nothing but Aperien blood in my veins, angel. What do you want?" Rina's scent soured, annoyance giving way to anger now, especially given her fear for Virtue. If that was the next thing coming down the pipe for this "justified" crusader. "Nizhny is independent. I don't answer to you."

Kushiel smiled at her, the patronizing look one might throw at a child speaking out of turn. "Perhaps, but the Accords of the Icelandic Citadel of Knowledge are universally respected, even where they are not enforced. Would you truly risk the ire of the unifying force in our broken world? Become known as the Independent who defied the general armistice that keeps the peace among the ruling powers?"

"The hells are you really after?" Rina snarled.

"I want justice," he answered simply. "All I've ever desired and served. This man you shelter murdered the human woman who secured his freedom mere hours after his release, then fled the ESC." His gaze flicked to Gunnar's, the weight of it making his skin prickle at the threat. "I will take him back to the Manhattan Penitentiary and bury him in the dark where he belongs."

The room warmed, the angel's eyes brimming with golden light, a halo ringing behind his head, chasing shadows from the dark corners of the room. "Will you stand in my way, Katerina Yaga?"

Gunnar growled, because he sensed Rina kind of wanted to do something stupid, like grab her sword and take a swing, and there was no way the pair of them could go toe to toe with one of the original Aperien angels, spawned from likely the strongest mythos to manifest into reality. Kushiel could kill them, easily.

Leave Nizhny without a leader, the door wide open for fuckers like Dimitri to lay claim. Audrey out here in the dark with monsters alone.

"She didn't know," Gunnar said.

Those gleaming eyes snapped to Gunnar's black gaze, and Kushiel's smile was luminous. "Ah, well, such a straightforward solution, then." The angel didn't turn back to Rina. "John Dust 78102 is a parolee, his freedom as a vileblood only guaranteed if he conducts his life free of new crimes." A deep chuckle, the room sweltering. "Are you aware of many lives this creature has taken to justify his freedom?"

"As I understood it, all that came before his parole. That human you're saying he killed after he got out, didn't she die in hellfire?" Rina asked. Gunnar silently thanked her for leaving Audrey out of this, at the same time gritting his teeth. Why was she pushing him? "Vilebloods aren't demons."

Kushiel didn't even blink. "There are always ways."

"You got proof he did it?" Rina pressed. "You want to push this in my town? Bring the Citadel in. You've got the clout, so call in an Archivist and see what they think about Accord adherence. Do it properly."

Kushiel huffed in disbelief, echoed in his scent. "You would risk your livelihood for this thing?"

"Two seconds ago, you were barking about the rights of vileblood. You really here for justice, Kushiel?"

The angel's bolstering died back, the warmth leaving the room in a rush and the golden light receding. "You're truly a fool then, perhaps mad as your mother?" Rina sneered at that, but Kushiel was unbothered, still in disbelief. "You truly believe that if I called down a tribunal upon this pathetic swatch of sticks and swamps and monstrosities, righteousness would fall to your side? You would stake your future, all you've built, on the word of the worst of the abominations to walk God's green Earth since we became blessed with reality?"

"Lots of pretty words, when all you're really saying is you've got the bigger stick," Gunnar drawled.

The angel was on him a second, hand around Gunnar's throat, lifting him from the floorboards and crashing him to the wall. Heat wafted from his skin, the raw, century's old fury an aroma Gunnar would never forget. His eyes were glassy, far, far away. Gunnar really understood Kushiel at that moment, and how little he had to do with what drove this Aperien's entire existence.

"We should have taken babes to the sword during the war, but we chose mercy. We should have slain your kind in the womb, but we feared to become the same as the monsters," Kushiel whispered, teeth grinding. "Instead, we watched those deserving give their lives, again and again, until we finally put your source to the blade, one after another. And yet, they live on. In you, in the vilebloods overflowing the hells and walking free, all because one human girl loved a monster."

It stung more than it should have, his mention of Audrey, but then Kushiel dropped him. Gunnar hit his knees, inhaling and wheezing against his half-crushed throat.

The angel let out a sour laugh, ruffling in his wings as he smoothed his suit jacket. He turned to Rina then with a nod, his scent ripe with decision. "If a tribunal is your wish, you will have it. But consider what you protect, and what other evils might be brought to light when the gaze of the untied fall critically on your precious little haven for deviants.

"The demons chased from the Velvet Emporium. Do they truly cage their feedings? The berserkers self-exiled from true civilization. Do they still bring humanity into their fold, breaking the most sacred of the Accords to protect the dreamers who gave us life? And your pack of beasts, dire wolves of all things, breeding unchecked.

"You believe a tribunal is the answer? That all those you shelter would pass muster?

"Or you can hand over this single vileblood for the justice long overdue and keep those you shepherd safe in the dark, where they belong. I expect your answer before the train departs."

And then Kushiel left, hands folded behind his back, his slip in demeanor a memory as he strode casually back down the stairs, the room chilled in his wake.

Chapter 34

"That fucker," Rina snarled as she dragged Gunnar to his feet. "You alright?"

"Yeah, I'm good." Gunnar coughed a few times, rubbing his throat.

"Shit," Rina muttered as she paced, diving into Russian for a slew of more creative cursing. She rubbed her face a few times. "Theodore was sure he'd been careful and covered your steps. All the news about Audrey being burned alive, you as the prime suspect."

Gunnar chuckled. "Yeah, that hellfire attack in the middle of the night took out a whole damn city block trying to get to her for being a terrorist. The ESC was a shitshow over it. Then I was a high-profile case right after the change, freedom granted from a tribunal." He sighed. "Figured this was about as far as we could get from all that. Maybe we should have taken that job shoveling sand in the Sahara."

"Maybe," Rina said with a half-laugh, but her scent was distressed, and Gunnar couldn't blame her a bit. "All this though . . ." she kind of trailed off, lifting a hand.

"He's lying. My guess is he found out I was alive, so he sent those two out here for an excuse to check in. I was in his prison for ten years, down deep in solitary holding, nothing but sustains and the dark."

"Heard of those places," Rina muttered. She shuddered, her scent ripe with a fear he'd never tasted from her before. "Virtue is . . ."

"Innocence told me enough. Kushiel led the Velvet Emporium

purge."

"When the Accord passed banning non-consensual soul feeding, it also allowed for punishing transgressions committed prior to the Accord." Rina scoffed. "No matter all the Aperiens, hybrids, and dusters that fed carefully or had never hurt or killed anyone. Or how many might have died without sneaking a bite. Part of all this, being out here so far away." Rina sighed, and she suddenly smelled old and very, very tired. "I wanted to protect her and her brother. To have a place where we could all exist, even if the rest of the world didn't want us."

Gunnar grunted. "Not sure Innocence is worth the trouble, but I'll admit he's grown on me a bit."

Rina laughed. "Yeah, he does that."

They sat in silence for a minute, the only sound Rina's tapping boot. The general noise from the tavern below, packed with train day patrons and the other residents of Nizhny milling around minding their own business, scratching out a life that had no clue was under threat.

"I don't think he knows Audrey's alive," Gunnar said, rubbing against the discomfort in his chest. "But he means his threat, about rallying a tribunal, and he'll come after Nizhny with everything he can if it comes to that. I can't ask you to pick me over that, Rina. Over everyone else in this damn town. I'm not worth it."

Rina closed her eyes, leaning her head back with a long sigh. "No, you're not. One person might be enough, but . . ."

"I'm not that person, not for you."

"No, you're not."

"Can you promise me something?"

"I'll keep her safe, Gunnar. Audrey's one of us."

"Alright."

"You're not going to tell her, are you? Not even say goodbye?"

He tried to imagine the moment. How she'd scream and cry for him, probably talk about loving him all over again, and he wasn't sure he'd be strong enough to walk away from that. Easier not to think about it all. If he was lucky, Kushiel would send him back down into a hole, and he'd sink down into nothing.

"Better she doesn't know. She gave up everything to get me out. She throws her life away for me again, it's just the same shit all over."

"I think you're an idiot, for what it's worth," Rina said, and then she had one arm around his shoulders, pulling him into a tight hug before he could stop her. "But I won't let her follow you. I'll call in my favor to Theodore, if that's what it takes."

He patted her back, the whole thing awkward, giving her a stiff nod as he turned to leave, his mind racing, trying to figure out if he might see her just one more time before he left, without her knowing. . .

No, too much risk. He'd walk downstairs, tell Kushiel they'd leave in the morning, convince him the best move was for them to both go to the train so the angel could chain him up and keep watch so Gunnar didn't change his mind and run.

After all, that's what vileblood did, right? All the bad things.

Like leaving Audrey behind without having the balls to say good-bye.

Gunnar didn't look back at Rina, just shut the door behind him. Ignored when Aster called his name when he reached the bottom of the stairs. Inhaled the familiar scent of the tavern, wondering if he'd remember it a few years down the road. Then he frowned, because he didn't smell the angel anymore. Must be waiting outside, and Gunnar stuffed his hands in his pockets and stepped toward the front door.

Paused, because he smelled Audrey. Not an old trace from her coming to the tavern, no this was fresh, but she wasn't here. He frowned, then cursed under his breath. Late lunch, she'd said. Aster called his name again, but he shoved outside, cursing at the falling snow, thickening by the second.

A hundred different scents assaulted him, the open market slowing down because of the weather, train visitors milling around with the Nizhny residents. He scanned fast, looking for white wings and a short human girl he'd know at a glance, but nothing. He inhaled deeper, searching, then caught what he was after.

Audrey, Kushiel. They'd both been here, right on the station entry way, within minutes. Innocence as well, he realized. All three scents tangled together. And three sets of fresh prints headed up the rails, away from town, north.

Then Gunnar smelled the blood.

He chased after the scent, breathing in heavy clouds as he rounded the station's corner, toward the wolf pack dens—empty, since the pack stayed away on train days—and there was Innocence, crumpled against the white building.

"Hey," Gunnar snarled out, sliding on the ice to his knees, grabbing the man by the shoulders and giving him a rough shake. Innocence hissed in pain, blood flowing freely from his broken nose and slit lip. Gunnar slapped his cheek a few times. "What the fuck happened?"

He swatted at Gunnar's hand. "Gods, I think he broke both my legs."

Yeah, they both bent the wrong way at the knees, bone gleaming between torn flesh and fabric. "Where's Kushiel?"

The incubus's eyes flared bright, but his scent was floundering, a breath away from passing out. "He ignored me. Eyes only for you, Gunnar dearest."

Innocence coughed, leaning heavily to the side. Gunnar held him up by his shoulder; his lungs sounded wrong. Might have broken ribs, too.

"Came back down, all smug. Then . . ." Innocence wheezed, head falling back on the wall. "They saw each other as soon as she walked in, and I have never seen an angel as shocked. Audrey ran. I followed, tried to stop him . . . but . . ." He gave a bitter laugh. "Just a duster, me."

Gunnar snorted. "You're a fucking idiot, thinking you had a shot against an angel. He could have killed you. Surprised he didn't."

Innocence chuckled, the sound pained. "Yes, well, it is quite irritating feeling obligated to be brave. I do think today fills my quota for the next century or so, hmm?"

Gunnar glanced north, wondering why the fuck Audrey didn't run toward the market. Probably didn't want anyone to get hurt. Shit. "Can you get yourself to the station?"

"Really, Gunnar, I thought you were a smart ma—that hurts, you barbaric *shit*!"

Gunnar hauled Innocence up anyway, because he didn't have time, but he couldn't leave the fucker here. If he saved Audrey by leaving Innocence to die after he tried to buy her time, she'd never let him live it down. "He chased after her? North?"

"Yes," Innocent grunted as he carried him to the station. They were drawing attention now, a few shouts coming from the market, members of the Clan running toward them. E watched from his station, his brow creased, and Gunnar swore his eyes glowed, molten metal in the distance. Gullin stood next to him, apparently returned from his latest trip. "Walking, of course, the prick he is." Innocence hissed in pain as Gunnar shifted him so he could kick open the tavern doors. "Gunnar . . ."

"Yeah, I know I'm just a duster too, but fuck if I'm letting him hurt her."

Gunnar called to Aster, who already ran over, and helped Innocence sit against the entryway wall. The incubus caught his wrist, his expression furious.

"Go get your girl, Gunnar."

Chapter 35

Gunnar raced north, the angel's scent tracking in pace with Audrey's, but the pair didn't mingle, Audrey's at a clear run while Kushiel followed in less of a rush. He hadn't grabbed her. He couldn't imagine, after all the angel's big, angry talk, Kushiel had his sights set on a casual conversation with Audrey about the Accords.

As far as the angel knew, she'd died in that apartment fire, and Innocence said it had shocked him when she walked in. All Kushiel's focus, despite the lies on his scent, had been on Gunnar. If the angel knew him and Audrey had been together all this time, why not use the lever from the gate, exactly what Gunnar feared right now. Kushiel's disgust for Audrey had always been clear, her actions anathema to everything he stood for. In the ESC, they'd declared Audrey dead, and Theo never gave the heads up that changed.

Gunnar didn't want to consider how well an angry, avenging angel might take Audrey being alive.

He kept his pace reasonable but quick. Audrey might not have had much time to react, just ran, but he wasn't sure why she'd headed toward their cabin. She certainly wouldn't put the chuchuna family in danger. That she was running away from everyone meant she was trying to spare them from Kushiel's wrath, which meant he scared her, whatever he'd said or done when he saw her, enough that she didn't come into the tavern.

Fuck, she'd probably run to protect him.

But she also had to know he'd come for her, so if Audrey expected this to end in a fight, she was running Kushiel onto Gunnar's home turf, giving him the slim advantage terrain would offer.

Gunnar tried to ignore his strangling pulse. He'd go with the fucker, he'd already decided, but if he hurt her . . .

If it came to blows, Gunnar was going to die in this fucking forest, which really wasn't how he'd seen this day going. He huffed; he would find the end of his rope the day Audrey told him she loved him. And she was nuts, but he found he really wanted to be around to talk some sense into the woman.

Maybe he should have waited when everyone was shouting at him, yelling questions at him, but he couldn't. He had to move, had to go after her, there was no other option. Getting Innocence help had taken all the willpower he could muster.

She hadn't stopped at the cabin; by the look of Audrey's tracks, she hadn't even broken her pace as she skirted their home and fled deeper into the taiga, so into the snow-capped woods of his hunting parcel he went.

It was eerily still, as if anything alive had fled as soon as the angel crossed into the forest proper. Yeah, an angry Aperien had that way about it, making even the air itself reconsider breathing. Gunnar followed the trails he had worn in the terrain in the past months, both Audrey's and the angel's scents growing stronger with each step, the heavier snowfall blocked by the bowers. Audrey had only been out this deep a few times, but he'd made a point of showing her the lay of the land when they moved up here, just in case. It was how she'd found her way to the leshy so easily. And now his smart girl kept to the terrain she knew, trusting him to follow.

Voices echoed through the trees, Gunnar's skin prickling with so much laden power saturating what should have been cold air, but as he closed in, the snow turned to slush under his heels, the temperature rising unnaturally and fast. It made it harder to hide his approach, but he was downwind, at least.

"How you cannot see your folly, even now, baffles me." Kushiel, of course, because why would an angel do anything without giving a fucking lecture first?

Gunnar's heart stuttered a bit when Audrey replied, her voice breathless from running, but otherwise she seemed unharmed. "I don't know what is so hard for you to understand. I love him."

Gunnar gritted his teeth, not seeing what the hells good that argument would do her, winding his way through the shadowed trees, trying to get a good look before he dove into this mess.

"You *love* the creature created specifically to bring about the demise of your species." Kushiel mocked her, the tsk accenting his words.

"No, because that's not what he is, and you know that. You're just too angry, or hurt, or stubborn to face the truth. The Vilestars were created to wipe out humanity, but all of them are dead and gone, along with their creators. The vilebloods who remain are not the ones you fought that war against."

"Naivety is the prevailing trait of humanity. The vilebloods are the intended sum of the equation, the continuation of the war in the absence of the progenitors. They are the legacy left behind to perpetuate suffering, and yet you, a *human*, champion them." The disgust from Kushiel was white hot, snow and ice sloughing from the trees and raining down on the clearing.

Audrey leaned against a tree on the far side, cheeks flushed but holding herself tall. "That might have been Lucifer and Lamashtu's intention, but that intention failed. Gunnar is not the monster they tried to create; he's the man who saved my life, who went willingly to prison for a life sentence so a girl he didn't know could live."

Kushiel laughed, the humidity climbing, his beautiful white wings trembling with barely controlled rage. Gunnar smelled it now; he was beyond furious, beyond frustration. He smelled like brimstone, like avenging angels sent in mythos to punish and burn. Retribution, in his mind unequivocally justified.

"Yes, please, tout how saving one life grants absolution from all his other crimes? From all the dead in his wake?"

"Isn't that the foundation of your entire mythos? Forgiveness?"

Kushiel went silent for an excruciating breath, then chuckled, the sound a low rumble in the landscape. "Perhaps it was, at some point in humanity's fabrication and imagination. To cling to the idea wishing washed away all sins, but that, well, that was before every other product of humanity's twisted minds came forth into existence in parallel." Another huff, another tsk. "But that concept was never for the angels, gods or monsters. Humans didn't see fit in their imaginings to extend such grace to anyone but themselves."

"That's what this is about?" Gunnar said as he stepped from the tree line. "Shit's not fair?"

Audrey's eyes widened when she saw him, her relief as clear as her fear for him. Him, not herself, because that's just who she was, wasn't it?

Kushiel faced him, the crisp control he expected on the angel frayed at the edges. His hair was tousled, the gilded curls sweat-damp against his forehead. His wings twitched with each movement, agitation saturating every inch of his near eight-foot frame. Mud saturated his white dress shoes, the damp climbing his ivory slacks, the suit jacket open and the top button of his shirt undone. The air cloyed around him, the faint outline of a halo ghosting the mist as he shifted.

The angel's smile. Well. Gunnar seen few things quite as monstrous.

"Perhaps," Kushiel mused, his eye color the gilded sky between sun beams, a blue so rich it defied the color spectrum. They shone, glowed, looked like they'd bleed if he didn't blink. "Perhaps it is all so simple for mortal minds. I've already lived longer with grief than the human lifespan. When this girl who undermined the Accords that protect humanity is dust and memory, her love for you dead and buried and forgotten, I will live on, forced to remember those who died so she had the chance to exist at all. Are you human enough to be so naïve, *Gunnar?*"

He canted his head, tsking again. "Or are you monster enough, like me, that the years will stretch and you'll spend them remembering how she died, all because she believed you to be something you're not?"

No, Gunnar damn well fucking wouldn't. "You came all the way out here for me. Here I am. Put me back in that hole you like so fucking much. I won't even fight you."

"Jonathan!" Audrey raced forward, stalling when he held up a hand, her expression frantic, the panic in her scent reaching him over the melting loamy earth and Kushiel's searing fury.

"The Accord changed, damage done," Gunnar added with a shrug, but he focused on Audrey as he spoke. "But you can have me with some bullshit broken parole. She's got nothing, esquire or not. And if she really thinks she loves me, she wouldn't throw her life away a second time."

"I didn't throw away my life!" Audrey yelled. "I regret nothing! The Accord was wrong, and not just because of Jonathan and what he did or didn't do!" Her anger turned on Kushiel. Gunnar cursed under his breath, trying to get there first, but there she was, five-foot-nothing, grabbing at the angel's arm so he turned toward her instead of Gunnar.

"Your grief, whatever you lost, does not justify this!"

Gunnar's entire body twitched when Kushiel lashed out and caught her face, his fingers wrapped around her jaw in a vice. Audrey didn't flinch, didn't blink.

"You know nothing of loss, little girl."

"Jonathan didn't kill the people you loved. Making him suffer won't bring them back," she said, her expression and voice gentle. "I'm sorry for what you lost. I'm sorry for what the Vilestars War cost the world, to stop something so horrible."

And she reached with those delicate little fingers of hers to touch the angel's chest. Kushiel blinked down at her hand.

"But you are among the best of what humanity imagined," Audrey said, so soft, barely a whisper. "And you're right; your mythos demanded but didn't give, not to your kind. And even if you wanted, your God is among many, many dead Aperiens. You can't ask him for forgiveness, but you can forgive yourself."

The heat wavered, a heartbeat, maybe less, before the rage that poured off Kushiel felt like sunburn on every inch of Gunnar's exposed skin.

"You," Kushiel said with a hiss, then a low laugh. "You dare to presume? You're a menace, and you should have burned in that hellfire for your sins. I don't seek *forgiveness*." He shoved Audrey away hard enough that she stumbled to the dirt, and when Gunnar advanced with a snarl, Kushiel turned on him, that specific Heaven burning at the fringes of his existence. "I want suffering returned in full. And as the dead cannot deliver, I will take from the living instead."

"You burned my apartment building," Audrey said, anger in her voice now. Gunnar almost laughed; he really needed to work with her on her survival instincts if they both didn't end up dead in the next five fucking minutes. "You killed hundreds of people!"

"And not the one I wished. Though it simplifies things now, doesn't it?" Kushiel reached between his shoulder blades, pulling a sword from nothing, the blade sliver-white and radiating holy energy—until he ran his fingers over the enchanted metal, wreathing it in winding, living hellfire.

"Why so surprised, vileblood?" Kushiel mused, cutting the blade once the through air, moisture sputtering and hissing, afterimage burning the mist, the smell of hells and hunger chewing at Gunnar's senses. "You think an angel spends a thousand tales and centuries of myth overseeing perdition and doesn't learn to wield the instruments of eternal punishment?"

Then he laughed again, his smile nothing but cruelty.

"It hardly matters, any of it. Even faced with a town of the shunned who would speak truth to truth seekers? Mere complications of which I've grown tired. Laws and justice are manmade fabrications, the Accords created in good faith to protect those who would eschew their silver-plated salvation. I will deliver my own justice, for myself, by my hand, here. Now."

He pointed the blade at Audrey, the hellfire rippling at the tip, and she shrieked, backing away in the mud, her fear reminiscent of the night she'd nearly died. Kushiel didn't advance further yet, his gaze never leaving Gunnar's, the halo of sunlight and purity an open, ever-burning volcanic pit.

"I will put Esquire Audrey Doe to the sword for endangering humanity with her misguided crusading. Do you intend to interfere? A crime which will certainly violate your parole, vileblood?"

"Jonathan, wait—"

"Yeah, I really fucking do," Gunnar bit out, pulling his hunting knife, Audrey's gift, free from its sheath.

Kushiel smiled, the angel's satisfaction a living, breathing abomination.

Then his gaze flicked over Gunnar's shoulder.

"So do we," Rina called.

Chapter 36

Gunnar hadn't sensed Rina's approach with Kushiel's power show, but he spun as she stepped from the trees, her father's great sword resting on a broad shoulder. She stood tall, her expression nothing short of the Independent who didn't take shit from anyone.

The dire wolf pack fanned out around them, intermingled with the berserker spirit forms—wolves, boars, and bears gleaming blue, save for one extremely large, solid golden boar with a flowing mane. Virtue emerged behind Rina's left shoulder, winged and demonic, an inky shadow against the tree line.

Quite the contrast to E on her right side, the dvergar dressed in his everyday smithy garb. Zhadan joined them with a snarl, the chuchuna frothing at the mouth. From the sky, high above the canopy, the harpy cried out in maniacal rage. Aster hung back, pale and wane in the confines of the pines but saturated in the magic she drew from the Earth under her heels.

"I think you're full of shit," Rina added.

Kushiel chuckled, waving the burning sword, snowmelt hissing and steaming, pine needles curling and smoking. "This is truly the stand you make, Katerina Yaga? Do you think it will matter, these details, when an angel swears upon Heaven on high against the word of a human girl, a vileblood, and a backwater town of miscreants?"

"You keep going on and on about Accords, but they're only binding under the major powers. Independents are outside Citadel Jurisdiction—which I believe your kind supported at the formation." Rina shrugged, but Gunnar knew her well enough to read her unease. "You really think you're going to get an Archival Tribunal called to the ass end of nowhere so you can settle some personal vendetta?"

"No," Kushiel said. "What I'm going to get, with certainty, is a rally of fools challenging a power outside their depth and dying on some thread of nobility, or pride, or perhaps even a misguided idea about love." He waved a hand, casual as the forest wept around him, the entire landscape curdling under the hellfire brought to bear. "And not a soul will question if I was within my rights to deliver justice."

A dry chuckle, kind of dusty, broke the posturing, and Gunnar stared with everyone else as E climbed onto a rock and dusted off his meaty hands.

"Funny thing about a lot of big Aperiens really," E said, then coughed, clearing his throat as if this whole talking thing was a bother to the man. He extended his arm, right hand out and open, and just sort of held it there as he spoke. "Mythos come in all shapes and sizes. Some gods were big, some not so much. Some creatures sounded plain terrifying on paper, didn't really amount to much once they had to exist.

"Your kind, angels, you all manifested in loud, swinging and screaming and fighting amongst yourselves, different versions of the same damn thing all so focused on being right." Another chuckle from E. Gunnar felt a prickle run across his skin, static rising in the air. "Y'all had muscle though, power in widespread awareness of your stories. Took little for angels and holy books and saints to take the front seat against all those dark demons and devils and evils people hadn't thought about for a long, long time. Everyone knew your faces, had global branding, the Pope in Rome before the Vatican got destroyed with the rest of the European sky."

Thunder rumbled, close enough to make the trees rustle, the sky above the canopy darkening. E smirked, lifting a bushy eyebrow while he smoothed his beard with the hand that wasn't still extended. "Made y'all cocky, I'd wager. And made you forget that being part of a popular religion isn't the only source of Aperien power.

"Some of us are just a lot fucking older."

E cocked his head, the air swimming, cold against the hellfire's heat. Electricity crackled between the smith's eyes, the rock grounding him, bouncing between various trunks as a low whine poured through the air, right before an object flew through the clearing and connected with his open palm with a crack.

Everyone stumbled back a few paces with the force, even Kushiel lifting an arm to shield his face as the air pressure eased and the static continued to build, E's eyes swimming pools if crackling light, his veins pulsing with blue energy, an unassuming hammer clenched in his extended fist.

"Is that . . ." Audrey asked, her expression wonder-struck despite their current situation.

"Yeah," E said.

Rina shook out her hand when electricity wicked out and nipped at her sword. "But isn't he . . ."

"Dead? Yeah."

"Why does that weapon answer to you?" Kushiel's was expression curious, reminding Gunnar of a cat who just saw something it wanted to eat, but after it got to play with its dinner first.

"Because I made it." E swung the hammer once through the air, the sky rumbling in answer. "Now, are you done threatening my home, angel?"

Kushiel bowed, a mockery in spades. "I have only just begun."

E nodded once, said, "Fair enough," and swung the hammer—Thor's hammer, Mjölnir—toward the dirt.

A column of lightning tore the air, and Kushiel expected it, bringing his flaming sword up to deflect the electricity sideways into the trees, a dozen pines splintering and crackling, the thunder deafening enough everyone flinched away.

The angel wasn't ready for the golden boar who tore after the strike, slamming into his chest full-body with a roar that sounded more man than beast. They went flying, tangled together, taking down a few more trees in their wake before full chaos broke out.

The dire wolves and the Úlfheðnar harried, in and out of the fray with biting strikes and retreats as Kushiel wrestled with the boar, deflecting most attacks with concise slices, his free hand firmly locked on the boar's right tusk as it thrashed.

"Fools," the angel grunted out, the air warming further, storm clouds fighting against gilded heavenly light, before the boar skittered away with a horrible shrieking squeal, smoking from head to hoof. "Burn these sinners from my path, and the righteous will prevail."

He swung his sword, pained yelps sounding right before a blaze of hellfire wrapped around about fifteen trees and set them up in torches. Gunnar smelled burned fur, flesh, felt ripples in the air when a berserker lost hold and was forced back into their body, like bubbles popping. He gritted his teeth, eyes watering and nose aching from the pine sap smoke.

He needed to get to Audrey. Now.

The angel hovered, easily deflecting another shot of lightning from E, a second and third set of wings blooming from his back as he laughed.

"Demoness, you think you can wrestle the flames of Hell from my hands? I'll burn everything back to the darkness from whence you crawled."

He heard Virtue curse, another light beam searing through the canopy, and Gunnar couldn't do shit as Rina threw herself in front of Virtue and both of them slammed into the slushy ground, barely avoiding the lash.

Flowers tangled up, growing fast and wild, the cornflower wraith's scent bursting, but the vines were nothing but an inconvenience to the angel, swatting down Aster's magic with ease—yet she was here, with the rest of them, fighting for Audrey, and for him.

Gunnar swung a little wide, still moving in Audrey's direction, because Kushiel had turned to her again.

"All for one girl, all this trouble," he murmured, beautiful rage and deadly purpose as he pointed his gleaming, flaming sword in her direction. "If only we could know for certain if we needed your kind anymore. If only we knew if imagination made real still required the source, if the dreams need the dreamers once the dreams are born? You are far, far too much trouble."

Gunnar felt Rina shoulder up to him, and they exchanged a nod and launched forward.

Kushiel met them both, taking the hit from Gunnar's smaller blade, even though the angel's hiss told him he didn't expect it to cut so deep into his side, as he countered Rina's heavier swing blade to blade. Blue flashed around them as the Clan surged at his back, but then Kushiel's fist met Gunnar's face, and he flew about fifteen feet, hard into a burning trunk.

Winded, he rallied in time to see Kushiel kick Rina in the chest. Her ribs cracking echoed through the clearing as she let out a guttural shout, rolling head over ass through the mud, her blade spiraling away into the brush.

Virtue's scream was feral, the succubus rushing forward in a fit of shadow, claws, and fury, and she got a hold of Kushiel, anchored in for about ten seconds. Her gaze flared, the light blinding as she fed on the angel's soul. Kushiel roared in shock, then a burst of light so intense followed that Gunnar buried his face in his arms.

He lifted his head as soon as it faded, struggling to stand, Virtue at Rina's side, trying to get her up on her feet. Howls sounded in all directions, the angel's fury gone from purpose to anger and indignation so heated it was suddenly all Gunnar could scent.

His throat and face bore the worst of Virtue's assault, but the wounds were already stitching closed, and Gunnar got the distinct impression Kushiel didn't feel like playing anymore. His gaze searched now, hunting, and when it landed on Audrey, who kneeled next to a wounded wolf, desperately trying to help it run, Kushiel's eyes narrowed.

Gunnar got about two steps toward her when the ground shook, the forest parting, and the leshy emerged, twice as tall as any of his trees. His arms were giant trunks, and both of them came pummeling down on the angel's head.

The force set Gunnar back on his ass again, then struggling up to his feet again, but grinning to himself now despite the chaos; his smart girl brought the fight right where they needed it to be.

The dust and smoke and needles cleared, revealing Kushiel on his knees, both arms bracing the sword over his head, the leshy's arms creaking with the force of ancient, deep-seated mythos. For the first time, Kushiel's expression flickered with . . . surprise? Concern? A bead of sweat on his temple.

But then the angel hissed in what sounded like infernal.

All the hellfire sucked away from the surrounding trees. The leshy went up in a bonfire.

Its scream shook the fucking world. The leshy reared back, and

Kushiel swung high, right through one of the enormous tree trunk legs, and the treeman took out a swatch of forest as he went down, branches cracking and snapping and breaking, the hellfire roaring like a starving horror.

"No! Aspen!" Audrey screamed. Gunnar was about fifteen feet from her, but he already knew.

Too far.

Kushiel's attention snapped to her, his expression a sneer, blood matting down his gold curls, the halo too bright, and he strode toward her, slashing at anything that dared come within his reach with deadly accuracy. Spirits flagged and vanished, and wolves circled wide, whining and howling and bleeding.

And Gunnar ran as Kushiel reached Audrey, threw himself in front of her, because really, there was nowhere he'd rather be than between her and anything in the world that would ever, ever try to hurt her.

"Gunnar!"

Rina screamed, and he saw her just over the angel's shoulder, throwing her father's sword to him, Virtue barely holding her on her feet. Gunnar caught the hilt right as Kushiel's blade buried into his chest instead of Audrey's, barely missing his heart, so he didn't flat out die on impact.

Felt like he was dying, though, holy steel making his blood burn—like the holy part tried to cleanse his cursed blood through white hot intention at the same time the wreathed hellfire turned his skin, flesh, and muscle around the blade to ash.

Instinct drove him through the pain, the disconnect of being unmade and alive within the same handful of heartbeats.

Gunnar's brain managed a lazy observation; the great sword was magic, a gift from a giant.

It felt light as his dagger, and Gunnar swung upwards with everything he had left, staring into Kushiel endless blue eyes, wells of hatred so deep he almost felt sorry for the Aperien for being so consumed.

The blade went right through Kushiel's neck, separating his head from his spine.

Then Gunnar was pretty sure he did die, but at least he got to hear Audrey one last time, one last "Jonathan!" before everything went black.

Chapter 37

Realizing he wasn't dead was a strange thing for Gunnar.

When he took Kushiel's holy, hellfire blade through the chest, he'd been pretty sure that was it. Box checked, story over. Yet here he was—sort of. Unlike his time in solitary, where his awareness had been steady, if removed, Gunnar was having trouble tracking time, his surroundings. Anything, really. Pain came and went. So did light. So did consciousness.

He wondered if he was still dying, just slower than expected.

Whatever the case, two things stayed consistent.

First, the scent of sunshine.

Audrey was alive.

Knowing that single fact let him rest, otherwise he would have clawed his way out of this torpor by now, whatever the cost. He inhaled, pain lancing through every inch of his muddled existence as he chased the trace of her, to confirm she was still alive, safe.

Second was her voice, which picked the perfect time to speak.

"Everything is okay, Jonathan. Rest as long as you need. I love you."

She did that every time, he realized as his body relaxed, and his thoughts grew fuzzy and disconnected, right before they went dark. Every time she spoke, she ended by saying she loved him.

"I know sustain potions are horrible, but I don't know how long you need to recover. I love you."

"I don't know if you can smell the cookies or not, but you don't get any until you wake up, just so you know. I love you."

"I'm sorry. I know this probably hurts, but the bandages need changing. I love you."

"I'm here. Whatever you're seeing, it's just a dream. I'm here, I'm alive, and I love you."

"I miss you. Please come back to me. I love you."

Hells of a motivator.

Gunnar had no fucking clue how long he'd been out of it. All he knew was as he woke for the first in what felt like another damn decade in torpor, his mouth tasted like shit and he smelled worse. He blinked a few times, built-up crud scratching at his eyes. Lifting his hands to scrub at his face was a chore, muscles stiff and the skin on his chest too tight. He ached, bone deep, and he let out a wheeze as he tried to chuckle.

Sure, he'd been wounded over the years, been in shit shape on more than a few occasions, but his vileblood let him shake off most wounds. Pain was always manageable, no matter how bad, since it was temporary. He healed fast, too fast for infections or fevers to take root, was immune to almost all diseases of the human sort. He'd never tested if he could regrow a severed limb, but the point was he'd never really dealt with wound recovery because his body just took care of it and quick. Give him the chance to duck into torpor, and he healed even faster.

Now, though, *fuck.*

Gunnar knew he wasn't all the way right. He ached everywhere, the most where he'd been run through by Kushiel's blade. He knew instinctually he'd lost muscle mass, his body screaming in protest at the effort it took to prop himself up on an elbow. His chest felt heavy, wrong. Different. With a grunt, he slumped against the headboard and tried to find his bearings.

His room, looked like. Curtains closed, but late morning given the shadows and bright sky. Gunnar inhaled a few times, senses a bit addled; they always were when he wrestled out of torpor. He found a large glass of water on the nightstand, gulped it down. It helped, the sensation of cold spreading through his chest waking him up the rest of the way.

The fight against Kushiel rattled around in his skull, all that fucking mess, but the most important bits: Audrey was alive, and Kushiel was not.

Where was she, anyway? Gunnar listened for a minute, but the house felt empty. He frowned a bit; even in torpor, it felt like she'd been next to him the entire time. He tried to recall the last time she spoke, something about train day, that she needed to go to the station.

I love you.

He fucking hated train day, he thought with a grumble, but his patience ran out within seconds, his mind shifting around, muddling through, just needed know where she was, when she'd be back. A snort, and he swung his legs over the bed, self-disdain twofold at being needy as hell and dizzy from sitting up. When his head stopped spinning, he ambled to the door, pushing it open, and called out to her even though he knew in his bones she wasn't at the cabin right now.

Gunnar scrubbed his face. Train day, she'd mentioned. Coming today? Leaving?

Who came in with the train this time?

He licked his dry lips. Train days had been shit for a while running now. First Dimitri, then Mateo, then Kushiel. Gunnar ran a hand through his hair, fingers tugging at greasy knots.

He really had no idea how long Audrey'd been gone, but the question of where she was now and if she was safe beat against his skull in a drum, his skin tingling head to toe at the intruding thought something had happened to her while he was out of it.

They had Nizhny, though. Friends. Good people, they wouldn't have let anything happen, but then again, Audrey wasn't theirs to protect. She wasn't anyone's responsibility but *his*.

He stumbled toward the door, pushed his feet into his boots, and hit the rails.

Cold bit at his skin, but he didn't care. A drum beat to match his pounding heart: Audrey, Audrey, Audrey.

He didn't run only because he couldn't. He tried, got winded after a few steps, and settled into a brisk walk when the spots in his vision settled down. Now Gunnar trudged and grunted and growled his way toward the station. Felt good, the icy air biting at his face, his bare arms. Right now, he needed the extra anchor to his body after floating.

Train day meant he'd been down and out at least a week—if today was the train day after Kushiel's arrival and not weeks further out.

Fuck, how long had he been useless? How long had he left her alone?

She wasn't alone, he repeated to himself, and although it was foreign and strange, he really couldn't keep on denying it. The whole damn town had showed up to save them, and it hadn't been just for Audrey, not this time.

Didn't change the clawing tightness in his chest. It went deep, didn't fit with the injury pattern. It wasn't the cold burning his laboring lungs. A different tightness, felt like his heart being squeezed to a pulp.

Gunnar licked his lips again, forced himself into a jog when the station appeared on the horizon. He just needed to see her, to know she was alright. Needed it more than he needed the oxygen he struggled to breathe in, more than the heat leaking from his exhausted body into the frosty air. He just *needed*, needed on a level that made no fucking sense, that didn't have description beyond right now or he was going to lose what was left of his fucking mind.

The rails were empty at the station's edge, meaning the train had already left, which meant strangers had been in town for an entire day while he slept. Another growl left his lips. Fucking careless on his part. He stared at the space where the train pulled in each week, his mind running in circles, all of which ended with Audrey tied up or hurt or dead and tossed into one of those storage cars.

Or maybe she'd gone and done something stupid, like leaving Nizhny because she didn't want him to get hurt on her behalf again.

Gunnar rubbed his chest, struggling for air, that tightness growing, pain lancing through his body. Panic, he realized. He was panicking.

He was standing in the middle of the train tracks, clutching his chest without a coat on, like a useless fuck.

"Jonathan?"

He spun wildly, and there she was, standing on the station's front stairs while Virtue held the door open for her. Audrey, a laundry basket balanced on one hip, two large bags in the other arm. Hazel eyes were wide, shocked to see him. She looked pale, deep circles under her eyes, her hair in a messy, lopsided bun.

She looked fucking perfect.

The tightness in his chest abated, the pain receding, and suddenly he could breathe again. Gunnar huffed between a laugh of relief, exhaustion, sheer idiocy, he didn't know. All he *knew* was that she was over there and he was over here, and that was bullshit.

He jogged over as she asked, "Where is your coat?" before he was on her, scooping her up in his arms as she shrieked at him. The bags dropped, the clean laundry tipping everywhere. "Jonathan? What's wrong?"

He buried his face against her neck, inhaling until it hurt. Sunshine, his sunshine. He really was a fucking idiot. He felt the blush creeping up her throat as he nuzzled against it.

"Are you okay?" Her arms wrapped around his neck, those soft fingers brushing his skin, but she was tentative and worried.

That wouldn't do. He set her back on her feet, cupped her face in his hands, made sure he had her full attention. She blinked up at him, owlish, her brow furrowed in concern.

"Everything," Gunnar said, swallowing a few times before he went on. "That's what you mean. To me. Everything."

"Jonathan . . ." Her entire expression softened, the way he bet she looked every time she'd whispered she loved him while she'd taken care of him and waited for him to wake up. To come back to her, she'd said.

When he kissed her, she let out a tiny sob against his lips. He brushed his nose along hers, rested his forehead against hers. Inhaled that bright, beautiful scent of her joy, everything he'd never believed he'd deserved, but it was for him and he wanted it, and he was going to take it. Protect this, right here, this feeling, the gorgeous smile when he leaned back to look down at her, the adoration and love she'd offered him.

"Everything," he repeated, firm. Almost angry in the way he said it, needing some kind of confirmation she understood. She nodded, her cheeks warm against his palms.

"About time," Virtue said, leaning against the station's open door.

Audrey laughed, burying herself in Gunnar's arms and hiding her face. He let her, looking over at Virtue with a shrug as he kept Audrey close.

Audrey rubbed at his bare arms. "You shouldn't be out like this in the cold. Virtue, is there a blanket?"

"I'm fine."

"Don't you dare. You've been unconscious for a week!"

Gunnar winced at the firm poke she landed right on his chest.

"Oh gods, I'm so sorry!"

"I'm fine," he repeated, and this time she scowled at him but didn't poke him again.

"You'll get him home and warm sooner if you just go now," Virtue offered, her expression amused.

Gunnar held Audrey tighter to him. "Everyone . . ." He swallowed a few times, not sure how to ask what the fight with Kushiel had cost Nizhny.

"Everyone is recovering," Virtue said, and he knew it wasn't the full story, but he wouldn't get it now, standing on the taiga without a coat. With a wave and a knowing smile, the succubus ducked back into the station.

Audrey sighed, then gathered up the spilled mess—food mostly, some bandages, and what looked like a few potions, and left the laundry to be washed again. She refused to let him help or carry anything, and for once, he didn't argue. They headed home, walking shoulder to shoulder, the silence comfortable considering his confession moments before. Audrey kept a casual pace, chewing on her bottom lip. Didn't much matter, really. She was here and safe, and he couldn't find himself much bothered about anything else.

But then she sniffled and cleared her throat. When Gunnar looked down at her in question, she shook her head, not looking at him.

"I'm sorry."

"For what?" He couldn't think of a damn thing she had to apologize about.

Another sniffle. "I wasn't there. I promised you I'd be there, but then you woke up alone."

"It's fine."

"It is not." She stopped, glaring at him over her bags, her eyes glassy with unshed tears. "I should have waited until you woke up, but we were out of food and I figured you'd be hungry once you did . . ." She stalled when he rested both hands on her shoulders.

"I did wake up worried when you weren't there," he admitted, "but not because you broke your promise. Shit keeps happening on train days, so I think hearing you talk about it drew me out of torpor. Then you weren't in the house, and all I could think about was maybe something happened."

He didn't mention the fear she might've left him, which seemed stupid now.

"Nothing happened. I literally didn't leave the house once until this morning. And it wasn't until after the train left." She scrunched her nose. "Train day has definitely lost a lot of appeal."

"Yeah, fuck it." He smiled when she laughed, then cupped her cheek so he could wipe away a stray tear. "We're alright, Audrey."

She leaned against his palm with a sigh but then straightened up. "Well, almost. You need to get inside. I can't believe you came out without a coat."

They walked on, so close their bodies brushed with each step. "I run hot."

"You're ridiculous."

By the time they got home, Gunnar had to sit down at the table, breathing labored, his entire body dead weight, but he didn't retreat to his room. Instead, he watched Audrey bustle around the kitchen, putting the food away and cleaning up, talking at him about ten miles an hour about everything he'd missed (nothing, the settlement quiet since Kushiel's dramatic show) and about how everyone was doing (well, considering).

The severity of wounds varied. Innocence was all but healed up, grumpy he'd missed watching Kushiel die. Rina and Virtue were both fine, if inseparable, and Aster was staying with the leshy to help heal him and his forest. Gullin took some of the worst of it, but apparently his connection with E allowed for swift healing. He'd left on the train this morning again, and so had the blood mage from the Dominion. Tomas's blood madness had been cured, and he was now focused on fretting over Innocence, much to the incubus's delight.

The wolf pack had a few losses during the fight, and one of the Clan got caught in the hellfire and died. Njal, one of Hertha and Frode's sons, who Gunnar'd spoken to on only a few occasions. They had sent him off with a proper Viking funeral, Valkyries and all, the day after his death. Audrey had offered condolences and thanks for them both and suggested they pay a visit to the Clan tomorrow.

She chattered about the food next, everything she'd picked up, including Aster's Shepard's pie with extra meat, just like he preferred, and served him a portion with a mug of hot chocolate—no coffee, not while he needed more sleep.

"I've slept enough," he grumbled as he ate. She sat across from him now, drinking her own hot chocolate.

"Torpor isn't really sleep. It's more like a coma."

He grunted.

"I know you're tired," she added. Her grin was mischievous when she added, "Besides, you look horrible."

"You don't look so hot yourself."

"That's rude."

"You were rude first."

A little hum, not disagreeing with him, and she took another sip. Silence stretched for a few minutes while he ate and Audrey fiddled with her mug. "I haven't been sleeping well," she admitted. "I was too worried about you."

Gunnar set his fork down, wiped his mouth, and took her in for a minute. Exhaustion was all over her—the rumpled clothing, dark circles, unkempt hair. She seemed thinner too, which he didn't much like. And she still smelled worried, even though he was sitting right in front of her.

"That bad, huh?"

Audrey gave him a weak smile. "Yes."

He extended his hand, palm up, and she didn't hesitate to take it. He squeezed, stared at their joined fingers as she wove her tiny ones between his. "Thanks," he said, his voice raspy. He cleared his throat a few times, having a hard time looking up at her. "No one ever watched out for me before you."

"You're welcome," she said, her voice barely above a whisper. "It's the same for me, you know. Before you, no one ever cared about me."

"That's not true. You had Theo. The druid who took you in. They cared, and everyone here damn well cares about you too."

Her smile was patient as she added her other hand to their tangled pile. "They all came after you, Jonathan. After you saved my life that day in the slums." He wanted to protest—surely there'd been someone, but she shook her head. "I know I never talk much about my life before that night, but there really isn't much to tell. My parents sold me into an indenture factory contract." She shrugged. "I have no memories of them. The factory keeper who had my contract wasn't cruel, but he didn't care. He bought up lots of orphans, put us to work as soon as we could hold tools. After a few years, I ran away because the older boys were abusive and stole food from kids who were smaller.

"After that, I lived on the streets, but I had no one. I never mattered to anyone. No one cared what happened to me. Not until you showed up in that alley." Another shrug, a soft smile. Those gentle eyes, undoing him. "And for whatever reason, I mattered to you."

"Yeah, you did." He chuckled. "Still can't explain it, not really, but no fucking regrets."

After a pause, Audrey said, "I mean it, you know that, right?"

His mouth went dry.

She stared right into him. Firm. Unblinking. Confident and unwavering. "I love you. It's okay if it's not something you can say back to me, but I need you to believe me."

He wanted to, but it still felt so strange to him. "You going to get pissed if I ask you why?"

"Why do I love you?"

He shifted in the seat but kept his hand with hers. "Yeah."

Audrey's smile was still gentle, her scent warm with sunshine and what he guessed was love, and amazingly enough, the two things were alike.

"I loved you when you saved me. For intervening on my behalf, for being willing to stay with me so I didn't have to be alone when I died.

"But then you did more, and you made sure I lived at the cost of your freedom. I loved you for being selfless. I loved you for giving me a life. I loved you for giving me a purpose.

"I loved you because even when you didn't believe I could free you—and I know you didn't, don't even try to deny it—you agreed to let me try. I loved the ways you were kind and gentle to me even when you were chained to the table."

She closed her eyes, letting out a slow exhale, memories shivering over her skin and scent, and he knew what she was remembering before she said, "And I loved you for caring, for putting my well-being first when they tried to intimidate me over that stupid silver tooth-pick."

"I wanted to kill them," Gunnar muttered.

"I probably shouldn't love you for that, but I do." Audrey laughed and just kept going with whys and reasons, like there wasn't an end to this list of hers. "But I fell entirely in love with you the night my apartment burned down. I knew you wanted to be free and alone, but when I lost everything, you decided you wanted me safe more. And you've kept me safe, you make me feel safe, and I love you for that too.

"I love you for the home you've made for us. I love you for knowing how I take my tea, even though you'd rather die than drink any your-self."

She kept smiling at him, wiping away tears now—why was she crying? And she still smelled like love, and sunshine, and happiness. He stood, frowning at her as she shook her head.

"I love you for how you smile at me, for letting me sleep in your bed so I don't have nightmares, for being funny and smart and for taking care of Zhadan when he worried about Lyubava."

She laughed again when he caught her face in both hands, growling down at her, wanting her to stop and keep going, he wasn't sure which. Both?

"I love you for letting me sleep in your shirt," she said as she grinned up at him, "for helping me give out cookies, and for being grumpy at me when I don't eat enough. Is that enough whys? I have more, I can do this all day if you—"

He kissed her. Seemed like the right thing to do, and it was, making her giggle against his lips.

"Alright," he mumbled against her mouth. "Alright, I believe you."

"Good," she said, kissing him again, then his chin as she dropped onto flat feet. "But I don't love how bad you smell. Go take a shower, then we can get both get some sleep."

"Hmmm." He held her face, kissing her again, nibbling at her bottom lip. She laughed again, trying to push him away.

"Please, you stink!"

Another growl, but he leaned back. "Fine, but only if you join me. Gonna need help."

He motioned to his chest, then his back. She blinked once, that pretty blush going up to the tips of her ears, the shyness in her scent about as good as the rest of it, and he somehow kept a straight face.

"Still feeling pretty weak and all that." Audrey narrowed her eyes, so he added, "Can't reach my back."

She swallowed once, still blushing despite her small grin as she turned him by his shoulders and pushed him toward the bathroom. "Alright, alright. No need to be a baby."

Gunnar laughed this time but let her nudge him along.

Chapter 38

Turned out he needed help after all. Wrestling out of his shirt, given the tightness in his chest muscles and newly healed skin was unpleasant, and Audrey was right there to chide him about it.

She turned on the shower, then came over to him, tugging at his sleeve. "Let me help. Isn't that why you dragged me in here?"

Gunnar grinned under the shirt as she helped him out of it, because he hadn't gotten too far in his thoughts in the kitchen besides not wanting her out of sight just yet and *naked*. He was still grinning when she finally got the shirt off, and she rolled her eyes at his wolfish expression.

"Turn around so I can get these bandages off. And no complaining."

He grunted down at her, five-foot nothing, bossing him around, realizing he liked it, enjoyed having anyone care enough—love him enough—to nag. He obliged her, rolling the word around in his head, over the list of things she'd tossed at him for all the reasons she loved him, how she claimed she could have just kept right on going.

Sounded like everything, and he pondered that word for a minute. The one he'd thrown at her the second he saw her alive and well, and the pain in his chest eased. Maybe *everything* was love; hells if he knew.

Gunnar watched the steam curl and the water circle the copper tub's drain. He'd never thought he could love, never thought he was worth love either, but Audrey'd insisted on proving him wrong. Maybe she did on the other side too. Didn't seem so strange, after listening to her reasons for loving him, that maybe all the reasons he had about her—everything—amounted to the same damn thing.

The bandages clung to his skin, Gunnar wincing as the layers separated, the skin underneath still a bit raw. Smelled bad too, she wasn't kidding. Then the bandages were off, but Audrey said nothing. When he turned, she just stared at him, her hands clenched under her chin as her gaze roamed over his chest.

Gunnar glanced at his reflection in the polished mirror. It was ugly, the gash in his chest still red around the edges, thick scar tissue in a raised ridge. The entire region was discolored, darkened and pocked from healed blisters. Right, hellfire—it burned deep and fast, and he'd been impaled on a burning blade. Scarring entirely covered his right pectoral, wrapped over his shoulder, down most of his bicep, and when he peered over his shoulder, it went halfway down his back too.

A perk of his vileblood, he rarely scarred, so it was strange to see such a vast stretch covering his body, to know the marks wouldn't fade in a few days.

He met Audrey's gaze in the mirror; she was pale, shaking as she walked around him and flattened a palm on his chest where pale, flawless skin met the fresh scarring.

"I thought you were going to die. You *were* dying." Audrey shook her head when he protested. "Let me get this out, please." She wouldn't look at him, just his chest, so he gave her a quiet nod, and she went on after a shuddering inhale. "When Kushiel died, the hellfire went wild, and it melted his sword inside you. It was . . . boiling, the metal . . . and you . . ."

Gunnar folded his hand around hers. Audrey swallowed, blinking a few times as tears slipped free.

"Virtue took control of the hellfire and pulled it out of you, and then E stepped in." She patted his chest. "There wasn't time to explain. He worked the metal inside your body so it stopped the bleeding and kept you . . . kept your body together."

Another thick swallow as she went on, "He came by to check on you a few days after. I've never seen him so animated before. He said he hasn't forged anything new in a century, and that he's never forged anything inside a living being before. But I think the fact that E is proud of his work is a good sign you're okay?" She let out a watery laugh, and he squeezed her hand again, then she grinned up at him. "Does this make Mjölnir your brother?"

Gunnar snorted. "Guess we'll have to ask E."

"Gullin too."

"What now?"

"If E made Mjölnir, I'm guessing Gullin is Gullinbursti," Audrey said. Gunnar just shook his head; he didn't read nearly as much about mythos as she did. "E was worried about you. We all were."

"I'm right here, sweetheart," he said, unable to stop himself from wiping away the fresh tears, tucking her hair behind her ear. "You're not getting rid of me that easy."

"Easy, huh?" She sniffled and wiped her face. "I'd hate to see what you think is difficult." She wrinkled her nose. "How about we just not?"

"Yeah, alright," he said, tugging her against him. She fit perfectly, curling up against his chest, her head tucked under his chin, her sigh long and tired. "Come on, why don't you wash my back and you can tell me more things about me you like."

"Love," Audrey corrected.

"Besides, you stink."

"Only because of you."

"Hmm, so you showered while I was resting?"

His only answer was a glare, and Gunnar grinned as he dropped his pants, knowing that would stall more arguing. Sure enough, she went quiet as he stepped into the shower naked and pulled the curtain closed.

He hissed as the water hit his skin, which felt stretched thin over the wound, and he frowned a bit, not liking the idea of having this magic metal in his chest. He supposed he'd be thanking E as much as bitching at him later, because he was alive and Audrey was too, and that was really all that mattered.

He felt the cold air as she stepped in behind him, and as much as he wanted an eyeful, he ducked his face in the water. They had time. For now, he just wanted to be close to her.

She washed his back, her gentle touches soothing as she checked everything was healed. Audrey let him wash her hair, and he found himself reminded of the night he killed Mateo, when they'd been here in the shower because she'd begged him to stay. The first night they'd slept in his bed together.

Washing the sickness and sweat from his body freed his senses to take in her scent in more detail, including the touches of embarrassment and desire as she stole glances at him when she thought he wasn't paying attention, the pink dusting her cheeks, neck, and shoulders from more than the warm water.

Once they were out of the shower and wrapped in towels, Gunnar couldn't help another peek at his new body, which looked a bit better without the dried blood and dead skin.

"You don't mind scars, right?" He called after Audrey as she went to change the bedsheets.

She laughed when she came out with the dirty linens, tossing them in a pile on the floor for now. She wore one of his shirts, swimming in it is as usual.

"Are you really fishing for compliments?"

"I almost died, remember? Maybe I need a little ego patting. Maybe you should tell me more about those things you like about me."

"Love," she corrected again, effortlessly.

He followed her into his room. Theirs, he decided, because he found he liked the idea of the arrangement being permanent. "Well, lay it on me."

She rolled her eyes as she tucked the fitted sheet on the bed. He leaned against the doorframe, arms crossed, towel tied low around his hips. She still blushed, and he decided if he loved anything, it was that color on her skin.

"Fine. I love your recent scars, because they mean you're alive," she said, very matter-of-fact and not looking at him as she worked her way around the bed. "I also, um, have always loved that you're very tall."

"That so?"

"Yes. I love how you always make me feel safe, and you . . . your, um . . ." She cleared her throat, changing the pillowcases, glancing at him sideways now and then. "The physical side is part of that."

"Hmm. Because I'm tall."

"Yes, and . . ." She turned waved a hand in his direction. At his body, top to bottom. "And muscly."

Gunnar laughed. "Anything else?"

"Please, like you don't know how handsome you are."

"I don't know how handsome you think I am."

Audrey finished making the bed, tossing the blankets in place rather hurriedly. "Entirely too much so."

Gunnar grinned as he prowled over to her; despite her embarrassment and fatigue, her scent remained playful, and her desire, well, it sweetened everything about her beautiful scent. He caught her by the hips, pulled her close, enjoying the way she fit against his body.

He purred the word, "Interesting," knowing she'd feel the low rumble of it in his chest against her back.

Sure enough, she shivered, goosebumps dancing across her bare arms, and he inhaled against the top of her head as the burst in her pheromones rolled over his senses. This was unfamiliar territory, not strangling down his want for her and instead acknowledging it. Baser urges he normally reserved for fucking, the physical act and release.

He already knew it would be a fundamentally different experience with her, which thrilled him, sent a hum deep in his bones that made his cock half hard every time he looked in her direction, while at the same time he felt raw and desperate in a way that he was starting to think had nothing to do with sex.

All of which could wait.

They were both exhausted. Audrey'd taken care of him for a week. Her desire and curiosity and wandering eyes might drive him mad, but for her, he'd wait. And if all Gunnar ever got was this, a quiet embrace and her trusting him enough to sleep at his side, in his bed, he'd take it.

"I love the beast in your blood," she breathed, so soft he thought he'd misheard. Then he frowned, ready to argue, but she'd already turned in his arms, the soft pads of her fingers resting on his lips. "Use your senses, Jonathan, not the defenses you've built to survive."

He took her wrist, moving her hand away from his mouth. "They're the same thing."

"That's fair," Audrey said, unflinching as she stared up at him. Her wet hair hung loosely around her face. "And it doesn't make me love it less. Don't argue." She lifted a brow. "Don't tell me what I feel."

Jonathan pursed his lips, but his scowl was not as firm as he wanted.

"I love the beast in your blood because it's part of *you*. I love how you use that part of yourself to be the monster you despise in order to protect what you care about. To protect the place we call home and the people who live here. To protect me."

She took her hand back from him.

"I love how it helps you know me and what I need." Her cheeks went redder. "You went to Virtue because you worried your urges would scare me."

Gunnar winced despite himself; he wasn't ashamed, yet, "She's a friend," he said, honestly. "We helped each other, but that's it."

"I know. I know about her and Rina," Audrey said. She still didn't look at him, not directly. "I was jealous, but not in the way you'd think. Not because of the sex. Well, I mean . . ." She covered her face with both hands and laughed, the sound strained. "Yes, but also because she got to share part of you I didn't."

"Audrey."

She shook her head, fierce when she met his gaze. "I love you for stopping when I asked after I kissed you. It was so easy, being touched by you, finally having that part of you. To be under your attention. To be desired by you, but I couldn't. Not then." Audrey exhaled a shaky breath. "And I love that even though I . . . I want that again, to feel that with you, and I think you want that with me, you're going to insist we sleep because I'm exhausted, and you'd rather take another hellfire sword through your chest before you do anything you worry I'd regret tomorrow."

The truth of it all was in her earnest gaze, the way she looked into him despite blushing furiously, but he couldn't have ignored the honesty in her scent, the sheer stubborn will.

"I love you," she said, flattening a hand on his chest, over his heart, over the scars, over the metal fused and forged under his skin. "Every-thing about you, everything you are. Everything."

A little grin, a little wrinkle of her nose as she watched him blink dumbly at her as understanding settled in, and he realized he was a fucking idiot, but she didn't push him to give it a voice. Not yet. She just gave him a sleepy smile and tugged him to bed.

Chapter 39

Gunnar cursed as he jerked out of a deep sleep, immediately annoyed at being caught flatfooted, at being so damn exposed so many fucking times so close together. His instincts were a few seconds ahead, cataloging the sound as he rubbed his face.

"What's wrong?" Audrey asked, curled against him, her voice tired but clear.

"Nothing, just . . ." He grunted, stretching a long arm out and peeling the curtain back. Deep night, but the sky was clear, moon and stars bright.

The motion caught the attention of their late-night visitors. The deer all lifted their heads at once, the faint crunching of their steps going silent. A dozen or so, looked like. After a few seconds, they walked on. Beside him, the tension left Audrey, her scent warming—pleased at being woken up by damn deer.

For whatever reason, Audrey whispered when she said, "Reindeer? Caribou? They used to travel in big herds around here before the Aperien event. Hundreds of thousands of them, Aster said."

She craned her neck to see better, watching until the last one passed by the window, and Gunnar left the curtain half open.

Audrey rested her chin on his chest. "That's a good sign for the area. They would have been easy food for the all the monsters. Maybe they'll come back some around Nizhny now that it's safer."

"Hmm." Gunnar ran a hand through her hair, which was still a little damp. They hadn't slept very long. "Sorry I woke you. Not used to sleeping so deep."

"It's okay. You're still recovering."

"I'm fine."

She patted his chest, avoiding the scars. "You just said you don't normally sleep so deeply. Don't you think it might be because your body needs more rest?" He grunted. "That doesn't make any sense? None at all?" Another grunt, knowing she saw him grinning. She snorted, rolling over to put her back to him. "You're impossible."

He didn't like that warmth leaving his side, so he chased it, laughing at the squeak she let out when he pulled her against his body, arm banded against her waist and trapping her to him.

"That something else for your list?" Gunnar ran his nose along her neck, smiling at the hitch in her breathing when he did.

"I'm not answering that. It would only make you worse."

He nipped at her jaw, and she squeaked again, but she also leaned into him. He liked that. Gunnar soothed the spot with a soft kiss, liked the little sigh she let out even better. A few seconds later, she giggled, and he caught the scent of mischief against her contentment.

"What's funny?"

"The fearless Jonathan Gunnar scared awake by a herd of—*Don't you da—!*" She cut off in a shriek as he found her ribs, tickling the hells out of her as she squirmed and laughed, kicking at him and slapping at his arms. "Stop, stop! Jona—" A scream as he really dug in, laughing at how hard she struggled. "I'm sorry!" Another hysterical laugh, then a hiccup. "I'm sorry, I won't tell anyone I swear!" He relented, letting her catch a few breaths, but then she said, "No one will ever know you're afraid of deer!" This scream about broke his eardrums. Tears ran down her cheeks now, but she wasn't sorry, not one bit, and he damn well knew it, even when she huffed, "No, no, you're brave, so brave, the bravest!"

"Listen here, you little smartass."

"I love you!"

Gunnar stopped, the words new enough that hearing them still startled him. That's all it took, and Audrey slipped free and jumped off the bed, fleeing the room with a victorious, breathless cackle. He blinked a few times, then chuckled.

"It's dark. Don't stub your toe again."

"That was one time!"

"This house has two rooms and a closet." Gunnar threw back the sheet and stood, taking his time, trying to keep the thrill of a hunt racing through his blood at a reasonable level. Different kind of prey, he mused. "You really think you can hide from me?"

He heard a faint giggle, muffled. Holding a hand over her mouth to keep from laughing outright. Gunnar grinned, prowling on silent cat feet. The only thing she really had on her side was her scent saturated the entire place. It wouldn't do her much good. Her heart raced like a rabbit; he could hear it from the bedroom.

Not that he wouldn't play, draw this out a bit.

The hall was better lit, the curtains back in the main sitting area and kitchen, so she'd see him coming. He wandered to the kitchen, unconcerned, getting himself a glass of water. Took his time drinking, looking out over the taiga, wearing only his shorts. Knowing she watched him, he could feel those eyes wandering over his bare skin. Heard her lick her lips, how her breathing didn't quite settle from all the tickling, not even when he gave her plenty of time to relax. Her desire was sweet against his senses.

It made him glad for the reprieve, because she might want him, but that didn't mean he could fuck her against the kitchen counter, which painted one hells of a picture.

At least not yet. Not until he learned her, if she let him. Then his mind was off like a shot, imagining what he *could* do to her, what she might like, how responsive she'd been to the barest touch, to a simple kiss.

Gunnar almost missed her sneaking down the hall.

Almost.

When he turned on her, her eyes went wide and she bolted, but he caught her at the doorway to his room, hefting her off her feet and against his body with a laugh as she shrieked again.

"You keep that up, Zhadan's going to come beat down the damn door," he mumbled against her hair. She dissolved into more laughing, breathless in his arms. "You really think that'd work?"

"No, but it was fun," she said, giggling, but then the mirth tapered off. He knew she looked at the bed, their bed, and the rumpled sheets.

Her scent shifted, nervous now, unsure in a way he rarely scented on her skin. He let her slide down his body, her feet soft on the floor, but he kept her close, arms around her middle. Leaned in to kiss, then nuzzle her cheek. "Nothing happens you don't want, sweetheart."

Her voice was barely a whisper. "I know."

He nudged under her ear, a sweet spot, her scent stronger there. Soft, perfect skin under his lips, goosebumps shivering across her skin at the slightest touch. She leaned back into him when he did, but when she stiffened slightly in his arms, he knew why. He'd been hard since she bolted from the bed, giggling and laughing and leading him on a little chase. Appealing to his beast almost innocently, but he knew better.

She was innocent, but the game wasn't, not entirely. Not when she wanted him to catch her. Not when she knew damn well he smelled her growing arousal.

But wanting him didn't mean she was ready for him.

"Back to sleep?" he asked against her throat, her pulse thrumming under his lips, inhaling as he spoke.

A fresh burst of nerves, anticipation. A swell of desire he had to grit his teeth against to keep himself from grinding into her ass.

And she said, "No," with a firm voice, but a faint trace of fear splashed his senses.

"What's got you scared?"

He felt her wince, then she sighed. "I'd never even kissed anyone until you. I don't know what to do."

"Was a damn good kiss, I thought." Gunnar couldn't help a small chuckle.

She let out a huff, both hands clutching his forearms around her middle, her throat warming against his lips as she blushed again. "You know what I mean."

"Sure, get being nervous about that, but that's not what I asked. You're scared. Not the same thing."

Audrey looked down, fingers tracing patterns only she could see as she thought about it. He needed to know before they moved forward.

"I always assumed I got there in time, in that alley."

"You did," Audrey said. "It's not anything like that, I promise." She swallowed again. Her hesitation was killing him, but then she whispered, "I'm afraid I'll disappoint you."

His first response was outright anger, the idea she was anything but perfect? Fuck her feeling like that, but he held back, because he knew the truth was far more uncomfortable, especially when he considered his own head space.

Gunnar smirked, only because she couldn't see him. "You ain't the only one."

Audrey laughed, a startled little sound. She turned in his arms, frowning up at him. "If you're looking for more compliments, I really don't know what to tell you."

Fucking hells, those wide, innocent eyes, her genuinely confused expression. She really had no idea what else lurked below his skin, not when it came to sex.

Not in the way his mind raced wild at thoughts of sex with *her*.

He'd known it, deep on a primal level his intellect refused to admit, how she'd been his from the moment he put his mouth on her that first time. How she'd answered the missing piece in him Virtue could never fake, that no working woman had ever satisfied.

And Audrey, in her inexperience, she didn't know the extent of what she offered him.

Gunnar had never tasted anything as erotic as her natural submission to him. What the beast in him had craved his entire life, and could never buy, because it came with a requirement: love and trust, and she laid both unequivocally at his feet.

Part of him wondered if blood madness felt anything like *this*, the all-consuming urge to take, give, shelter, protect. To make her entirely, unerringly *his*.

Yeah, pretty sure he'd always wanted her to be his. *Mine*, always on the tip of his tongue, in the front of his mind.

He'd fucking possess her in a way no magic could protect from, if she'd let him.

But first he needed to be certain, needed her to understand.

"Nah," he drawled, running his teeth on the tendon between her neck and shoulder, trying to keep himself grounded. "Meaning I'd disappoint you."

"What? Why?"

Gunnar cupped her face in both hands, trying and failing to keep the raw need for her from his expression. Traced his thumb over her bottom lip. "I worry I might scare you with how much I want you, the things I want to do to you."

She shifted a bit, her cheeks apple red, the blush stretching up to the tips of her ears. "I . . ." She opened and closed her mouth but said nothing else.

"Need you to understand, though, while it might seem like I'm in charge of all this," he said as he inclined his head toward his bed. "It's all you, sweetheart. You want to stop, I stop. You don't like something, you tell me, I stop. I'm too rough, you tell me, I stop."

Audrey swayed on her feet but pressed her lips into a thin line before she said, "Well, the same is true for you." Her chin lifted. "If you don't like something."

His brave, perfect girl. Gunnar chuckled, leaning forward until his lips brushed her ear. "There isn't a damn thing I don't want with you, Audrey." He savored the way she arched into him. "But if you let me, you want me, I'm going to take you to my bed, and we won't be sleeping anytime soon."

She shivered, her already rich scent deepening, and it was all he could to do to stay still, waiting, until she whispered, "Okay," into his shoulder.

Not quite enough, so he tangled a fist in her hair, tilted her head back to get a good look at those beautiful eyes, at the slight glaze, the way she licked her lips as she stared up at him, lost, and yes, wanting.

"You want me, sweetheart? We can't undo this. I want the words."

A slow blink as she held his wrist, squeezed. Nervous, not scared, as she whispered, "I want you." Then she decided to really fuck with what was left of his sanity when she added, "I'm yours."

Chapter 40

Gunnar was pretty sure, for all the shit that'd happened in the last few weeks—the brushes with death, the angel, and the manticore venom—*this* was what would kill him in the end.

I'm yours, from her sweet mouth. Audrey.

He lowered his forehead to hers, her breath warm on his lips as he mumbled, "I don't deserve you," and kissed her before she argued.

There it was, the trust, enough for her to sink into him, into their kiss. To let him cradle the back of her head in one hand, her jaw in the other, and angle her head just so, and he owned her mouth.

No fight, just beautiful, consuming submission, and he drank it up with tongue and teeth, gentle, soothing after each nip at her lips, each bite and suck at her tongue, and Gunnar kept his eyes closed, pretty sure his vision was tunneling as all the blood in his brain fled to his cock, hard enough to drive nails already.

From a kiss.

No, this was more than a kiss.

Everything.

He growled against her mouth, and she gave up those little noises for him again, precious whimpers and gasps and sighs, both hands holding his one wrist. She tried to keep up with him, yielding as he guided her, taught her, showed her how to lick back at his mouth, and when he drew away, trying to give her a second to breathe when she rocked into him, she whined.

"Perfect," Gunnar whispered against her kiss-plumped lips, brushing his over her cheeks, her nose, her forehead. Felt how the praise warmed her already flushed skin, how she tried to shake her head in protest, but he didn't allow it. "Perfect," he repeated, firmer, a rasp in voice now as he dragged his nose along that elegant neck. "And mine."

He kept worshiping her throat, sucking against her pulse point enough to mark, a hummingbird between his teeth. Hated what he put on her skin would fade, but just an excuse to place more, really, any time she liked. And she liked, if the way she squirmed, the way she restlessly shifted her thighs together was any indication.

If her fucking scent didn't give it all away; fucking hells, he wanted to bury his face in her cunt. And he would. Oh, how he would.

Slow and gentle, he reminded himself again and again, intellect and instinct oddly aligned. For all he'd threated to ravish her minutes earlier, she was *his*.

Nothing had ever belonged to him before. No one ever wanted him enough to fight for him, to believe in him, to keep him. Exquisite, that might have been the right word for the woman in his arms, in his heart.

Everything.

Gunnar groaned at the thoughts, the rolling mantra, at her scent, the hot want on the air, her desire sweet as everything else about her. He'd never shake it, never get it out of his system, and he'd never fucking try.

He scooped her up by the thighs, and she gasped, falling forward against him. Soft, warm skin in palms, those perfect tits of hers pressing against his chest through his shirt—damn if that hadn't been driving him crazy, her wearing his clothes. Her arms flew around his neck, her legs squeezing his hips.

More of that scent. Wet for him already, he'd bet his ass on it. He felt the radiant heat of her core against his stomach. A few fumbled steps forward and he lowered them both to the bed, careful to keep his weight from crushing her. He hissed, his hips cradled between hers, his erection pressed against her virgin cunt.

"Oh gods," Audrey's voice went shrill, grasping at his shoulders at the intimate contact, and he shushed against her lips, soothing, drawing her in to a tender kiss. Letting the moment stretch, let her acclimate to what it felt like to have him over her, his body above her, and she trembled, then relaxed, feeding him with more of those perfect noises.

He kept the kiss, one hand tracing down her body, lifting the shirt up high enough that he could run his thumb along the line of her cotton underwear. Practical, no frills or a show. Just who she was, his perfect girl. She tensed again, and he broke the kiss to nuzzle into her throat, against her jaw.

"Alright, sweetheart?"

"Yes," she whispered, her single word a tiny pant.

He bit at the collar of the t-shirt, tugged. "Seems uneven."

Audrey blinked up at him, hazel eyes luminous in the moonlight, the curtain still pulled back from watching the deer. He knew how he looked; dark hair falling forward, hungry black eyes, but she saw him, not the monster.

No, she'd showed him, hadn't she?

He was a man, not a monster. He'd just been a slow learner.

Gunnar grinned down at her; she was a damn good teacher.

"What?" He didn't know if she was asking about his shirt comment or his stupid grin, so he leaned back and tugged at the shirt, helping her sit. She let him, didn't protest as he peeled it from her body. Knew his expression darkened when the moonlight hit her pale skin, as she settled back on the mattress, dusky nipples perking with the chill.

He shook his head when her arms lifted, clear she meant to cover herself, and she stalled, then folded them over her stomach instead. Found himself lost for a few seconds, gaze roving over her slight curves, the scar on her left bicep from the hellfire attack in the ESC, the faded marks from where she'd been stabbed the night he saved her the first time. Her delicate hip bones, the white cotton and the promise underneath. Gunnar breathed like he'd just fought for his life, realizing she studied him with the same intensity.

He watched her watch him for a few seconds, knowing she lingered on the scars covering his chest. Without thinking, he reached down and took one of her hands, pressed it over his heart.

"I'll always keep you safe. Don't matter what it costs."

"I know," she whispered, fingers tracing the raised skin, her eyes shining now. Tears? When he frowned, she shook her head. "It's silly, but . . . I never felt safe, never in my whole life until you." A tear raced down to her hair, disappeared. "Thank you."

Gunnar caught her hand, kissing her fingertips. Holding them against his lips, just watching her, captivated.

Everything, well, it really was simple, wasn't it?

Lowering down, he pressed his forehead to hers against, inhaling the happiness, the sunshine radiating from her skin, her desire for him so much more than what he'd ever really understood the desire to be. He kissed where the tear traced, then her cheek, then near her ear.

Told her he loved her.

Everything, he repeated, and her soft sob before she grabbed his face and both hands and kissed him for all she was worth. It took his fucking breath away. Then she giggled, he chuckled, then growled and sucked another love bite into her neck, because all this?

He wanted her more than he'd ever wanted anything in his life.

"Let me love you, sweetheart," he said, pressing his lips to her clavicle, sternum. A lick along the underside of her breast, a tender suck on the side, before he palmed her entire tit and laved her nipple, savoring her desperate little cry, a breathy mewl making his cock twitch against her hot center.

"Fuck, more of that," he growled, switching sides, teasing back and forth until both nipples were red and wet and swollen, and Audrey gasped his name between frantic pants. "More of you."

He tugged at her underwear for emphasis, patting her hip gently as he pulled and she lifted for him, and fuck if he didn't take his time, running his palms over her pert ass, giving a squeeze, before pulling the garment off and tossing it aside.

Gunnar had to pause, kneeling over her, squeezing his cock to keep from going off at the site of her, naked under him. Truly felt like an animal, groaning as he palmed her thighs and pushed them apart.

"Jonathan!" Her voice jumped an octave, surprising coloring her scent, her entire body tensing.

"Gorgeous, look at you," he growled. She turned her face away, covering it with her hands, and he let her, for now. Delicate between her legs like everything else about her, the patch of curls above her sex slick, her cunt swollen and ripe for him, so much so her inner thighs were damp with her want. "Smell so fucking good." He kept one hand heavy, holding legs her open, as he brushed her with a single knuckle, she rocked her hips, chasing him. "That's right, beautiful. I'm all for you."

"Jonathan . . ."

"Too fast?"

"No," she whimpered, "Just . . . I'm . . ."

"What, baby?"

Audrey shifted her hips, restless, hungry. All of it radiated from her scent, obvious on her glistening folds. He touched her again, spreading her a bit, finding her clit and giving it a slow circle. She let out a choked noise, still covering her face.

"Tell me," Gunnar said, his voice a low rumble, easing off to a featherlight touch. His mouth fucking watered, but he needed words.

"You're staring," she whimpered out.

He chuckled. "Yeah, sweetheart, I am." Shifting his weight, he settled between her thighs, his chest against the sheets, that pretty cunt a breath from his mouth. "Are you telling me to stop?"

Her laugh was strained, a whine to it. "No, I . . . it's okay?"

"You're perfect, woman," he growled, nipping high on her thigh, running his tongue higher, hips jerking into the mattress as he tasted the arousal on her leg. "Fuck." Took a few breaths to steady himself, soothed a hand up and down her leg, squeezing gently as he hefted it over his shoulder, then the other. "You touch yourself?"

Another whine—embarrassed, he could tell, and fuck if it wasn't adorable and sexy, both. "You're really asking me this right *now*?"

"I am."

A huff, mumbling from behind her hands, "Yes, but never here. Because you'd know . . ."

Yeah, he'd have smelled it, no question, and the thought made him grin. But also, "Nothing to worry about now," he chuckled out, and before she could protest, he licked a stripe across her cunt, groaning at the same time she let out a startled moan.

"Fuck," he grunted, his vision spotting again, pressing his hips hard into the bed, trying to avoid humping the fucking mattress. "Your taste . . ."

The sounds she made for him; he might have thought her in distress if he wasn't mapping every inch of her cunt with his tongue and lips, drinking up everything she offered him. Twitching and shifting, whimpering, gasping, and it only took about a minute for those hands to drop, grabbing at nothing until he gave her a hand to anchor herself. She squeezed hard enough his knuckles ached, and hells if he didn't fucking love it.

Took his time too, learning her. Learning how sucking hard on her clit was too much for her, but when he ran his tongue just inside her, she shuddered each time—but it distracted more than built her up. How she let out her embarrassed little whine when he spread her open with his free hand but pressed herself into his face when he licked her up and down, then swirled a few times on her most sensitive spot. How she squeezed his hand harder when he traced a finger around her opening, how she trembled, her scent thickening, sweetening.

Fuck, he wanted to go down on her for hours, but he had a feeling once he made her come, she'd need him to let off, and she was climbing quick. And he also needed to prep her a bit, because she was small. Tiny.

He was not.

Gunnar teased again, slicking up his finger before he dipped inside, testing, enough of a barrier there still she'd bleed when she took him. Gunnar tried to shove the thought away, focused on what he could do to ease the inevitable discomfort. They both groaned when he sunk in further, even one finger a tight fit, but her body pulled at him, so hot and wet.

He was about to lose his fucking mind.

Gave her clit a good suck, earning him a little gasp, but the distraction let him get all the way into her, savoring how she pulsed around his finger, his dick aching, and he curled, grinning at her shocked cry, how her back nearly arched off the bed. He put pressure against her hips with their tangled hands, holding her down.

"Oh!" Gasps, faster now, all the wild noises and knowing he'd be the first and only man to hear this? To own this, to give her this. Almost laughed, how close he felt to coming, grinding against the bed while he ate at her.

A few more slides and he found the exact spot she needed, felt the change as her muscles tightened head to toe, her thighs trying to close around his head, and suddenly it was the only thing in the world he needed, his woman coming on his mouth.

Careful, he added a second finger, her reply a more strained, less comfortable sound, which immediately faded into pleasured whine, then another little "Oh, oh gods," and then she tipped, spilled into bliss because of him, and he carried her through it, gentling only once the clenching stopped and her cries turned to desperate little sobs. He pumped his fingers a few more times, pressing, stretching, and easing before he left her body.

Damn, she was vision, and he couldn't take his eyes off her face as he climbed up over her body, limp and sated, those pretty cheeks flushed bright, her gaze hooded and shiny, her lips parted as she panted to catch her breath. Then she reached for him, touching his cheeks, his jaw, his hair, tugging him in for a kiss.

"Sexy," he growled against her lips, and she laughed, breathless, and then her breathing hitched when she felt his cock, heavy against her. Her eyes fluttered shut.

"Jonathan," a little gasp again, fingers tightening in his hair.

He rubbed her hip, hitching her thigh up, slicking himself with her come. "You want this?" Half question, half sudden disbelief. His mouth on her, sure, but this . . .

No hesitation, just a reedy, "Yes, Jonathan, please . . ."

He grunted, a tingle racing through his body, down his spine, and settling low on his back, heavy in his balls, and he took himself in hand, stroking a few times, lining himself up and pressing.

Then he stalled, blinking down, fixated on where their bodies met, his senses ratcheted to the sky when she tensed again. Licked his lips, kept soothing up and down her leg; hells, she was soaked for him, ready, wanting. He . . .

Gunnar blinked again, trying to anchor himself, his mind in a scattered haze.

When Audrey whispered, "What's wrong," her beautiful scent touching with concern, fresh nerves, sudden embarrassment, he shook his head. Closed his eyes.

"I don't want to hurt you."

Relief in her scent; she understood at least his hesitation had nothing to do with *her*. Those soft fingertips were petting him, soothing *him* now. "I know it will, a little. It's okay. I want this. With you."

Gunnar nuzzled into her palm. "Tell me, if . . ."

"If I need to stop. I will. I promise." Truth, entirely, and when he still hesitated, she whispered, "Love me."

Fucking hells, she'd end him.

He didn't know how or when, but this woman, everything began and ended with her now. He laced his fingers with hers, gripped her hip tighter, and rocked forward, enough to slip inside, feel her part for him, welcome him, and he kept the momentum despite her whimper of discomfort, needing this part over as fast as she did.

Inside her, well, all the imagined heavens couldn't have possibly compared, and he wasn't buried to the hilt yet. He pinned their joined hands to the bed—he needed to keep himself upright before he fell onto her, into her, got lost for the rest of his damn life.

Then he smelled her blood.

"Fuck, sweetheart. Audrey, baby, okay?" He kissed her forehead, left his lips there, tasting the sweet and salt of her skin, trying desperately to keep still. The leg he wasn't holding wrapped around the outside of his thigh.

"Yes, I'm . . ." A little hiccup, a whine. "Don't . . . don't stop, I'm okay."

Shit. *Fuck.*

He moved his arms under her shoulders until he cupped her head in both palms, his mouth against hers, not kissing, just breathing.

She smelled like truth and love and trust, so he pressed forward into her, the stretch of her around his cock like nothing else. Her gasps at his lips as he adjusted the angle, pulled out a bit, then buried himself, all of him, into her beautiful, perfect body.

"Jonathan," she gasped, then again, his name, her head titled back against his palms, his lips against her chin as he fought to be still, a shudder running through them both. "Jonathan, oh gods . . . it's so . . ."

"Good," he slurred against her skin, her sweet skin, a growl slipping out when she shifted under him, fluttered around him. Fucking hells, all of them, she was so, so fucking tight. He was about to lose his grasp on reality. "Fuck. Fuck, sweetheart," he mumbled as he licked at her jaw, the side of her mouth, barely coherent. "You feel so fucking good, so fucking good."

"Yes," she whimpered at him, for him. She must have felt it, the way he trembled now, every muscle in his body fighting the urge to thrust, to claim, to move. Then she whispered, "Love me," again, and the sound he made in return wasn't human.

The first stroke, he kept slow, steady, an even slide out and back into her, and she grabbed at his arms as he moved, and they both moaned, and then his fists tightened in her hair, and he had to kiss her, needed her mouth.

Rolled his hips, again, again, deeper. Somewhere between fucking into her and making love, he decided, because the feral way he held her, the way he ravaged her mouth, was at odds with how controlled he kept his thrusts. She kept getting wetter, tighter, with each movement, as discomfort faded from her scent.

She was all want and need now, and love, and sunshine, everything.

Another growl, a harder thrust, and she titled her hips up to meet him, and he was in *deeper*, and this time her cry rattled through his skull to his hindbrain, the animal in him all male pride at the sounds he pulled from her.

"Audrey," he snarled, nipping at her lips, their faces not even an inch apart as he took her, her eyes tightly shut. "Look at me, sweetheart." He didn't recognize his own voice, hoarse with need, and then she looked at him, her expression all fascinated, drowning pleasure.

He did that to her. He'd do more.

It about killed him to pull away enough to snake a hand between their bodies, but now that he knew how she sounded when she came, he needed it again. Now that he knew what she felt like around his fingers, he'd fight ten more angels to feel her around his cock.

"Oh . . ." A frantic little sound, her gaze snapping to his, her skin flushing darker, all the way to her tits, which jerked each time his hips met hers. Confusion, surprise, then realization.

"That's right, sweetheart. You're gonna come around my cock."

Audrey made a strangled little noise, turning her head to the side, trying to hide, but she couldn't, not from him. Not from the burst in her scent, the flutter around his cock as he pressed, lengthening his pace, because there, right there, he felt each twitch in her body when he rubbed just where she needed. Quickening his fingers, giving her clit a little pinch to keep her attention.

"Look at you, taking me," Gunnar rasped, then almost laughed, as he added, "Owning me." She blinked up at him, her expression wild, almost panicked, and the second she started to crest, he added, "Letting me love you like you deserve, sweet girl."

And she broke for him, under him, gorgeous in her pleasure, watching her an almost out-of-body experience. That alone kept him from coming with her, the focused, rabid desire inside him to wring every bit she'd give him from her body. Her cunt clenched over and over, her back bending off the bed as she gripped the sheets and sang for him.

He slowed as she did, stopped when her cries shifted to little mewls, and lowered himself against her body, both of them sticky with sweat. Gunnar kissed her, her neck, her cheeks, little pecks everywhere he could reach until she gave him a sated, delirious giggle. She nuzzled at his cheek and he nuzzled back, tasting her scent for any lingering pain or discomfort, pleased to find none.

Then she shivered, which caused her cunt to tighten around his cock, and he groaned against her neck.

"Jonathan?" Half-question, half-pant, her fingers playing across his biceps, shoulders, running through his hair. "What do you need? What do I do?"

He huffed against her throat. "Just need you," he mumbled, laving just under her ear, another shiver racing across her skin as his hips pumped lazily into her.

"No, I mean for you. How do I make it good for you, too?" Concern touched her scent, even as the aftershocks still made her tremble under him.

Another laugh; he felt almost drunk and loved how her voice hitched with each stroke; fuck, he could do this all night. Maybe they would. "Baby, if this was any better for me, I'd be dead."

"Be serious!"

"I am."

"But you didn't . . . how do I . . ." She frowned then, looked like she might cry, shaking her head when he growled and went after her lips again. "How do I make you . . . you . . ."

Ah, he got it now. Shushed her, again when she tried to protest, and said against her mouth, "I've been barely keeping myself from coming this whole damn time, sweetheart." When she kept frowning, her confusion clear, he nipped at her chin and rolled his hips again, which got a little frustrated, pleased noise from deep in her throat. "Almost came when I tasted you the first time." A lick along her jaw, and she was still trying to argue with him. "Woman, I'm not done with you yet. I don't want to be done with you yet.

"I want to fuck a few more orgasms out of you before I come, Audrey. Trying to pace myself, take care of you. Keep it slow, for you."

Despite being as frazzled as he felt, he could tell, her breathing still erratic, Audrey told him, "No."

"No?" He chuckled at her, teased, "That's not what you want?"

"No," she whispered, her desire and nerves and the sweet scent that was just her and love encompassing him. "I don't want just what you think I want. I want you to . . . to . . ." Oh, he knew he was in trouble then, the determined look in eyes, the little jut of her chin.

Then she went and said, "Fuck me like you need."

Gunnar stilled, resting his head on her shoulder. Had to bite down on her shoulder, a little harder than intended, right where that tendon met her shoulder, right where he'd like to leave a bruise that would take weeks to fade. Maybe something more permanent, that beast inside of him wanting to make sure she knew, everyone knew, she was his.

She gave a little moan when he did, and his cock throbbed. He ground his hips against hers.

"Careful, sweetheart." He traced the indents he'd left on her skin with his tongue, darker pleasure zinging up and his spine, gathering in his groin. "You need to mean it when you say things like that to me," he slurred, couldn't help himself, he was slipping. "Especially when

I'm buried in your perfect cunt."

"I mean it," she whispered, her lips against his hair now. She brought her arms around him, hugging him close. "I want all of you."

He bit again, harder, pulling on her hair to open her throat to him more, inhaling deep, searching for the truth, and there it was.

She had no idea the power she had over him. Power he'd willing given her, because he'd never tasted anything like the knowledge she could break him, and he'd let her.

Gunnar slipped from her body, drawing a surprised protest that turned to a little squeak as he rolled her on to her stomach, nudged her legs apart with a knee. Drew her up on her hands, ass and hips in the air for him, a hand smoothing up her spine as he crawled behind her.

Yes, yes. This. Fuck, she was a sight, wet and on display, swollen from the pleasure he'd already given, empty and wanting more of him. All of him.

He caged her under him, his chest against her back as he caught her jaw, turned her face toward his, panting against her cheek, against the corner of her mouth. Tasting her scent with his open mouth.

"Mean it," he repeated, his voice guttural. He ran his cock along her, reveling in the violent shudder than wracked her entire body.

"I meant it. And I promise I will stop you if it's too much."

The world, Gunnar mused, he'd destroy it for her.

He thrust his cock back where it belonged, his vision tunneling at her call, her strangled moan as he held her face, kept himself up with one arm anchored to the bed, savoring the feel of her, how she gripped him like a vice, and even though he'd opened her virgin body to him, she was still too tight to be fucking reality. The animal he was, deep down, was rapidly slipping the leash he fought with day after day, minute after minute. Every second when it came to her, but she'd extended the invitation; that's when he realized she might be his, but she was the one who held the leash now.

"Perfect," he growled against her mouth, his last coherent thought as her fingers wove between his against the sheets, and he let her have him.

He fucked her like he never dared to dream about, walking the edge as he slammed into her from behind, over and over, keeping her mouth right there, right at his, so she could taste every one of his strangled growls, his aching groans, her name pouring from his mouth, along with *mine, mine, mine,* echoed back in her desperate pants of *yours, yes, yours.*

When he came, Gunnar about went blind, because she followed him over the cliff with his name still on her lips, the name she gave him, her body arching and draining him fucking dry. She gripped his hand tighter as they fell together, her tears sweet when they reached his lips, her scent wild with pleasure, feral almost, and not a hint of regret or pain or fear.

"Jonathan," she whispered, a little sob, a hiccup. Exhausted, but happy. And his.

"I know, sweetheart," he said against her skin, his head swimming. "I know."

"I love you."

"Everything," he confirmed, nuzzled her cheek. "You're everything." Dizzy, but then he recalled how women liked to hear the words, not an equivalent, so he added, "Love you, woman," and her little, contented sigh?

He'd keep it forever.

Epilogue

"'Truly?" Innocence said with a scoff, burrowing deeper into his absurd fur coat, two-sizes too large at the very least.

"Never heard someone bitch so fucking much," Gunnar offered, tugging Audrey closer to him, who giggled against him.

"Please," Innocence said, sniffing. "All of you, barbarians." He gave Audrey the side-eye. "My sympathies to your cold extremities, dearest."

Tomas laughed, finishing his lap around the stakes and ropes set up about fifty feet from Gunnar and Audrey's cabin—which extended in the opposite direction with markers for their expansion.

"It's really not that cold today," the kid offered, grinning ear to ear when Innocence waved him off, grimacing.

"You'd better make it worth walking all the way up here," the incubus sneered, flippant, and he turned and headed down the rails toward the station.

"It won't be done for a few weeks yet!" Tomas called, still laughing, and Innocence flipped him off and kept right on walking. After watching him depart, Tomas looked back at them, his expression hesitant.

Gunnar rolled his eyes. "Told you eight fucking times already. It's fine." He pointed north. "Your parcel swings wide, but it makes sense to keep the houses close up on this end. The chuchuna are just over the hill the other direction.”

“I know, I just . . .” Tomas looked to Audrey, who only smiled, her scent pleased—just how Gunnar liked it.

“It will also make it easier to keep up your lessons,” she offered. “For reading and for processing.” She shrugged against Gunnar, warm. He liked that too. “That way you don’t have to drag your kills farther than needed either, since you’ll be using our supplies while you learn.”

“But why?” Tomas asked, earnest as he was in everything. Gunnar wondered, now and then since Mateo’s death, if he’d only ever saw the kid as a threat because of his so-called brother. Completely healed from the blood madness, Tomas’s scent radiated nothing but hope. And gratitude.

Audrey glanced up at a Gunnar, her nose wrinkled.

Cute, she wanted him to answer. Pain in the ass.

“Because you deserve the chance, and my woman here can’t do anything by halves.” She pinched his stomach, but he ignored her. “Not a lot of us get that, so don’t fuck it up.”

“Jonathan!” Audrey laughed as she moved away from him, shaking her head. He just grinned at her. “I’m going to make lunch. Lyubava and Zhadan are coming by with the cubs. Do you want to join us?”

“Okay, sure,” Tomas said, smiling now. Audrey headed off, and Gunnar watched her go but felt Tomas’s eyes on him.

“What’s on your mind?”

Tomas shouldered up next to him, gaze wandering by their cabin, the stakes that marked where he’d make a home, and the chuchuna family trudging through the fresh snow.

“I don’t know, just worrying, I think.”

“Anything in particular?”

He scratched at his nose, adjusted his scarf and hat. Gunnar needed to work on all the kid’s ticks, get him less twitchy, but it would come with time. Found he didn't mind it, the idea of helping Tomas find his stride. He'd fit in well here, and the right things drove him; he wanted to protect Innocence, protect the place he called home, same as the rest of them out here on the taiga.

"Kushiel was important in the ESC."

"Important period, yeah."

"What's going to happen about that?" Tomas glanced up at him, concerned and open.

The dead angel buried in the leshy's forest, he meant.

Gunnar shrugged, because he didn't know. None of them did, not yet. "We have a connection with the Citadel, the archivist who helped change the Vilestars Accord."

"The one Audrey worked with, right?"

"Yeah, that's the fucker." Gunnar smirked when Tomas choked out a laugh. Then he sobered, fixing his gaze to the sky, clear and wide. For now. "We'll see what he thinks. Something'll come, no doubt."

Tomas nodded, crossing his arms again, straightening his spine a bit. "Guess we'll need to be ready then, whatever comes."

"Yeah," Gunnar drawled. "We will."

The Earthen Calamities Series:

Dreams on the Taiga: A Novella

Dreams on the Taiga: Audiobook

Blood on the Taiga: Nizhny Book 1

Cursed on the Taiga: Nizhny Book 2

Legends from Ashes: A Novella – Free Newsletter Signup

Feathers of Trials and Truths: The Acquisitionist Book 1 – Coming June 2025

www.eandersauthor.com

Acknowledgements

A huge, hefty first off goes to Jocelyn Lindsay, one of my very best friends, fellow writer, and book coach extraordinaire. Fifteen years ago, when we first met, I never would have considered self-publishing. I had a dream in mind for what my goals as an author looked like, so much so I lost sight of the forest for the trees. We had few candid and crucial conversations about dreams and what we think they mean and what they really are in January 2023. My view broadened from one constantly narrowing path to how I "should" be an author, to a vast landscape with a hundred different evolving ways for how I "could" be an author. Thanks for asking me to be brave and look up, Jocelyn. I couldn't have gotten here without your support and confidence in me and my dreams. There's not a day that goes by that I'm not grateful to have you in my life for at least a hundred reasons.

To my beta readers: Jennifer (magic fruit check point), Heather (fastest beta on the entire planet), Rena (ninja eyeballs), Cameron (who gave me the best tagline ever: *The Witcher meets Legends and Lattes – but spicier!")* and Matt (who will 100% run my Wikipedia if I'm ever rich and famous).

To Emily McKay for hours of double doubling (you realize you're doing this forever now, right?) and all things being a writer with ADHD. To Beth Revis for many years of being an inspiration, both as a person and an author, and her husband Corwin for being my very first fan back in 2009. To Lorin Oberweger for being a fantastic teacher, editor and writer, and for catching me when I needed it most. To Donald Maass, because no joke, his craft books and workshops changed my writing forever.

To my writer people, past and present: Lightforge City, The Wonderful Murders, fellow BONI attendees over the years (and staff Veronica Rossi and Brenda Windberg), the River Ward fandom when Cyberpunk released for the BEST first time fanfiction writing experience (most importantly Heather, Dany and Trishi). More specifically: Jennifer (again, this time for many years of my shit), my brother Jack, Kath, Deb, Simone and Joyce. To all the other writers out there who I've crossed paths with over the years, thank you for being part of my journey.

To Shanna and the 100covers team for my book cover and all my graphics, including my Fantastic Frog logo. To Lori Diederich for proofreading. To Phoebe Ravencraft at BPF, who gave me the most informative 30 minutes, followed by the nerdiest 30 minutes, and helped me craft an amazing book blurb. To everyone at 20BooksTo50k 2023 for the inspiration, education and positive energy. To Sam Stark for the stellar job on my first audiobook and showing a newbie the ropes.

To my parents, Julie and Bill, who've always supported me no matter my path. To my son Ethan, because nothing overhauls your life and teaches you what's important more than having a kid! To Nick, for always wanting more details about my worlds, for that butter knife fight choreography in his parents' foyer like 20 years ago (oh god), and for always making me say my made-up names aloud. To my brother Scott and sister-in-law Darci, because when I called you guys to tell you I was self-publishing on a random Friday, you both cheered me on so hard I cried after we hung up. To my many frogs, because they bring me little bits of joy every day (Winky is my favorite, don't tell the others). To Gibson, the first total stranger to subscribe to my newsletter!

And farthest from the least, as mentioned in my dedication, my husband Erik. Without him, this wonderful era of my life, for all the mess, wouldn't be possible. I love you.

About the Author

E Anders lives in the Pacific Northwest with her husband, son, two cats and sixty-three fantastic frogs.

Her newsletter, FANTASY AND FROGS, features: updates about her published and upcoming fantasy novels in THE EARTHEN CALAMITIES series; pictures and videos about her many pet frogs; links to free eBooks from other indie authors; and random things she loves that are not limited to but mostly - as you probably already guessed - about books and frogs.

https://www.eandersauthor.com/theauthor